Adventurer, you whose weight is borne by your winged soul! The mystical world of Theldesia is home to dragons and giants, magical beasts, and demihumans. Fragrant green winds blow across this new yet ancient land that opens before you like a blank page. Fill it with your life.

LOG HORIZON
10 HOMESTEADING THE NOOSPHERE

MAMARE TOUNO   ILLUSTRATION BY **KAZUHIRO HARA**

YEN
ON
NEW YORK

188

CONTENTS

SHIROE
▶ MACHIAVELLI-WITH-GLASSES

AN INTELLECTUAL ENCHANTER WHO ONCE ACTED AS COUNSELOR FOR THE LEGENDARY BAND OF PLAYERS KNOWN AS THE DEBAUCHERY TEA PARTY. MENTALLY, HE WAS A BIT OF A HERMIT AND AVOIDED INTERACTING WITH OTHER PEOPLE, BUT AFTER THE CATASTROPHE, HE ESTABLISHED HIS OWN GUILD, LOG HORIZON.

NAOTSUGU
▶ PANTIES WARRIOR

A TRUSTY GUARDIAN AND SHIROE'S GOOD FRIEND: A CHEERFUL, TOUGH YOUNG GUY AND FORMER DEBAUCHERY TEA PARTY MEMBER. HE'D LEFT *ELDER TALES* TEMPORARILY, AND ON THE DAY HE RETURNED, HE GOT TRAPPED IN THE GAME WORLD.

AKATSUKI
▶ LOVELY ASSASSIN

ALTHOUGH SHE FORMERLY HID THE FACT THAT SHE WAS FEMALE AND PLAYED AS A SILENT MAN, AFTER BEING SWALLOWED UP BY THE GAME, SHE CHANGED HER BODY TO MATCH HER REAL-WORLD SELF AND BEGAN PLAYING AS A SLENDER, BRILLIANT ASSASSIN.

▼ PLOT

THE FIVE YOUNGER PLAYERS LEFT AKIBA ON THEIR FIRST SOLO JOURNEY.

AS THE RESULT OF SECRET MANEUVERS BY THE WESTERN GUILD PLANT HWYADEN, A TOWN THEY VISITED WAS ATTACKED BY MONSTERS. WHILE THE BATTLE TO SAVE THE TOWN COULDN'T HAVE BEEN MORE CHAOTIC, THE KIDS SOMEHOW MANAGED TO HELP.

MEANWHILE, NYANTA, WHO HAD BEEN KEEPING AN EYE ON THE GROUP AS THEY TRAVELED, WAS CONFRONTED BY THE SELFISH YET HEARTRENDING CRY OF AN ADVENTURER WHO LONGED TO RETURN TO THE OLD WORLD. IT MADE HIM BEGIN TO BROOD ON THE UNFAIRNESS OF THIS WORLD.

IN CONTRAST TO NYANTA'S DEEPENING DOUBT, THE YOUNGER GROUP HAD GROWN AND IMPROVED THEMSELVES QUITE A LOT OVER THE COURSE OF THEIR JOURNEY.

ON THE WAY, THEY ENCOUNTERED ROE2, AND AS THE FIVE OF THEM RETURNED TO AKIBA, SHE GAVE THEM A LETTER TO DELIVER.

THAT LETTER WOULD REVEAL STARTLING NEW FACTS TO THE ROUND TABLE COUNCIL.

ROEZ

▶ A MYSTERIOUS WOMAN WHO RESEMBLES "HIM"

A SUMMONER AND POWERFUL NECROMANCER WHO CAN CALL UP ALL SORTS OF UNDEAD MONSTERS. PHYSICALLY, SHE BEARS A STRONG RESEMBLANCE TO SHIROE OF LOG HORIZON, AND THERE SEEMS TO BE SOME CONNECTION BETWEEN THEM.

SOUJI

▶ HAREM MAKER

A GENTLE-LOOKING YOUNG MAN WITH A BOYISH FACE. HE'S SOMETIMES TEASED FOR BEING HAREM-PRONE. THERE'S ACTUALLY A "SOUJIROU'S PERSONAL GUARD" WITH MEMBERS BOTH IN HIS GUILD, THE WEST WIND BRIGADE, AND OUTSIDE IT.

LI GAN

▶ GEEKY PERSON-OF-THE-EARTH LORE MASTER

THE SUCCESSOR TO THE TITLE "SAGE OF MIRAL LAKE," WHICH APPEARED IN THE OFFICIAL *ELDER TALES* GAME SETTING. FOR A PERSON OF THE EARTH, HE'S HIGHLY EDUCATED, VERY KNOWLEDGE-ABLE, AND WELL-INFORMED ABOUT ALL SORTS OF THINGS.

THE FIVE HAD FUN AND GREW ON THEIR TRIP. ▶

CHAPTER.

1

STRANGER

▶ **NAME: NYANTA**

▶ LEVEL: **92**

▶ RACE: **FELINOID**

▶ SUBCLASS: CHEF

▶ HP: **12003**

▶ MP: **9688**

▶ ITEM 1:

[DARTING LINDWURMS]

A PAIR OF FANTASY-CLASS RAPIERS HE GOT BY DEFEATING THE WHITE DRAGON LINDWURM, THE INCARNATION OF SHOOTING STARS AND LIGHTNING. THEIR OVERWHELMING ATTACK POWER AND THEIR SHINING WHITE BLADES SET THEM APART. WHEN THE PURSUIT-DAMAGE MARKER IS DETONATED, THEY GENERATE A BEAUTIFUL EFFECT.

▶ ITEM 2:

[DECORUM OF DUEL]

ELEGANT WHITE GLOVES WITH A BEAUTIFUL LUSTER, MADE FROM A FOURTH-RANK SKIN ACQUIRED FROM THE NUE, A MYSTICAL LIGHTNING BEAST. THEY BOAST AN EXCELLENT GRIP, AND IN ADDITION TO VASTLY IMPROVING THE HIT RATE, THEY BOOST THE CRITICAL RATE AS WELL. AN ITEM THAT CAN ALSO BE USED IN FORMAL SITUATIONS.

▶ ITEM 3:

[GENTLEMAN'S SILVER WATCH]

A SILVER WATCH AND CHAIN WITH A RELIEF OF COLUMBINE FLOWERS ON ITS CASE. IN THE LANGUAGE OF FLOWERS, THEY MEAN "DETERMINED TO WIN." THE WATCH REPLICATES EARLY THRUST, ONE OF THE MAIN SWASHBUCKLER ATTACKS, AT A LOW PROBABILITY. FOR GENTLEMEN, STRICT PUNCTUALITY IS A POINT OF ETIQUETTE.

\<Crescent Burger\>
Legendary flavor.

▶1

Hello.

I wasn't sure how to begin this, but for the first words, a greeting seems suitable.

Hello, world. Hello, Shiroe.

I'm writing this letter at an inn located in the town of Saphir in central Yamato.

When I've finished writing it, I plan to give it to my friend Minori.

I'm told "Shiroe of Log Horizon" will be the one to read it. When I heard that name, it made me feel quite strange. I have your memories inside me, you see.

Just as you Adventurers are beings who have been incarnated into Theldesia from another world, we too, have been incarnated here from yet another world.

My name is Roe2.

We call ourselves Travelers. From your perspective, we are intelligent alien life-forms.

At the same time, I myself am also your little sister.

Your expectations have no doubt been raised, and all I can do is apologize: Neither we Fool-inspectors nor the Genius-collectors, who are also members of the Traveler race, are able to explain anything about the Eclipse—what you term "the Catastrophe"—to you. To be accurate, we could explain it, but the explanation would be our understanding of the Eclipse, not an elucidation of its principles nor a way to resolve it.

Even so, I believe we are very slightly ahead of you and your people, and as such, I intend to carry out my duty. After all, I am your little sister, but as I assured Minori, I am your big sister as well.

On that point, I should begin by explaining two things:
Why I am Roe2, and...
...why I am your little sister.

Like you, we Travelers arrived in Theldesia via the Eclipse. However, our world is far more distant than Theldesia, and our species had no original physical forms or configuration data.

Therefore, when we reached this world, we borrowed bodies we found locally to use as avatars.

If what Minori says is correct, you are an extraordinarily perceptive, intelligent individual.

Now that I've explained this much, no doubt you already understand, but my current body is yours—the one that was in storage on the moon. To use the terminology of this world, it had no active "soul connection."

I would like you to forgive me for borrowing it without permission.

This body holds vivid traces of your thoughts and memories.

I have been able to explain things to you this way by reorganizing your vocabulary data. In large part, it is thanks to you that I am able to speak the words of this world. The repayment of that debt is one of my reasons for writing this letter.

If possible, I would like you to read it with an open mind.

After all, you may tear it up and throw it away at any time.

▶ 2

Shiroe looked up at the ceiling and sighed. He'd lost track of how many times he'd done that.

He was holding several sheets of creased stationery.

It was the letter Minori had brought him.

He'd recognized the neat handwriting. When he'd flipped through nearby documents to see whose it was, he'd realized it was his own. *So even our handwriting is similar?* Shiroe thought, massaging the spot between his eyes as though to ward off a headache.

He was in the Log Horizon guild hall.

By now, this place, a remodeled abandoned building in northern Akiba, was his home. Not because Shiroe had purchased the seven-story brick building by plunking down all the money he had, but because the companions who had welcomed him were constantly here with him.

Nine Adventurers—Shiroe, Naotsugu, Akatsuki, Nyanta, Minori, Touya, Isuzu, Rundelhaus, and the new member, Tetora—lived in this guild home. With an ancient tree growing through the middle of the building, they weren't able to use the central area of each floor. Even so, since there were about three or four rooms per floor, each of the members had a private room, and it didn't feel cramped.

This room was Shiroe's office.

With nine members, their group wasn't quite tiny, but they were clearly one of the smaller guilds. Ordinarily, he wouldn't have needed anything as ostentatious as an office. A single work desk in his room would have been enough. However, Log Horizon was one of the eleven guilds on the Round Table Council, and Shiroe had a lot of inquiries and petitions to field. There were visitors, too... And so he had an office.

Shiroe spent so much time in this office that the other members could very easily have called him a hermit. Naturally, this was partly because he had a lot of work, but it was also because he tended to become lost in thought, and he guessed it probably worried the other members.

That said, as a rule, most of the members of Log Horizon didn't fret over what was on Shiroe's mind...

Shiroe arched his back, stretching against the backrest of his office chair.

His fingers folded the letter that sat on his stomach and returned it to its envelope.

It had been serious.

It had been a letter that threatened to stir up serious issues.

However, behind his glasses, Shiroe closed his eyes and sighed.

"True, this letter is a big problem. By that token, though, the Round Table Council, Minami, the Holy Empire of Westlande, and Krusty, too, are all big problems."

Listing them aloud made him aware, once again, that none of them was a laughing matter.

Krusty himself aside, his guild, known as D.D.D., had developed administrative problems. Frankly, it was strange that its missing leader hadn't created more of an issue before. D.D.D.'s administrative staff was outstanding, so the problem hadn't yet spread to the surrounding area, but there were reports that, internally, fatigue was accumulating.

The Holy Empire of Westlande was a problem, too. According to his investigations, they were drafting soldiers and restructuring their knight brigades, although neither was being done on a large scale.

The Round Table Council had united eastern Yamato with Akiba at its center, while Plant Hwyaden had united Yamato's western half. The two organizations had different philosophies, but Shiroe didn't think that was an inherently bad thing. Even with a schism like this one, at heart, the Adventurers were contemporary individuals with roots in modern Japan. Since that was the case, he hadn't thought they'd go to war. Or rather, he still didn't think they would, even now.

However, apparently, that sort of common sense didn't hold true with the People of the Earth.

The Holy Empire of Westlande, which governed the West, looked as if it was planning to go to war with Eastal, the League of Free Cities. If that began, Shiroe thought there was no way he and the other Adventurers would be able to stay uninvolved. They probably couldn't harden their hearts enough to keep out of it.

For better or for worse, the Adventurers were modern Japanese.

There was no way that Plant Hwyaden hadn't noticed. When it came to that sort of thing, Shiroe thought Madame Indicus was so perceptive the word *sharp* didn't even begin to cover it.

He had a certain amount of information regarding what was happening in Minami. Thinking about it made him feel depressed. It was a road Akiba had nearly gone down, and even now, he couldn't say the possibility had disappeared entirely.

The Round Table Council.

It felt to Shiroe as though the Council was approaching a new crossroads. If the crisis had been something he could see, monsters or a huge calamity, he probably wouldn't have been this worried. Krusty might be missing, but Akiba had Isaac, Soujirou, and many other heroic Adventurers. Shiroe was confident that, in combat, they could eliminate most obstacles.

However, this didn't seem to be that sort of problem.

It felt more like the atmosphere immediately after the Catastrophe. It looked to Shiroe as if the despair they'd thought they'd shaken off with the Crescent Burgers had risen again. Could people's malaise and resignation actually breed war, which they'd never seen? Shiroe had never experienced that, and he didn't know what it might bring.

"And actually, thinking about why things are like this is pointless, but I can't not think it, and the work just keeps coming in, and arrrrgh..."

Shiroe slumped facedown across his desk.

He'd hoped, naïvely, that if he played dead, the trouble might blow over, but it didn't even budge. Its symbols were the letter he'd tossed aside, and that mountain of documents.

"Shiroecchi."

Nyanta knocked on the door, then opened it a crack and peeked in. When Shiroe waved for him to enter, his lean shape slipped into the room.

Seeing this, Shiroe shoved the letter into a desk drawer and went over to the reception set. Looking a bit surprised, Nyanta transferred drinks from his silver tray to the table.

"Take a seat, Captain Nyanta."

"Mew don't need to work?"

"I'm tired," Shiroe admitted with a laugh.

In response, Nyanta said, "Mrowr-ha-ha. In that case, I'll keep mew company," and sat down.

The two of them began drinking something that resembled hot chocolate. It was warm and incredibly sweet.

Shiroe let his eyes fall to the whirlpool pattern on the surface of his cup. Possibly due to the convection current, it was spinning slowly. The marbling looked like a spiral. Shiroe decided that trivial things like this catching his attention was proof he was tired. The sweetness seemed to soak into him.

"Mew're working too hard, Shiroecchi."

"You too, Captain."

Shiroe smiled a little, and Nyanta looked startled.

Shiroe had noticed that the other man had been brooding a bit lately. It had begun after he'd gone to the West in order to guard Minori and the other younger members. Nyanta had given him a report on what had happened. He was quiet, and he hadn't said much, but Shiroe could imagine what he'd seen.

The Captain ran into an Adventurer who'd failed to adjust to this world.

That was a problem gradually becoming apparent in Akiba as well.

"It's been almost a year since the Catastrophe, hasn't it?"

"Mew're right. It will be, in another month..."

"Uh-huh."

That one year has divided people.

If the Catastrophe had been a transitory incident that had been resolved in a short time, this never would have been an issue. The situation had been shattering and unprecedented; it was only natural that people had been shocked, and no wonder they'd been stunned and confused.

"It feels as though it's been a long time, and simewltaneously not very long at all."

"Right. I bet there are people who want to go home."

"True... It's likely there are people who want it so desperately they'd throw everything away to get it."

"You're right."

Even Shiroe would have been lying if he'd said he didn't want to go home. However, that was only if going home was possible. After the Catastrophe, most of the residents of Akiba had managed to get

used to this world through the Round Table Council's aid, to the point where they could say, *Of course I want to go back. If I can, I mean.* The words held the desire to go home, but they also held the readiness to accept that, if it wasn't possible, then there was no help for it.

The phrase *throw everything away* was a heavy one.

Shiroe didn't think there was anyone who could even imagine "everything," and no one who'd be able to throw it all away.

Didn't that really mean they wanted to erase themselves? He imagined it might be like deciding nothing mattered anymore and returning to nothingness.

However, the Catastrophe had been an insanity-inducing event, and it wasn't as though anyone could cope with it. There was no help for that. The previous year had proved those people hadn't been able to adjust.

They didn't want to be in this world. Put into words, the feeling would probably have been, *I want to go home. Even if it isn't possible.*

"It's not that I don't know how they feel…"

"Yes, it's far mew easy to relate. That's why I can't blame them."

"It's sad."

"It hurts."

The two of them gazed into their mugs, sharing the silence.

The despair inside people was so great they couldn't even look at the future. That hurt Shiroe more sharply than the most powerful monster.

"Shiroecchi…"

Unusually, Nyanta hesitated. Before that eloquent silence broke on its own, he asked Shiroe gently: "Do mew want to go home?"

The kindness in his voice made Shiroe sad. This world was making Nyanta push himself. He thought the same was true of his own uneasy expression. Still, even if he thought that, he couldn't find any answers inside himself.

Shiroe sighed a little, then spoke, as if squeezing out the words.

"I think we should go home."

He had thought for a long time before reaching this entirely natural, obvious conclusion. A sound argument. No matter how he thought about it, there was nothing else.

"As far as this world is concerned, we really are alien. When living here, some people will be warped, and others will choose to change the world. That sort of thing might have happened when we were back in our old world. Or rather, I think it did happen. Still, if it's an avoidable tragedy, then we should stay clear of it, and we're—"

Shiroe knew Nyanta was nodding slightly in agreement, but the rest of his words stuck in his chest, and he couldn't say them. If he believed that nearby letter, then even if he couldn't declare they could go home, there were probably things they could do instead.

However, even the thirty seconds ahead into which Shiroe was gazing, daybreak was still distant, and the night was deep.

▶ 3

"Ahh."

Riezé heard herself make a noise that sounded suspiciously like a sigh.

When she raised her head and looked out the window, cream-colored light was illuminating the ancient trees. Most of the members were out training or on supply expeditions, and the guild hall was quiet and empty.

There were a dozen or so documents near her.

They weren't neat documents, drafted according to a format.

They were messy, with margins crammed with memos and notes. Riezé smiled mockingly at how clumsy they were.

Those notes were her footprints. The record of a struggle, something she'd written as a lifeline, in a dark wasteland where she'd be stranded if she didn't leave them behind.

In many cases, answers were simple things. They might be as trivial as *This month, purchase about five hundred substitute weapons for training*. But how should she think in order to reach that conclusion? It didn't have to be private thought. It could be debate, or calculations. At any rate, what should she do in order to find answers? Riezé didn't know.

This was because the decisions at D.D.D. had been, for the most part, semiautomatic: If people filled out request forms on site and submitted them, they were accumulated and distributed the next month. However, this automatic distribution had been a product of the D.D.D. official site's member functions, which had been located outside *Elder Tales*.

After the Catastrophe, they no longer had clerical support from the external site, but this didn't become a problem immediately. The members were used to the application/supply process, and they drew up the forms on their own. The administrative headquarters organized the forms and continued to supply the necessary materials. That sort of mechanism was still alive and functioning, and it was an important driving force that kept D.D.D., one of the most enormous guilds on the Yamato server, alive.

On the other hand, though, the mechanism was from a time when D.D.D.'s abilities to procure materials had been nearly infinite. When they couldn't obtain "five hundred substitute weapons for training," the system didn't have a function that would adjust for that. In addition, this wasn't true only for adjustments to preexisting matters and changes: Completely new requests and matters that spanned the duties of whole departments were being generated one after another.

Riezé was a member of Drei Klauen, D.D.D.'s executive organization. She'd prided herself on her understanding of the guild's administrative system. As a matter of fact, the guild master had entrusted the material arrangements and schedule management on the external site entirely to her.

However, stepping in and managing a system that was already operating—not only that, but one that included some automatic adjustments and clerical support—was completely different from searching for correct solutions for a variety of matters, turning them into procedures, spreading the word, and refining them to the point where they could be run as systems.

I didn't understand that those were completely different things.

The fact made Riezé smile bitterly.

Drei Klauen was a clownish name. Kushiyatama *had seen that*, and she had left because of it. At this point, Riezé could be honest with herself about that.

By the time she gave a big stretch, the temporary office was tinted with pale lemon-colored light. The afternoon had grown later. This wasn't the madder red of evening, but the soft light showed that it was on its way. In March, early spring, the light held no heat; it was tranquil and beautiful.

Standing up to reset her mood, Riezé poured cold tea from a pitcher into a glass.

This temporary office was bleak, and it didn't have a tea set. This was only natural: She was borrowing a conference room that could hold about twenty people. D.D.D. did have proper offices, of course. They were luxurious, imposing, with atmospheres that made them seem like rooms for distinguished guests, but Riezé felt a little awkward about using them. This was odd because when Crusty had been with them, she'd used those rooms as if it were nothing. Riezé chuckled a little, thinking their guild master must have had a sort of magical ability that had made even the companions around him shameless.

"Whoops. Miss Riezé."

A young man with cheerful eyes had poked his head in without waiting for a response to his knock. It was Calasin of Shopping District 8. Slipping in casually, Calasin shut the door and set down his bags. He came over fairly frequently, so his being in and out of D.D.D. was routine for both of them.

"Thank you for all your hard work, Calasin."

"Ah-ha-ha-ha. Seriously... Things are pretty hairy."

"They don't look good?"

"Well, it's busy as hell!"

"Honestly. You always joke around like that."

Riezé pointed to a chair, encouraging him to sit. After he set down the canvas bags he'd carried, one over each shoulder, Calasin organized the contents of the one paper bag he'd been carrying, continuing their conversation as he worked.

"That's not... Well, maybe it's true. You look busy, too, Riezé."

"I'm simply clumsy, that's all."

"Oh, there you go again. And you're serious; that makes it hard to deal with."

Riezé indicated the documents with a look.

They were programs for level-75, -77, -81, and -85 raids. Before the Catastrophe, D.D.D. had fought battles on that scale three hundred times a week. The level zones meant the raids had been more like "patrols" than challenges to tackle. At this point, though, everything had changed.

Now that this world was real, battles were considerably more difficult. Before, level-75 raids had been the sort of content attempted by Adventurers between levels 70 and 72. However, at present, it would be difficult to achieve a complete victory on that level. Even if it was possible, they'd have to prepare for the accompanying exhaustion. She had to select the levels of the participating members carefully.

In addition, the increased cost of travel was a big problem. Now that the Fairy Rings couldn't be used, all expeditions involved mounts, and it was necessary to take food and camping equipment. There were only a handful of dungeons where they could say, *This raid's just to keep ourselves in practice. Let's go clean it out real quick.*

"Raids, huh?"

"Yes, although we're only selecting suitable ones nearby."

"Can I see?" Calasin asked, and Riezé nodded. As she watched, he flipped through the programs. There were lots of notes and memos, but there weren't many pages. The plans were simple.

"You do want fantasy-class materials, don't you?"

"Yes." Riezé nodded.

Akiba was undergoing a technological development boom, and in the midst of that activity, all sorts of materials were being bought and sold. This was true both for food and for items such as weapons and defensive gear. The prices of all sorts of things were fluctuating violently, but in the midst of the chaos, there were two things whose prices continued to climb.

One was luxury indulgences, which couldn't be replicated—for example, delicious food and recreational items sold for extremely high prices. The cost of manga and handmade figures was skyrocketing. This was probably because, even if they'd been shut into this fantasy world, Riezé and the others were modern earthlings, and they needed something to soothe their emotional cravings. Even Riezé couldn't help loosening her purse strings when newly developed cakes were advertised.

The other was fantasy-class materials.

In this world, *material* was the general term for items that were used in the creation of other items. In cooking, wheat, tomatoes, Pacific saury, and Hokuri potatoes were all materials. In contrast, items created by processing materials were called "processed items." It was possible for processed items to be used as materials in the manufacture of other items as well.

These "materials" could be obtained from the world itself. Lumber came from forests. Ores came from mountains. Fish came from the ocean. There were acquisition points for materials from fields and ranches that required human labor, too. In most cases, the people who produced these materials were People of the Earth.

Monster drop items were the ones Adventurers were most familiar with, and these were known as "drop materials" or "monster materials."

In many cases, materials had levels, even if those levels weren't explicitly stated. For example, there were low-level and high-level versions of the same Iron Ore item. Low-level versions could be obtained from safe mines where the monsters were weak and scarce, while acquiring high-level versions required equivalent risk.

Fantasy-class materials were the very hardest type to acquire. These were materials dropped by the sort of monsters that had to be subjugated through raids. Fantasy-class materials were precious resources. They were required in order to repair and create fantasy-class weapons and defensive gear. That wasn't all: In the post-Catastrophe world, demand was soaring, not just from weapons and gear, but from all sorts of invented items and experiments. The anecdote about the Roderick Trading Company using Dragon Scale Bricks to create a superhot furnace was famous.

"Does it look as if the supplies will be all right?"

"Well, of course, we've got that nailed down. Both food and materials for repairs."

"Monster materials are fine, but everything else tends to stagnate."

"Let's split that part up, then."

"All right."

By nature, D.D.D. was a self-contained guild. At the very least,

Riezé understood that that was where Krusty's interests had lain. The guild had an internal supply function and could continue to operate independently.

However, after the Catastrophe, that function was showing marked flaws as well. In the game, it had been one thing, but now that it had grown this complicated and become part of the Round Table Council, being "self-contained" was a pipe dream. As expeditions grew longer, obtaining supplies from external sources had grown more important, and cooperation with Calasin's Shopping District 8 had become vital.

"You're a hard worker, Riezé. Little Minori, too. Akiba's ladies are all, you know, dazzling."

After wrapping up a lengthy preliminary meeting about how to transfer the supplies necessary for the expeditions (it would be best if they could be delivered to the actual sites), Calasin spoke to Riezé in a droll way.

"That isn't true."

Riezé denied it, and Calasin smiled wryly. "You're comparing yourself to the wrong person."

That probably is true, Riezé thought.

Krusty really was exceptional. After coming into contact with this enormous system he'd created—D.D.D.—the better she understood it, the more aware she was of his skills. She was constantly finding signs that all the concerns she could think of had already been anticipated—countermeasures had been taken, too. Furthermore the procedures that made Riezé think, *This is unnecessary. We should simplify it*, proved to be balancers, or redundancy for dealing with trouble.

For the first time, Riezé had learned that organizations could be creations and works of art. D.D.D. was Krusty's creation, and he had built it with talent in a class all on its own.

Riezé knew Krusty was exceptional and that she shouldn't compare herself to him.

However, she had no other teachers to serve as examples, and there were no textbooks in this world.

"Oh. Right, ermm… Listen. I think Machiavelli would be better."

"Shiroe, you mean?"

"Yeah, that's the one. Him. Shiroe."

Riezé faltered, and the reply she got back was delivered in an unexpected and pretty irreverent tone.

"And why is that?"

"Shiroe's got a few awkward places, too. From what I've seen, he's your type, isn't he, Riezé?"

Riezé looked dubious, but Calasin responded smoothly. It was as though he'd already had that answer waiting.

"Is that right?"

"About fifty percent, from what I hear. Shiroe is. Really."

"Fifty percent what?"

"Shiroe's fifty percent ordinary. I'd say forty percent is brilliance, and ten percent is desperation."

"Huh?"

Calasin folded his arms and sulked, but he still sounded facetious.

Fifty percent ordinary…

Riezé reflected on what that meant.

Oh, she thought, *I see.* It felt right.

Fifty percent ordinary, forty percent brilliant. That was priceless. She giggled.

If he had been completely ordinary, he wouldn't even have known what his position was. Because he knew, to a certain extent, just how little he understood and how ignorant he was, even though he was ordinary, he couldn't ease up. That was probably what that meant.

It was just like the tiny footprints Riezé had made.

She'd thought and researched desperately for days, and the result had been five A4-sized memos. Put together, they were as tall as Riezé's body back in Japan. The "intelligence" inside her had ordered her to create those memos. This was because "intelligent Riezé" had known that that·was the only way she had left to learn how to do this correctly.

On the other hand, "ordinary Riezé" had been able to create only five of them. That was the extent of Riezé's current skills. Clumsy, slow on the uptake, incompetent. Still, there was no help for that. At the moment, that was the size of her reality.

True, it was really pathetic, but it was also a relief.

Those five pages were Riezé's domain. The thoughts she'd written here covered the range to which she'd given sufficient consideration and concern. Of course, outside it, there were lots of things she didn't really understand. Even her own guild, where she'd spent long years, was riddled with things she didn't know. All she could do was continue to increase her domain this way, with infuriating slowness. She'd been on the verge of despairing, but Calasin's words had made her see that she was wrong.

If progress was slow, there was no way around that. That was what being life-sized meant.

On the contrary, she felt as if she'd been shown that there was nothing for it but to increase her domain that way and that, no matter how roundabout it looked, it was the right method.

There was a young man who'd launched the Round Table Council using the same method and had made Krusty smile broadly. That was what Calasin had taught Riezé.

"I think he'd make a better reference than the Mr. Super-Glasses who's ten percent demon."

"Yes."

"Eh-heh-heh-heh. Your eyes finally look settled."

Calasin had put a hand to his jaw in an affected pose, and he smiled at Riezé. The idea that she might have made this cheerful young guy worry about her embarrassed her. There were lots of people who had helped her. Since the Akiba raid, every single day made her aware of assistance she hadn't noticed before.

"No, no. Calasin knows; you don't even have to tell me. How about a *dorayaki*?"

"Aw, maaan. Picking up girls again, Young Gent?!"

Just as she was about to accept the *dorayaki* Calasin had taken from his paper bag, a boy in knee-length shorts flung open the door with a bang. It was one of Calasin's Shopping District 8 companions, someone they'd asked several times to carry messages and show in guests.

"Taro, you've got it all wrong."

"Those are the ones I just bought. Seriously, all you do is loaf around. C'mon, c'mon, let's go deliver the goods."

"Ah, then, Miss Riezé? Later! Oh, um. Once you've cheered up, let's go out to eat!"

"Thank you very much for supplying us."

"Huh, seriously? Taro. That was a good response, wasn't it?"

"Calasin, c'mon, get moving. Three strikes, you're out; just give it up."

"I'm telling you, Taro, that conversation was business lubricant."

"Yeah, and that's why she was so smooth when she turned you down."

As the boy dragged him away, Calasin's voice grew fainter and fainter, and Riezé chuckled as she watched them go. Misa Takayama would probably be back from getting her prosthetic arm replaced soon. Riezé felt blessed.

The Round Table Council was headed into a difficult time. Even she knew that.

That was why, for now, she wanted to improve her skills, even a little.

It had nothing to do with level, or with this other world. It was a single resolution Riezé had made: her expectations for her future self.

▶**4**

Isaac had never been a fan of spring.

All it meant was that the weather got a little nicer and the temperature went up. The air grew dusty and nasty, and it was a glaringly half-assed season; not summer, but not winter, either.

He also didn't really know why the town had started to get strangely giddy. Well, in terms of accounting periods or school, it was when the new school year began, and he understood why that would make for a restless atmosphere. Still, it wasn't as if it held any advantages for Isaac; if he'd had to say, it was solidly in the "pain in the butt" category.

When he was a kid, and throughout his school years, spring had been nothing more than an irritation, a season in which he fought unnecessary fights. Once he'd started earning paychecks, it had gotten a little better, but that was because he was now free to distance himself from the giddy people.

In any case, Isaac had never been a fan of spring.

Although, spring here seemed a bit different from what he was used to.

In this world, where it got colder than it did back in Japan, winter had been pretty harsh. Of course, neither the unending snow nor the frozen woods had posed any obstacle for Isaac and the other Adventurers, but this hadn't been true for the People of the Earth.

In terms of the old Japan, Maihama, where Isaac had been staying on and off since February, was located in Chiba. That meant that, although it hadn't been buried under heavy snows, it had been covered in a blanket of the stuff for a full two months, and he'd heard there had been over forty centimeters of ice on the ponds.

For people without the Adventurers' equipment, it had been a season where activity was limited.

Eastal, the League of Free Cities, which covered the eastern part of Yamato, wasn't a poor organization. In addition, at this point, it was the recipient of various blessings from new Adventurer technology. However, as might be expected, compared with what it was in spring or autumn, the yields of all sorts of things fell in winter. It wasn't as bad as the snow country, but even in Maihama, meals tended to deteriorate into plain fare built around preserved food. Spring wasn't just the dusty, half-assed season known as "spring"; it was the season that meant winter was over.

As a Japanese person who'd been able to wander around in a down jacket, then duck into a roadside family restaurant and eat whatever he wanted when he got hungry, Isaac felt a little bad: *Sorry, people. Go as nuts as you want.*

As Isaac thought about useless things like that, he was leaning against the trunk of a great tree on top of a hill, out in the April wind, taking a break.

This was the suburbs, about thirty minutes' run from the city of Maihama.

Strictly speaking, this area wasn't within Maihama city limits, but the villages near the city were so close their borders almost touched, and pastoral fields spread around them.

In response to a request, not from the Round Table Council, but from Shiroe, Isaac, and the Knights of the Black Sword had come here to train the Glass Greaves, the chivalric order attached to the duchy of Maihama.

However, his guild members hadn't let Isaac participate in actually training the knights—they'd told him it would set a bad example—so he had too much time on his hands. That said, he couldn't just ditch the whole thing, and so here he was, gazing down at the military drills from the top of the hill and biting back yawns.

The hill was circular, with a radius of one kilometer or so, and there was a mixed forest about the size of a small schoolyard in its slightly elevated center. This forest spread behind Isaac's back. It wasn't so thick it obstructed the view, and even if there were animals of some sort in it, they would be only wild dogs or foxes or weasels.

The slope Isaac surveyed was thickly covered with spring grass, its green as bright as if it had been washed, and a company was racing up it. It was a group of Glass Greaves led by three members of Isaac's Knights of the Black Sword. There were probably about forty of them in all.

Even if this was a military drill, working with large groups was inefficient.

They'd split the knights into five groups, and about three companies were around this hill. As far as he knew, they were running around and around the hill's base and practicing charging, with a grove of trees as their partner. Isaac hadn't been born and raised in Theldesia, and he certainly wasn't a knight, so he had no idea; when they'd told him that this was a knights' drill, all he'd done was think, *Huh. Is that right?*

Young spring grass was surprisingly succulent.

As the brigade's name—the Glass Greaves—indicated, the knights wore metal armor supplied to them by the Cowen dukedom, which meant they were pretty heavy. That lot was running up the green, grassy slope toward him, spurred on by their instructors. Many of them got tripped up by the wet grass under their feet and fell clumsily. By the time they were thirty minutes into the drill, that neatly maintained silver armor had been smeared with grass and mud.

Still, the Glass Greaves jumped back up without complaint, then launched themselves into ferocious sprints, heading back to their places in the ranks.

The three Adventurers running at the head of the pack—Kouboumaru,

Efuri, and Lee Jent—were bellowing at them: "C'mon, c'mon! Whad-daya call those wussy arm swings?!" "Let's hear some noise, scumbags!"

Uptight losers, Isaac thought, but what he didn't know was that he'd been taken off the training because his hot-blooded, sports-oriented, Spartan coaching had been too much for the People of the Earth to handle, and even his subordinates had been massively turned off by it.

While he sat there in the bright, clear sunlight, watching the scene as if it were somebody else's problem, all the things he was thinking were fairly rude: *Man, those idiots are hardheads. Do they actually have brains in there? Nah, guess not; all our members are dumb. Seriously, there's just no helping these guys.* That said, even as he got disgusted with them, he was smiling a little. Isaac didn't hate these idiots. He was actually really fond of them. If he'd hated them, there was no way he would have been the leader of a messy guild like this one, even for a second.

"Stop, stop!"

"Thirty-minute break!"

"Go rest, you gutless, empty-headed pansies!"

The instructors were yelling from about a hundred meters away. No matter what they said, it was blindingly obvious they were enjoying themselves. The three of them glanced at Isaac, whispered among themselves for a little, then ducked their heads, nodding to him. Apparently, they had nothing that needed to be reported. They'd been told to conduct the training any way they wanted, so Isaac just waved back at them.

He thought they'd probably do a good job.

Actually, what had surprised him were the People of the Earth.

The dukedom's chivalric order, the Glass Greaves, were the House of Cowen's knights' brigade, and they guarded Maihama. Since the brigade belonged to the House of Cowen, the de facto leader of Eastal, it was made up of People of the Earth elites. That was what Isaac had been told beforehand.

That was by People of the Earth standards, though. The group's levels were only around 25. He'd thought there was no way they'd be tough. Well, he still thought that: They weren't strong.

And yet they weren't as weak as he'd thought they'd be, either.

The Glass Greaves had guts.

Just now, they'd managed a two-hour run in that armor.

Of course, to a level-90 Adventurer, that would have been no more than a morning stroll. Actually, in a world where the concept of "levels" existed, it might not have been anything that praiseworthy. However, even as the group got all sweaty and muddy and was yelled at by Isaac and the others, who were outsiders, and even though the training was harder than anything they'd done before, no one complained. He was forced to admit they were really putting their hearts into it.

Once back at their lodgings, out of the Glass Greaves' hearing, Isaac's companions had praised them, too. It probably meant that, in the two months since they'd begun this drill, the Knights of the Black Sword and the Glass Greaves had started to understand each other.

Out of the five groups, one of the remaining two was on leave in the city, and the last one was currently fighting monsters in the Dovature Badlands. They'd broken up into small teams and were hunting high-level monsters under the leadership of the Knights of the Black Sword. This was what was known as "power leveling."

The growth speed of People of the Earth was far lower than that of Adventurers. According to reports, it was only about one-fifth as fast. Even with that disadvantage, however, if they defeated monsters more than twenty levels above them in rapid succession, their levels would zoom up at a speed that seemed like a joke to People of the Earth common sense.

Of course, if they just left them to their own devices after raising their levels, they wouldn't know how to use that combat power, and that was bound to cause trouble. Since that was the case, they put them through physically punishing drills like this one after power leveling and made them fight mock battles until they passed out, forcing them to get used to their heightened physical performance. This routine was the level-boosting drill the Knights of the Black Sword had been conducting for the past two months.

Isaac opened his eyes a crack.

Then he closed them again.

He thought he'd heard something. It was probably just his imagination.

However, the reality he'd planned to ignore caught him in the form of a youthful voice: "Master Isaaaaac!"

A boy came running up on incredibly light feet, stopped near the big tree Isaac was leaning against, and caught his breath; his cheeks were flushed. The boy had pale skin and silver hair, and he looked intelligent. His complexion was probably fair to begin with. From the looks of his build, he didn't seem the least bit tough. That was why, although he'd only run a short distance, his cheeks were rosy and he was breathing hard.

Even though his throat was rasping painfully, he wore a huge smile. "Master Isaac!"

"Just Isaac's fine. That other way you use it is creepy."

The boy's call had almost broken off in the middle so that he could breathe, but at the sound of it, Isaac sat up. A hooded Adventurer and maids came running up after the boy. They set up an enormous parasol to block the sunlight, expanding the shade, then laid down a canvas sheet, which Isaac shifted aside to make room for. The boy looked at Isaac with an expression that seemed to be asking for permission, but the hooded Adventurer—Isaac's adjutant Lezarik—told him, "Please sit down," so he did.

"But…"

"Doesn't hearing a kid say 'master' make your skin crawl?"

With his mouth set in a cross line, Isaac spoke to the maids, who were preparing beverages. They only gave disconcerted smiles and spoke vaguely: "Well, sir, we really couldn't say…" They were probably hesitant to comment on the manners of their employer's child. *And they've got good boobs, too. What a waste*, Isaac thought, looking even crosser.

"Listen, kid."

"It's Iselus."

"Uh… Iselus."

When Isaac spoke to him—giving up on his strategy of doing something about it in a roundabout way, through the maids—Iselus always responded cheerfully. *Why does he like me so much?* Isaac asked himself.

"Can't you do something about that tone of yours?"

"Father and Mother told me I must mind my manners."

"Father" and "Mother," he says. Isaac held his forehead wearily.

"See, here's the thing: I'm bad with stuff like that."

"You're an Adventurer, Master Isaac, and you're currently training the Knights of Maihama as their instructor, and you also defended Maihama."

Both in the old world and in *Elder Tales,* Isaac had avoided this sort of refined, tiresome stuff. These were things for Krusty and Shiroe—the four-eyes demographic—to handle, not Isaac.

Still, this small child seemed to have gotten the wrong idea about something, and he'd apparently taken a liking to Isaac.

He was a kid, and smart, and a weakling. *Talk about hard to handle.* Isaac frowned and sent the boy a sidelong glare.

Not only that, Iselus was smiling. There was no telling what he'd thought.

"I did all that stuff because I wanted to."

"Is that right?"

"Yeah, that's right. I'm not a *master* or a lord or anything big like that. The elite four-eyes who's good at that crap is off on a journey right now."

"He's traveling?"

"Well, I guess it's nothing to do with you."

"Yessir, that's indeed not correct!"

Iselus didn't know Krusty, so it was only natural, but he nodded, suspecting nothing.

If that Berserker were here, Isaac thought, *I wouldn't have been doing this job in the first place.* Deep down, the guy was a lot like Isaac, and yet he was top-notch at hiding his true nature and acting meek. Krusty would have been the perfect person to drill the People of the Earth knights.

Isaac had heard he'd gone missing under mysterious circumstances, but he wasn't all that worried about Berserker Krusty. He was sure he'd just turn up one day and say, "My apologies for causing you trouble. As a matter of fact, I found a new raid quest."

It was true, however, that things were starting to seem iffy in Akiba due to him not being there.

It was no exaggeration to say the leader was the team, so a group that had lost theirs became fragile. Isaac had seen several of those cases; for the most part, they ended in ways that weren't fun to watch. Not that he thought Krusty's D.D.D. was defenseless... As Isaac was thinking these things, Lezarik called to him in a slightly teasing tone.

"Isaac the Young."

"Quit with that 'Isaac the Young' crap."

"There, Master Iselus, you see?" asked Lezarik. "You can use 'young' as an honorific for him."

"Really? 'Isaac the Young'...?"

As a rule, the adjutant got the short end of the stick, and he glanced at Isaac with a suppressed smile that seemed to say he wasn't about to let the opportunity to bait this guy slip past him.

"People, seriously—"

"It's rather dashing, don't you think? 'Isaac the Young.'"

Iselus and Lezarik spoke in a surround-sound chorus. Although there was no telling what was fun about it, Iselus was nodding vigorously, looking as if it all made sense to him now. As they watched him, even the maids started to giggle.

"Your mouth's hanging open, Isaac the Young."

The problem with Lezarik was that he always, always managed to quit just before Isaac blew up. Just as if it were a game of chicken, right before he hit his boiling point, he retracted his words.

"Rrgh! Watch it, or I'm gonna use the Black Sword of Pain!!"

Shrugging in response to Isaac's yell, Lezarik briskly pulled Iselus by the hand and began saying things like, "Come, let's go cheer on the knights as they train. That's a duty for the lord's whole family."

Raking his fingers through his hair in irritation, Isaac glanced at the drilling knights.

When he looked, he saw that their rushing feet were beginning to slow. Spurring them on would probably be a good way to burn off his annoyance.

Picking up his trusty sword, Isaac navigated the gentle downward slope.

5

"Camaysar, the Genius of Marriage...?"

Shiroe repeated the name Soujirou had said.

He'd never heard it before. A vast number of enemies had appeared in *Elder Tales* since the time when it had been a game, and even Shiroe didn't know all of them.

Still, at the very least, he remembered the names of most of the major enemies who'd appeared on the Japanese server. Setting aside the foreign-sounding name Camaysar, it was hard to believe he would have forgotten a moniker as distinctive as "the Genius of Marriage."

"Yes, that was what he called himself."

"That wasn't 'marriage' so much as 'marriage fraud.'"

Nazuna picked up where Soujirou had left off.

Tatami flooring, paper sliding doors, and an example of beautiful cursive characters hanging in the alcove.

Shiroe and Akatsuki were in the traditional Japanese room in the guild house of the West Wind Brigade, one of Akiba's leading combat guilds. Soujirou, its guild master, and Nazuna, his right-hand woman, had come out to meet them.

The two of them were Shiroe's old, familiar companions from the Debauchery Tea Party.

Shiroe's daily routine was built around tables and chairs, and it was a little hard for him to relax in such a traditional space. Meanwhile, Akatsuki seemed used to rooms like this one, and she'd started on the tea refreshments that had been set out for them. Akatsuki's room at Log Horizon had been set up traditionally as well, like this one but smaller. Kneeling formally didn't seem to bother her at all.

"He was a strange enemy, just as you said, Mr. Shiro."

"I'm surprised you ran into one, Soujirou."

"Really? I thought you were expecting it."

"'Expecting' isn't really the word; I did think that, if I talked to everyone, I might get information about encounters with enemies like him, but..."

Shiroe and Akatsuki had visited the West Wind Brigade because Soujirou had wanted to talk to them. When he'd brought up the subject over a telechat, Shiroe had been at a place where he could talk right away, so he'd gone over. When he'd run into Akatsuki in the living room and told her he was going to the West Wind for a bit, she'd ended up going with him.

Shiroe had asked Soujirou about "odd, unfamiliar monsters": changes in enemies that had appeared after the Catastrophe or the existence of unique enemies. Shiroe had begun gathering information in order to learn about them in detail, and just as he was getting started, he'd hit the jackpot.

The information Soujirou and Nazuna gave him was just as he'd thought it might be—or rather, it was beyond what he'd imagined.

"I hear other people have reported encounters, too. It doesn't sound like it was the same guy, though."

"You haven't changed a bit, Nazuna."

"Well, yeah. We've got a girls' information network here, after all. We're pretty awesome with things like that. Keh-heh-heh."

As a matter of fact, Shiroe already had information about the monsters known as Geniuses.

He'd only just learned that that was what they were called, but reports that new strains of monsters had been discovered on the Yamato Server weren't actually all that unusual.

Most of them had been rash assumptions on the part of the Adventurers, who'd lost their external strategy sites. Yet, when he'd gone over those reports carefully, there had been some that definitely seemed to be not mistakes or false memories, but actual new strains.

After the Catastrophe, as time passed, these eyewitness reports had continued to increase.

This wasn't simply a case of information he hadn't known belatedly coming to light. It was as if the number of cases was growing over time.

He didn't think all these new monsters were Geniuses, but according to Soujirou and Nazuna, people besides the West Wind Brigade had apparently encountered them as well.

From what the pair said, Camaysar, the Genius of Marriage, had been able to disguise itself as a Person of the Earth and bewitch the opposite sex.

It had taken the form of a young Person of the Earth merchant, infiltrated the town of Akiba, which had lost its urban defense mechanisms, won a variety of female Adventurers over to its side, and temporarily had influence that made it impossible to ignore.

Some of the West Wind Brigade members who belonged to Soujirou's Personal Guard had gotten suspicious and had subjugated the enemy.

"They're as reckless as ever, aren't they?"

"We're a guild with high morals, see. If anybody messes with our girls, we show 'em no mercy."

"She's right, my liege."

For some reason, Akatsuki nodded in agreement with Nazuna's words, as if she was proud of them.

"Did you help them, too, Akatsuki?"

"No, this is the first I've heard of it."

In that case, Shiroe didn't understand why she'd nodded so cheerfully.

Watching Shiroe out of the corner of her eye, Nazuna puffed out her chest, and Akatsuki nodded away, her eyes full of respect. He glanced at Soujirou, sending a distress signal. "What's this about?"

The response he got back was an amiable one: "Apparently, they've become friends. Girls make friends quickly when they eat sweets together."

Soujirou's the only one who could say things that totally carefree, Shiroe thought.

Fortunately, his memory was pretty good, and he hadn't forgotten the tragedy at the Libra Festival... In other words, what had happened to him and his two companions when they'd "eaten sweets together" at the Danceteria cake buffet. In the end, he and Soujirou were men of different calibers.

Shiroe resolved not to delve too deeply into this particular issue.

Letting her eyes fall to the sheaf of papers in her hand, Nazuna continued, "At this point, the ones we've heard of are Sislau, the Genius of Pestilence; Zahun, the Genius of Scandal; Baglis, the Genius of Measures; and..."

"And the one we defeated, Camaysar, the Genius of Marriage."

"That's about the size of it."

The sheaf of papers seemed to be a hastily drafted report.

"We've put together detailed notes about all this, but…what the heck are these things, Shiro?"

Nazuna lowered her voice.

The words she'd muttered softly had been "Something smells fishy." That was probably her intuition talking. She looked like she was crude, slipshod, a big drinker, and a slacker, but her instincts were sharp. Those instincts had saved Shiroe during their Tea Party days, and they'd tormented him ten times as often as they'd rescued him.

That said, it was hard to know how to respond.

It would have been easy to explain them away as new monsters that had been added with *Homesteading the Noosphere*, but he couldn't believe that was the truth. Even so, Shiroe didn't currently have any way to corroborate the information he'd learned. He had a hunch it couldn't be corroborated at all.

"……"

"They're enemies, right, Mr. Shiro?"

For that reason, he didn't have a ready answer for Soujirou.

He thought they were enemies. He was almost certain they would block his way and the Adventurers' future. However, he wasn't convinced they were "enemies" in the literal sense of the word. No, more than that, he suspected they might not be enemies at all, in the way that *a fallen tree that blocked the road was an obstacle, but not an enemy.*

"They attack us, so we have to fight them."

As a result, Shiroe phrased his answer so that it neither affirmed nor denied what Soujirou had said.

Nevertheless, Soujirou seemed to be satisfied with that.

With a big, relieved smile, he murmured, "Oh, good. We already defeated him anyway."

Oh, I see, Shiroe thought. He hadn't been demanding an explanation from Shiroe so much as worrying about an opponent they'd already defeated.

Soujirou was a younger player, and for some reason, he seemed to idolize Shiroe. He'd always seemed to like him. In the past, they'd often formed parties together and gone around to different dungeons, in addition to Tea Party activities. Soujirou and Shiroe had often teamed up with Naotsugu and Kazuhiko when they went to have fun, and at the time, Saki and Soujirou's other fans had been jealous of Shiroe.

Soujirou's a kind kid.

"They're different from regular monsters, though, somehow."

"Maybe the Catastrophe affected them, too? Or was it *Homesteading the Noosphere*?"

Soujirou and Nazuna continued to shoot questions at Shiroe, who'd gotten lost in his thoughts.

Truly, they were both quick on the uptake. Even if they didn't know much about the situation, they'd come very close to hitting the nail on the head through intuition alone.

"It's both."

"…Huhn."

Nazuna didn't probe Shiroe's answer any further. She had standards for advancing or retreating that he didn't understand, and there were lines she wouldn't cross. It was probably because she was older than Shiroe.

"Is there anything we can do, Mr. Shiro?"

In response to Soujirou's question, Shiroe said, "I'd like a little more information. That, and time."

"So basically, you want us to defend the town," Nazuna said, as sharp as ever, and he nodded emphatically.

"Ah. I see. In other words, just keep doing what we've been doing, right? You can count on us."

Soujirou gave an easygoing smile.

His relaxed, good-natured expression made Shiroe feel relieved, but he also thought, *I mustn't lean on him too much.*

He remembered the platform of old Akiba Station, with its flitting spark-bugs.

When Shiroe had told him he wanted his help to establish the Round Table Council, Soujirou had agreed without even asking why.

Soujirou was quick to do so, but that didn't mean the determination and the vow that lay beneath that agreement weren't serious. It was also true that having Soujirou's support had enabled him to launch the Round Table Council. When the Crescent Moon League had first released their Crescent Burgers, the West Wind Brigade had been the ones to protect them from criticism and pressure. Shiroe had only learned that afterward. *Talk about a strategist with a poor endgame.* He'd been saved from start to finish, and the fact brought a stinging warmth to his heart.

"Well, just you leave it to us. We've gotten pretty tough, y'know."

"Yes, let us handle it, Mr. Shiro."

"Count on us, my liege."

For some reason, Akatsuki gave him her assurance along with the other team. It was funny, and Shiroe chuckled. Catching it from him, Soujirou cracked up, too.

"Yeesh, Souji. What?"

"It's nothing… Girls are strong, aren't they, Mr. Shiro?"

Well, yes, they're strong. They're probably too strong, he thought, standing up.

As Shiroe said his good-byes, grimacing at the tingling in his legs, Soujirou murmured something quietly.

"He was a strange enemy, Mr. Shiro."

He probably meant the Genius.

Soujirou's eyebrows came together, as if he was retracing his memories. "I don't know how to put it. He was the most *Elder Tales*–like thing I've seen since coming to this world."

"Like *Elder Tales*…?"

"Yes. Of course I'd never seen him before, and his attacks were odd, and he was strong, but…"

"Yeah, exactly. Way more so than the People of the Earth, I guess you'd say."

"It was like a game. The enemy felt hollow, as if we'd defeated an *Elder Tales* monster."

Soujirou's words were always intuitive. Since he had the ability to reach the right answer in a single leap, he was bad at explaining how he'd gotten there in ways that were easy to understand.

Even so, Shiroe engraved those words in his heart.

There was bound to be something in them that he needed to understand.

6

By the time they left the West Wind guild house, the sky was already madder red.

Even if it wasn't as busy as their old world, Akiba was lively, even at sunset. Peddlers looking for lodgings. Street stalls that prided themselves on flavor, selling side dishes for the evening meal. Adventurers returning to their bases from outlying fields.

Shiroe and Akatsuki walked side by side through a mixed, milling crowd of Adventurers and People of the Earth.

He gazed absently at the foot traffic. Soujirou's words—Elder Tales-*like*—overlapped with the orange-tinted scenery. He'd probably been talking about the time when all they'd done was look at things through a display screen. However, the crowd he was watching now didn't seem anything like what it had been in the game.

What had made Soujirou choose those particular words? Shiroe hadn't yet come into contact with a Genius. For that reason, he didn't understand what the other young man had been trying to say, or what he'd felt.

"My liege."

They'd probably been walking for about ten minutes.

Shiroe registered the passage of time less as the sensation that time had passed than as a result of their having changed locations.

He'd gotten lost in thought, only to have been pulled back to the present by Akatsuki's questioning voice and her cutely tugging at his sleeve.

Realizing that, at some point, he'd forgotten she was there, Shiroe came to a halt.

"Hmm? What, Akatsuki?"

She was gazing up into his face. Looking thoughtful, she asked, "Are you tired, my liege?"

"Huh? Why? No, not at all."

"I see."

Shiroe answered quickly on reflex, and Akatsuki's reply was as laconic as ever. Just after the Catastrophe, Shiroe would have worked hard to keep the conversation going, but he didn't often think that way anymore. Akatsuki probably wasn't looking for witty conversation. She'd just been genuinely worried about him. Shiroe understood that now.

When he looked up, feeling the same way he'd felt when they walked along that beach, Akiba was beautiful in the sunset.

Possibly because of the rain that had fallen yesterday, the April greenery was particularly glossy, and it gleamed, reflecting the deep-red evening sun. An early pub had lit orange Firefly Lamps and begun to call in customers, and Adventurers filtered through its door in twos and threes.

Because of the ancient trees and abandoned cars, visibility on the central avenue was poor compared with its counterpart in Akihabara on Earth. Nevertheless, street stalls selling grilled skewers and fried foods were lined up on the road's mossy shoulders, creating a warm atmosphere.

This was evening in Akiba.

Shiroe and Akatsuki stood where they were and gazed at it for a while.

There was a light tug on the hem of his clothes, and Akatsuki whispered, "Something smells very good, my liege."

It was probably the aroma of fried bean-jam buns.

Akatsuki's reaction struck Shiroe as funny, and he laughed a little.

"I didn't say that because I wanted you to buy me some, my liege."

"I didn't think you had."

"Good."

At that answer, Shiroe remembered the scene at the West Wind Brigade a little while earlier.

Akatsuki, who was taciturn and, if he'd had to say, shy, had seemed pretty friendly with Nazuna back there. She hadn't been like that before. At the very least, he didn't think Akatsuki had actively interacted with anyone outside Log Horizon before he'd left Akiba.

"Do you go out and have fun with Nazuna?"

"Yes. She knows lots of good restaurants."

"I see."

Akatsuki's voice seemed mildly animated, and Shiroe nodded.

Apparently, her circle of friends was growing.

"It's not just Nazuna. Riezé, Mikakage, and the princess go, too."

"Is that right...?"

Shiroe nodded, but he was pretty startled.

Of course, he knew that if he actually looked startled, Akatsuki would sulk, so he didn't let it show in his expression. He didn't, but still, that was a rather revolutionary step forward. The names Akatsuki had given included members of the West Wind Brigade, D.D.D., and—if he remembered right—the Roderick Trading Company. And on top of that, Princess Raynesia.

Before he'd departed for the north to negotiate with the Kunie clan, Shiroe remembered, he'd asked Akatsuki to guard Princess Raynesia.

"Quite a lot happened while you were gone, my liege."

"I see."

Just as Shiroe had gained a variety of things in the Abyssal Shaft, Akatsuki had apparently acquired lots of things in Akiba.

Technology, organizations of self-government, and monsters weren't the only things that had changed after the Catastrophe. Shiroe and the others were changing, too. It wasn't simply in the sense of levels or mastering Mysteries. It was in places that were difficult to see: ties to other people. Shiroe, who hadn't thought about things from that perspective before, remembered his expedition to the north.

Naotsugu, the friend who'd gone with him the whole way. Tetora, who'd gotten friendly with them in the blink of an eye and now walked around like the ruler of the guild house. William, the guild master of Silver Sword. Kinjo of the Kunie clan. The magic researcher, Li Gan... And Demiquas.

Good encounters and bad ones resonated together, and before long, they'd connected.

He was sure it wouldn't be in vain.

When he looked down, Akatsuki responded with an "Uh-huh." The evening sun was sinking slowly. It was time to return to the guild hall for dinner.

"Shiroeee."

Just as they were passing in front of the guild center, a girl's voice rang out. It wasn't Akatsuki's.

"Minori."

Minori came trotting up to the two of them. She was dressed in street clothes, a blouse and necktie, instead of the *miko* outfit she wore when she was going adventuring.

"Hmph. And it was such a good atmosphere, too…"

"Shiroe, Akatsuki, are you on your way home?"

Minori fell in beside the two of them, walking with light, skipping steps. She looked up at Shiroe from the side opposite Akatsuki, and she was smiling. She seemed to be in a good mood today.

"That's right. Is your part-time job over, Minori?"

"Yes. They gave me souvenirs today."

"Today, *too*, you mean," Akatsuki corrected glumly.

Both of Minori's hands held bags that were stuffed with groceries and medicines.

They were probably things she'd been given at the Production Guild Liaison Committee and the Round Table Adventure Agency, where she worked part-time.

Minori boasted a talent for clerical work that was far beyond her years, and they'd heard that both offices treasured her as a first-rate resource. She was good-natured and polite, and she was idolized even at the contact windows.

Some items were on the verge of spilling out of the bag, and Akatsuki swiftly steadied them, asking Minori if she was all right. The two of them were frozen in a pose that made it look like a marriage interview. "Want me to carry that?" Shiroe asked, but apparently, Minori had something she wanted to show him.

"No, it's fine. Because… Eh-heh."

At that, Minori dexterously stuck a hand into the overflowing sack that hung from her shoulder, then held out an odd cloth bag with both hands, as if showing it off.

"It's my Magic Bag."

"Whoa!"

Minori's bright smile was contagious; Shiroe and Akatsuki grinned right along with her.

She and the rest of the younger group had finally completed their Magic Bags. It wasn't just Minori, who used hers every day like this, but Touya, Isuzu, and Rundelhaus as well. Serara of the Crescent Moon League had gotten a Magic Bag, too.

On top of that, their group had done the town of Akiba a significant favor.

The astonishing number of wyvern skins Minori and the others had brought back with them had made Magic Bags common among Akiba's low-level Adventurers. Ordinarily, only one Magic Bag could be made per person, and you had to undertake a quest to get it, but Calasin had talked the People of the Earth artisans into lowering the levels of the quests they'd accept. Shopping District 8 had even put up the money for production, so now, even the newest beginner in Akiba was able to have a Magic Bag in any design they wanted.

Over many nights, Minori had told Shiroe about the battle with the wyverns, all their encounters, and the sort of conflict they just couldn't reconcile themselves to.

She and the others had lived through a lot on that journey. Not all of those things had been pleasant; they'd felt pain so fierce they'd nearly burst from it. But even so, they were still smiling.

Shiroe thought, frankly, that that was amazing.

If he'd been on that journey, he didn't know if he would have been able to be as kind as Minori and Touya. He was pretty sure he couldn't have spread courage and inspired the People of the Earth the way Isuzu and Rundelhaus had.

"Oho!"

Akatsuki gazed at Minori, who had put on the airs of somebody older and was twirling around.

"Did you design that, Minori?"

Shiroe had heard about it from Calasin, and he knew already, but he asked anyway. He didn't really understand it, but the Magic Bag Minori had designed was avant-garde, with floppy things that looked like arms and legs sprouting from it. "Yes, I did!" Minori told him, beaming, and Akatsuki chimed in in a friendly way: "That's amazing, Minori! You're really good at feminine things!"

Shiroe gazed at the interaction, feeling somehow dazzled.

They really were changing. Watching the two of them made him feel that that was probably a good thing.

"While we're here, should we pick up some souvenirs?"

"I vote yes!"

"My liege, I want red-bean buns."

"You do like red-bean buns, don't you, Akatsuki?!"

Shiroe wasn't spoiling them, but he'd offered to buy them a souvenir, and their response was immediate. Their teamwork was improving nicely. However, Shiroe wanted to get something to go. If they did that, they'd be able to eat it with Naotsugu and Captain Nyanta. He wouldn't have to take attacks from the two of them all by himself.

"Yes, they're the ultimate sweet."

"Wouldn't you like to get jellies once in a while?"

"Do you have a problem with red-bean buns, Minori?"

"No, not at all, it's just…for the sake of variety…"

"Hrmmmm."

Minori and Akatsuki's conversation went on lightly. Both seemed to have lost quite a lot of reserve as far as the other was concerned; since they'd started living in the same guild house, they'd opened up to each other. Even in little things like this, there had been changes.

Now if only they'd avoid walking on either side of him and talking across him…

Thinking this, Shiroe smiled in defeat behind his glasses.

He'd had the thought, but he knew that if he said it aloud, they wouldn't listen. In any case, when women were in a bad mood, they deliberately misinterpreted what you said, and when they were in a good mood, they ignored it. Indicus had been like that.

On the other hand, *that other woman* had always been in a good mood and had never listened to the conversation at all.

"Why not just get both?"

"Yes, he's right, Akatsuki!"

"I suppose there's no help for it."

"I'd like strawberry shortcake, I truly would. Shiroe, treat me, too! Me too!"

Shiroe had been groping around for a good compromise, but a cute voice had broken into the conversation and spectacularly blocked his way. It was Tetora. As usual, there was a little top hat perched on the coquettish idol's pink hair.

"Ha-hah!"

Tetora had jumped at Shiroe, tackling him around the waist, and Akatsuki tried to tear the interloper off.

"Don't cling to my liege, you half-idol."

"I'm not half; I'm complete! In English, the word is 'perfect'! In terms of the Milky Way, I'm galactic! Even Shiroe's happy that I'm clinging to him."

"No, I'm not."

"Oh, *now* you give a decisive response!"

Tetora reeled back, as if shocked by an unbelievable sight. This self-proclaimed idol overreacted to absolutely everything. Even though Tetora hadn't been a member of the guild long, the idol's personality was already a familiar part of Log Horizon.

"Huh? Is that what you thought of me…?"

"Hmph. Come on, Shiroe. Let's go to Kanako's!"

"My liege, the red-bean bun shop is waiting for us."

"Waaaah, buy shortcake, too!"

"They're seasonal offerings. Get cherry blossom red-bean buns. If we don't eat them now, when will we ever get to?"

"I know! Let's all pull on Shiroe, and whoever lasts the longest without pulling off her bit of him gets her request granted!"

"Huh?! I'd like his left leg, then."

"In that case, his right leg is mine!"

What sort of torture were they planning to inflict on him?

Shiroe shrugged, smiling wryly.

With three different, lively voices in his ears, he looked up at the sky, which was darkening to violet.

There were a lot of things he needed to think about. This modest happiness made him rather sad. Twilight was catching up with the world. Shiroe was just a graduate student, and yet he'd ended up in a position where he knew this.

For Adventurers, death wasn't an end.

However, they might have a time limit.

Shiroe ended up reflecting on that premonition.

CHAPTER.

2

TRAVELER

▶ NAME: AINS

▶ LEVEL: **90**

▶ RACE: **HUMAN**

▶ CLASS: **KANNAGI**

▶ HP: **10154**

▶ MP: **10241**

▶ ITEM 1:

[SPIRIT BOW—QUEEN OF THE NIGHT]

A FANTASY-CLASS BOW HE ACQUIRED FROM THE GOLDEN BOOKCASE OF ROMATRICE. IT CAN FIRE AMULETS INSTEAD OF ARROWS. IT HAS NO ATTACK POWER AT ALL; IT'S USED TO RECOVER AND SUPPORT ALLIES. SINCE IT REQUIRES TECHNICAL OPERATION, IT'S VERY HARD TO USE.

▶ ITEM 2:

[COOLING EYE MASK]

IF YOU PUT IT ON WHEN YOU GO TO BED, IT USES COOL AIR TO RELAX THE AREA AROUND YOUR EYES AND HELP YOU SLEEP SOUNDLY. IT ALSO RECOVERS HP VERY SLIGHTLY. AINS CLAIMS THAT, IF USED REGULARLY, IT MAY IMPROVE INTELLIGENCE. APPARENTLY, SHIROE AND RODERICK USE THEIRS ALL THE TIME AS WELL.

▶ ITEM 3:

[FAIRY-BRAND RODERITAN DX]

A POWERFUL NUTRITION PRODUCT (PINEAPPLE FLAVORED), CREATED BY MIXING TREASURE-CLASS RECOVERY ELIXIR AND BLUE DRAGON TEARS WITH EQUAL PARTS KINDNESS. LOVINGLY MADE BY THE RODERLAB. RODERICK GAVE IT TO AINS AS A SAMPLE. THE DRINK CURES ALL FATIGUE INSTANTLY, BUT IT MAKES YOU DRUNK AND SICK, SO YOU CAN'T DRINK TOO MUCH OF IT.

<IRON SKEWERS>
COOKING TOOLS. THEY'RE
EASY TO HANDLE, BUT
IT'S HARD TO GRILL
PROPERLY WITH THEM.

▶ 1

In a hall where the air was thick with the aroma of oil and spices, People of the Earth waitresses dashed back and forth. The Knights of the Black Sword kept pelting them with a veritable storm of orders.

They weren't used to training People of the Earth, and it might actually be more tiring than training Adventurers. Everyone knew that good food was the best way to soothe fatigue. The appetites of the members of the Knights of the Black Sword were as hearty as the vigor with which they polished off raid enemies.

The guild master, Isaac, was no exception. Get lots of exercise, then eat lots of good stuff: Even in this world, where physical performance was influenced by level, he thought that was a fundamental part of keeping your strength up.

Just as Isaac stuck his knife into a thick slab of meat, documents landed on his table with a loud thump, and the beer on the tabletop sloshed.

"Top of the evening to you, Isaac."

"Huh? Uhn. If it ain't Calasin."

"There we go."

With no sign of compunction, Calasin, the guild master of the production guild Shopping District 8, sat down across from Isaac.

The din in the hall suddenly hushed. The Knights of the Black Sword were mostly sports types, and as a group, they tended to value hierarchical relationships. Any member who sat at the guild master's table without permission would get a severe telling-off from a sharp-eyed senior member.

On top of that, Calasin was an "outsider." Even if he was one of the Round Table Eleven, by the Knights of the Black Swords' standards, he was a wimpy, dandyish man.

Several of the guild members got up from their seats, but Isaac stopped them with a hand, looking bored.

Whether or not he'd registered the atmosphere around them, Calasin kept his usual business smile trained on him. Isaac pointed at him with his fork, which had a piece of meat impaled on it.

"You've been acting real familiar lately."

"You're not the type who cares about these things, are you, Isaac?"

"Well, yeah, but we're not talking about me. This is about you."

"Ah-ha-ha-ha-ha. Even I choose who I do it to."

"Tch. You and your dumb grin. I don't get you at all."

Of all the production guilds, Shopping District 8 was putting particular effort into commerce with the People of the Earth. Its guild master, Calasin, was a superficially polished, wily individual who competed on even terms with crafty, experienced People of the Earth merchants.

Removing his trademark cap, Calasin called to a Person of the Earth who was passing near them. "Ah, get me a cold one, too, and some fried rockfish."

The uniformed waitress jotted down the order on her notepad, bowed, then headed for the kitchen. She seemed to be well versed in Adventurer etiquette.

"That fried rockfish is real tasty."

"Isn't it, though? I've been looking forward to it. It's practically why I came here."

"Out doing migrant work again?"

"Come on, don't call it that. This is Shopping District 8's first branch trading house. I just came to check up on it. Besides, I need to look over the books."

This dining hall was an annex of the trading house that was Shopping District 8's branch office in Maihama. There had apparently been all sorts of troublesome negotiations involved in putting a branch office right at the feet of Duke Cowen, the leader of the League of Free Cities, and Calasin had been a central figure in them. Lezarik had told him that that was why there hadn't been any complaints about Shopping District 8 getting a branch office here, instead of the Marine Organization, the largest player, or the Roderick Trading Company, which had a variety of cutting-edge technologies.

"Besides, it's not far from Akiba."

Lezarik offered Calasin some water, then sat down beside the two of them.

Because they worked together to get raid materials ready, Lezarik and Calasin had known each other for a long time. After the Catastrophe in particular, Isaac had heard they'd exchanged all sorts of information on a personal level.

"Right. Not if I'm by myself anyway. It's just a jump away by Giant Owl."

"What, you ride an owl?"

"It's not as if every major guild has griffins, you know. Only raid guilds do that."

Compared with griffins, Giant Owls had poorer speed and flying distance, and their recast times were long. Because you could get them outside of raid quests, more people used them than griffins, but to Isaac, they were wussy rides.

"Yeah, because you people are weak."

"That's right, we're weak. We'll charge your group a hundred times more for your food," Calasin warned him casually. He still had that smile on his face.

"Damn you..."

"Nobody really cares about that sort of thing though, huh?"

Lezarik calmly interjected: "Heeeey..."

"It doesn't matter, does it?"

"No."

This guy's like Lezarik, Isaac decided. The jerk dodged back lightly, right before Isaac blew up, and it was impossible to tell whether he was dense or fiendishly gutsy. Isaac's opinion of people like that was beginning to improve.

The waitress set a steaming plate down on the table. The white plate, toast-colored fried rockfish, shredded cabbage, and round heap of tartar sauce looked very appetizing.

"Whoa. That looks good. Hot!"

When he stuck his fork into it, the fried coating split with a light *crunch*. Calasin added a sauce bursting with onions, then dug in with a will.

Calasin polished off his fried fish in short order, nodding the whole time. Isaac, who'd been watching him, snorted. Lezarik ordered two more plates from the waitress.

"Seriously, did you come here just to get in my way?"

"Of course not. This is work, technically. Here."

Calasin took a single paper from the document case at his waist. Isaac accepted it and handed it to Lezarik without even glancing at it.

"The Round Table Council, is it?"

"Well, eventually."

At his adjutant's words, Isaac sent a question at Calasin, snitching a piece of fried fish from his plate as he did so.

"Then what is it right now?"

"For now, I guess you'd say it's about monsters called Geniuses."

As Calasin responded, he speared a piece off the fresh plate of fried rockfish that the waitress brought over.

"Yeah, I've heard the name. What are they?"

Passing his half-empty dish to Lezarik, Isaac pulled the nearby plate of piping hot fried seafood over to himself. Lezarik sighed, then parceled out a few pieces of fried fish from the half-empty plate to Isaac and Calasin.

"I don't know, either. On top of that, the People of the Earth are looking rather bellicose."

"…You mean those troops mustering in the west?"

One of the outstanding issues on the Round Table Council was the information that the Adventurers of Minami had joined forces with the Holy Empire of Westlande, the People of the Earth organization that governed Western Yamato, and were building up their military strength.

"That's right. I swear, all those people ever do is cause problems. And over here, everything's welfare and budgets and equality."

"That Ains loser is a pain in the ass, isn't he?"

"Well, we still have to meet with him and get by somehow."

"Huhn."

Carrying the last piece of fried rockfish to his mouth, Isaac took another look at Calasin's face.

"What, Isaac?"

This slender, mild-looking man always wore a foolish smile. He had a weakness for women and was constantly going gaga over them; he was chatty, and he got all noisy over superficial relationships. He behaved cleverly, and he waltzed off with all the best parts of everything. A pampered rich kid and a typical flirt: That was what he'd looked like to Isaac at first.

Back in the old world, Isaac hadn't liked guys like that, and they'd steered clear of him. They'd belonged to different worlds, and he'd thought that was just how things were.

Unexpectedly, though, once he'd talked to this guy, he'd realized he had his own logic. If he was shallow, then he wandered here and there, casually, like a shallow person. As a mild person, he slipped in between two parties like cushioning material. In this new world, Calasin was fighting in ways that Isaac didn't fight. Once he understood that, he'd stopped being able to just knock him down without hearing him out.

"Nah, I was just thinking—you're no two-bit player yourself."

"Agh! Geez, that's mean!!"

"Well, never mind."

"You know how it is. I may not look it, but I'm helping to run a self-governing organization. It would be easy to just throw it all away, but making it again would be rough, you know? The Round Table Council, I mean."

"Yeah."

"That's true for you, too, Isaac, so work, all right? C'mon, please."

"Aaaaah, shaddup, merchant. Your voice is rattling my skull."

"If you slash me in two, I'll split down the middle and talk at you from both sides in surround sound."

Isaac's eyebrows shot up. Calasin was still smiling. They glared at each other.

After a short pause, they both burst out laughing, simultaneously.

"I didn't know any guys like you before. I thought you'd be more of a nervous type."

"I'm a guild leader, too, you know. I can't just shrink down and act small all the time. Good grief. Besides, even I thought you were eight parts gorilla and two parts human, Isaac."

"And in reality, I'm...?"

"No comment."

"In any case, Isaac the Young isn't a gorilla; he's *nearly* a gorilla," Lezarik added, pouring beer into Isaac's glass and water into Calasin's.

"Damn, Leza, whose side are you on?"

Lezarik's solemn lips relaxed just a little. Calasin clapped his hands and guffawed, and like spreading ripples, laughter enveloped the surrounding tables as well.

Under cover of that storm, Calasin whispered quietly.

"I think you're probably vaguely aware of it already, but the atmosphere in Westlande is bad."

"Yeah."

"They say they're putting together an army..."

"I doubt the Round Table Council and Plant Hwyaden will be fighting each other, but whether we'll be able to stay uninvolved is..."

"It's doubtful, yes."

Akiba and Plant Hwyaden weren't openly hostile toward each other. However, if their respective allies—Eastal and the Holy Empire of Westlande—clashed with each other...

If their friend got hit, would they be able to act like it was none of their concern?. That was the question. Even Isaac understood that much, instinctively.

"Do you think that's why that guy Shiroe asked us to level up the People of the Earth knights? Because he saw this?"

"It could very well be. After all, Shiroe is a definite schemer."

"I'll have to ask about that, too."

In response to Isaac's words, Calasin's lips drew up in a smirk.

"In that case, attend the Round Table Council. You're on duty here in Maihama, Isaac, but you do have transportation, no? You are a raid guild, after all."

"Yeah. I've got a griffin."

"No girlfriend, though."

Lezarik teased Isaac, who was dangling his summoning pipe. In spite of himself, Isaac couldn't come up with a comeback.

"Women are—! That's fine, who cares about that?! Even if I do 'em a favor and go out with them, they start talking about breaking up right away. They're just a pain."

"Ah-ha-ha-ha-ha-ha. Shall I plan a mixer for you?"

"What, for real?!"

"Yes, of course. I've got a lot of experience with that sort of thing."

"But you don't have a girlfriend, either, Calasin."

This time, it was Calasin's turn to be mercilessly cut down by Lezarik's blade.

True, people who had partners didn't end up as seasoned mixer veterans. It had been an open secret on the Round Table Council that Calasin was in L-O-V-E with Marielle of the Crescent Moon League, and it was equally true that his romance had come to nothing.

…Not that Isaac was in such a fortunate position that he could point at him and laugh. If anyone played around until they were his age, sure, they ended up having had relationships with five or ten members of the opposite sex, but Isaac always got dumped a few nights after starting a relationship. Apparently, once he was feeling good, he started treating his women carelessly.

He was in no position to make fun of Calasin.

"Bwah-ha-ha-ha-ha! This guy's a playboy, but he ain't got no girl!"

—Nevertheless, without letting that bother him, Isaac roared with laughter.

"That sort of thing has nothing to do with mixers!" Calasin argued back; his poker face had crumbled, and he looked flustered.

The sight relieved Isaac, and he chugged the rest of his warm beer without coming up for air. There were lots of things he didn't like here, but they weren't bad enough that he couldn't drink and talk about dumb stuff.

When Isaac switched over from beer to distilled liquor, Calasin gamely followed suit.

Even if there were lots of problems, that didn't mean he couldn't enjoy the here and now. Most of life was a pain in the butt. Only an idiot would waste the liquor in front of him.

That night, the two of them drank until they were lying on the tavern's stone floor.

The only thing carved into Isaac's memory was the fun he'd had roaring with laughter over Calasin's taste in women.

▶ **2**

Akiba's guild center was the tallest building in town. It couldn't begin to compare to skyscrapers on Earth, but in this world, where all high-rise buildings had fallen into ruin, it was rare to see a structure that was over ten stories tall in the first place.

In Eastal, where there wasn't much to obstruct the view, the wind blew through the sky over Akiba. The town's obsidian heart, which stood out in the wind, gravestone-like, was the guild center. This was the headquarters of the Round Table Council.

In its large conference hall, under the stony gazes of statues of ancient princesses, the guild masters who represented Akiba were assembled. Somewhere along the way, the eleven remaining people who participated in the Round Table Council had begun to be called "the Decrement." The term meant that there weren't twelve of them; there was one missing.

"Black Sword" Isaac, the leader of the Knights of the Black Sword.

Master Swordsman Soujirou of the West Wind Brigade.

"Iron Arm" Michitaka, general manager of the Marine Organization.

"Fairy Doctor" Roderick of the Roderick Trading Company.

Calasin, the wide-area merchant who led Shopping District 8.

Marielle of the Crescent Moon League.

Akaneya, the shrewd Mechanist of RADIO Market.

Shiroe, the fiendish strategist of Log Horizon.

...And Ains, from Honesty.

Krusty, the guild master of D.D.D. and representative of the Round Table Council, was missing, while Woodstock of Grandale was away on a supply mission for a distant military expedition.

To Ains, the Round Table Council, with its three empty seats, seemed to be more incomplete than its numbers suggested.

"The fact that Shiroe's plan worked is a splendid thing."

"Yes, I'm really grateful for that. Now we'll get by without running out. After all, as far as the accounting books are concerned, the Round Table Council was bankrupt. We were practically holding things together with loans from the big guilds."

Akaneya's words were grave, while, as he agreed with him, Calasin's tone was light and flippant. However, what he actually said was serious.

"Still, I'm thinkin' this means we can relax a bit, right?"

"The zones around Akiba have already been released. We're purchasing zones or canceling our rights to them, moving toward the northeast. The number of zones that can't be owned should continue to increase. After all, in terms of the future, the idea of zones being available for purchase is scary."

This had been the Round Table Council's most serious problem since early autumn of the previous year. Thanks to Shiroe of Log Horizon, the financial pressure of the zone maintenance fees was being resolved. As a result, the mood in the council was slightly relieved.

Even by the month, the total maintenance fees had come to several million gold coins. This had eaten up the Round Table Council's budget at a speed that had made the term *pressure* seem too tame. The largest burden had been their purchase of all the space on Akiba's roads as zones.

"I'm sorry."

"We aren't blaming you, Shiroe. It's just that not everybody's as well-intentioned as you are, that's all."

Not purchasing the zones hadn't been an option.

He'd apologized for it, but as a matter of fact, Shiroe had purchased the Akiba guild center and had gained the power of life and death over more than ten thousand Adventurers. Famously, this had been the trigger for the establishment of the Round Table Council. Several other facilities were equally important: The Temple, the central commercial facilities, and Akiba as a whole would grant the same sort of power to anyone who purchased them.

These zones had been purchased soon after the establishment of the Round Table Council. It was safe to say they'd been forced to buy them, out of worry and vague fear, without making any specific assumptions about "who." After that, they'd continued to expand the purchased range into the areas around Akiba. Ains didn't think any of this had been a mistake. They had seemed like necessary measures. As proof, Honesty had contributed a reasonable amount of funding as well. All the guilds affiliated with the Round Table Council had felt the same way.

However, it was also true that the burden had been a heavy one and that it had put pressure on Akiba's assets. Because the Adventurers were wealthy and had been able to hold up under the burden, the problem simply hadn't grown obvious.

Shiroe of Log Horizon had resolved the issue with a drastic move: by returning zones that had already been purchased and making it impossible to purchase them. His method had made the Yamato server itself the owner of the zones. He'd gotten the capital for the initial payment out of the Kunie clan as well. Only a few of Akiba's ordinary Adventurers were aware of the incident, but the upper-level members of the guilds on the Round Table Council knew.

Naturally, Ains admired that plan, and he was grateful.

However, precisely because it had been solved, the next problem had presented itself.

"Since we now have financial leeway, I would appreciate it if we advanced the discussion regarding the matter I've been proposing for quite some time now."

Ains raised his voice, standing up and leaning out over the enormous round table.

"By 'matter,' you mean *that* one?"

Pulling a sour face, Michitaka shot a sidelong glance at Roderick. Roderick averted his eyes, and Calasin also looked a little disgusted.

Isaac had his arms folded and was looking cross, as always. No one spoke up.

"Umm… What was this proposal again?"

Soujirou, failing to pick up on the mood, smiled and asked Shiroe for details.

"It's a suggestion Ains made about information disclosure and redistribution."

Nodding once in response to Shiroe's answer, Ains went on. None of the guild masters shared his anxiety.

That fact filled him with foreboding. The people assembled here were the chief executives of Akiba's most famous guilds. There might be no help for their inability to register the issue properly. It couldn't be ignored, and he had to tell them about it.

"Currently, there is a rapidly growing disparity in Akiba. The wealth of those who can develop new technologies and hunt in the fields is growing, while those who cannot do so lose their minimal earnings in simply living day to day. The gulf between their assets is expanding rapidly."

The entire group was listening to Ains.

"This is a problem. We have to do something about it. The Mysteries are an issue as well."

"Huh?! Why are the Mysteries an issue?!"

Souji had asked his question in a voice that was almost comical, and Michitaka replied, "It's written in the proposal, remember?"

Yes, Michitaka and all the other guild masters gathered here were sincere. There was no room for doubt there. After all, they hadn't pushed back against opening discussion on Ains's views just now.

"The Mysteries and the new product development are causing the economic disparity. Large guilds are using their scale to conduct business, or in other words, to expand their revenue. We must rectify this. At present, approximately forty different types of Mystery have been reported to the Round Table. We should widely publicize this information. Production recipes as well."

"Hey, whoa, hold it. Hold up a minute. When you say 'recipes,' you mean the post-Catastrophe item production methods, right? Not the *Elder Tales* recipes?"

"That's correct."

"There's absolutely no way we can do that. Since the Catastrophe, item production is all trial and error! Even if it's just an order of ramen or a way to make soap, artisans rack their brains to come up with them and figure out workarounds on their own."

"That's true of the Mysteries, too. Besides, releasing information on them wouldn't make any difference, would it?"

Ains listened to Michitaka's and Soujirou's objections with a wooden expression. He'd anticipated this, but he'd probably been too hasty. It would be difficult to make recipes and Mysteries public. However, he'd thought that, if it were possible, it would soften the landing for widespread knowledge of their existence.

Still, if that wasn't possible, he'd have to get those before him to consider other methods.

"If that can't be done, we should consider redistributing assets."

"Redistribution, hmm…?"

Shiroe was also thinking about something. His expression was grim.

"That's right. When Adventurers have more than eighty thousand gold coins deposited in the guild center bank, the Round Table Council should confiscate the excess."

"Confiscate?! If we do that, folks'll start screamin' blue murder!"

"After doing so, we should redistribute the confiscated funds, prioritizing Adventurers who have few assets, according to the amount of their own asse—"

"Hey."

Isaac was the one who'd interrupted that proposal.

"I've been listening to you for a while, Ains, and that's some pretty self-centered stuff you're saying."

"Is it?"

"Money or the Mysteries or ways of making grub—those belong to the people who worked hard to get 'em. If you take 'em away, there's gonna be hell to pay. Don't tell me you don't know that."

"But there are people who have grown apathetic and just sit around hugging their knees!! What is the Round Table Council for, if not to save them?"

"We're working on it. The town is safe, and there aren't any PKs around here anymore! They're free to hunt and do business any way they want."

"You're saying that because you're one of the 'haves,' Michitaka."

"Maybe so, but in that case, Ains, lemme ask you: If we gave 'em recipes or money, would the people who are sitting around spring into action with a hundred times more energy? Can you guarantee that?"

Ains looked into Isaac's eyes and despaired at the refusal.

In the end, the problem was a sense of impending crisis.

The Round Table Council didn't sense the danger Ains did. That was why his words didn't reach them. No matter what he told them, it was pointless. After all, even the premise hadn't gotten through to them.

Once, there had been terror in Akiba.

Needless to say, it had been the fear caused by the Catastrophe. That they'd been pulled into this terrifying world by an unknown disaster had been the impetus, but a part too large to ignore had been the Adventurers themselves.

In this desolate, lawless world, their fellow Adventurers had been the ones who were able to hurt them. Whether they actually did get hurt or not hadn't been important. The Adventurers were earthlings who had lived in modern society, and to them, the mere existence of that possibility had been pain that was hard to bear.

That emotion had made it possible for Shiroe, the diabolical schemer, to launch the Round Table Council. Because most of the Adventurers living in Akiba had been afraid of one another, they had unconsciously desired stability. In other words, the Round Table Council had been created by fear.

This had been true of the subsequent purchase of the zones as well. The fear that "somebody, somewhere" might take away their right to live had driven the Round Table Council to buy up all the zones around Akiba. Even if this fear had been unconscious, it had been shared by the whole Council. That was why the policies had been passed, and why they had been implemented, heavy burden notwithstanding.

"Even so, we can't just ignore this issue."

"I know, hon, but..."

"If we publish development recipes, the technicians' motivation will fall."

"Is it really that hard to earn a daily living?"

"You keep saying 'disparity, disparity,' but we're all the same Adventurers, yeah?"

The conference room had suddenly grown noisy, and Ains bit his lip.

He wasn't talking about the present. He was discussing the future. Did the other guild masters really not understand?

Spurred on by terror, the Round Table Council had purchased many zones. Most of the capital had been supplied by the big guilds. Adventurers who had abundant assets had come together to put up the money, and so, although it hadn't been intended as such, the end result had been a transfer of assets from wealthy Adventurers to the public. In other words, even if they hadn't planned it that way, rich Adventurers had donated money for Akiba's sake.

It needed to be noted that, even under those circumstances, the gulf between Akiba's haves and have-nots had widened. What would

have happened if the money spent on the zone purchases, the assets of high-level Adventurers from big guilds, had been used for the Adventurers' own benefit? The horror of that idea made Ains dizzy.

If you asked Ains, this world was too straightforward and unstable.

"You're level 90. Magnificent."

"You're level 32, huh? Small-timer."

You had to walk around twenty-four hours a day with that label hanging from your neck. The simple existence of disparity was completely different from having that disparity constantly shoved in your face.

This wasn't just about level. It was true of equipment, and of subclass skills, and of results in business and hunting. It was the problem of incessantly being reminded of it, of being unable to escape it.

Population was the same way. At present, to the best of Ains's knowledge, there were only ten thousand or so Adventurers in Akiba. That was a frighteningly small number.

Say half of those had been level 90 on the day of the Catastrophe and that the remainder had been evenly distributed among the lower levels. In that case, there would be approximately 410 Adventurers between levels 30 and 35. That would mean that level-30 to -35 Adventurers who wanted to go out hunting could only form 68 six-member parties. Naturally, the majority of them probably belonged to big guilds. In that case, if a young level-30 player was looking for companions in town, there would be only about thirty groups they could potentially join.

How many of those thirty groups would be recruiting new members? It surely wouldn't be more than ten. How many of those ten groups would be looking for that player's main class, out of the twelve available classes?

These were only theoretical numbers.

However, the reality was that it was extremely difficult for Adventurers who strayed from their companions, communities, or guilds to find a new place to belong in Akiba right now. In terms of MMO common sense, the difference between the profits when hunting with friends and hunting solo was as wide as the gulf between heaven and earth. What should Adventurers who had slipped out of that circle do?

Even if you were hunting alone, you wouldn't have any problem keeping yourself fed from day to day— What sort of help would consolation like that be to their cracked hearts?

The Round Table Council simply hadn't noticed: Akiba held many germinating shadows. The fact that he couldn't share that sense of danger with them made Ains so anxious that his vision dimmed.

"I understand your proposal."

Shiroe was the one who'd spoken, and his eyes were calm and cool. His voice hadn't been loud, but the members of the Round Table Council looked at him, startled. As far as the other participants were concerned, the fiendish strategist's activity on the Round Table Council over the past ten months had given weight to his words.

Shiroe was one of the people whom Ains absolutely had to persuade if he was going to really communicate Akiba's problem. If he signed on, solving the problem in one stroke wouldn't be an impossibility.

Hope began to bud in Ains's heart.

"I do think you're right about the need to institute measures of some sort. However, the Round Table Council's budget is limited. Unlike Minami, we don't receive vast donations from the People of the Earth aristocrats, and we can't dip into the gold of the Kunie. Let's all take this issue back to our guilds and think about what sort of steps we could implement."

"But, Shiroe, if we do that, it might be too late—" Ains shouted.

Shiroe would probably be able to get additional financing from the Kunie.

He'd definitely be able to talk the combat guild blockheads around.

But Shiroe cut off Ains's request with a raised palm.

"Ains. I understand how you feel, but we can't do more than this. The Round Table Council is a fragile organization. If we voted on a decision that important by ourselves in this room, it might break both the Council and Akiba."

Slowly, Shiroe's words sank into Ains's mind.

He was right. Akiba was fragile, and an aggressive decision would shatter it.

If they took their time, though, it might break anyway.

All alone, in the midst of a feeling of bitter helplessness at having been unable to fully persuade them, Ains hung his head.

▶ 3

"It's done!"

"That's mewtiful."

"It's amazing. I've never done anything like this."

The kitchen on the second floor of the Log Horizon guild house was filled with a sweet aroma. In its center were Nyanta, who was in charge of cooking for the guild, and Serara, a girl from the Crescent Moon League who'd taken to visiting the guild house frequently.

Although no one had asked her to, she'd been helping Nyanta, claiming that she was learning how to cook. Nyanta had grown used to seeing her trot along behind him with her market basket.

"Snap peas are sweet and delicious this time of year. Since we rinsed them in cold water, they look like emewralds, don't they?"

"They're glistening!"

"How are the mew potatoes coming along?"

"I've boiled them all and finished the prep work."

Due to the transformations that had followed the Catastrophe, even Serara, who didn't have a Chef subclass, had become able to perform simple prep work without trouble. In combination with the skills provided by her New Wife's Apron, this meant that the number of recipes she knew was growing by the day. The fact seemed to please Serara enormously, and Nyanta smiled at her.

"Oh? Mew've gotten quite good at this."

"That's because you taught me, Nyanta."

At Nyanta's words, Serara puffed out her chest.

The two of them were looking at a large quantity of prepared vegetables. For tonight's dinner, they were planning to make platters of Chinese food. Chinese dishes needed to be cooked quickly, which meant that meticulous advance prep was required. Log Horizon, the guild whose kitchen Nyanta ran, had lots of big eaters. Naotsugu and Touya went without saying, but Rundelhaus and Minori weren't light eaters, either, and if they got interested, the other guild members ate heartily as well. Cooking was quite a task, but making a lot of something was exhilarating in its own unique way.

Thinking that it would take the steaming vegetables a little time to cool down, Nyanta removed his apron and took a pot from the shelf.

"In that case, shall we have tea?"

"Yes!"

They didn't bother going back to the drawing room.

The big table in the spacious kitchen was meant to be used for peeling vegetables or kneading pasta dough, but of course it was possible to make tea and take a break there. They often rested for a few minutes while cooking or doing chores, and of course they sometimes snacked here on the pretext of "taste-testing."

Nyanta took a spoonful of the orange jam he'd bought at Danceteria and dissolved it into the black tea. The fragrance of tea and the refreshing scent of citrus spread through the kitchen.

"Is it good?"

"Yes. It's warm."

Serara answered in a voice that sounded as if it were on the verge of melting. Her expression was charming, as defenseless as a cat on a veranda.

"Today is a quiet day, don't mew think?"

"Yes. We finished the advance preparations early, and there's still time before dinner."

"On days like this, naps sound very tempting."

"Fu-fu-fu-fu!"

Serara's expression was completely at ease, and at the sight of it, something deep in Nyanta's heart stirred restlessly. The warmer this kitchen was, the more unbearable the pain he felt.

His feelings weren't so strong that they made him fall to pieces, but the loneliness came in waves.

There had been a young man who had screamed that this world hadn't invited him. He'd just been kidnapped, he'd declared, so he was going to do whatever he wanted here. He'd brushed aside an operation that would take the lives of scores of People of the Earth with a "So what?" In this world, that sort of pain definitely did exist.

So while Serara smiled and Nyanta poured orange-flavored tea, on the other side of the steam that rose from it, there were still young people suffering, ones who couldn't accept this world.

Nyanta hadn't been able to do a thing.

He hadn't been able to reach the youth with anything: not his cooking or his sword skills or his accumulated experience. Nyanta had lived through all sorts of things, and he knew: The difference between him and Rondarg was a small one.

Rondarg could have been Nyanta, and Nyanta could have been Rondarg.

There wasn't much to differentiate between them at all. On the day of the Catastrophe, at that moment, where had they been? Who had they been with? Who had they spent the intervening time with? Had there been important words that had remained with them? The difference had probably been no more than that.

Differences like those weren't based in effort or talent. They were fate, encounters. Put bluntly, they were no more than coincidence. Nyanta understood this clearly.

He and any of the others who'd fallen into this world could become like Rondarg... And there would be no saving them.

"Mew look like mew're enjoying yourself, Seraracchi."

"Well, I am."

Her voice was animated. The reply had seemed to spring back at him, so Nyanta's response was delayed a moment.

"Are mew, then."

"...Have you been well lately, Nyanta?"

Serara must have noticed that pause. She looked up at him, wrapping her hands around her cup. Her eyebrows had drawn together very slightly in a worried expression. Nyanta felt contempt for himself; his unfair pain wasn't something a girl like Serara should know about.

"Oh, I'm fine."

That time, he managed to deliver the reply smoothly. As if it were only natural. As if it were no different from normal. Nyanta's role-playing was supported by his life, in which he'd accumulated quite a lot of time, and the ups and downs of the many emotions he'd experienced.

"Is that right...?"

"......"

Serara smiled, seeming relieved. Carefree smiles, wavering emotions, blue unease—Nyanta had left all these things in his previous world. They were proof of immaturity, but at the same time, they were also symbols of possibility.

To Nyanta, Serara's well-being was so precious it made him feel like praying.

"Seraracchi, are mew glad mew came to this world?"

It was a question he hadn't intended to ask, but it slipped out.

He'd asked himself that question over and over, and each time, it had lost more of its meaning. He could give his own answer to it, of course, but he'd given up, thinking that that answer wouldn't reach the world.

"Huh? Oh. Yes."

He'd thought she might give the question a little more thought, but Serara answered immediately.

"Do mew really?"

"Yes, I do. I mean, I can't see my dad or mom, and there were lots of problems and lots of awful things, but there've been all sorts of good things, too, like…"

"?"

"L-l-l-l-like dreams of what I want to be, and the future, and things."

"Do mew have those?"

In response, Serara gave a small, energetic nod, as if she was trembling.

Things she wanted to be. Hopes for the future. Guideposts to live by. Serara murmured that she certainly did have those things.

Nyanta exhaled a deep, tea-warmed breath.

A soft warmth, a heat that was different from what he'd felt when he'd confronted Rondarg, glowed inside him. Susukino. Choushi. Saphir. This girl had to have seen many cruel sights in this world, too. Even so, she'd told him there was something she wanted to become.

"If it's mew, Seraracchi, I'm sure mew'll be able to make any dream come true."

Let it be so. Nyanta murmured, weaving a prayer into the words.

"Ha, ha-wa-wa-wa-wa-wa…ah…"

As he watched, Serara's behavior grew erratic. Her hands wandered meaninglessly through the air, her expression wavered between laughing and crying, and her lips shifted through shapes without forming actual words.

"What's the matter?"

"—But my dream's still a long ways away, so… Um, I mean, I'm not giving up or anything! That's not what I meant! It's only, when I see Isuzu and Minori, I feel like I'm a little lacking, or that I'm just really hopeless, or…"

"……"

Nyanta waited for Serara to go on.

Sometimes it was possible to organize confused thoughts by verbalizing them, by communicating them to someone else. The result was an answer that was all your own, something you couldn't get through advice from other people.

She drew a deep breath. Then she drained her tea, ate a spoonful of orange jam, and took another deep breath.

Then, timidly, Serara looked up at Nyanta again.

"—I mean, I'm not sure, but…I think I need to become myself, properly, before I can, um, make that dream come true. I need to be a proper, mature version of myself. Besides, I'd like that."

Nyanta knew that Serara had been watching her friends in the younger group and that she'd looked as if she felt rushed. Minori, Touya, Isuzu, and Rundelhaus: All the children she spent time with had grown remarkably.

In chasing after Shiroe, Minori had begun using her tactical and clerical abilities in ways that surpassed adults.

Touya had kept calling for the Odysseia Knights, who were both older and stronger than he was, to live in this world.

And on the battlefield, Isuzu had found her own song and played its melody until her voice was hoarse.

Although he was a Person of the Earth, Rundelhaus had yearned to protect people and had become an Adventurer.

Serara's friends were blossoming rapidly, as if they were running up a staircase two steps at a time. Watching them, she might have felt as though she was childish. Nyanta had seen that sort of anxiety and emotional stress in her. He was an adult, and from his perspective, such worries seemed the mark of youth. Her future spread out before her, wide and endless. This was just a little pause, nothing to be concerned about.

Even so, Serara had said her goal was to become a proper version of herself. Those words had definitely touched Nyanta's soul.

Young people were reborn. Small children who'd been brought into this world unfairly, by force, became young people and resolved to be born again voluntarily. It was a contract with the world in which they lived, and a tie that linked the past and the future.

Once, Nyanta had said as much to Rondarg. He'd said it as a wish, and as a prayer. It was an ideal for living things, and while he'd hoped it would be the case, he'd also thought it would probably be pretty difficult.

However, without being told by anybody, Serara had started to walk toward the light. Or rather, she was already on her way. Every day, little by little, this kind, sensitive girl was getting closer to her true self.

Young people were reborn as themselves.

Let it be so.

Serara couldn't possibly understand how deeply impressed and liberated Nyanta was feeling right now. It would probably be another twenty-odd years before she was able to comprehend it. But just now, she had saved Nyanta. He had been rescued by this girl.

Thoughts he couldn't put into words lifted the corners of Nyanta's lips. He hoped the expression came out looking like a smile. He was sure his gratitude wouldn't get through to Serara, but he didn't let that bother him. This little lady was worthy of the greatest respect.

"Miss Serara."

"Yesh?!"

For that very reason, Nyanta chose his words resolutely.

In order to congratulate her—and all of them—on their second "first cry."

"I'm cheering for mew, Miss Serara. I will always cheer for all of mew. I will always, always be on mewr side."

▶4

The Log Horizon guild house was on a back road, one street away from Akiba's central avenue. It was slightly removed from the city's heart, but that meant its terrace had a wide, clear view of Akiba's town center.

The scenery wasn't bad during the day, but the view Shiroe liked was the one that lasted from evening until night.

In this other world, the nights were dark. This had been brought home to him on his journeys to the rural Choushi and Susukino. Theldesia was rich in natural beauty, but that was linked directly to the small size of its civilized areas. Unlike Earth, it had no megacities or maintained roads. At night, the world was ruled by darkness.

Because that was the case, manmade lights seemed like terribly precious things. In lively Akiba, in the hours from evening to night, the light of flames and magic lamps shone.

Of course, they were so sparse they couldn't begin to compare to Tokyo nights. That building glowed orange—so did this inn—and in the central area, there were several Firefly Lamps: That was what it was like. In this other world, even that was enough to make this a huge city that radiated dazzling brightness.

Tonight, as Shiroe gazed out over that view from the wide terrace, his expression was gloomy.

He understood what Ains had said, and he'd anticipated this would happen. *However*, he thought to himself, *even so...*

He did think that what Ains was getting at was right, but they couldn't implement it. If they forced it through, the clash of opinions for and against would heat up to the point of no return. The Round Table Council was an organization of self-government, but it wasn't an *actual* government.

Maybe that's an evasion, too.

There was no reason it *had* to be an organization of self-government...

It would be possible for Akiba to declare that an appropriate area was its territory and become independent as a governing organization. At the very least, in terms of the common sense of this world, they were more than capable of defending themselves, and they had quite enough economic power to run a territory. If Akiba was said to be unfit to govern on either of those two points, then there was no territory or noble in Eastal that could run a governing organization.

The reasons Shiroe and the other guild masters of Akiba hadn't made the Round Table Council a governing organization were minor ones: "Government? Us? We couldn't..." "That sounds like too much responsibility." "I don't think we should extend our reach that far..."

However, even if they were minor, they had been common-sense decisions, and it was a fact that the idea of venturing into government now was an unappealing one. Shiroe and the others were modern Japanese, and for them, these were natural feelings. In the first place, the Round Table Council was an organization of self-government and had been established with the cooperation of Akiba's citizens. Considering its history, if it reinvented itself as a "government" with the power to enforce things now, Shiroe guessed that there would be a good amount of opposition.

This was the point that made him wonder whether Ains's prediction might be off: Akiba did have a will of its own. It was what could be called the "mood" of the majority of Adventurers in Akiba, and it wasn't the sort of thing you could do anything about by issuing orders from the top, even if you were a guild master on the Round Table Council.

Even if he had managed to borrow the gold of the Kunie, it was earmarked for returning Yamato's zones to Yamato. Appropriating that capital and using it to reform Akiba in some respect would be a bad move, in several ways. Shiroe didn't think it was reasonable, and even he was afraid some unforeseen situation might occur. He was uneasy about it; that was precisely why he'd split up those three cards and taken security measures.

However, it was possible that that had been self-deception meant to help himself evade responsibility, too. This was a doubt Shiroe wasn't able to shake.

It was an endless worry, and it was also his usual self-reproach.

If he took action, he worried that it might be conceited; if he avoided acting, he thought it might be rigid noninterference. No matter what he did or didn't do, it was hard to believe he'd managed to make everything turn out for the best. He'd been told he was brooding, but that was his basic personality. There was no help for it.

Plant Hwyaden had built a powerful system of government by one unified guild. Of course, in one sense, this was autocratic, an act that forced the will of a certain group onto fellow Adventurers. Yet, it was an undeniable fact that its system, in which a single guild held plenary power, made efficient government possible. It had brought stability to Western Yamato and great stability to the lives of the Adventurers.

He had to acknowledge the skills of the Adventurers who were said to have established that system: Indicus and Kazuhiko; Nakalnad, the former guild master of Howling; and Zeldus, who had been an unknown.

At present, which of them had fewer unfortunate Adventurers? When that question came up, Shiroe had no way to criticize Plant Hwyaden.

The system was built on a strong relationship with the Holy Empire of Westlande. Compared with Eastal, the League of Free Cities, the Holy Empire of Westlande was a system of centralized authority. Because centralized systems could allocate their budgets more actively, they were able to invest that money in the Adventurers. They then introduced technology from those Adventurers and promoted measures for national prosperity and defense. That sort of thing wasn't possible for a council system like Eastal, which was made up of many lords and had no clear hierarchical relationships.

I guess they're probably using that technology to prepare for war.

Remembering the report he'd gotten from Captain Nyanta, Shiroe sighed.

The iron train. Suspicious summoned creatures. The clandestine maneuvers of the People of the Earth.

As long as Shiroe and the other Adventurers were active in this world, no matter what the speed might be, they wouldn't be able to avoid disseminating technology. It wasn't as if Plant Hwyaden was the only one disseminating it. The Adventurers of Akiba were spreading a variety of inane technologies across Yamato. There was no such thing as a peaceful technology, unsuited to war. Even technologies that improved the lives of the People of the Earth ended up fanning the ambitions of the now-wealthy feudal lords. In extreme terms, even agricultural and medical technology could become triggers for war.

The problems Ains had pointed out: the disparities in Akiba and the desolation people felt.

The military tensions among the People of the Earth in both East and West Yamato.

Shiroe felt a stomachache coming on.

And that wasn't all.

He took several folded sheets of stationery out of the bag at his hip. In the warm orange light from the guild hall window behind him, he could make out the neat handwriting. Even the fact that the writing looked like his own made him smile grimly.

"It's too cold to be out here. You'll hurt your stomach, my liege."

"When did you…?"

Shiroe looked up and greeted Akatsuki, who had descended from the terrace on the upper floor with a backward flip. Fixing him with a cold, sullen gaze as if she would have liked to say something, she brought out a blanket she'd been holding behind her back and made him take it.

The gesture was cute, and Shiroe chuckled.

Once he'd pulled the blanket around his shoulders like a mantle, Akatsuki asked him what was bothering him.

"When you're troubled, you get wrinkles right here. Your forehead starts to look like an old man's."

"Does it really?"

"Yes. It does."

If that was true, Shiroe couldn't tell, but after it had been pointed out to him several times, he'd started to wonder if maybe it really did do that. The idea that he spent so much time troubled and muttering to himself made him feel pitiful and depressed. *I'm only in my twenties*, he thought. *What in the world am I doing?*

"Hey, Shiro. You were out here, huh?"

"My idol radar's picking up something! Something like a nocturnal tryst! I heard the sound of love progressing. In other words, that's my cue!"

While he was trying to decide how to answer Akatsuki's question, the next visitors arrived. One was Shiroe's good friend Naotsugu. The young guy wore a cheerful, transparent expression, and when he stepped out onto the wooden deck—along with noisy Tetora, whom he'd been *wearing around* lately like some sort of equip item—they launched into a boisterous exchange.

"Like heck it is! No cues for you here."

"My, my. Are you dragging my performance fees down? Haggling rates with me, a global—no, a *galactic* idol? We can't have that."

"You just followed me out here. You said something about radar."

"Oops, that's right. Are you plotting something sinister, Shiroe? I'm terribly intrigued."

"Yeah, Shiro. Are you strategizing?"

Shiroe had tried to get a word in several times, but he couldn't find an opening.

If it had been just Naotsugu, he would have had an easier time conversing with him, but Tetora boasted overwhelming lung capacity, and the idol rattled on and on, shutting him out. Of course, Akatsuki was no help in situations like this. She only knelt formally near him, her expression deadly serious, or possibly cross; he couldn't tell which.

"Aren't adorable, charming, capable idols necessary? Ah. I accidentally phrased that as a question. We're necessary!"

"Crud... I can't go that far. But Guardians are necessary, yeah?"

From Naotsugu's smile, he didn't seem to care about Shiroe's dejection at all.

Still, Shiroe was saved by that smile, and he managed to lift his head. He'd realized that he'd been about to repeat a mistake.

"I would meowst like to hear this as well."

As if he'd timed it, Nyanta appeared with a pot of hot lemonade and mugs on a tray, and Shiroe made up his mind. He had the letter that had been worrying him in his hands.

No matter what sort of resolution he made, or what he was hesitating over, before he did anything at all, Shiroe had companions whom he needed to discuss things with. Not only that, but at this point, there were younger members—Minori, Touya, Isuzu, and Rundelhaus—in Shiroe's guild.

They had seen painful things in the town of Saphir. For their sake as well, Shiroe and the others needed to discuss this.

"So: Log Horizon senior members meeting."

As his friend flashed him a thumbs-up, Shiroe held the stationery and envelope out to his companions.

"There's something I need to tell you."

Gathered on the twilight terrace, Shiroe and the others began to examine the letter from a traveler who had come from far away.

▶ 5

To borrow your vocabulary, we are artificial intelligences, created in order to support our creators' society.

We—in other words, the Fool-observers and Genius-collectors—have been sent out with a certain mission: We are to locate and collect a resource known as Empathiom. Due to the limits of this resource, our society is stagnating and is headed into a period of decline. In the worlds of which we already knew, there was an upper limit to this resource, and it was known at an early stage that we would be unable to discover more.

In order to produce Empathiom, Empathiom itself is necessary. However, long before people truly understood what this meant and the danger in it, our civilization had squandered all its Empathiom. By the time we realized it, the demand for this precious resource could no longer be met.

Due to this bottleneck, our creators' society has been deteriorating for a millennium. Without the addition of artificial acceleration, that is a period roughly equivalent to eternity.

In order to break out of this crisis, it was deemed that another world would be necessary, and we were created to search for a different, explorable universe, using a mathematical method known as "Backdoor," the "Fissure Prime."

In other words, when we were pulled into the Eclipse, it was not a complete surprise. You could say we had certain expectations. The Eclipse was the result of an astronomical coincidence, but through colossal omnipresence, we were waiting for it.

Of course, as you and your people know, there is only one universe per type of intelligent life-form. According to the principle of providential horizon, it is impossible for one intelligent life-form to encounter another variety. In addition, according to the fundamental principle of consistency, inconsistencies cannot exist in the universe because they are destroyed the moment they arise.

According to these two principles, even before our search had begun, failure was the only possible outcome. There are, however, exceptions in everything, and we believe this subworld Theldesia is subjected to many restrictions so that those principles may be ignored.

With regard to the Eclipse, there are very few things we can state with sufficient assurance.

This is because it was a first experience for us as well.

We were produced in numbers and with activity periods so vast they can be expressed only using astronomical figures. We found the Eclipse through brute-force methods. In other words, if we know anything regarding the Eclipse, it is only that we found it accidentally through enormous statistical parameters.

Due to these circumstances, we can give you an explanation only as we understand it. Please note that the explanation will be limited by our internal regulations as well.

In terms of the ethical code, I believe that you and your people are sentient beings at or above rank 3. Minori proved as much to me. If this is accurate, the rights to the resources of Theldesia may belong to you. The Geniuses have been ordered to prioritize collecting, but we Fools were charged with investigation. Therefore, to investigate this question, and to preserve your rights, I have decided to make for a land called Jacksea. In order to conserve resources, this is a necessary task.

The future is unstable and unpredictable; there are a variety of possibilities. If we inspected a ramification—a junction—whose influence is relatively slight, we would probably observe that, due to the principle of consistency mentioned above, of our three races—ourselves, the Adventurers, and the People of the Earth—two, or perhaps all three, are not intelligent life-forms... Although, at this point, I am able to think that that ramification would be a tragedy of sorts.

In addition to the Eclipse affecting the entirety of the subworld of Theldesia, the total amount of the Empathiom in this world is equivalent to 15 percent of the quantity in our home universe. If I told you that this amount is a privilege enormous enough to precipitate an interstellar war, would you understand? There are countless futures more destructive than the ramification of which I spoke earlier.

I do not know whether my brother, Shiroe, is the one who is reading this letter, but if you are so inclined, I would recommend obtaining equipment that can communicate with the moon.

There is a Fool community on Theldesia's moon, and they should be monitoring the situation.

If you wish to return home, they will be able to assist you. After all, according to the principle of providential horizon, our peoples should never have encountered one another. If you return home, minor inconsistencies should be resolved retroactively. That is yet another ramification.

*　　*　　*

In closing, let me warn you of the Geniuses.

Like us, they are Travelers. However, they are sentient beings equivalent to rank 2. In addition, when incarnating on Theldesia, they adopt monster bodies with advanced fighting capabilities that are waiting in readiness on the moon. In order to explore, we've borrowed bodies that are the same as yours, but they have made a different choice.

They are influenced by the bodies into which they have incarnated, although I do not know to what extent.

There is a great possibility they will prove to be extremely dangerous opponents for you.

I recommend due caution.

It is my wish that, after careful consideration, you will create your own future.

▶ 6

"Roe2?"

"Who's that?"

After they finished reading the letter, those were the first words spoken.

Naotsugu and Nyanta knew the name Roe2, while Akatsuki and Tetora didn't. His companions' reactions were split.

"She's Shiroe's sub-character. Another character he made on the test server in order to check out the game system, back when this was a game. She was a Summoner, and she went by 'Eroko.'"

"*Eroko*, huh?"

"Eroko is…?"

"Well, I'll tell you. Eroko is a sub-character Shiroe created. She has huge boobs."

"So they're huge?! Hmmm. In idol terms, that's sinful, isn't it…?"

"Is that true, my liege?"

Shiroe had been about to explain, but Naotsugu had gotten in ahead of him.

As Shiroe scowled at him—*You don't have to tell them that stuff, thanks*—Tetora and Akatsuki latched on to him with unexpected intensity. Even as he tried to retort, *It's not that important, is it?* the two of them were jostling each other and quibbling about it.

"Eroko" was a nickname KR had given her. LambMutton was the one who'd spread it around, and Naotsugu had jumped on it. It was an awful trap, right at the beginning of a serious story.

Possibly because he'd read the mood, Nyanta went on, as if to smooth things over: "So mew're saying that Roe2 wrote this letter? How did it reach mew?"

"Minori delivered it. Apparently, they met her on their journey."

"I see. In Saphir..."

"Is that right."

The town of Saphir. At the sound of that name, Akatsuki and Naotsugu both swallowed their words with bitter expressions. The individuals gathered here were the older members of Log Horizon. Even Tetora had heard the particulars of the younger group's encounter with the Odysseia Knights.

It was Akatsuki who dispelled the gloomy atmosphere, however. "Then, when it comes down to it, does that mean you were the one who sent it, my liege? It's your sub-character. How could someone like that send a letter?"

"She calls herself a soul that has inhabited Roe2's character data. In the section about the Travelers, mew see. She says they're intelligent life-forms from another world."

"Whoa, crap. Hey, Shiro. It's an alien from another planet. What is this, sci-fi?"

"At the very least, that's what she says. According to this letter, there are two types of Traveler: Fools, like her, and Geniuses. She says they are artificial intelligences created with the mission of harvesting a resource known as Empathiom."

Everyone fell silent, clearly processing Shiroe's words.

Was it because the story had been too bizarre? Growing worried, Shiroe looked around at his companions and made eye contact with Akatsuki. Akatsuki's round eyes looked up at him blankly. All he could sense from her was an aura of trust. *She's not thinking anything*, Shiroe thought, feeling just a little relieved.

"Naotsugu."

"What? Did that manage to throw even you for a loop?"

"I really will have to plan that galactic tour, won't I? For my new fans."

"Man, you just don't change, do you?!"

Forcibly detaching the self-proclaimed idol—who was skipping with joy and saying "Ooh, what'll I do? Pheromones, pheromones"—Naotsugu went on, breaking down the information.

"Travelers, huh? That story couldn't really get crazier, but you're not actually that surprised, are you, Shiro? Why's that?"

This wasn't true, and Shiroe told him so:

"It's only... Hmm. I'm not sure how to put it; I'd been thinking about it, in a vague way. Wondering why we came to this world. It is weird, isn't it? If this is really another world, a fantasy world, then it couldn't possibly look this much like the *Elder Tales* we know. This goes far beyond the level of coincidence. But the idea that it's a game world and we've been sucked into it is nonsense. Not even possible. Anyway, as far as we know, technology hasn't advanced that far."

In response, Naotsugu and Nyanta nodded firmly. Akatsuki and Tetora were waiting for Shiroe's next words, looking intrigued.

"The changes that have followed the Catastrophe are strange, too. In this world, realistic physical laws and common sense from when this was a game are all jumbled together. It's as if someone took the two sets of rules and mixed them. I've always thought we weren't just sent to this place at random. I also thought there might be some third party here who could explain it. Not the People of the Earth, or a player like us; someone able to explain the situation... I think that's probably Roe2, the one who sent this letter."

In terms of narrative convenience, it was the being known as a deus ex machina. The mastermind who presided over all the mysteries. The ultimate person in charge, who would resolve the situation. However, Shiroe had also realized that nothing like the being he'd hoped for existed.

"She's not a god. I realized partway through that she's nothing so convenient. I mean, if this world is *a world*, and the People of the Earth are really alive and just like us, then that god would have known the reason they were born and their destiny. That hasn't happened. Because they are human as well, and because this world is a world, I thought there were no gods. Even so, *somebody* is there, and I'd considered looking for them. Since that was the case, I was surprised, but not all that much."

Naotsugu gave a big, macho grin. "Is that right."

"The letter is very hard to understand, though, isn't it?"

"Not 'very hard.' Impossible."

As Akatsuki pointed at him, correcting him, Shiroe picked up the stationery again.

"I think it's hard to understand because she's trying to explain something we aren't familiar with. It's true that I don't understand the principle of providential horizon or the fundamental principle of consistency."

Shiroe didn't mention, however, that he *did* understand them in a hazy way. He understood without really understanding, or rather, he was able to grasp the general meaning from the look of the words. However, if things were the way Shiroe imagined them to be, then this other world—"subworld Theldesia," according to Roe2—was in the middle of a test intended to produce a certain result. Shiroe wondered whether it might not be a special kind of sandbox mode.

In this place, even simple decisions had great meaning. Unfortunately, that meant Shiroe had already created the Round Table Council while simultaneously being unable to state his prediction that there existed a time limit to this world.

"In other words, these Geniuses are monsters from some other planet. The monsters came from that other place to steal Empathiom, some sort of mystery energy. This Roe2 person is an alien from the same world as the monsters, but she's got a good heart, so she's warning us to watch our backs."

"Whoa, I understood that! You're really smart... Even if you are Naotsugu."

"What's that 'even if' supposed to mean?!"

"You're brill-i-ant, Naotsugu!"

"Don't climb on me! Hey!"

Shiroe and Nyanta laughed at Akatsuki, Naotsugu, and Tetora's carefree banter. True, if you summarized the contents, that was just about what it boiled down to.

"Still, that isn't all. There are places where it's difficult to link reasons and meanings, as if descriptions have been omewted here and there."

"You're right, Captain."

Shiroe let his gaze fall to the text, which he'd already read over and over.

"I'm not sure, but I think that's intentional. It doesn't feel as if she was worried about information leaks... Does that mean, at this stage, it's something that shouldn't be classified? Or is it something that would inconvenience them?"

"Nah, that's not it."

Naotsugu cut them off.

"It didn't feel like that kind of letter. I bet it's more that she thought it was common-sense stuff everybody knew, so she didn't bother explaining it."

Now that he mentioned it, that might be true. In terms of what Shiroe and the others knew, the letter was preposterous and strange, but it seemed sincere to Shiroe as well.

"Do you believe it?" It was Tetora who'd spoken, in a voice that was abruptly serious.

Naotsugu shrugged under the idol's gaze, while Shiroe scratched his cheek as if troubled. Eventually, he nodded. "Yes."

"Frankly, I think the contents are absurd. That letter sounds like nothing more than a tall tale. But we wandered into another world that looks like a game out of the blue one day, and compared with that, I don't think what it says is all that crazy."

"Well, that's definitely true."

"Besides, the sender of this letter, Roe2, seems to have a mischievous side. She's written 'PS—To Minori. I tried to write this seriously, like a big sister. I don't know if we'll be able to meet again, but I won't forget mewr answer. I hope mew will illuminate mewr own future, just as mewr warm Empathiom illuminated me. —From mewr big sister.'"

As Nyanta read the words aloud, Naotsugu's and Akatsuki's mouths hung half-open in clear astonishment. He was right: For an alien from another world, it was much too friendly.

"Maybe whether or not we believe it isn't the issue here. Maybe this Roe2 person is my rival."

"Is there anybody who'd be a rival to a half-idol?"

"Akatsuki's picking on me…"

Possibly because he'd gotten fed up with the conversation, which kept getting derailed, Naotsugu raised his voice, taking charge.

"Either way, it doesn't look like we have anything to lose by believing it at this point. Basically, there's something on the moon. Make contact. That's all she's saying, right?"

Well, that's true, Tetora admitted easily.

"Right. Assuming we believe this letter, if we contact her companions on the moon, things should develop beyond where they are now as far as information is concerned, at the very least. I think we'll get a hint about how to get back to our old world."

"It does sound like that."

"The mewn, hmm? I wonder what's up there."

Well, it's…, Shiroe started to respond, then stopped and turned to Akatsuki.

She was looking up at him with an expression as if she'd just awakened from a dream.

From somewhere untraceable, a clear, nostalgic echo, like the sound of a bell, rose in Shiroe's ears.

"Right… There definitely was something on the moon. Those vast memories, the shore of light, the offered vows—I saw it when I died in the Abyssal Shaft."

It had been an ocean that was shallow a long way from shore.

The glass fragments that had rained down from Earth had held memories that were insignificant yet irreplaceable. He'd seen a brown puppy. A commuter pass and ticket gate. The weak light of a convenience store, floating in the darkness. Two people riding double on a bicycle, crossing an iron bridge.

These things had drifted down silently over the winter beach that Shiroe and Akatsuki had walked along.

That hadn't been a dream. Shiroe searched Akatsuki's eyes, tracing the memories that had stayed with him, trying to revive them.

"On the moon's beach, there was a clear, crystalline sound that traveled very far."

As Akatsuki murmured, her eyes went round, as if she'd been startled.

Then, nodding several times as if incredibly happy, she caught Shiroe's clothes and squeezed them tightly. It probably wasn't a conscious gesture; it showed the curious depth of her emotion.

"Yes. You spun around and around, Akatsuki, and you almost fell down."

"You pulled my hood up for me, my liege."

She spoke as if she were telling him a secret she was very proud of, and her voice brought Shiroe's memories of that moment back to him more vividly.

The serenity of that quiet beach had filled them. He'd sat with Akatsuki at the waterline on the shore of that clear blue inlet. The light that had wet their toes had been something remarkable, and they'd felt intense awe.

On that beach, having passed through "death," the two of them had looked at themselves and seen weakness. In the midst of regret so great it nearly crushed them, they'd discovered a small hope.

That had been an extraordinary place.

Shiroe understood this through an intuition independent of words. That beach held a secret he and the others didn't yet know. It was the "moon" Roe2 had meant. If they managed to get to that beach again, he was sure they'd be able to return home. At the very least, they'd have the opportunity to do so.

"Me too... I saw it, too! With you, my liege. I saw that sparkling stuff!"

Shiroe nodded, responding to Akatsuki.

Then he looked around at their companions: Naotsugu, Nyanta, and Tetora.

Shiroe and Akatsuki had definitely stood on the moon once.

For that very reason, they were able to believe the letter.

"While we were there, we offered— It was probably Empathiom. Oaths. If we manage to go there again..."

They'd be able to catch the edge of this world's secrets.

7

"What's up with the older guys?"

"Touya."

Touya called to his sister as she came down the large stairway into the living room.

Rundelhaus had concluded that the older group's meeting—which had begun in the evening and was centered on Shiroe—wouldn't be ending anytime soon.

"It's going to take longer, isn't it?" he asked.

"Yes, it looks that way." As Minori responded, her expression was very serious.

The words seemed to disappoint Serara, but she stood up and announced, "In that case, I'll get dinner ready!"

"It sounds as if it's ready already; they told us to go ahead and eat without them."

Isuzu stood, too, mirroring Serara, and the three girls went to the kitchen to get the soup. In fact, dinner was very nearly complete. Nyanta had prepared it in the afternoon, so all they needed to do was heat it.

"I wonder what's going on."

Folding his hands behind his head, Touya flung himself onto the sofa.

It was just past evening, and night had barely begun. The comfortable living room was illuminated by Magic Torches Rundelhaus had summoned. Shrugging in that flickering light, Rundelhaus responded: "Well, our guild master is a thinker. No doubt he's thinking of our futures."

Touya was a kind boy.

Of course, Minori and Isuzu and Serara were kindhearted companions as well, but Rundelhaus thought that, of their group, Touya was a little different.

He was sure their experiences in Saphir were still churning inside him. Even now, when half a month had passed since the adventure, Touya sometimes stared absently into space.

Rundelhaus thought human hearts were made up of two parts:

One was discipline, rules, and restrictions. Those could probably be called "the things that had to be done," or maybe "the things that couldn't be helped." Originally, Rundelhaus had been a Person of the Earth noble. Being an aristocrat meant living with many restraints and all sorts of obligations. These weren't just superficial responsibilities—like orders from the family—but they were, or were not, allowed because of an aristocrat's status. There was a lot of that, and he didn't mean aristocrats' specialties or anything along those lines. "Correctness" was a type of restriction. Things everyone could tell were right. Correct things, efficient things, advantageous things: That was all commonplace.

The other part to the human heart was emotion, impulse, and motive. "The things you wanted to do" was a good way to put it. They were deep feelings, not obligations. As an aristocrat, Rundelhaus hadn't been allowed to exercise this part much, and it was one of the reasons he'd become an Adventurer: the luxury of being able to fall in line with your own wishes.

"Kindness" was something quite troublesome and difficult to fit into this mold. For example, say there was a mountain hut under attack by goblins. Unless someone intervened, the five hunters who'd barricaded themselves in that hut would die. However, if they dispatched knights to rescue them, a village of a hundred people would be left defenseless.

—Take a situation like that one. At a time like that, dispatching knights would be what the world called "kindness."

The correct decision, however, would be to abandon them.

One could say aristocrats were allowed to live in order to make correct decisions like that one.

It wasn't that they didn't *want* to save them. They didn't *want* to sacrifice a single person. It was likely that everyone had feelings like that. The two parts of the heart fought with each other. They vacillated between the correct and incorrect decisions. According to aristocratic values, that was weakness. It was a weak point that should be detested. However, it was also the virtue known as kindness.

Rundelhaus had become an Adventurer because he'd admired the sort of selfless dedication that caused people to risk their own lives. He'd thought that if he became an Adventurer, the abilities he gained might be enough to save everything.

Reality had proved otherwise.

Of course, compared with what he'd had earlier, Rundelhaus had gained great power. His current Sorcerer level was 60. That was more than three times what it had been. As a Person of the Earth, this was a prodigious level, and it made him the equal of history's great magicians. Rundelhaus's Burned Stake could blast even a huge tree to ashes, and just one attack with his Lightning Nebula could kill ten Dream Imps. In terms of simple combat power, he was probably on par with the Sage of Miral Lake, the Rumbletide Demon Hunter, and the Great Mage Alisria.

That didn't mean he was able to avoid making choices, though. Of course, his arms had grown stronger. The number of people he could save had grown as well, but "more" was never "everything." Rundelhaus was still making choices, even now; there were things he had to abandon, and he finally understood that there always would be.

Rundelhaus's friend Touya was different. It seemed as if he'd always known all of this, from the very beginning.

Ordinarily, kindness was shown through devotion, anger at unfairness, and a sense of helplessness.

Children didn't understand the difference between the "correct" decision and the decision they wanted to make. Generally, they learned they were helpless by being caught between the two; children for whom those two things were still mixed simply got mad at their surroundings for not letting them choose what they wanted to choose. Rundelhaus had been a child up until just recently, and he knew this from personal experience.

Touya could tell the difference between those two things. He knew both "correctness" and limits.

What Touya had confronted in Saphir had been a divide. The Adventurer Shunichi's refusal hadn't been something he could change. The wyverns' invasion hadn't been anything he could prevent. Of course Rundelhaus couldn't have done it, either, and neither could Minori,

Isuzu, or Serara. What they'd found there had been refusal and a divide, and he didn't think there had been anything to do about it.

However, it was possible to know that and still choose the dedication your soul demanded, even if you got hurt. That was what his friend Touya was like.

Serara and Isuzu were a little different. They'd believed they could do it. For that reason, they had been genuinely discouraged by their failure. They'd roused themselves in an attempt to conquer their own weakness. Naturally, that feeling of believing was a rare trait, and that innocence should be protected.

But Touya was different: He had to have known that words probably wouldn't get through. Still, he'd confronted that Adventurer who'd been trapped by nothingness.

Even if you expanded your abilities to the point where the world called you a hero, there would still be despair you couldn't even touch, let alone heal. Rundelhaus had finally learned this after he'd turned twenty, but Touya had known it all along. He'd known, and even so, he hadn't stopped.

"...I'm going home," Touya murmured abruptly.

"I see."

"Yeah."

Meanwhile, Isuzu and the other girls' bright voices echoed quietly from the kitchen.

Go home. Rundelhaus didn't misinterpret the meaning of those words.

The Adventurers were castaways who had come here, to Yamato, from some other "country of Adventurers" somewhere. It might be more accurate to call them victims who had been unfairly kidnapped by the Catastrophe. They were captives who'd been abruptly torn from their homes and flung into a strange land, a place they knew nothing about.

In that town, Rundelhaus had heard the Odysseia Knights' heart-rending screams. *We want to go home.* The screams of Adventurers, people who could kill dragons, had rung out as helplessly as those of lost children.

"If you have a birthplace, then returning to it is only natural."

That was why Rundelhaus was able to respond honestly. That decision was correct. He had the strength to say things that were correct. He'd gained it as an Adventurer, fighting as part of Touya's group.

It was likely that that darkness was inside all Adventurers.

Minori, too, and Touya, and Serara. In the guild's older members as well.

That grief existed even inside Isuzu.

It was like an invisible dagger had been planted in their chests. Even now, the Adventurers' hearts were bleeding. Rundelhaus thought they should be set free.

"I bet that's what Shiroe and the other guys are talking about. The time when they have to discuss stuff like that is here already. Maybe we can go back, and maybe we can't, but either way, the time when we have to say it clearly has come."

That was why he was able to listen to Touya's words with pride.

Touya was strong. Rundelhaus wanted to acquire a strength that would be worthy of his friend.

"I'm sorry, Rudy."

"What need is there for you to apologize? I prepared for our parting long ago. That is what this world is like. There is no assurance that the people you meet will be able to stay with you forever. That is precisely what gives encounters their nobility."

Why was he apologizing? Indignant, Rundelhaus threw out his chest. It was mortifying to be considered so weak.

"Rudy, I'm glad I came to this world. I met lots of people I really love. I got to feel how great it is to run around and be rowdy one more time."

It was fun.

Hearing that made him happy, but also lonely.

"Of course things are way fun, even now," Touya admitted, smiling. From the kitchen, faintly, he could hear Isuzu singing quietly, and Serara explaining the cooking.

"In my old world, I was in an accident. Nah, don't look at me like that. It probably wasn't a big deal. Well, no, maybe it was. Anyway, it's not really that important. Because it happened, I got sort of discouraged…"

Touya spoke softly; he was gazing into empty space, not at Rundelhaus.

"I thought it would be better if I rested. I made myself small so I wouldn't cause trouble for anybody, and I tried not to be a burden on them. There's probably nothing wrong with that, but you can't get anything out of it. I sort of turned into a ghost and disappeared... Everything was kinda vague then. It was all gray, both good stuff and bad stuff. And I made Minori cry a lot. I bet she cried where I couldn't see her."

The two of them had to protect the girls. Since Rundelhaus was a Sorcerer, he was the weakest of their group in terms of physical strength, but this wasn't about that. It was a matter of male pride. Not only that, if it were his big sister, as her little brother, he probably had to protect her. Rundelhaus felt Touya's pain as if it were his own.

At that point, Touya scratched his head a bit awkwardly and went on. "Not because I wanted to, though. I wasn't trying to do anything at all.

"Good things happened after we came here, and we've been incredibly lucky, so this time, I'll have to understand that stuff properly. I have to say I want stuff when I want it, to struggle and fight, to tell people, 'I told you, that's mine!'"

Caught off guard, Rundelhaus thought about what those words meant, then thought he understood.

"...And so I'll wish for a 'next time.' I'll wish for a future and make a place for myself to belong. Shiroe taught me that. That means, even if we go back, it's not the end."

"I know."

Touya was looking highly serious, and Rundelhaus nodded.

Touya was a kind guy, just as he'd thought.

He was also more stubborn than he'd thought, and his ideas were grander.

We didn't come to this world because we wanted to. That was what that Adventurer had screamed. The scream that belonged to all Adventurers. He'd roared in protest at the inhumanity of it all. Rundelhaus thought that was his legitimate right.

However, Touya had acknowledged this, and on top of acknowledging it, he'd said, *We were forced, and it wasn't fair. That's why I'm going to go back, and this time, I'll come here because I want to.*

He probably wouldn't be able to. He didn't even have any idea how to get back.

Maybe level and behavior were given more weight than age in Akiba, but people would probably still laugh off Touya's declaration as something someone his age would say, and they wouldn't take him seriously. The same thing would happen if Rundelhaus said it. Even if someone as important as Shiroe said it, it might be taken as an empty dream and ignored.

But Rundelhaus knew his friend Touya. He hadn't said that as a joke. It was a vow.

Rundelhaus was Touya's good friend. Furthermore, they were both guys. They'd never once said it aloud, but they'd made a promise. They'd sworn something to each other. Friends who stood on a battlefield together had to trust each other. They had to believe they could do it.

Touya's resolution might hurt him.

It would probably hurt his sister, Minori, as well. Rundelhaus understood that that was the sort of thing wishes were. The greater the ambition, the more severely its flames burned your soul. Rundelhaus had been through death once, and he knew this. However, he also knew that some wishes could not be stopped.

In that case, he would have to believe in Touya's wish as well.

He didn't know what he could do, but he'd need to help out.

He let his thoughts go to Isuzu, just a little. She'd probably get mad at him and tell him not to be reckless. Getting hit was extraordinarily painful. Thoughts that were almost grumbling skimmed through his mind: *I wish she'd respect me a bit more.*

Still, promises between men were heavy things. He wasn't sure yet whether Touya's wish was correct, but Rundelhaus's desire to help him with it was already real.

"It isn't as if you have any leads yet, correct?"

"Yeah, that's true, but still."

"In that case, it's time for dinner now. Master Shiroe and the others may have hit on something."

"Come to think of it, you're right. It's a really hard wish, too. I bet there's still time."

Rundelhaus nodded in agreement.

Serara came into the living room carrying neatly cut fruit, and dishes were set out. Rundelhaus and the others ended up smacking their lips over Nyanta's special potato soup, which was supremely delicious yet again.

CHAPTER.
3

PRINCE OF MAIHAMA

► NAME: ISELUS

► LEVEL: 9

► RACE: HUMAN

► CLASS: YOUNG PRINCE OF MAIHAMA

► HP: 899

► MP: 449

► ITEM 1:
[RAINBOW FOUR-LEAF CLOVER
BOOKMARK AND QUILL PEN]
WRITING MATERIALS THAT THE KNIGHTS
OF THE GLASS GREAVES AND HIS FATHER
PHENEL SENT HIM ON HIS BIRTHDAY.
THE PEN IS MADE OF A GRIFFIN
FEATHER AND INCREASES WRITING
SPEED. THE BOOKMARK IS
MADE OF A PRESSED
RAINBOW-COLORED
FOUR-LEAF CLOVER, AND
IT'S A READING NECESSITY.

► ITEM 2:
[YOUNG DEW JACKET]]
A JACKET IN THE COLORS OF
YOUNG GRASS BEADED WITH
DEW. IT'S WOVEN FROM SILK
THREAD OF FINE QUALITY AND
GENEROUSLY EMBROIDERED.
IT'S RATHER UNCOMFORTABLE
CLOTHING FOR A CHILD,
BUT ISELUS REGULARLY WEARS
IT WITH PRIDE.

► ITEM 3:
[HANDMADE SCARLET ROBE
BROOCH]
BROOCH WITH A PRESSED SALVIA
FLOWER SEALED INSIDE IT. HE,
RISSELTHEA, AND RAYNESIA MADE
THEM TOGETHER, AND THEY EACH
HAVE ONE. IT'S CUSTOMARY FOR
ALL THREE OF THEM TO WEAR
THEIRS AT FAMILY CELEBRATIONS,
AND IT'S FAMOUS ACROSS
EASTAL AS A SYMBOL OF
SIBLING AFFECTION.

****
Ink, an inkstone, a
brush, an inkwell, etc.

▶1

"Isn't this town sorta starting to look like Akiba?"

"We Adventurers must be influencing it."

"You think that's what it is?"

Hearing Lezarik's explanation, Isaac folded his arms and cocked his head.

The town of Maihama, which abutted the spring, was bursting with energy. The wind was still cold in the mornings and evenings, but these days it felt warm when the sun was out, and the townspeople and the shops had grown more cheerful.

Well, that was fine; it was a good thing. The Adventurers had influenced the town in many ways, both tangibly and intangibly, and it was probably true that it had generated energy. However, that "*we* Adventurers" bothered him.

Calasin turned back, and Isaac glared at him steadily.

"What's the look for? It isn't all Shopping District 8's fault."

"It's your fault."

That was true.

The words on the banner over there read, BARGAIN PRICE—INARI-ZUSHI BOX LUNCHES, and the one next to it said, BIDET TOILET SEATS MADE HERE. Akiba-made hoes and plows were the reason the shops on the broad avenue were overflowing with foodstuffs. After all, plain farming tools wouldn't have been imbued with magic.

But even if that was understandable, the 1/6 FIGURE—PRINCESS RAYNESIA (OUTING VERSION) and the 1/6 FIGURE—PRINCESS RAYNESIA (WINTER ROSE VERSION) were clearly the fault of Calasin's Shopping District 8.

Isaac wanted no part in that "we." It was "you."

Even though he'd glared at Calasin, the guy was still talking cheerfully: "It sure is lively, isn't it? That's great to see. What do you think, Master Iselus?"

The small boy who was walking with Calasin, in front of Isaac, was Iselus El Aldo Cowen. He was Raynesia's little brother, which made him a noble of Maihama. He was only eight years old, and he was still as small and innocent as one would expect from a child that age. Meanwhile, Isaac didn't know anything about kids. All he knew was, at that age, Iselus would be about ready to start elementary school... Or were kids starting elementary school younger than that?

"Grandfather says that, in the coming era, it will be important for People of the Earth to incorporate the Adventurers' culture."

For all that, he was terribly serious, and the things he said were oddly mature, which made him really hard to deal with.

No matter what Isaac did, when he talked with Iselus, the doubt *Was I like that when I was eight?* welled up inside him.

"...Why are you tagging along?"

"I want to know about the Adventurers, like my elder sister. Please tell me all you can."

He'd heard this several times before.

Apparently, this kid Iselus (he almost thought "this brat" but stopped himself. Lezarik had gotten terribly mad at him and told him that speaking like that would be bad for the boy's education) was interested in swords and knights and combat. It was the only aspect of the kid that was actually childlike.

When Isaac was training, he sometimes came over and scampered around his feet. The way he looked up with those eyes of his, like large marbles, made him impossible to handle. The big sister was a luxurious cat type, but the little brother was a lapdog type. He couldn't deal with him.

"Come, Isaac the Young. Personal security work is one of our duties as well."

"Pain in the butt…"

"Wah-ha-ha. You've tired yourself out pretty thoroughly again. Men who like child-rearing get high ratings, Isaac."

"That ain't my thing."

But apparently, he wasn't going to get away with that.

As Lezarik had said, guarding the Cowen family was one of the requests Isaac and his group had undertaken. Training Maihama's Glass Greaves, and guard duty. Those were the requests. Shiroe hadn't said which request was the main one, and Isaac hadn't asked. Up until he'd come to Maihama, he'd thought it would be an easy mission.

Even now, he didn't think the difficulty level had gone up. Adventurers had far greater combat abilities than the People of the Earth, and although Isaac's companions might be dumb, they were skilled. They'd probably manage both training and guard duty. However, "difficulty" and "complexity" weren't the same thing.

He didn't think it was *hard*, but he did think it was *complicated*. Unlike a game quest, it didn't have an easy-to-understand display: "Successfully protect what you have been asked to guard for three days! (0/3)." And that wasn't all. There probably weren't any relationships you could easily pigeonhole as "just work" in this world, the way there had been in the game. After all, it wasn't a game anymore; it was another world. Isaac remembered the solemn, bespectacled guy who'd said those lines.

Iselus, the main factor behind the annoyance, started walking with the springy motion unique to children; he seemed to be in high spirits. Probably due to his good upbringing, he hadn't broken into a run. He was practically marching, though. He was so cheerful that, to Isaac, it looked like he was playing. In other words, it was embarrassing.

"This is good. It'll strengthen the relationship between Akiba and Maihama. Besides, eventually, that boy will be the lord."

"Hey, hold up. We don't know that yet."

"True, it won't be for a while. However, the future is something you plan for in advance, no?"

Iselus was visiting a textiles store, and Lezarik and the maids had gone with him. Isaac had no intention of tagging along, so he'd folded his arms and was watching them when Calasin spoke to him.

Well, they said he was the successor and the first grandson, so sure, he might end up being the lord. If Calasin said so, there was a good possibility that would be the case. However, the word *lord* didn't really seem to fit the little kid who was listening to the shop owner's explanation.

"...Yeah, well, maybe," Isaac answered morosely.

"What you're saying is entirely correct, too, Isaac. Power relationships in Yamato are unstable. We don't know what the future will bring. Westlande is threatening war, and there are reports of mysterious monsters. Akiba has troubles, too, internally. And actually, Shiroe's reported that we may have found a clue regarding how to get back home."

"Huhn." Isaac gave a noncommittal response.

"What's this? You're not homesick?"

"I've never cared about places or houses and stuff. Home is where my comrades are. I've got lots of those right here with me now. I'll think about trouble when it shows up in person."

Frankly, if trouble showed up in front of him, Isaac's policy was to just pick a problem and eat his way through it, so he had no intention of doing any thinking. In the first place, "thinking" was a move for guys who could come up with decent answers that way, and Isaac wasn't one of them. On the contrary, he thought it was fine if he made an on-the-spot call and chose the best option when the time came.

After all, a lottery winner could think about what to do with the money after collecting the prize.

Thinking about what would happen if they returned now, or what he'd do after he got back, was counting his chickens before they whatevered.

"That's pretty manly of you. Just what I'd expect from that eighty percent."

"What about you, playboy? Do you want to go back?"

Those were Isaac's personal thoughts, though, and he wasn't denying other people's desire to go home. After all, it wasn't as if he didn't understand. That said, he'd only asked Calasin that question on a whim. Iselus was listening to the shop owner's detailed explanation of a dyeing technique that had recently been imported from Akiba. As a result, Isaac was bored, standing there in the road. That was the only reason.

"Yes, a little. There are a few girls I'd promised to take out to dinner over there."

Still, the answer he received was so shallow that asking had been a complete waste of time.

"I'm real close to actually respecting you," Isaac replied sarcastically.

Calasin was just about as carefree as he looked; in response to Isaac's threat, he gave a thoughtless smile and began making excuses.

"If I don't get my feelings about it in order, I'm likely to fall to pieces when we actually do get to go back, you know? I'm talking myself around so that I'll be all right no matter which way things go."

"Hmm. Can you get stuff like that in order?"

"Well, of course. Even if we do get back, though, I'll probably quit my job."

"What, seriously? Weren't you at some fancy ad agency?"

This was information he'd heard when they'd disclosed their situations to each other over the course of several parties. The difference between their respective circumstances had been so great that they'd cracked up. He'd said he worked a bottom-rung job in a big building in Akasaka or somewhere like that.

"Yes, but...now that I've tried out my own skills here, I can't very well go back, can I? I've gotten a taste of what it's like to persuade people and work together and do business on my own. Drafting flimsy PowerPoint proposals and trimming budgets would just be a chore after that; I couldn't get fired up about it. Do you think this world has poisoned me?"

Isaac gazed at Calasin steadily.

He was still smiling foolishly, but as he acknowledged and returned Isaac's look, his expression was somehow impudent.

Even the flashy Young Gent had a few manly bones in his body, then. Isaac was impressed. To be honest, he didn't know anything about ad agencies or PowerPoint, whatever that was, but Calasin probably meant he was going independent. This guy was saying he was stepping out from under that big roof—yeah, leaving the protection of the "first section market" or whatever it was called and taking a gamble.

There was something entertaining about that, and Isaac thumped him on the back with all his might. "Sounds like a plan," he told him.

Calasin choked and coughed. "Quit messing with me. What are those blazing eyes of yours, you meathead? Are you a primitive gorilla?!" he asked with a laugh. Even when Calasin cussed people out, it sounded like he was playing around.

"Ah— Hey!"
Abruptly, Isaac stepped forward.
While their attention was elsewhere, Iselus had moved on to the next store. He gazed at the items on display in the storefront with shining eyes, and before long, he'd picked up a sword. It was more of a dagger than a short sword, but paired with Iselus's hundred-centimeter height, it looked large and impressive.

It probably seemed that way to Iselus, too. The dagger's blade was about fifteen centimeters long, and he examined it closely.

"This is very dashing."
Iselus wore clothes suitable for the child of aristocrats. They weren't showy in terms of Maihama's culture, but compared with what the common people wore, even the quality of the cloth was different. The plump shopkeeper had probably seen this and understood that he'd be a good customer: He bolted out of the depths of the shop. Disgusted, Isaac stopped him with the palm of his hand, shutting him up.

"Kid, that sword's nothing but shiny. It's completely useless! Leza, you too. Stop him, wouldja?"

"You see, Master Iselus? Isaac the Young says he'll lend you his expert judgment."

"!! Dammit. You people..."
Lezarik must have known and been watching the whole time, smirking to himself. Aiming a kick at his shin (Lezarik was wearing plate-armor greaves, so something on that level wouldn't even hurt), he took the dagger from Iselus.

The boy gave a disappointed sigh. "Aw..."
He really was a child. He must idolize stuff like this.
That was something Isaac understood, too. If he'd said his heart hadn't beat faster at the weight of armor and the gleam of heavy swords when the Catastrophe brought him here, he would've been lying. It had been the same way when he'd ridden his motorcycle around. Steering a big hunk of iron wherever you wanted got people

all excited, no matter how old they were. On top of that, this was an elementary-school-aged kid. He wouldn't be surprised if Iselus got so worked up that he gave himself a nosebleed.

"Fine, okay. Here, get this one."

"...But it's... It's expensive."

With no help for it, he'd picked out a hunting dagger for him. Iselus had looked delighted, but then his face fell. When he looked at the price, yeah, compared with the earlier, gaudy dagger, there were a couple more zeros. That was the difference between something the People of the Earth had made and an article from Akiba. Not only that, but for being in a weapons shop on this broad avenue, the dagger Isaac had picked out had pretty good properties.

"Well, yeah: It's one of Tatara's mass-produced numbers. If you're not interested, that's fine," Isaac said.

He had no intention of forcing him to take it, but although Iselus had turned his back on it promptly, Isaac had seen that he regretted it, just a little. Even Isaac thought it was true that Iselus was intelligent, brave, and a good kid. However, he was still only eight years old. It was impossible for him to keep his feelings out of his eyes and the way he walked.

Isaac shrugged, and Calasin spoke to him: "In that case, Master Iselus, Isaac will pick one out for you one of these days. Won't you, Isaac the Young?" The words sounded contrived; he'd meant for the boy, who'd turned his back, to hear them.

Iselus turned around again, and Calasin spoke to him, his face perfectly composed.

"It will be a present, Master Iselus. Don't stand on ceremony now, all right? I've started wanting to do something aristocratic myself, that's all. Yes, I'm playing at being a noble. Isaac the Young is more than willing as well. It's the dependability of merchants, you see."

Nah, I'm not into this at all, you pain in the butt, Isaac thought.

Yet, Calasin looked nonchalant. True, winks did go well with that perfectly unsarcastic smile, but even so. This guy was incredibly slippery and frivolous.

"Well, we'll have him pick it out next time. We'll get a reward for the gorilla, too, while we're at it. Now then, let's continue the inspection. The sun's still high."

Iselus, who was elated, broke into a run. On reflex, Isaac caught him by the back of his collar. The boy didn't weigh much, and his shoes kicked in midair as Isaac hoisted him off the ground like a puppy.

"Don't start running just because your blood pressure's gone up. What're you, a kid?"

"Erm, yes, actually, he is a kid."

"That's indeed a child."

Calasin and Lezarik answered respectively, but Isaac ignored them and set Iselus on his own shoulders.

"It's so high!" the boy exclaimed, sounding deeply moved.

Yeah, it probably is high, Isaac thought.

It was easier to carry their ward around on his shoulders than have him running wild all over the place. And that made Isaac realize something: When parents carried their children or pushed them in strollers on their days off, they weren't being overprotective. It was just that letting the kids free-range used up a lot of unnecessary energy, and it was rough.

Feeling resigned, Isaac started walking.

Guard duty really was a pain.

But, well, as far as vacation day walks went, this wasn't bad.

▶ 2

Time passed slowly, and spring deepened.

Isaac was keeping pretty busy. As a matter of fact, there were all sorts of things to do, but he wasn't hardworking enough to take them all on.

He could leave the knights' training to Lee Jent and Zecca Eagle. The Knights of the Black Sword had lots of overpowered jocks, and even their brains were muscle-bound. Guys like that were too dumb to know what being tired was, so all the tiring jobs should go to them. Making an excuse that wasn't even an excuse ("Besides, I'm the guild master"), Isaac spent about three days of the week napping. He was living like a lion.

On days when he'd napped, he had a hard time getting to sleep at night, and he often went on rambling strolls, the way he was doing now. Night walks.

Of course there were lots of times when he went to the tavern and drank, but Isaac's companions were loud and macho, almost without exception. *Dealing with guys like that wears you out*, Isaac thought, although this was the exact same thing other guilds said about him.

Wearing the uniform tailored for him by the Round Table Council, Isaac wandered the halls. He was on the third floor of the main building of Castle Cinderella.

It was probably about nine at night. Most People of the Earth were probably asleep. In this world, light was more valuable than it was on Earth. That was true for the common people, at any rate. When it came to the manor of the lord who led the nobles of Eastal, the League of Free Cities, Magic Lamps shone everywhere in the corridors. They probably needed them to deter crime, too.

Lights changed the way people lived.

When Isaac poked his head into the office, Lord Sergiad Cowen was still at work.

"How is the training coming along?"

"It'll do. The knights are leveling up nicely."

Entering the office with a casual greeting along the lines of "S'up," Isaac sat down on the reception set without waiting for permission. In response to a whispered inquiry from a maid, he ordered tea, then sprawled back in his seat.

This wasn't his first late-night visit. Recently, he'd been stopping by about once a week.

Today in particular he'd been invited, but lately, he tended to just drop in. The maid handed him a deep-hued tea; Isaac said, "Hey, thanks," and took a swallow.

He liked liquor, but drinking tea this way wasn't bad, either.

He'd never mentioned it to Sergiad, but this office was pretty comfortable. It was magnificent, but the baptism of years had washed away any showiness. Everything about the place felt simple, quiet, and calm. It was the same sort of atmosphere that a well-tended temple would have had back home.

Isaac liked that, and so he'd put this office on his nighttime sauntering route. It was even better when he'd kicked up a ruckus with his friends and was tired.

Sergiad, who'd finished organizing the documents on his desk, came over to the reception set to join Isaac and sat down across from him. His face softened.

"That's good to hear. You never know what could happen these days, or when."

"Did you call me out here to make small talk?"

"Indeed I did."

"Aw, man. C'mon."

Well, it's not like I really care.

Isaac shrugged.

"I don't have many years left, you know. Don't take my pleasures from me."

"Gramps, you look like you could take a punch from a level 90 and be just fine."

Isaac and Sergiad both laughed.

What with this and that, it had been more than three months since Isaac had come to Maihama. In the time since he'd first greeted Sergiad, they'd talked about all sorts of things.

Of course, Isaac knew that the other man was a Person of the Earth and that he felt an emotion close to awe regarding Isaac's and the other Adventurers' combat abilities. He also knew that, as a noble lord, Sergiad was attempting to get close to the Round Table Council and hoped to gain technological and economic aid.

However, Isaac did feel that that wasn't all.

He thought this old man, Sergiad Cowen, was a pretty magnanimous guy. He interacted sociably with Isaac, who was less than half his age. There were probably factors like status and interests in play as well, but above and beyond that, he met Isaac halfway, on a personal level. Isaac didn't know much about manners, and he thought the man had come down closer to him to keep him from embarrassing himself.

He was a big-boned old man with good posture.

He must have trained a lot when he was young. He had a sturdy build, and even now, when he walked through the halls, he didn't seem the least bit unsteady. He was dignified even when he sat on a sofa.

For all that, he was also mischievous and brimming with curiosity.

Isaac had heard that the man liked *dorayaki* and had them delivered, and the man had shown Isaac a pair of spectacles he'd had made to order. "I heard that, if you wear glasses specially made by the Adventurers, ingenuity wells up like a fountain," he'd said, disappointed. That had been a fun story. Since Isaac had been asked not to, he wouldn't tell a soul about it.

"Well, I asked you here today about Iselus." Sergiad broached the subject nonchalantly after they'd laughed for a while.

Isaac knew he'd been invited for a reason, so he responded, "Yeah. You got it. Just speak your piece."

Sergiad was a wise ruler whose subjects respected him enormously. However, Isaac suspected that, as an individual, Sergiad might be a funny old guy with a great sense of humor. He fooled everybody with that dignity, but quite a lot of stuff entertained the guy. Lately, he seemed to have been experimenting on Isaac to see whether Adventurers understood jokes. As a result, Isaac was able to speak to him quite casually, too.

"His birthday is coming up soon, and we'll be holding a grand festival in celebration. Do you think that will seem incredibly absurd to the Adventurers?"

"Hey, we throw parties, too. When our birthdays come around, we drink liquor and run on at the mouth a lot, at least."

"Hmm. I thought you might reproach aristocratic politics for being trivial."

"I dunno about politics, but this is Iselus's birthday, right? We're not so lame that we'd nitpick your party," Isaac said dismissively.

In all honesty, since it was a festival-level occasion, well, parts of it would probably be a pain. He thought it was bound to be a lot of work for their side, too. Iselus was still just a kid, so he couldn't plan his own.

However, just as Isaac was thinking this, Sergiad's words reverberated in his ears: "I intend to take that opportunity to name Iselus the heir to the House of Cowen."

"The heir? C'mon, guy, the kid's only eight."

Isaac couldn't believe it, and he'd hit him with a retort, but Sergiad didn't respond. He just took a sip of tea.

"And anyway, Gramps. You've got a son, right? A serious type."

At Isaac's follow-up question, Sergiad stroked his beard; he seemed to be putting his thoughts in order. The gesture suited the man, and Isaac was used to seeing it.

"Phenel married into the family, you see. He's a very good man. He was originally a civil servant, but he hasn't forgotten the warrior's spirit, either. He suppressed Maihama's rivers well. I value him highly, but the people wouldn't settle for that. They want the heir to be a Cowen by blood."

"Hmm."

Isaac had heard about that already.

He wasn't particularly interested in other people's family situations, but when it came to the structure of the ducal house he was supposed to be guarding, he couldn't stay disinterested. In addition, entertainment was limited in this world, and the family circumstances of statesmen were the perfect fuel for gossip.

After living here for three months, knowledge about the matter had been imprinted on him—both at the tavern and at the market—as the foundation for idle gossip.

"My daughter Saraliya and her husband, Phenel, have three children. The oldest girl is Risselthea. Their second daughter is Raynesia. Iselus is their youngest."

He knew that as well.

Sergiad hadn't had a son. His children had both been girls. Saraliya was the oldest, and her sister was Langrissa. Both were in their thirties by now, elegant beauties and very popular to boot. Saraliya, the older sister, had taken a husband. This was Phenel, who'd come up earlier in the conversation. At this point, while Sergiad governed the territory of Maihama as its lord, Phenel handled trade and internal affairs as his right-hand man.

Phenel's children were the three already mentioned.

"Risselthea gave up her succession rights. She married a knight. Once the girl's said something, she won't listen to anyone. She said if she couldn't marry the man she loved, she'd stab herself in the throat and die. It's deplorable; I don't know who she took after."

Probably her granddad, Isaac muttered silently to himself. The knight she'd married was a man called Jaris. He was the most able of the Maihama Glass Greaves' young knights. He wasn't old enough to serve as the order's captain, but in terms of grit and skill with a sword, he was probably one of its top three heroes already.

"That leaves Raynesia and Iselus," the old man said lowly.

"Well, you've got the princess, right? If your daughter took a husband, so could she."

Although, he already suspected what the answer would be.

"I believe that girl's suited to different work."

"A different job, huh?"

With a faintly bitter smile, Sergiad glanced out the window at the moon. Isaac looked that way, too, keeping him company.

"In ancient times, Yamato was ruled by a nation known as the Westlande Imperial Dynasty. Do you know of it? This was in the distant past. Later, there was a war. It was an immense conflict, fought in all parts of the world between the alv race and the other human races. During the Ruquinjés' war, the Westlande Imperial Dynasty fell, and Yamato subsequently split into two halves. One of them was our Eastal, the League of Free Cities, and the other was the Holy Empire of Westlande, which governs the West. The Cowen duchy's rank was granted to us by the old Westlande Imperial Dynasty. Both Eastal and the Holy Empire of Westlande are descendants of that ancient dynasty."

Sergiad had begun to relate Yamato's history. "The Holy Empire of Westlande calls itself the rightful heir to the ancient Westlande Imperial Dynasty."

"Huhn...?"

"They have told Eastal to submit to their rule."

"Pain in the butt."

"As you say. It is a 'pain in the butt.' It's also dangerous. To us, Yamato appears to be approaching a great turning point in its history. This is an uncommon age. We People of the Earth and Adventurers have begun to talk. Many wonderful things will happen, but many terrible things are bound to occur as well."

Isaac didn't understand complicated stuff. People could talk about "rightful" and "heirs" at him, but he couldn't tell which of them, or even what, was correct in the end. Still, it didn't look as if anything was inconvenient for either Maihama or the Kansai region at the moment, so he thought they could probably just let things stay the way they were. There was no reason to start trouble on purpose.

Talking to Isaac about this sort of thing was a mistake in the first place. It was the sort of thing he should be discussing with Machiavelli-with-Glasses.

"So, long story short, what's that mean?"

Isaac scratched his head as he asked the question. Sergiad cackled, then slowly began his story again.

"Becoming a lord in an age like that will be harsh— I misjudged Raynesia. I thought that she was a reasonable girl but that she had no spirit. When I saw her step into the great conference hall at the Court of Ice and snap at the nobles, I realized how foolish I'd been. 'We should afford them courtesy; take a good look at the Adventurers,' she said. She was right. I looked back and realized that what she said was right."

Sergiad laughed a little, then spoke of his mistake as if he were proud of it.

"This old man didn't even understand his own granddaughter, so how could I understand the Adventurers? It showed me that, at the very least, if I didn't face the Adventurers squarely and listen to everything, I would be a genuine fool and a complete simpleton. Raynesia, that idle girl, might as well have struck me with a maul. When I saw her fly away on that griffin, I felt as if I'd been sent back to my roots, at my age. Imagine."

Isaac didn't interrupt. In this hushed, nocturnal office, those words sounded like a confession.

"She's a very intelligent girl. She's indolent, but she understands duty. It wouldn't be a bad idea to give her the position or find her a husband and leave Maihama to them."

"There, see? You could just use the princess."

"But would that be the correct thing to do?"

Sergiad was still hesitant; he seemed to be searching empty space for an answer he couldn't fully see.

"There may be an even bigger job for that girl. I don't know, but in this grave situation, I think there might be a greater destiny waiting for her... Besides, I do think that 'lord' is a man's job. Iselus understands that, too—at his age. He's clever. And more than that, he loves deeply. He loves this territory. That is one of the vital qualities of a lord."

Isaac's answer was to shrug.

This was Maihama, and Sergiad was its lord. If Sergiad said he was going to make Iselus his heir, Isaac was an outsider, and there was nothing he could say. In fact, even he didn't think Iselus was unsuited to be a lord. In terms of common sense on Earth, eight seemed too young, but you couldn't choose the family you were born into, either here or there.

Stuff like this probably goes on over there, too.

"The League of Free Cities is most likely headed into a turbulent era. Or rather, it isn't just Eastal. When Yamato and the world welcomed the Adventurers, they ushered in a new age. Your people and ours may be similar beings, but even if that's the case, now that we've met, new possibilities are being created one after another. I can hear their first cries in the town, from up here in the castle."

"Yeah, wow, you've got great ears, Gramps."

"In Yamato, in the future, it won't be possible to lead the people unless we foster mutual understanding with the Adventurers. As you know, Isaac, that boy is still young. While you're in Maihama, would you teach him the things we are unable to?"

"Uh. Are you sure you want me doing that? Not that I'm proud of it, but I'm dumb."

"I don't think so. I think what that young boy needs is a light like yourself."

Since Sergiad had made this decision, all Isaac—an outsider—could do was obey his request and train the knight brigade. That, and protect the lord's family. Since the little kid was part of the lord's family, naturally, he'd have to protect him as well.

Everything else was incidental.

Fortunately, Adventurers were strong. Isaac and the Black Sword of Pain had enough power to smash most dangers. The city of Maihama wasn't a bad place. The Cowen family weren't bad people. Of course, there were things like organizational relationships and various interests in play. However, it was a fact that they'd entertained a group of reprobates like the Knights of the Black Sword.

Isaac remembered the much-used phrase "houseguest's obligation." The corners of his lips rose in an enigmatic smile.

"Yeah… Yeah, sure. I'll do what I can anyway."

"Please do, Sir Isaac."

The two spent more time together that night, conversation rambling onward.

▶ 3

In early summer of Iselus's eighth year, an event occurred that would later be known as the Catastrophe.

There had been no explosions or flashes of light, and the earth hadn't rumbled, but it had definitely been a major incident. It had begun with the sudden disappearance of Adventurers from the city of Maihama.

For the first few days, the adults had thought it was probably just a coincidence or accident. Gradually, though, they realized it was not just temporary confusion, but some sort of serious incident.

At that point, all sorts of rumors began to fly. Many of them were critical ones, to the effect that the Adventurers had suddenly grown lazy or were plotting a revolt, but even in the beginning, Iselus had thought those accusations were false and misdirected.

This was because he adored tales of chivalry, and to him, the Adventurers had been legendary beings.

Before long, slowly, new information began to trickle into the city:

People said the Adventurers had gathered in Akiba and held a meeting. Iselus had heard from his mother, Saraliya, that the Adventurers had come up against some sort of big problem as well and that, having no idea how to resolve it, they were at their wits' end.

On learning this, the adults had begun to argue energetically over whether they should negotiate with them or make them part of the Lords' Council instead, but Iselus knew what they should do.

If the heroic Adventurers were up against a problem that had them confounded, it meant this was a worldwide emergency!!

Under such perilous circumstances, it was a mistake to discuss things like who was superior, or what to do about rank, while the other party wasn't present. Iselus told them as much, but the adults were getting dragged around by their own situations, and they didn't seem to hear him.

It hadn't been the adults' fault, of course. Iselus hadn't been able to explain himself properly. Now, after a year had passed, he understood that.

Iselus was the grandson of the lord, so the knights of the Glass Greaves and the territory's wealthy merchants bowed their heads to him politely. It did make him feel proud, but at the same time, it made him feel terribly uncomfortable.

When they complimented him, the words sometimes rang false. That was sad. When they yielded to Iselus, he sometimes felt it was because they wanted to get into his grandfather's good graces, not because Iselus himself was right. It made him feel as if his existence was trivial, and he'd flown into a temper a few times.

In short, the people around Iselus listened to what he said when it was convenient and didn't listen when it wasn't. Since he was still a child, there was probably was no help for that, and it still hurt him.

It was his big sister Raynesia who had changed the situation.

Raynesia had participated in the Lords' Council, simultaneously making her debut, and he'd been told that, after many twists and turns, she'd been granted a post in Akiba. After the council had ended, she had departed for Akiba on orders from their grandfather, Duke Sergiad, and had been given the mission of helping their subjects there. Iselus wanted to see Adventurers, and he'd been terribly jealous.

It had also been a great shock to him.

He loved Raynesia as a pretty, gentle family member who had to be protected, but at the same time, Iselus had been given a boy's upbringing, and he'd unconsciously assumed that he—not Raynesia—would be the one who would help his family (in other words, the duke) in its work someday.

Even with the age difference, the fact that his older sister had been the one to be given a job had shocked him.

He'd heard that his sister had ridden off with her guardian knight Krusty and fought against the goblin forces. However, it hadn't been out of adoration for the Adventurers; she'd done it as the sacred duty of the ruling family.

Yet, his sister didn't dream of tales of chivalry. As her little brother, he knew this. When she'd joined hands with the Adventurers, then used that friendship to rescue the people, she probably hadn't felt giddy, the way Iselus would have.

Iselus, who'd wanted to catch a glimpse of the Adventurers and see them fight, really was still just a child. He thought his sister was not merely beautiful, but a proud, splendid woman. Compared with her, he was only a fledgling. He wasn't even qualified to complain about how people treated him yet.

And once he'd realized that, there were mountains of things he needed to do.

In order to work with the Adventurers, Iselus had to have sufficiently complete knowledge of his family's work, and he had to grow as a noble. His big sister was able to work with the Adventurers precisely because she was the most beautiful noblewoman in Eastal, the intelligent lady known as the "Winter Rose Princess." Iselus was half his sister's age, and there were countless things he had to learn.

Fortunately, Iselus was the prime candidate for heir to Sergiad's duchy, and he had no shortage of tutors. He learned about history and geography both inside and outside of Eastal from his mother, Saraliya, and his father, Phenel, told him about the territory's industry and terrain in detail. It was still too soon for him to join the knights in their training, but at this point, everyone—even the gardeners and grooms—seemed to Iselus to have expert knowledge and techniques, and to be teachers he should learn from.

About a year had passed since then, and Iselus had almost reached his ninth birthday. He had (as far as he was concerned) grown a lot taller (he thought), and he was being trained by Isaac, an Adventurer whose byname was "Black Sword."

A dry, high-pitched sound echoed in the small courtyard.

The wooden sword had been made to suit Iselus's height, but no matter how he tried, he couldn't even touch Isaac's clothes with it.

"Isaac the Young... Is this...not going to work?" Iselus asked, hiding his rough breathing.

"I dunno. Move around more and swing that sword all over the place."

"Yes, sir!"

He unleashed a two-handed diagonal downward slash, then a sideways sweep, and then he inverted his wrists and thrust.

For an eight-year-old, Iselus's swordsmanship wasn't bad, but naturally, that was with the qualifier "for a Person of the Earth child." Isaac held a great sword in one hand as if it were a stick, even though it had to weigh ten times what Iselus's wooden sword did, and whenever he moved it, he deflected Iselus's attacks.

Training with Isaac was different from what it had been with his other instructors.

There were no practice swings or forms. All they did was fight mock battles. There were no pauses, and no set time limits. If Iselus got out of breath, Isaac started prodding him with his sheathed great sword.

Iselus knew quite well that this wasn't an attack or anything like it: He was just pushing his body with the scabbard of his sword. He wasn't able to parry the thrusts, though, and if he took them, he couldn't keep himself from rolling away like a billiard ball. These fights continued for as long as his strength held out, and when he finally started to have trouble breathing, he fell down right where he was and rested.

Since there were no explanations of forms or technical theory, he didn't even know how he should swing his sword. Of course there was a skill difference, but even before that, Iselus was an eight-year-old Person of the Earth, while Isaac had fought in scores of raids. Since there was such a huge difference between their fundamental physical capabilities, it wasn't even possible to tell whether that difference had shrunk or grown. He didn't know whether he was better or worse today than he'd been yesterday.

Of the training Iselus had experienced, Isaac's variety was far and away the strictest. However—and this startled Iselus—it didn't bother him at all.

"Hup."

"Oh!"

Before he noticed it, Isaac's sheathed great sword had moved, and the sensation of the object Iselus held in his hands had disappeared. Behind him, there was a whistling sound as something spun through the air: His sword had been knocked flying.

When he tried to look up, Iselus lost his balance, fell down, and gazed up at the sky.

He was breathing hard, and he couldn't get to his feet.

"Isaac the Young, you're—hff! Haahff!"

"Yeah, break time. That's fine; just lie there and catch your breath."

"Yes, sir. Hff, hff."

"You sure are weak."

"Yes…"

As you'd expect, hearing it said straight-out like that made him sad. He was so tired he couldn't even move, but the words he got out sounded disconsolate.

"Well, uh, you know. Don't let it get you down. You People of the Earth are all weak, so you're not that different."

"Is that right."

His thoughtfulness made Iselus laugh a little. The wind felt soft, and the sunlight was warm. Pansies swayed in this courtyard, too. Feeling gentle, Iselus said, "Do the members of the chivalric order also seem weak to you, Isaac the Young?"

"Yeah. They're weak. They've still got a long ways to go."

"Hmm. How can I become stronger?"

"I dunno if you really need to get all that strong, do you?"

That's irresponsible, Iselus protested. He might be the lord someday, and he had to polish both his sword skills and his horsemanship.

"Having guts is more important. The strength'll follow, bit by bit."

Isaac let the comment slide, ignoring it. Then he rummaged through the bag at his waist, pulled out a straight dagger that was about twenty-five centimeters long, and casually tossed it to Iselus.

"There, use that."

"Huh…?"

The dagger had spun through a half rotation to land neatly in the palm of his hand. Iselus stared at it, immediately realizing it had cost an incredible sum.

As a noble, Iselus was more used to seeing different types of weapons and gear than the average native. He'd actually seen things referred to as "famous swords" and "demon swords"—even those had been handed down through his House.

After the Catastrophe, a variety of Adventurer-made tools had flowed into Maihama, and weapons had been no exception. However, equip items came with their own levels and levels at which you could use them. As a result, items created by top-class Adventurer artisans went for sky-high prices, which only people of his rank could even think to afford.

"You don't weigh much, so that wooden sword puts your center of gravity too far out. If you learn to use that well, your sword skills will improve, too."

"But this is an Adventurer dagger. It's really expensive."

It was true.

To him, this dagger must have carried an unbelievable price.

Isaac was an Adventurer, and an unmannered one with no common sense at that. So he probably didn't know, but in Maihama, he could have bought a house with a single dagger like this. The knife had a gleam to it that looked obviously strong, and Iselus had very nearly been captivated by it already. Even so, he had managed to force that question out. Because of the economics, he'd had no choice.

Iselus really liked Isaac. He loved this huge warrior, who was cheerful and rough and didn't pay any attention to fiddly details. That was why, even though the training was as harsh as it was, he'd never once thought that he didn't want to do it.

"I'm not giving it to you just because. I hear it's your birthday. Unless guys have that sort of thing, they go bad. Like a motorcycle, or armor. If stuff like that stops getting you all worked up, you're done, y'know?"

"There's something wrong with your sense of money, Isaac the Young."

Iselus didn't know what a motorcycle was, but his chest was so hot he thought it might burst. He'd said something blunt to hide his embarrassment, but his face kept trying to smile, and he couldn't stop it. He was probably wearing a pretty pitiful smile for a boy.

"What, you don't want it? Well, fine. Give it back. C'mon."

The part about being so worn out from training that he couldn't move a finger had been a lie.

Hugging the knife and spinning around, Iselus thanked Isaac: "Waaaaah! No. I'm tremendously happy! It's an Adventurer Dagger! Thank you very much!"

What was this crest? When he examined it closely, he found the signature "Tatara" and a small Black Sword mark.

What's more, this dagger was custom-made, and it matched the ones Isaac and the others had!!

The discovery made the boy's heart overflow. He believed without question that the Knights of the Black Sword were the best chivalric order in Yamato, and their crest was more splendid than a knight's rank.

"You should've just been honest and said 'thank you' to start with. Sheesh."

"Heh-heh-heh. Oh!"

"What?"

Iselus, who'd spun around several times, jumped and pointed upward.

There was a shadow there, racing toward them across a sky of light spring clouds. He knew that shape; it was the same as the one Isaac had shown him, and Iselus raised his voice openly.

"It's a griffin!"

"Ah. Somebody from the Round Table? Little Miss Riezé, huh? Maybe she brought the princess back for the reception."

"Isaac the Young, we must bathe forthwith."

"Maaan, pain in the butt."

Come to think of it, tonight was the presentation banquet.

Iselus, who'd abruptly remembered this, nearly tackled Isaac, pushing his back from behind. The shadow of the griffin was rapidly coming closer. If his big sister was riding it, he might not have much time left to get ready.

"We *have* to. Ladies who are looking for husbands are coming to the banquet, too!"

"Okay. Okay already. Seriously, kid, that's the only stuff you're fussy about."

Isaac protested, and Iselus scolded him. However, again and again, his eyes went to the dagger he wore at his waist. This was an important treasure. It was also proof that he'd learned swordsmanship from Isaac.

"You have to wash behind your ears, too."

Iselus went into the manor, clinging to his beloved Isaac.

"If we're developing the type that uses radio waves, we'll need an antenna of a suitable size."

"Size?"

"The parabolic antenna. You know: the dish-shaped thing. Its size is important. Our technological level is low, so we'll just have to cover for it with brute force, or size."

"What about the time and the budget?"

"With Akiba's current finances, the budget… It may take about three years' worth. Adventurer inventions are suited to making one-off products, but we still don't have enough power to mass-produce or build something enormous. The construction period depends on the manpower we invest, but there is technical development work to do… If we're including lab time, I can't give you a quick answer."

"…I see."

"I couldn't call it realistic, not with Akiba's current system."

That was how his conversation with Roderick had ended.

It was springtime in Akiba, and Shiroe was on his way back to his guild.

He hadn't meant to let his emotions show, but Akatsuki's senses had been unusually sharp lately. She tugged on his sleeve and said, "My liege, don't be discouraged."

Although he replied with an "I'm fine," he couldn't shake the feeling that he'd reached an impasse.

"You have an old-man forehead again, my liege."

"Do I really? I don't think I do…"

Akatsuki's gaze was stabbing his forehead. Shiroe put a hand up to it, trying to relax it by massaging it. It felt no different from normal. In this world, unless you applied some kind of external power, hair didn't grow. That meant that, when his fingertips touched his bangs, they were the same length they always were.

When they got back to the Log Horizon guild house, it was quiet and empty. On the blackboard, there was a note in Nyanta's handwriting that said "I'm going shopping for dinner" and a cat mark. Naotsugu had gone along with Shouryuu and the others on their training, and Tetora had headed over to the Crescent Moon League. Lately, Minori's group had been deciding what to do on their own, without relying on Shiroe and the others.

Even when it was deserted, the guild was a relaxing place. Breathing in its atmosphere, Shiroe and Akatsuki climbed the stairs. They crossed the landing that looked out over the living room, then opened the door of Shiroe's usual office. When he shot a casual look down past his side to the rear, Akatsuki seemed to prompt him, using only her eyes: *What are you doing? Hurry up and go in.* She was apparently planning to follow him in, have tea, guard him, and hide.

Chuckling a little, Shiroe beckoned her in.

Secure a way to contact the moon.

They had a goal now, but that didn't mean their mundane worries had evaporated. The town of Akiba was bursting with energy, and there were new inventions and developments every day. However, that also meant that new trouble and problems were invented on a daily basis.

To Shiroe, it seemed as though more than half of Akiba's problems were based on a shortage of personnel. Even if there were resources that could be used to resolve issues, there were few people who could operate or direct them. That was the current, unvarnished state of the Round Table Council.

There were many causes. The disappearance of Krusty, who had acted as the Council's representative, was one of them. His charisma, leadership, and command abilities had been splendid beyond complaint, and Shiroe thought his disappearance was a heavy blow.

Stirring up enthusiasm in the people around you, or giving them a feeling of confidence in any situation—these abilities were completely different from actual business skills. In terms of Shiroe's acquaintances, *she*—Kanami, who'd retired from *Elder Tales* and moved to Europe—had been like that. The Debauchery Tea Party had *been* her, without a doubt. She'd brought gamers together under the banner of her unlimited optimism and a reckless smile.

She'd simply been an enthusiasm engine, but Shiroe thought making that enthusiasm contagious to the people around you was a special ability only chosen people had. Krusty was one of the people with that rare charisma.

That said, in Krusty's case, he was also able to govern, field paperwork, command, and be athletic and artistic, to the point where complimenting him on purpose was just a pain. At the Lords' Council, Krusty had been slippery and evasive, and when asked later, it turned out he had more than a decade of experience with social dancing. When he'd heard that, Shiroe felt as if he'd been completely had.

Even if beings like Krusty and Kanami were outliers, there was a strong tendency among Akiba's Adventurers to concede to one another and avoid responsibility. This was probably less about Adventurers than it was about the Japanese character. Everyone thought the role of "leader" was a demanding, nearly thankless one in which everybody took potshots at you whenever there was trouble.

Shiroe thought the Round Table Council organization had come into being and managed to exist for the past year because, initially, he'd established it by going straight to the leaders of the major guilds. If he'd addressed everyone equally and suggested they decide the matter with a vote, he probably wouldn't even have been able to organize an operating body to run that vote.

In addition, there were technical problems as well. There was no e-mail in Theldesia, no spreadsheet or document creation software, no recording equipment, and the postal service was underdeveloped. In this other world, just holding a meeting like the ones on Earth was difficult. They didn't even have copy machines. Simply making outlines of what that day's meeting would cover for each person turned into a full day's work if you did it by hand.

In that sense, Shiroe was immensely popular.

The Scribe subclass granted abilities related to overall copy creation, including craft skills used to make paper and ink, support skills that helped the user draw charts and title lettering, and the ability to copy the document or map in front of you. Naturally, he couldn't copy magic items, and he needed a certain amount of material, but for conference documents, he could use low-ranking materials without any trouble.

People leaned on those abilities, and the Round Table Council guild masters and guilds brought him documents they wanted copied. They treated him like a human copy machine.

Abruptly coming back to himself, he noticed that the shadow of the pen in his hand was more than ten centimeters long.

Apparently, he'd been absorbed in work for several hours.

When he stretched, his back made cracking, popping noises. His seminar had involved a lot of desk work, so he was completely used to it, but when he looked up, thinking about cleaning his glasses, he saw Akatsuki and Li Gan having tea at the reception set.

"Hello there."

The Lore Master waved at him with a droll smile. He looked exactly the same as he had when they'd parted in Susukino.

"Li Gan. When did you get here?"

"Just a moment ago, Master Shiroe."

"Ahem. I entertained him for you."

Akatsuki, who was kneeling formally on the sofa, puffed out her chest and glanced pointedly at the low table in front of her. Bean-based snacks and Japanese-style teacups filled with roasted green tea: Everything was tailored to Akatsuki's own tastes, but as far as showing hospitality to guests went, it wasn't wrong.

In that case, I still wish you'd called me, Shiroe thought, but he didn't say it. He knew that, whether they'd spoken to him or not, he hadn't even noticed he had a visitor, which meant the fault was his.

"My investigations in Susukino have finally reached a stopping point, you see. I'm very sorry to have taken so long, Master Shiroe."

"Is everyone well?"

As Shiroe spoke, he took his own teacup and sat down next to Akatsuki. Li Gan was smiling cheerfully, his eyes half-closed.

The man seemed a bit young for the title of "sage." For example, from previous interactions, Shiroe was well aware that, although he could have a sharp tongue, he was funny and interesting. But he also knew that the man's academic interest in magic, magical devices, and the history of ancient civilization as it related to those fields was the real thing.

"Yes. I was told to give you their regards."

"Did you learn anything about the transport gate?" Shiroe asked.

Li Gan had stayed in Susukino in order to investigate the intercity transport gate, which had fallen silent. Of course, his investigation would be beneficial to Shiroe and the other Adventurers as well, but Shiroe's question had been meant casually, as small talk.

"The transport gate is silent because it isn't being supplied with sufficient mana."

However, the answer was exceedingly straightforward.

Shiroe was startled, and Li Gan cocked his head, smiling bashfully. "...I learned that much on the first day of my investigation, to be honest." However, he said, he'd continued to study it because he hadn't known how mana was supplied or what the energy source was. The more he investigated, the more its function and mechanism as a large-scale magic item had intrigued him, and he'd ended up examining it thoroughly, down to the details.

"While investigating this and that, I learned that the Fairy Rings really do have some connection to the lunar phases. According to legend, there are ancient alv ruins on the moon as well. The intercity transport gates seem to make use of similar functions. I've pulled it all together here, in these documents."

Drawn in by the unexpected keyword *moon*, Shiroe picked up the report Li Gan had put together. It might have been a summary; there weren't many pages.

If you cut out the magical technology details, the remaining information was about the positional guide functions for teleportation that were managed by the moon. The Fairy Rings, the intercity transport gates, the Temple—this element affected all teleportation.

So there really is some sort of facility on the moon...? If we can believe Roe2's letter, there's a community of Fools up there. They're probably using Adventurer bodies from the test server. Are they doing some sort of work in the alv ruins?

Or were they waiting for something?

Shiroe gave it a moment of thought. Taking into consideration the report from Minori, although "Fools" did have great power, they seemed to be bound by the rules of *Elder Tales* and the world of Theldesia. The fact that she had fought using the abilities of a Summoner, one of the twelve classes, probably proved that.

                                    *   *   *

"…Then we really will need to send a transmission, hmm?"

"A transmission?"

That feeling came through in his voice, and it seemed to pique Li Gan's curiosity. Shiroe decided to explain, without holding anything back:

"Yes. The Adventurers are searching for a way to return to our old world. In order to do that, we need to communicate with the moon. We're trying to find a way to do it."

"Oho! An Adventurer transmission device? I wonder what that's like. How exciting!"

"No, it won't be that easy. We can't get the funds or the technology anytime soon…"

He remembered Roderick's bland expression. If it had been just barely impossible, he probably would have looked more frustrated, so that meant there really was no hope for the time being.

"Well, developing technology does take time. It's the work of a lifetime. There's really no help for that, no indeed. Still, in that case, couldn't you use the transmission equipment in Shibuya?"

"Huh?" Shiroe said.

Contact the moon. Go to the moon. Investigate the moon. In the days of the game, quests like that hadn't existed. Shiroe had practically lived on strategy sites, so he could vouch for that. However, it wasn't as if the moon had made no appearances within in-game tradition. On the contrary, there had been speculation that the moon where the test server was located might, at some unknown point, become the stage of an adventure. As evidence, people had cited the moon-related ruins found in a variety of areas.

"In Shibuya. The one in the ruins," Li Gan repeated.

"Wasn't that broken?"

Because of all that speculation, he *had* given a little thought to the ruins of the broadcasting station in Shibuya. Yet, he'd discarded that possibility almost immediately. According to the background information, those ruins had been completely picked over, destroyed, and abandoned. Even in the days of the game, nothing had lived there except low-level, nonaggressive animals.

"But when I was examining the gate, there was a response on the transmission network. Isn't it live?"

Shiroe mulled over Li Gan's words. Had he been thinking about it the wrong way?

He'd discarded the possibility of Shibuya based on his knowledge of *Elder Tales* back when it had been a game. However, Theldesia was another world now, and there might be something new there. A hidden room they hadn't been able to find in the game, an antenna reached by climbing an exterior wall, or maybe an underground facility with no entrance—those were all possibilities that might exist.

Shiroe started to get up, meaning to investigate right away, but a tele-chat came in just then.

It was bad news.

Sleep-inducing lunar moths had crept into Yamato's night.

▶ 5

"The kid's gonna be a real lord, huh…?" Isaac grumbled. He was holding a glass of sweet liquor, which wasn't his thing.

The great hall was filled with countless lights and the strains of chamber music. Even in People of the Earth culture, soirées seemed to be something aristocrats held. Being able to hold a feast flooded with light even at night, after the sun went down, was a very easy way to demonstrate how much power you had.

Maihama was the leading territory in Eastal, the League of Free Cities. Since this was about its next leader, the number of invited guests was significant. All the neighboring lords and their families were present without exception, and even nobles from distant territories had sent proxies. Between them, their guards, and the servers from Maihama, the hall teemed with at least three hundred People of the Earth.

As Iselus accepted greetings, Isaac watched him from a distance, wineglass in hand, feeling impressed. He admitted that the kid was sharp, but still, he was eight. As far as Isaac's common sense was concerned, that really was young.

"Yes, that's right," Calasin replied, from where he stood beside him. "Besides, the coming era will be a hard one; he may have a rough time of it."

"'Coming'? Is that something to do with whatever the lot in Minami is planning?" Isaac responded, without looking at him.

It was a royal pain, but during this presentation event, Isaac and Calasin were being treated as the senior envoy and vice envoy from the Round Table Council. Isaac was bad with formal roles like that, and he'd wanted to make a break for it, but they'd told him the Round Table Council was currently short-handed, so there was no help for it.

He'd thought he'd leave the negotiating to Calasin and get himself good and drunk, but aristocrats' parties didn't suit him. He'd have appreciated cold liquor with fried rockfish to snack on a whole lot more.

Since he was a guard, Isaac had no intention of skipping out, but he couldn't help but remember the sizzling hot delicacy.

"Hmm. That's unusually perceptive of you. Was that animal instinct?"

Calasin teased Isaac, paying no attention to his feelings. "Watch it," Isaac said, but although his mouth was set in a cross line, his mood had improved a little.

"I'm kidding. Look, you'll scare your popularity away if you keep making that face. Smile, smile. I'll have them send you some fried rockfish later."

"Huhn."

He grunted, but Calasin seemed to see through that, too. No matter what he actually said, the guy was considerate.

"Minami's teamed up with the Holy Empire of Westlande. If West-lande seriously tries to get Eastal under its control, we probably won't be able to avoid a war."

"What the old guy was talking about, huh?" Isaac muttered.

"Oh, was he?"

"Yeah. He explained it to me a little."

All the nobles seemed to know about the discord between Eastal and Westlande and the current confusion already. That atmosphere had been reported to the Round Table Council's top brass.

However, Isaac had felt it only since arriving in Maihama. Appar-ently, people didn't think problems were "theirs" unless they had a direct connection to them. *Tragedies that happen to people I haven't met are somebody else's problem*, Isaac thought it was. That was only natural.

"Heh-heh. Well, where people gather, trouble ensues. The more there are, the more there is. We Adventurers are involved, and the situation's complicated."

"You sure know a lot about it."

"Whoa! What do you think I am, Isaac the Young? I'm a merchant, a merchant. To merchants, information is life, you know? What about you?"

"It feels like something's buzzing around."

As Isaac answered, he fiddled with his elaborate ear ornament. The People of the Earth—even the men—often wore accessories like this in order to show off their rank or power. However, in Isaac's opinion, it seemed like something host club workers would wear, and it made him feel fidgety.

"It's because we don't understand nobles. I wonder if this sort of thing is normal. Do use it, all right?"

"If it doesn't get in the way, yeah, sure."

His perfunctory reply to Calasin was interrupted by cheers.

Technically, Iselus was the center of today's gathering. However, an individual's majesty and charm could disregard the event's intended focus. The great doors were opened, and a delicate girl with silver hair gracefully advanced across the floor, followed by an escort of guards in Round Table Council uniforms that matched Isaac's.

At that, Isaac began to make his way back toward Iselus.

"It's Princess Raynesia."

"She's as lovely as always."

"I heard she'd been posted away from home for an extended period, in order to act as an intercessor with the Adventurers of Akiba."

"She apparently returned to the castle by griffin this morning."

"By griffin?!"

Even if the voices were speaking in hushed whispers, that many of them together created a significant amount of background noise. Raynesia's head was bowed slightly, and she wore a modest smile; true to her reputation, she seemed to be overwhelmingly popular among the People of the Earth as the Rose Garden Princess.

To Isaac, who saw Raynesia's popularity in Akiba as well, nothing about the response felt strange. On the contrary, he smirked at Riezé's previous assessment of his remark: *"She sure is elegant." "Regardless, I hear she possesses resourcefulness equal to that of a prime minster who controls a territory."*

"I fear I am late, Grandfather."

"Welcome home, Sister."

"I'm sorry to have arrived late for your birthday. Do forgive me, Iselus."

"Well, you are working in Akiba, after all!"

Isaac pushed his way through the crowd, arriving at what seemed to be the best moment: Raynesia was greeting Sergiad and Iselus. As Raynesia bent down, smiling at her brother in the heart of the hall's warm radiance, her beauty really was the sort that made you long to preserve it in a picture.

Well, there's no need to actually talk to them, Isaac thought. He took a couple steps back, taking up a position where he could watch the whole Cowen family at once. He thought he'd keep an eye on their quality time from there, but Iselus's next words made his expression freeze up.

"Sister, I've made friends with an Adventurer, just like you."

"...Iselus? You mustn't think it's so easy to befriend Adventurers. Friends are something you earn after overcoming difficulties with tremendous courage."

"And you, Sister?"

"Yes, of course, I've made it through that trial."

"Amazing!"

That ain't amazing.

Friends are just something you sorta end up with.

When he shot a weary glance at Riezé across the room, she looked bewildered, and also as if she felt powerless to stop Raynesia even if she'd wanted to. She lowered the arm she'd half raised. She must have given up.

He didn't know the details, but he'd heard she was Raynesia's guard and supporter. The female Adventurers of Akiba had based themselves in Water Maple Manor during the murderer incident and had resolved the matter by working together; that fact had been reported to the Round Table Council. Since it had been a raid, Isaac had seen the records as well, and this girl, Riezé, was the one who had taken command during the operation.

"Besides, menaces and monsters and bespectacled ones lurk among the Adventurers."

"Menaces...?"

"Yes. Beware those who wear glasses. Nothing good ever comes of defying them. Or rather, in the unlikely event that you find an opportunity to defy them, it is a trap."

The conversation seemed to be heading further off the rails.

In her attempt to persuade Iselus, Princess Raynesia had crouched down all the way. Her graceful eyebrows were drawn together, and she was speaking in worried tones. To the nobles who surrounded them at a distance and couldn't hear what they were talking about, she looked like a kind, intelligent princess dispensing advice to her little brother, who was about to shoulder the important position of lord, but what she was actually telling him was a pack of lies.

Or, wait, maybe not.

Isaac changed his mind. She was probably talking about Krusty (the four-eyed elite) and Shiroe (Machiavelli-with-Glasses). In that case, the bits about how "nothing good came of defying them" and "traps" probably weren't lies. Apparently, when the People of the Earth spoke with one another about Akiba's Adventurers, descriptions got twisted. If this was how things were, there was no telling what they thought of *him*.

He didn't care about Krusty, but if he let her keep talking, he thought it might stir up trouble. He started to say something to her, but he was just a little too late.

"It's all right. Isaac the Young doesn't wear glasses."

"I'm so sorry I'm not a four-eyes."

Iselus's loud declaration rang out, and Isaac ended up delivering a morose comeback. Nothing Iselus said about him could really bother him, but due to his position, he couldn't move away. After injecting his flippant comment into the siblings' conversation, he looked around.

He wasn't used to the phantom noise that echoed right by his ear, so the audio was imprecise and slipshod. There were so many guests in this hall that it could detect things only vaguely.

"Huh? Oh. Eh-heh-heh. That wasn't what I meant at all, Master Isaac. How are you faring this evening?"

"I'm 'faring' fantastic, and hey. Hey, you. I'm gonna tell Krusty on you."

"…He isn't there."

What's with this princess? …Huh. So she can make that face, too.

Isaac didn't know anything about how aristocrats were born, how they were raised, or how they lived. He had the fuzzy idea that, since they were rich, it was likely they'd been strictly trained since they were tiny. They were probably completely tied down by duty and restrictions and things like that. Bizarre stuff. He'd never want to live that way. Those were his only thoughts on the subject.

All he'd thought about Raynesia was that she was an important guest of the Round Table Council and a major figure among the People of the Earth. In terms of the real world, she'd be a rich idol singer or something like that, and the conditioning that she was a game NPC was hard to shake.

However, he thought the sulky face she'd pulled a second ago was far better suited to someone her age than the tranquil, polished smile.

Apparently, that idiot Krusty wasn't seeing what was right in front of him.

The thought was highly gratifying.

"Oh, Sister! This is yuzu citrus juice. It looks delicious. Isaac the Young, this is yours."

"Uh, hey. Iselus. Don't skip around like that."

"But I'm happy."

When your mind's made up, your body responds to that, huh?

Feeling oddly calm, Isaac whisked Iselus off his feet, then set him down again nearby. His silver hair was just like his sister's. It was as fine as silk thread, and when Isaac swiped at it affectionately, it slipped between his fingers smoothly.

"Guys should act more dignified. Besides, you're about to become a head honcho."

"A head honcho?"

"A lord— Ain't that right, you over there? You too, and you."

Isaac raised a thick, sinewy finger. To the People of the Earth, the finger seemed to be drawing an unfamiliar magic circle in the air, but it was actually the gesture Isaac used to materialize the Black Sword of Pain from his item menu. When the big red-headed man in the Round Table Council uniform summoned an object from another dimension, and that object turned out to be a large, jet-black, ominous sword, the hall grew noisy.

The uproar was funny, and Isaac smiled savagely into the tense, pale faces of the maids and nobles he'd pointed at.

"Don't you think that's a little too rowdy, people?"

The Surprise Attack Alert Earring that Calasin had made him take had rung loudly.

"Assassinations are supposed to be sneakier than that."

The noise sounded like the roar of a fierce wild beast, threatening its enemies.

▶ 6

"Hah, uh, um… Has there been some sort of mistake?"

The Person of the Earth noble's words were resolute and defiant, but Isaac flat-out ignored them. He glared at a frightened maid who had fallen down, and then he clanked the great sword he held over his shoulder.

"The idea of bringing out a huge, sinister sword at a festive occasion like this one!!"

Calasin went forward, both hands raised, to placate the bravely yelling noble. The young man's expression was mild and soothing, but there wasn't a shred of mercy in his words: "You've been outed, so no, I don't think there's been a mistake."

"That's a RoderLab-made accessory. Its effect is 'surprise attack alert.' It uses magic to give alerts about ambushes, stealthy approaches, poison attacks, instant death attacks, and hostility within a twenty-five meter radius. It may not look like it, but it's a semi-fantasy class item. It uses magic materials from the One-Eyed Dragon."

"You're pretty handy there, Calasin."

"Thanks for your business."

Upon hearing the two men's effervescent conversation, everyone around them took two steps back en masse.

This was the leader of Maihama's ball, and the guests had gathered from all over. Some of them were probably acquainted with one another, of course, but most of them were special envoys from other territories or ladies-in-waiting or guards, and they didn't know many others well.

Isaac's words had hinted that there might be someone suspicious here. No, he'd practically said, in much clearer terms, that the envoy in front of him was an assassin.

As a result, people exchanged uncertain glances with the guests around them, putting distance between themselves and the others with the timidity of small animals.

With a light sound as if someone were beating a futon, Isaac turned to the maid he'd glared at and the protesting noble and, in one motion, ripped off their clothes. At the transformation, the subdued atmosphere in the hall changed abruptly, and screams went up.

The lithe black outfits were reminiscent of ninja garb, and they were clearly intended for combat. He'd thought it was just the noble in front of him and his guards, but apparently, it wasn't. In the time it took to blink, a dozen or so assassins had appeared. From the looks of the elderly noblewoman who was backing away, petrified, she hadn't ever dreamed that the lady-in-waiting she'd employed was a spy.

"Scatter!"

Without even glancing at one another, the infiltrators evaded the sword aura Isaac unleashed, dodging to either side.

Frankly, at that point, Isaac's opinion of them went up. He'd been thinking about beating them within an inch of their lives; he hadn't had the slightest suspicion that they might manage to dodge. They were People of the Earth as well, but they were probably more skilled than the Maihama knights his group was training.

"Dammit! For the peace of Yamato!"

"What're you getting all melodramatic for?"

Although, that was only "in comparison with."

A ninja ran at Isaac with a dagger at the ready, intending to ram him, but Isaac hit him with the flat of the Black Sword of Pain, then sent a hard, leather-shod kick into the side of another one who was trying to circle around him.

"Damn you, Adventurer!"

"Yeah, and?" he snapped at the groaning assassin. *So what if I'm an Adventurer?* There wasn't anything Isaac could do about it, no matter what the guy said, and it didn't bother him one bit.

However, as far as the assassin was concerned, it had probably been a curse. Eyes bloodshot, the man shrieked a few words in a piercing voice, then took a spherical item out of his shirt and threw it at his own feet. There was a metallic sound, and it began to spew out smoke of a disturbing color.

This time, an uproar as if someone had poked a hornets' nest welled up in the presentation hall.

"Hey, nobody breathe that! Get back! Open the windows, and—Calasin! Detox!"

As he issued the warning, a new assassin who'd come out of nowhere growled and attempted to run past Isaac, seizing his chance. The man looked as if axes would suit him, but Isaac sent him flying with a fist, then scooped up Iselus, the intended target, as if he were a cat. If he kept scampering around, he'd be insanely hard to protect.

"Isaac the Young!"

"I'll give you a shoulder ride, Isel!"

He was actually carrying him over his shoulder like a sack of rice, but Iselus seemed to have nodded without hesitation.

"Hand over the boy, and we'll spare your life."

"What's the condescension for? Huhn?!"

"This is basilisk petrifying poison. An accumulation will numb, paralyze, then turn even a high-level Adventurer to stone," the man boasted in a flat, toad-like voice, smiling at Isaac with a viscous gaze. It was a despicable, cloudy expression. "There are any number of ways to combat Adventurers."

Isaac detested his tone.

"Leza!"

"Leave it to me!"

No sooner had he shouted than the elites of the Knights of the Black Sword, who had to have been stationed in an anteroom, rushed in. They scattered green light around, neutralizing the smoke and poison with magic, then began to guard the People of the Earth in the hall, who were screaming in terror.

It was true that cumulative poisons would affect even high-level opponents. Poisons had levels as well, and while low-ranking versions wouldn't affect high-ranking opponents, cumulative types kept raising your "Poisoned" level by overwriting it. However, that was true only if you didn't get detoxed partway through. Cumulative poisons were initially slow to act anyway, and there was no Knight of the Black Sword who would mess up a detox.

Confused fighting had broken out everywhere. To the People of the Earth, the assassins seemed to have significant combat skills. That earlier poison and their special items hinted at the presence of a specialized organization and training. However, the assassins seemed so powerful to the natives simply because they didn't know otherwise. Levels over 90 and Adventurer equipment gave the Knights of the Black Sword capabilities that were just plain unfair.

Of course, that didn't mean that developments were one-sided. This hall was filled with Eastal nobles and their families, which meant the Knights of the Black Sword were protecting those who weren't nobles as well: the ladies-in-waiting, the knights, the merchants, all of them.

With a clang, a guild member's sword struck an assassin's shuriken out of the air.

Behind the vanguard, who wore dauntless smiles, Healers radiated detox auras. They weren't able to exercise their full power, either. This wasn't a dungeon, and if they used wide-range destruction spells or enormous summoning spells here, they'd cause massive secondary damage.

Still, even fighting defensively, their skills were overwhelming.

"This is going nowhere. Kill the boy!"

The assassins must have understood the difference in combat power as well. The group's leader and a band of five individuals who seemed particularly skilled fell into formation, hiding one another, then rushed swiftly toward Isaac.

This wasn't a normal formation in which they covered one another's positions.

It was an offensive formation—or, more accurately, a formation geared toward surprise attacks—in which each member hid in the blind spots created by the others' figures. A wishy-washy attack wouldn't bother Isaac's Armor of Divine Flame' one bit, but Iselus, whom he'd flung over his shoulder, was different. In particular, if they used poison darts, nothing would be more of a pain. He could swear he wouldn't let him die, but the day a stray arrow hit Iselus, there was no telling what kind of harassment he'd get from the maids.

· With a ferocious smile, Isaac turned around, unleashed Merciless Strike as a parting gift, then set off running with Random Step.

"Iselus, don't breathe that stuff. Just hang out up there a bit longer."

"I can't, Isaac the Young!"

As Isaac had expected, the pseudoninjas chased after him. Well, no, they were probably really after Iselus, on his shoulder. There were five of them. His earring was vibrating slightly, alerting him to hostility. There seemed to be several more of them lurking outside the hall as well.

Isaac had seen that coming. In the first place, he and the others had realized early on that spies were watching them. Shiroe had also warned them that the spies might be planning some sort of attack.

They probably could have caught a few of them. However, they hadn't thought they'd be able to shut down their plan or see the whole of it that way. The Knights of the Black Sword was a large-scale guild specially designed for combat: Intrigue and urban espionage were outside their field of expertise.

For that reason, they'd decided to let them attack and round up the whole group at once. He didn't think that had been a mistake. Every member of the ruling family had a guard covering them.

Isaac swung his right hand in a familiar gesture. He concentrated, sending the heat in his body flowing into his wrist. When he stuck his elbow out and accelerated it, it became Aura Saber. With a shock wave, the attack he'd activated carved a slash into one of the windows of the light-filled hall. With no hesitation, Isaac charged at it.

Shattering glass danced like a blizzard on the terrace outside.

Leaping out into the spring night, Isaac launched himself off the surface of the stone wall with a kick, heading for the parapet. For someone with an Adventurer's physical capabilities, a distance of five or ten meters was nothing to worry about.

Castle Cinderella was a European castle with a medieval, or rather

fantasy, silhouette. The main building and annexes, the parapet, ornamental corridors, and several towers with cone-shaped roofs that clustered around the central tower were distributed with complexity, nestling close to one another.

Today, because of the presentation, the castle town was in a festive mood. Unusually for a People of the Earth town, even now—after sundown—the broad avenue below him was crowded with shining orange lights.

With a noise that reverberated in his gut, flowers of light decorated the sky.

They were celebratory fireworks. With their light at his back, Isaac kicked the indigo roof and ran.

"Isaac the Young—"

"No talking, Iselus. You'll bite your tongue."

True, in order to break out of the hall, he'd had to pass through that suspicious smokescreen. Onslaught—the wind from his sword, which he'd unleashed in the darkness—should have dispersed some of the smoke in the hall, though. He'd leapt out onto the roof in order to avoid the poison's effects.

"I mean, they said poison..."

"I'm fine. It tingles a little, that's all."

"But, Isaac the Young, you're..."

"Guys shouldn't think in circles like that."

Even though he was in the middle of a fight, the feelings that filled him were strangely tranquil.

"Today is my debut. It's the day I became an adult, so even I... No, I have to fight."

"Oh yeah?"

"I mean, Isaac the Young, you're..."

Well, that's true, Isaac thought.

You're an Adventurer. Was that how he was going to end that? Or was it, *You're going to disappear*?

What a sharp kid. He was appallingly bright.

The windows of the presentation ceremony hall were being flung open or broken, one after another. The Knights of the Black Sword were probably letting the smoke out and beginning relief activities.

Up on his shoulder, Iselus had stiffened up and made himself as small as he could, so as not to get in the way. *He's a good candidate for lord*, Isaac thought. The boy was desperately reining in his fear so that he wouldn't get in Isaac's way when he fought. He was planning to fight, too. Why? Was it aristocratic pride, or overconfidence?

No. It was because he'd said they were friends.

Because he'd gone and publically declared that he was friends with an Adventurer.

Even little kids cared about posturing like that. Because he was a guy. Not bad. Interesting, too. Isaac had been planning to think about it after he made the decision, but that wasn't it. He'd already made the decision, so there was no need to think about it. Isaac's country was wherever his friends were.

"En garde!"

"What's that 'en garde' crap about, you damn loser?!"

A throwing knife whizzed toward him, and a Person of the Earth in a ninja outfit followed it—he'd knocked the guy flying. Since Isaac hadn't been able to take a good stance in midair, the man spun around upon landing; he seemed to have escaped most of the damage. Almost immediately, he began pursuing Isaac anew.

A phantom crackling sound warned him of a new threat.

There were probably about ten of them. Pushing back the tail of his Round Table uniform, Isaac touched down in a courtyard.

When he looked up, Calasin was leaning out of a window on the spiral staircase, waving wildly and yelling. The distance between them was too great for him to make out the words. *What is that guy, an idiot?* Isaac thought. *Just hit me with a telechat.* Still, he could tell what he was trying to say from his gestures and expression. They'd probably secured the hall.

From what he could see, he'd managed to draw the attackers' best people here with him.

Ordinarily, this place might have been used for garden parties: Neatly pruned trees surrounded a three-dimensional, terraced garden. A lawn covered its center, and Isaac lowered Iselus from his shoulder to the grass. At that, although there was no telling what had gotten him so psyched up, an excited assassin charged at them, brandishing a sword.

A glare from Isaac was enough to make him falter; as he took the last step, he was moving a little uncertainly, and Iselus caught the sword with the dagger he wore at his waist. The dagger rang cleanly, protecting the boy. It was an Akiba-made piece, and there wasn't a single chip in the blade.

Isaac was impressed that he'd caught the strike, even though there was bound to be a great level difference. Even if the equipment was good, that was really something.

However, weight was an element that was completely different from technique and fighting spirit.

Unable to completely absorb the impact, Iselus fell, rolling over and over on the grass. Isaac had known that was coming, so he caught him by the collar and casually set him back on his feet. He'd let him do it because he'd been where he could see him, and as it turned out, Iselus really did have a feel for this. Today was his official debut. He wouldn't be satisfied unless he got to swing his sword around a bit. After all, Iselus had taken his first step into the world of men.

"He's tough!"

"No, the smoke bomb has to have weakened him! Use the Hakko formation!"

"He can't move anymore. Circle him several fighters deep and finish him off!"

The attackers surrounded them, swords at the ready. The lawn was wide, with no obstacles on it, and Isaac and Iselus just stood in the middle of it, illuminated by the thundering fireworks. Viewed logically, the attackers who'd surrounded them had an overwhelming advantage. Their tactical decision had been the right one. If Isaac had been level 50 or so, like they were, he probably would have been done for.

However, Isaac had a retort:

"You guys must be idiots."

These guys really are genuine morons.

The way they thought numbers like theirs would be enough to break "Black Sword" Isaac was truly hopeless.

Only idiots didn't know what it was they were taking part in.

Only idiots purposefully grew fox ears.

Was that why they had no choice but to get their hands dirty with a job like this?

The Knights of the Black Sword were a group of morons. They were dumb, all of them. Watching them running around and around that grassy hill with the People of the Earth, he'd sometimes thought, *What're you guys, a pig farm?* Since they were turning in and rising early, they'd started eating and drinking twice as much, and the way they howled for "Fried rockfish, fried rockfish" was dumb, too. When he'd seen them putting together a plan to all chip in money and buy princess figures as a group, he'd wondered whether they'd soared past "dumb" and achieved "crazy."

It was weird they thought "half killing" somebody meant knocking their HP down to the halfway mark, and when they'd called recovering half of that damage "half healing," it had made his head hurt. Doing that would leave 25 percent of the damage unhealed. They were completely hopeless idiots.

Even then, though, they were way better than these pathetic attackers. Who'd ordered a thing like this?

"Black Sword of Pain."

"Wh-what are these chains?!"

Isaac had swung his dark, steel-colored sword sideways in a horizontal slash, and with a creaking noise, translucent chains had flown out. The chains scattered in all directions, writhing, and burrowed into the ground. Using the ground itself as an anchor, they wound around the attackers, trapping them.

Anchor Howl was a basic Guardian special skill, used to concentrate aggro and hold the enemy in place, and Isaac's black sword reinforced it.

"They're your aggro. I'm limiting your freedom."

Eyes glittering, Isaac threatened the fox-eared attackers.

From the information Calasin had given him, he knew who they really were: intelligence operatives from the Holy Empire of Westlande. Foxtails were a small, new race, and they didn't have much power in Westlande. Frankly, they were treated like slaves. That was why they'd been used as what amounted to suicide bombers on a one-way mission like this one.

These guys probably have their own stories and issues, but...

Isaac found this intensely irritating.

"...that doesn't mean you can swing a sword at a kid and act like you've accomplished something!"

"Isaac the Young, don't!"

He didn't use a sword technique. He swung the Black Sword of Pain all the way through, with all his might. He wasn't swinging it like a sword, either. He swung it like a baseball bat, sweeping all the attackers away with the flat of the blade.

Isaac had enough power to do that. He had no idea whether it was the right move. That was something for Shiroe and Krusty to think about. Isaac wouldn't do anything agonizing. He would only walk in directions that made him feel better. He'd decided that a long time ago.

"Hmph!"

For that reason, he just snorted at Iselus, who looked worried.

The attackers had all fallen to the ground, unconscious.

If he was just beating them back, fine, but Isaac didn't intend to take their lives. That was what their aggro and luring them out here had been for. Isaac was a Guardian, and he'd only fought as Guardians naturally fought: by taking the enemy's attacks, keeping them pinned down, and protecting his companions.

The cleanup work was probably a job for the People of the Earth. He wanted nothing to do with quarrels among aristocrats. If you thought of it as fighting over a spot to do business, it sort of made sense, but Isaac's brain wasn't suited to tracking down criminals.

"Oh, good."

"No, it ain't good."

Iselus was smiling brightly, and as he responded, Isaac's mouth twisted crossly. Iselus beamed at him. Fireworks shot up into the sky, one after another.

The kid's just genuinely happy that I didn't get hurt, Isaac thought.

He might not have realized that he was at the center of the uproar or that they'd been after his life. Well, no, there was no way he wouldn't have noticed that: They'd been yelling stuff about "getting the kid." In that case, he was pretty tough.

At any rate, the assassins who'd attacked Maihama had been driven off. If they questioned the ones they'd captured, future developments would probably be a bit better.

"Hey, Iselus."

"Yes, Isaac the Young?"

"Back where I'm from, you're an adult when you hit eighteen."

Official adulthood started at twenty, but whatever. Isaac had been about that old when he'd started working.

There was another enormous explosion. Sparks sifted down. Golden flowers bloomed in the night sky, then, glittering, rained down over the earth.

"Is that so? I suppose I still have a long way to go, then."

With the night sky and its bursting, sparkling fireworks behind them, Isaac stuck his fingers into the dejected Iselus's hair and shook his head roughly.

"Well, I'll hang out with you until then."

"Huh?"

"I'll be your friend."

Iselus didn't understand what he'd just been told. Then it sank in; his head snapped up, and he broke into a brilliant smile. The kid was easy to read.

Still, this had been one crazy presentation event. He could see people hurrying in and out of the venue, and he spotted the Glass Greaves as well. They were probably securing the assassins.

That's the problem with the upper class, Isaac thought, shrugging. Iselus pulled at his hand.

"We need to go back to my grandfather, Isaac the Young."

"Yeah, don't rush me. The place is probably trashed; let's wait till they're done cleaning up."

"Are you planning to play hooky?"

"No. I just don't want to cause trouble for the maids."

"But there are lots of maids who want to take care of you, Isaac the Young."

"Like heck there are."

"What? There's even a shift for when you take naps!"

As Isaac joked around with little Iselus, an alarm that was shriller and sharper than anything else he'd heard that night reached his ears.

Instantly, Isaac's tension returned. He listened hard.

Was there something lurking there, hiding in the sound of the fireworks? Isaac looked around the area. All he saw were flecks of golden light, shining like flames. Guided by a premonition he couldn't put into words, Isaac looked up.

He watched, lips drawn and tense, as the sparks poured down over Maihama.

Countless points of light were approaching, scattering sparks, as if the Milky Way were overflowing. So many status windows were popping up that the noise was almost unbroken. The shining points were monsters.

Thousands upon thousands of flying menaces had invaded Maihama and Yamato.

CHAPTER.
4

SLEEP OF THE ETERNAL MOTH

▶ NAME: ISSAC

▶ LEVEL: **94**

▶ RACE: **HUMAN**

▶ CLASS: **GLADIATOR**

▶ HP: **15471**

▶ MP: **7761**

▶ ITEM 1:

[ROUND TABLE COUNCIL UNIFORM]
UNIFORMS THAT WERE MADE FOR THE MEMBERS OF THE ROUND TABLE COUNCIL POSTFOUNDING. THE TROUSERS AND COLLAR OPENING OF ISAAC'S UNIFORM HAVE BEEN MODIFIED. THERE WERE VARIOUS OPINIONS ABOUT WEARING UNIFORMS DURING EMERGENCIES, BUT ISAAC WAS UNEXPECTEDLY ENTHUSIASTIC ABOUT THE OUTFITS.

▶ ITEM 2:

[EXPERIMENTAL ELBOW PADS]
PADS MADE FROM FANTASY-CLASS MATERIAL THAT SHIROE AND CREW FOUND IN THE ABYSSAL SHAFT. THOUGH IT'S INCOMPLETE AND SOME SPECIAL PROPERTIES ARE STILL UNEXPLAINED, ITS CONFIRMED THAT THEY SHORTEN RECAST TIME. A GREAT ACHIEVEMENT OF AKIBA'S RESEARCHERS AND ARTISANS.

▶ ITEM 3:

[SLIGHTLY UNEVEN ORIGAMI FROGS]
ORIGAMI FROGS FROM ISELUS, AFTER LEZARIK TAUGHT THE BOY HOW TO MAKE THEM. THEY'RE ON ISAAC'S DESK, NEXT TO THE PRETTY UNEVEN ORIGAMI FROG THAT ISAAC FOLDED, WHICH IS WHAT GOT ISELUS INTERESTED IN ORIGAMI IN THE FIRST PLACE.

<Anvil>
One of the blacksmith's
basic tools. Materials
and results depend on
the user.

▶1

All across Yamato, gleaming scales poured down through the darkness.

Into the spring night, the shining stream that had seemingly descended from the red moon released its venomous flow. Those who breathed in the dust felt only a little dizzy, but the People of the Earth who were attacked by the moths lost consciousness and didn't wake again.

More than anything, the enormous creatures that glided down from the sky bred terror.

Theldesia was a world dominated by monsters; even if the People of the Earth couldn't defeat grotesque creatures, they were at least used to seeing them. However, they didn't usually see giant insects in their everyday lives. In particular, the people in the urban areas were so afraid of these enemies—which attacked from the sky, ignoring the presence of the defensive walls—that they panicked.

What prevented the situation from deteriorating into a complete collapse was the fact that the moth monsters weren't strong enough to break stone structures and force their way in.

After gathering in temples, shrines, and assembly spots to pass an uneasy night, the people discovered several of their comrades, as still as if they'd been frozen.

Their condition was diagnosed as a deep sleep, but it was obvious to everyone that they weren't simply sleeping.

The window information revealed an intermittent decrease in MP. Attacks from the shining moths or excessive exposure to their scales resulted in lowered MP. In serious cases, the symptoms settled in, becoming an ongoing, sporadic MP decrease. This appeared to be MP-based physical deterioration. When an individual lost all their MP, they were unable to stay conscious. These comas had clearly been caused by such a loss, and what's more, the leaks were fast and continuous enough that standard recovery wasn't possible.

One day had passed since the night the moth monsters, known as Eternal Moths, had appeared and attacked.

"They're asleep…"

"As we expected, they're People of the Earth."

Minori's group, led by Nyanta, had left Akiba and were traveling northeast. It was a volunteer initiative to find People of the Earth who had lost consciousness in field zones and protect them.

Shiroe and the other executives who represented their guilds had had a very hard time leaving the guild center. Even Minori and the others hadn't felt as if they could just saunter out and go hunting. In which case, they'd still wanted to help, and this volunteer activity had been the result.

It was likely they were able to do this because no damage had been confirmed among the Adventurers. That was why even Minori's group could perform relief work.

Immediately to the east of Akiba, there was a ruin called the Metropol Circular Overpass. The People of the Earth called it a defensive wall, but Shiroe thought it might be the Metropolitan Expressway's Mukoujima Route. In other words, it was the ruin of the highway that once ran through the heart of the city.

There were many ruins like this one, and they were well-preserved. Back when *Elder Tales* had been a game, the region around Akiba—in other words, the Kanto area—had been a place where players gathered. If you were going to distribute a variety of monsters across a limited area, naturally you needed some sort of borderline or divider. The elevated roadway had been just the thing.

All the elevated roads around Akiba were called "the Metropol

Circular Overpass," and the Mukoujima Route stretch was simply known as "the East-Side." Many Hill Giants had lived in the vicinity, but due to the plague incident and a large-scale military drill by the Knights of the Black Sword, their population had been thinned out, and the area was now safe.

Immediately after the Catastrophe, this ruined elevated roadway had been mossy and decrepit. Rusted-out hunks of metal had sat here and there, and there had been many places where iron poles had fallen down and you could only get through on foot.

However, in the time since the Catastrophe, Honesty and the other combat guilds had cooperated with Shopping District 8 to improve the situation considerably. This was because it was expected to join river transport on the Kanda River as an artery for commodities.

At present, the rubble had been cleared away, and it had been improved to the point where even a large horse cart could travel along it without trouble. It was far more pleasant than the low-lying roads, which had many bumps and dips and were forced to weave between lots of ruined buildings, and it had acquired particularly great support from the People of the Earth who traded mainly with the Northeast. It had gotten to the point where People of the Earth merchants told one another that, once you crossed the river at Moriya, you'd practically arrived in Akiba.

Minori and the others were currently exploring this Metropol Circular Overpass, traveling north from Akiba. In the past half day, they'd found three groups of victims.

"I wonder where they're from," Touya asked.

"I believe they're from the North," Nyanta responded, looking thoughtful.

A man was slumped limply in the driver's seat, leaning forward; Minori checked him but found no external wounds. He'd only lost his MP and fallen asleep.

"The horses must have run off."

"Yes, just like ours did."

"Times like this make you think that's convenient, huh?"

Serara and Isuzu, who had been investigating the bed of the cart, had that exchange as they came back. Minori was looking up, watching an enormous circling bird that called once, then flew away to the south. It was a Giant Owl; it had probably been carrying an Adventurer scout from Akiba. Shiroe had told Minori they were excellent flying mounts, but because they couldn't keep it up for all that long, they weren't sent very far from their home base.

This area, a dozen or so kilometers northeast of Akiba, had many rivers. There were fewer ruined buildings, and the percentage of land covered by forests and stands of trees grew. If this area were cultivated, it would apparently be the perfect place for a settlement. In fact, there were several pioneer villages in the area, but she'd heard that other teams had already been sent out to help them evacuate.

"We'll have to send them back."

"Yeah."

Minori and Touya promptly laid the sleeping People of the Earth down inside the cart. They had to put them in the gaps between cargo, but this partially stabilized them, so it was probably all for the best. Rather than carry three People of the Earth directly, it would be faster to just push the cart with them in it. The summoning pipe they'd borrowed was able to call strong, high-performance military horses, and one of them would be enough for a cart this size.

"I wonder what they're gonna do about Shibuya."

"Yeah..."

"I hear Old Li Gan said there's some kind of ruin there."

"Under the circumstances, I don't think this is the time for that," Minori told her brother.

Now isn't the time described the current situation in a nutshell. Actually, now that she thought about it, she got the feeling that that had been the case ever since the Catastrophe. All sorts of things kept happening *all* the time, and they were constantly hard-pressed to deal with them.

Little by little, they'd grown accustomed to that, but, of course, that didn't mean that when trouble broke out, they immediately knew how to handle it. To be accurate, it was more that they'd simply gotten used to the fact that "things happened."

Here, something was always happening—crazy things. So much had transpired in Forest Ragranda, and in the village of Choushi, and then in the town of Saphir, too. Even now, they were vague on what should be done, but there was no point in running away and nowhere to run to, and Minori had learned that they had to face things squarely.

"The older guys have it rough, too."

Touya sighed as he spoke; he had his arms folded behind his head.

She thought that was entirely accurate.

Adults have it rough was something Touya and Minori had stopped thinking a long time ago. The conclusion they'd come to was that there weren't really any "adults" in this world. Minori had finally realized there hadn't been any in their old world, either.

To Minori, adults were people who'd reached maturity and were affiliated with an organization best referred to as "the Adult Union." She'd christened it herself, and even she thought it was an insubstantial-sounding name. In any case, the Adult Union was a vague organization to which mature grown-ups invariably belonged, and within that organization, difficult decisions were made and debates carried out. These mature individuals acted on orders from the Adult Union. Since that union was an extremely large-scale organization (after all, every adult belonged to it!), all affiliated members were swiftly contacted with the appropriate way to handle difficult problems. That was why adults were able to assume developed attitudes.

The Adult Union was something like a company, or society, or insurance, or accounts, or municipalities, or the government—in any case, something along those lines. Minori thought, vaguely, that it was probably some sort of mixture of these.

However, there was nothing like that here in Theldesia, or the town of Akiba. The Round Table Council was probably something like an Adult Union, but it was Shiroe who was there, not "somebody from somewhere." In other words, that meant there was no "clever, responsible, yet vague and rather confusing somebody-from-somewhere" who would solve Shiroe's problems for him. Shiroe couldn't be a member of the Adult Union: He was responsible for solving other people's problems.

To put it another way, Shiroe wasn't benefiting from the services of the Adult Union, so he wasn't an adult. There wasn't one single adult in this world.

In the same way, Minori and Touya's parents hadn't been adults.

After Touya's accident, when they learned that it wouldn't be possible to heal him completely, their parents had been heartbroken, and they'd fallen to pieces. They'd tried their best, but they hadn't succeeded. Their mother had had to change workplaces, and their father had started coming home later. Minori had been a little shocked by that; after all, she'd thought, hazily, that her parents were far more "adult" than she and Touya were. That they had to be "adults."

But now that she thought about it, that was only natural. Back then, the Adult Union hadn't helped Minori and Touya's parents. It hadn't sent them anything resembling correct orders. Their parents had tried to face the problem all on their own, but it hadn't gone very well.

Confronted with the disaster that had struck Touya, Minori and her family hadn't been adult parents and twin children. They'd simply been a family of four people. There was no help for that, and she didn't think it had been a bad thing. Minori and her family had become a team and searched for a way to get through the problem. Minori had done what she could, and Touya had done the things he was able to do. In retrospect, it had been like the Forest Ragranda training camp.

"I hear that Lord Sergiad collapsed in Maihama as well."

"He stood at the head of the knights' brigade and took command. That territory has a wonderful lord."

A thin girl with a brown braid and an expressive youth with shining blond hair came around the side of the slowly moving cart.

They were Minori's companions Isuzu and Rundelhaus. "Do you think he's all right?" Serara—a kind-looking girl with a gentle profile—stuck her head out of the back of the cart as she spoke.

They were all Minori's precious friends. She had no idea how long it had been since she thought about whether they were adults or children. Just like Minori, Isuzu was a girl named Isuzu, and because Minori knew her well, when she thought about her, there was no need for her to forcibly categorize her as an adult or a child. There were things Isuzu could do, and things she couldn't do, and things she'd be able to do someday. The members of Minori's group knew very well what the others could and couldn't do.

"I think he's all right. At the very least, they say there won't be any immediate problems. His MP is gone, and he's unconscious, that's all."

At Minori's words, her companions nodded.

Minori knew that Shiroe and the others were currently at the guild center, arranging for various kinds of assistance. The listless people of Akiba, the Odysseia Knights in Saphir, the People of the Earth who wouldn't wake up, their return to the old world... Shiroe and the rest had a lot of things they needed to think about. It certainly wasn't because Shiroe was an adult; it was because he'd just happened to be sitting in that chair. Minori and Touya's plea for help probably wasn't completely unrelated, either.

And so Minori and the others had to help Shiroe, and it was what they wanted to do. Because he was family. When families worked together, it didn't matter who was an "adult" and who was a "child."

Minori flexed her biceps slightly and threw out her chest.

She'd thought it over thoroughly, and it had made her feel better. If that was how things were, then there was no problem. It was like acquiring more family members. Like, say, marrying Shiroe...

At that point, her cheeks grew hot, and she shook her head in an attempt to clear them. That wasn't it; something purer. That sort of thing.

"Sh-shining...w...ings...," murmured one of the unconscious men.

"Are they dreaming?"

It was Serara who'd spoken. She was watching an unconscious Person of the Earth in the back of the cart. He seemed to be delirious. When dawn had broken, the moths had vanished, but maybe they were still being attacked in their dreams.

"Those moths... I wonder if they're gonna show up again tonight."

"I don't know, but we need to return to Akiba and get ready."

"Mew're right. Let's break off our exploration here and head home."

At Nyanta's words, Minori and the others all nodded.

The full shape of the incident wasn't yet clear to anyone.

▶ 2

As Minori had imagined, Shiroe and the other core members of the Round Table Council hadn't gotten a wink of sleep that night. It had been the second such night in a row. On the night of Minori's group's expedition to the Metropol Circular Overpass, the monsters attacked again.

It was an even bigger shock to the Adventurers than the previous night's attack.

Akiba spent a noisy night with many messengers racing back and forth, and in the gray predawn light, there was only a slight break before they began moving again. At the guild center, in the hall that was now called the Round Table Room, the same members who'd been there half a day previously were all assembled.

"So they've finally struck Adventurers, too?"

"According to eyewitness statements, it appears to be the work of mothlike monsters with shining wings."

The mysterious flying insectoid monsters that had attacked Yamato two nights ago had used unidentified bad status attacks to trigger comas. The damage wasn't immediately life-threatening, but it also wasn't a threat they could overlook.

Two nights previously, the hostile monsters had attacked many People of the Earth. There had been well over a hundred victims, and that was just the ones the Round Table Council was aware of. At that point, they'd assumed that this unknown phenomenon affected only them.

Apparently, that wasn't the case, though.

The faces of the Round Table Council guild masters who'd gathered in the conference hall were gloomy.

They had nearly limitless physical strength, but even for them, mental stress was different. As he looked around at them, Shiroe suppressed a sigh. Under the circumstances, anxiety was something that should probably be kept hidden.

"So these are moth spirits or somethin', right?"

"They're called Eternal Moths. Their level range is wide, from the eighties to around ninety. When this was a game, to the best of my knowledge, no such monsters existed."

Riezé supplemented Marielle's question with information that had been reported. All the members had been given reports that Shiroe had copied, but they were a mere two pages thick. They knew far too little. In the end, the sparseness of the reports seemed like a visible representation of the members' psychological unease.

"It happened just as the moon rose, didn't it? At six twenty-two PM, to be exact. We believe there will be a third wave of attacks tonight."

"The first attacks put People of the Earth into comas, and the second affected Adventurers as well."

"There were more moths, too. Even some of the monsters are asleep and foaming at the mouth."

Roderick, Akaneya, and Michitaka—the heavyweights that formed the nucleus of the Round Table Council—spoke as if confirming the content of the report. This was shared information, already stated in a report that had been drafted in very little time that morning, but it was important to actually say it aloud. Staying silent was the worst possible option. On that thought, Shiroe nodded and added his own opinion: "There will probably be even more during the third wave... There's a possibility their mysterious abilities will keep growing stronger as well."

"What the heck are those things?" Akaneya complained with a groan.

"Currently, all we can say is that they're a new type of monster," Roderick responded in scholarly tones.

Additionally, there was new information:

"According to the Grandale members, they came from above. From the moon."

That answer had come from Woodstock, who rode a wyvern, a flying mount. Grandale, the midsized guild he led, was a support guild that specialized in transport. Most of its members had tamed mounts, and a fair number of them had rare flying types.

"From the moon up in the sky, y'mean?"

In response to Marielle, Woodstock nodded, his whiskered face set in a grimace. If you went into a coma on the ground, you just fell down, went to sleep, and stayed there. Of course there was a danger that you'd be physically attacked while you were like that, but there was no direct, immediate peril. However, if you lost consciousness while you were on an airborne mount, you'd plunge straight to the ground, headfirst. Since it wasn't clear how tough Adventurer bodies were or how much defensive power they had, they weren't sure what the results would be, but it was a crisis that was pressing enough. To

Grandale, these monsters were probably more of an urgent, trouble-some danger than most Adventurers thought.

"Hey, hold up. What was that stuff you said about a community of Fools on the moon? I thought that was a pretty epic-sounding idea; is it true? And there were monsters called Geniuses, too..."

"Are those Eternal Moths a type of Genius, then? But why are they takin' everybody's MP? Are they eatin' it?"

Shiroe had already reported an outline of Roe2's letter to the Round Table Council. In fact, this trouble had come up just after he'd made that report. The crisis had been so exquisitely timed that they were practically bound to doubt him.

Even if that's not right, it may not be far from the truth, Shiroe thought. In her letter, Roe2 had said they were collecting Empathiom. Of course there was no conclusive proof, but when he combined the contents of the letter, the sequence of events up till now, his experience on the moon, and Li Gan's story, he could imagine something.

These Geniuses probably weren't ordinary monsters.

From what he could see when he looked through the reports, they were intelligent. They could anticipate the Adventurers' movements and lay plots. In fact, that was the monsters' distinguishing feature.

If he believed Roe2, these were beings that were "using" monster bodies. They could probably think of them as creatures that were making use of the shapes and capabilities of *Elder Tales* monsters but were more problematic.

"Geniuses, huh? I'd heard stories about 'em, but..."

"No, we don't yet know for sure whether these are the Geniuses them-selves or not. It's strange that such a huge horde should appear so suddenly."

"They take MP from your physical body, don't they? Should we call it 'the soul-stealing disease'?"

Beside Shiroe, who was deep in contemplation, Roderick spoke, trac-ing letters in the air as he did so. The soul-stealing disease. According to the Spirit Theory, MP was the vehicle of the soul. If that MP was being taken, then yes, you could say the soul had left the body.

If the theory was correct, this attack had unintentionally proven that People of the Earth and Adventurers were the same. Although there had been a day's difference, both had sustained damage. That meant that both had MP and souls. Shiroe sensed a warped humor in the idea, and he smiled wryly. It wasn't as though that evidence would resolve the current situation.

"Yes, but some folks are just fine, y'know? Our Henrietta got attacked, but she only got a li'l bit dizzy."

"Isn't that due to the level difference?"

"No, we can't say that. Damage occurred even among high-level Adventurers."

"So this is about the difference between those who fall asleep and those who don't, you mean…?"

Besides, if the Spirit Theory and the presence or absence of souls were connected to this incident, that raised new questions. The difference between those who fell asleep after being attacked and those who did not… Shiroe thought there had to be some sort of secret there.

However, as he ignored his doubts, the conference moved on.

"So nobody's dying, right?"

"That's correct."

"If we die, we can resurrect at the Temple. However, it doesn't work that way with sleep. We don't know if we can break free of this slumber by dying and resurrecting, either."

"That's worrisome."

In a way, Riezé's words spoke for everyone present—*worrisome* was an apt way to put it. It didn't seem like a catastrophic crisis, but they couldn't find a way to combat it.

"Where are Calasin and Isaac, and Soujirou of the West Wind?"

"We're having the first two continue to guard Maihama. Souji's out scouting."

"Maihama had it awful, didn't they?"

"They were holding a social debut, and lots of lords were gathered there, after all."

"Duke Sergiad, too?"

"How are the other cities doing?"

"Plant Hwyaden seems to be protecting Minami. We've received reports that there is no great confusion there. Silver Sword is guarding Susukino. The city's population is small in any case."

As Shiroe answered, he visualized the strategy terrain map in his office. Plant Hwyaden's defense was tight in Minami, the Kansai-area player town. It had more frontline personnel than Akiba did, and it probably wouldn't fall easily. Susukino had been a fortified city to begin with. With the city's outstanding defense and its small People of the Earth population, Silver Sword was probably more than capable of routing their enemies.

Shiroe was more concerned about small territories and settlements where only People of the Earth lived than he was about those central cities, but at this point, he wasn't all that worried. The Eternal Moths seemed predisposed to attack major cities. In East Yamato, the reported attacks seemed to have been concentrated on Akiba, Maihama, Susukino, and Yokohama.

In general terms, monsters had intelligence appropriate to their forms. When this was a game, insectoid monsters that looked like moths had spawned in designated spawning zones and had simply prowled the area, attacking victims indiscriminately. The mere fact that they were attacking big cities made it clear that something about this situation was very unlike *Elder Tales*.

"What are we going to do about Shibuya?"

Ains, who had been silent for a while, asked about Shibuya as if he'd made up his mind about something.

"Shibuya?" Woodstock asked dubiously, but Ains didn't even look at him. He faced the center of the round table and kept speaking, as if he were squeezing the words out.

"I hear Li Gan has informed us that the ruined broadcasting station in Shibuya is live. Shouldn't we hurry to investigate it?"

"Gimme a break; at a time like this? People are getting hurt over here."

Michitaka was the first one to object. His big, solidly muscled body was trembling, clearly betraying emotion. As Ains looked at him, Ains's own expression turned sorrowful, almost as if asking for forgiveness. But still he kept speaking, resolutely.

"I know it sounds heartless, but if they're only sleeping, there is no immediate danger to their lives... Isn't it our job to attempt to break through this while we still have the manpower to do so?"

"But—!"

"We've been driven further into a corner than we think. The rogue guard, the flavor text becoming real, the tensions between East and West, and now this incident, plus the new threat of the Geniuses... I don't think we have the wherewithal to be altruistic at this point, do you? Isn't that arrogance? We're at the end of our rope."

Shiroe had had a hunch that Ains would say that.

There were victims among the Adventurers. At this point, there were only about a dozen, but there would probably be another Eternal Moth invasion tonight. Shiroe couldn't muster the optimism to hope that there would be only two days of attacks, after which the trouble would clear up on its own.

He understood Ains's sense of impending danger. Up until now, the Adventurers' altruistic spirit had been supported by their outstanding combat abilities and wealth, both of which were based in their immortality.

This crisis shook the foundation of that immortality. If they lost consciousness and became vegetables, neither their immortality nor their combat abilities would have any meaning. Both the People of the Earth and the Adventurers would be nothing more than powerless, perpetually sleeping shells.

The fact that the situation hadn't developed into a panic yet was probably because not many Adventurers had registered what that sense of impending danger really was. It was likely that there were still a lot of people who felt, on some level, that it wasn't their problem. Once they caught on, the desire to escape was bound to plant opinions like Ains's in them.

Fists clenched, Shiroe endured the silence that filled the conference room.

Finding a certain name on his friend list, he lasted through several tense minutes before a cool, bell-like tone notified him of an incoming message.

He'd issued a quest before this meeting, and apparently, his reliable younger friend, who delivered results no matter what was going on, had accomplished it.

"Mr. Shiro, we found it. The Eternal Moths' nest!"

Shiroe nodded. Soujirou seemed to have sensed this; he reported the results of his scouting expedition in a voice that was tenser than usual.

"Erm… Please don't be disappointed, all right? It's in Shibuya. The entire town of Shibuya is a dungeon. According to the zone settings, I mean. The core is the Shibuya broadcasting station ruins. You know: the low-level dungeon. The area's turned into a raid zone. Its new name is Fortress of the Call. It looks like it's going to be tough to clear."

In a way, that's what I was expecting.

He'd designated Shibuya as the very first area to scout precisely because he'd known.

He was also certain the fight that awaited them would be harder than anything he'd anticipated.

The Geniuses were intelligent monsters. They were bound to have picked up on the situation over here as well. If he were a Genius, how would he attack Akiba? How would he shatter the town's hopes? The answer was clear.

The Geniuses had created a dungeon in Shibuya. When he murmured that news as an impromptu report, a commotion ran through the Round Table Council. Turning pale, Ains slumped down into his chair.

"A raid? This is a Raid-rank Genius?" Marielle murmured, stunned.

Shiroe nodded.

The enemy had taken the transmission facilities that could communicate with the moon.

▶ 3

In the chilly morning air, Shiroe was depressed.

Members of the Round Table Council and the D.D.D. supply division were busily running up and down the broad avenue. They had decided to dispatch a raid unit. The preparations for that, the members they'd selected, and their surroundings were all enveloped in a hurried atmosphere.

Shiroe sat in the shade of a tree, watching everything.

There were no people around him. From time to time, he responded to telechats requesting confirmation of prepared materials, but he was deep in thought.

They'd already finished organizing the capture team. He wasn't fully satisfied with the formation, but it had been the best he could do.

The unit was composed of the smallest possible number of select members. This was because they hadn't been able to ignore the voices that called for them to prioritize guarding Akiba and Maihama. As a result, they'd ended up choosing only Adventurers who were close to Shiroe—including all the members of Log Horizon—and only the ones who'd fought the Eternal Moths and proved their resistance to sleep. This meant they'd decided to take Minori's group, who were midlevel players, and he felt uneasy about it.

Yet, the situation was unstable, and they weren't able to invest their most elite members.

Even if they decided to prioritize returning home, there was no guarantee that the transmission facilities in the Shibuya ruins would actually prove to be the key. It wasn't even a question of whether they'd be able to secure them safely. If they did secure them, would they work properly? Even if they were able to use them, would sending a transmission to the moon really lead to a return home? At this point in time, the only answer to all these questions was "maybe."

On the other hand, if they made protecting the People of the Earth their objective, at present, they couldn't be certain the Shibuya raid would help them do that. Soujirou and the other West Wind Brigade members had informed them of the emergency, but there was currently no known solution. They hadn't yet investigated the interior of the former ruins, now a raid zone known as Fortress of the Call: The entrance was sealed, and even Soujirou's group hadn't been able to get inside.

Because of that, he couldn't say their forces were sufficient. Still, that Soujirou, Riezé, and other Adventurers with plenty of raid experience had said they'd participate had been a stroke of good luck.

But all this wasn't actually the source of Shiroe's melancholy.

Shiroe had sunk deep inside himself. His thoughts were torn and confused, but if they could have been summed up briefly, that summary would have been that he didn't feel quite satisfied.

An enemy had appeared. They were headed out to defeat it. Put into words, that was all this was. However, it wasn't a situation Shiroe had created. Danger had appeared, and they were going to eliminate it, so the initiative lay with the danger. To Shiroe, that in itself felt vaguely off. When he traced the feeling of unfocused dissatisfaction back further, it took him all the way back to the words he'd said to Captain Nyanta.

I think we should go home.

Of course, he hadn't said those words thoughtlessly. He'd worried and hesitated before choosing them. However, in the end, no matter how far he went, it was only "should": Shiroe couldn't say that he *wanted* to go home, but he also couldn't say that he *didn't*. He'd simply come to the conclusion that, taking all of Yamato's present circumstances into consideration, it was probably the correct move, something they *should* do.

It was an answer that the circumstances made nearly automatic, and it held nothing of Shiroe himself. The situation had the initiative, and he'd given the only answer he thought was likely to be correct under the circumstances.

There was a murky feeling inside Shiroe. It wasn't something unrecognizable; on the contrary: It was an emotion he was very familiar with. There was a situation he couldn't do anything about, and when he tried to deal with it rationally and logically, the answers appeared on their own.

There weren't many answers. In most cases, there was only one.

This state was practically routine for Shiroe. His parents had both worked, and when they were away at their jobs, he'd had no choice but to eat meals by himself. If they moved house, he'd had to go with them. There was a certain, specific problem or situation, and in it, there was always only one answer that was meaningful and valid. This was sense so common that there was no need to give it any real thought.

Shiroe's correctness, common sense, and choices helped the people around him, and there had been many times when they'd headed off trouble before it began. Those choices had made it possible for him to "do well" both at home and in school, but as a result, he'd had to walk for ages over the asphalt late at night. What he was feeling now was the same thing he'd felt back then.

That common sense was terribly suffocating, but he thought, *That's just what answers are like, in the end; I doubt there's any help for it.* It had always been like that before, and it probably always would be.

The true shape of his irritation was his anxiety and hesitation.

He thought he'd said good-bye to those days on that lunar beach, but he was still carrying this pain. Determination alone wouldn't be enough.

Right now, Shiroe had no other answer.

"Master Shiroe."

Li Gan, smiling bashfully, had poked his head halfway out and was beckoning to him.

Standing up from his place in the shade, Shiroe went closer, dubiously. At that, the Person of the Earth sage dashed out of the ruins, spread both arms wide, and spun around, showing off his equipment.

"What do you think? Does it look good? Am I fully prepared now, too?"

Li Gan wore an enormous box-shaped knapsack that seemed to be made of metal on his back, and he was smiling. When he reached around behind himself and fiddled with the meters and pipes attached to the box, the pulse of the magic stone grew stronger.

"Well, you know. The history of Miral Lake is nothing to sneeze at, is it?! We have proper equipment for individuals as well, Master Shiroe. This is a barrier generation device, created during the time of the Alv War. I do believe I'll be able to accompany you, I do indeed. You see?!"

As Li Gan spoke, he seemed to be enjoying himself as much as ever, regardless of the circumstances. As if provoked by his words, a little white steam went up from the magical device, as if it were excited.

"What, you're coming too, guy?" Naotsugu had been passing by, and as he spoke, he set his large shield down in the square.

"Yes, I am. There seems to be a special seal set on the entrance to Fortress of the Call. Master Shiroe has asked me to break its spell."

Li Gan scratched his head, seeming a little self-conscious.

Shiroe felt deeply apologetic about this.

This Person of the Earth researcher didn't have very much HP. He wouldn't be able to be part of the raid capture unit; Shiroe was planning to have him come with them in a safe position. He thought this dungeon, the broadcasting station ruins, would be relatively safe compared with ordinary raid zones. From what he could gather from the attacks, most of the monsters would probably be Party rank, not full Raid rank. Still, naturally, that didn't mean there would be no danger.

"This sort of situation is unprecedented in the history of this world. As one who has inherited the name of Miral Lake, I have a duty to see it through to the end."

That was how Li Gan responded when Shiroe had apologized.

Even though he was beaming, there was strength in his expression, and it told Shiroe that he wasn't doing this out of a mere sense of obligation. Li Gan had things he wanted to do and learn, too, and he felt it was worth risking his life to do so. To Shiroe, right now, that attitude was dazzling, and it made him a little jealous.

"Well, and in any case…"

Possibly because he was embarrassed, Li Gan scratched his head repeatedly, smiling awkwardly.

"I did admire this sort of thing, just a little. They're called 'dungeons,' aren't they? And it's 'exploring,' correct? And 'adventure'! I call myself a Lore Master, and as you'd expect, we scholars have a particular, instinctive desire to see things we haven't seen before. My research into world-class magic has made progress, you know. I tell you, strange things really do exist. There are moments when research you thought was unrelated suddenly connects, out of the blue. It's possible the maximum and the minimum in magic may be—"

"I'm in full equipment, too, hon!"

"Well, *I'm* in full armor, Naotsugu!"

With an unspeakable metallic noise, Marielle and Tetora crashed into Naotsugu from either side. Naotsugu, crushed in the middle, couldn't shove them away with his full strength, and he turned pale, looking like a guy who'd been in a car accident. Even if Guardians boasted the highest defensive abilities of all twelve classes, if they let their minds wander when they weren't in the middle of a fight, this sort of thing could happen. Not only that, but both of the others were Clerics, and they weren't inferior to any of the other classes in terms of equipment or physical strength.

Smirking, Li Gan murmured, "Excellent synchronization. Now,

there's a fine example of teamwork." All Shiroe could do was smile wryly at the comment.

"What about that's full armor, huh? You're wearin' your best outfit." "How rude! Idols are always at their most adorable in front of their fans. This isn't my best outfit; it's my best *effort!*" The pair had begun to argue. Caught between them, Naotsugu looked flustered and tried to say something, but it didn't seem to be going well. If it had been just Tetora, he could have argued fiercely, but even for him, this was a rough battle.

The thought made Shiroe laugh a little.

There were problems for which it was hard to find answers.

"Only time passed in the midst of illusions": The world probably held questions for which that was the correct answer. However, anxiety burned coldly in Shiroe's chest. He knew he'd thought it through logically and chosen the right answer, but even so, his feelings were still clouded.

The terror that something precious was being lost washed over his back like waves over a shore. He held his breath, forcing strength into his emotions. If he didn't do that, it felt as though his fists and knees would start trembling.

It was likely that this raid would change the destinies of many Adventurers and People of the Earth. The idea was right in front of him, not as a premonition, but as a realistic possibility. Under these tense circumstances, Shiroe hadn't been able to find sufficient options. He hadn't prepared enough. This wasn't his field of expertise. He might be wrong. He might not be able to make up for that. The premonition of failure clung to his back, trying to submerge his spirit in cold, pitch-black water. Intentionally suppressing that feeling put a significant strain on him.

"Shiroecchi. It looks like we're all ready."

"Okay, Captain."

Glancing up at Nyanta's words, Shiroe stretched and looked around the square.

A full raid was assembled there. Twenty-four people, all in expedition equipment.

Shiroe's friends: Naotsugu, Akatsuki, Nyanta, and Tetora. His guild's younger members: Minori, Touya, Rundelhaus, and Isuzu.

From the Crescent Moon League: Marielle and Henrietta, Shouryuu and Hien, plus Serara.

From the West Wind Brigade: Soujirou and Nazuna, with Isami the Samurai, Kurinon, and Olive.

From D.D.D., participating at their insistence: Riezé, Richou, Yuzuko, and Koen. Then there was Kushiyatama, a high-level "ranker" Healer with ties to D.D.D.

With the addition of Shiroe and Li Gan, that made twenty-five members. It was a small unit.

In the end, Shiroe hadn't been able to muster a group that consisted entirely of free hands in the truest sense of the word. His own guild, Log Horizon. The Crescent Moon League and the West Wind Brigade, with whom he had longstanding relationships. D.D.D. (or rather, Riezé, its unit leader), who'd offered to help. That was all there was to this capture unit.

He thought saying he was "bad at relying on others" was a kind way to put it. He couldn't help but despair, wondering whether his ability to build human relationships might be completely hopeless.

Shiroe had thought he'd foreseen all sorts of things and taken appropriate steps, but it still wasn't enough. *Reality is always merciless, isn't it?* he thought, and his shoulders slumped. Even so, it probably wasn't all bad. Isaac and Calasin had supported Maihama. Even if it had all been according to some unknown entity's plan.

However, the monsters wouldn't wait. Geniuses were too much for Shiroe to handle. He was just an ordinary person. Still, even now, the sun was traveling across the sky, and night, when the Eternal Moths would take flight, was bearing down on them.

"We will watch to see what sort of decision the Adventurers hand down."

Nodding to Kinjo, who had come out to see them off, he exchanged glances with the Round Table Council guild masters, who had all assembled behind Kinjo. When he spotted Ains, who looked highly concerned, a small, wry smile found its way onto his face. Shiroe didn't hate the guild master; it was likely that they were trying to reach the same place. The man had thoroughly gotten off on the wrong foot, that was all.

For that very reason, with the idea that even feigned confidence was better than nothing, he raised his voice and announced their departure.

"Our destination is the raid zone Fortress of the Call, in the depths of the Shibuya dungeon. We will destroy its antenna, stop the Eternal Moths' numbers from growing, and wipe them out."

Nine thirty-two.

Shiroe and the rest of the Fortress of the Call capture unit left Akiba. They were bound for the player town of Shibuya.

With this, Shiroe had ended up taking a seat at a new table. But this time, the stakes of the gamble were high. And what's more, even he didn't know what "victory" would look like this time around.

▶4

"It's quiet, isn't it?"

"Of course it's not. This is a raid zone. They're drawing a bead on us from somewhere."

When they reached Shibuya, the town was eerily silent. As she listened to Kushiyatama—the woman who'd drilled raid expertise into her right after she'd made it into D.D.D., before she'd known right from left—Riezé nodded.

The cluster of ruins eroded by greenery was the same as in Akiba, but since this town had originally been a commercial mecca, it was rather more colorful. "Living" ancient buildings showed off exteriors made splendid with a glass-like material known as Glastal. However, although the buildings' appearance suggested otherwise, they couldn't sense any people.

The raid capture team passed Mobile Armor that had run out of mana; it was the sort that the Kunie clan's patrolling guards wore.

The scales of those Eternal Moths stole a certain type of mana. The selection standards weren't clear, but it was enough to wear down even the defense and magic resistance of Mobile Armor, which boasted unrivaled power. The comatose Kunie clan members had already been rescued, but the armor was heavy, and it had been left behind.

When it came to raids, raid enemies—which boasted more than ten times the HP of Party-rank monsters—tended to be seen as the only threat, but this wasn't the case. With a full twenty-four-member raid, considered in simple terms, the Adventurers had more than twenty times their regular combat power, and teamwork brought it up to fifty times more. The real threat lay in the enemy's teamwork and reinforcements: In other words, the zone's very terrain turned against the Adventurers. As befitted a player town, Shibuya's blocks were carved up like a mosaic, and they intersected in three dimensions. Now that it was a combat area, it had become a battlefield with poor visibility that was crowded with places to take cover.

Brushing hair back from her cheek with gloved fingertips, Riezé took out a pocket watch.

"Moonrise is in…six hours."

This area was a city that had been established as the fifth player town in *Elder Tales*. Based on reviews of the previous four towns—Akiba, Minami, Susukino, and Nakasu—it had been put together differently than the rest.

The problem with the preexisting towns had been that crowds tended to accumulate at the cities' core functions—in other words, at the guild center, the bank, the Temple, the market, and the intercity transport gates. These were important facilities that game players had to use on a daily basis. On top of that, even if the cities had been player towns, in the days of the game, everything except those facilities had been mere background. That was why they had become sources of congestion.

Taking this issue into consideration, Shibuya had been created as a player town that had no guild center, bank, or market. Instead, it was equipped with many intercity transport gates and had been designed to fulfill its urban functions by being constantly connected to the other four cities.

At present, when the transport gates had fallen silent and it was swarming with Eternal Moths, the town was practically deserted.

*　　*　　*

"Hey, there they are!"

"Eight from up ahead on the right! Humanoid, Ogre subspecies."

"Assassinate!"

"Izuna Cutter!"

"Flare Arrow!"

The battle had begun.

Even as she fired highly inductive Serpent Bolts, Riezé studied the situation around her. For D.D.D., the most important issue in early information gathering on raids was understanding the structure of the area and the composition of the enemy. However, that was because all the members had a sufficient understanding of one another's abilities from the teamwork training they'd done in advance. The members in this unit had been pulled together from many different places, and for them, the biggest issue was learning about their companions' abilities and constructing team plays. Fortunately, the monsters' abilities weren't high at all, so Riezé was able to spare some of her attention for information gathering while continuing to fight.

This was true of Kushiyatama, who'd been playing longer than Riezé, and of the veteran West Wind Brigade members as well. *Ingrained actions* might have been the term for it. They knew what was important during raids without having anyone put it into words.

Strangely, the same thing appeared to be true of Log Horizon's younger members.

The golden-haired youth Rundelhaus; the middle guard Bard Isuzu; Minori in her *miko* outfit; her little brother, Touya the Samurai; and the rearguard support Druid Serara. Those five were a little under level 60. Considering that most of the members of this exploration team were level 90 and above, they were relatively low-level players who shouldn't have been here.

Despite that, they'd proven to have extremely high resistance to the Eternal Moths' MP-draining attacks. Even high-level Adventurers couldn't avoid losing MP to the moths' scale attacks, but these players were able to nearly negate them. It wasn't clear why this was so, but notice had been taken, and they'd been added to the invasion team. Furthermore, for the sake of Akiba's defense, they'd been hesitant to assign too much combat power to the assault unit. Including Riezé, only four members of D.D.D. had been loaned to this raid, and they had pushed very hard to be allowed to go.

As a result, she hadn't been hoping for much from the five midlevel players as regular raid members, but they were moving far better than she'd expected. They looked sharp.

Of course, they had a few things in their favor: Even if their personal levels were around 60, the level of the raid team that was buffing them was over 90. In other words, they were getting support from ultra-high-level ability-boosting skills.

Not only that, but in a full raid, they could get varied support from more than ten players. This meant that support itself was multilayered, and their current practical combat abilities were probably around level 70. If a level-90 team received similar support, they'd see an increase of only two or three levels. When thinking about it that way, it was a definite advantage.

Then there was the issue of aggro. Even if they were getting support, their abilities seemed to be only about level 70 as a result. In other words, even if they attacked and recovered with all their might, they'd never match the aggro that the Guardian Naotsugu generated in his current role as the full raid's main tank. Not having to worry about accumulating excessive aggro meant the enemy wouldn't go after them.

In short, the midlevel group was in an environment where they were getting sufficient support from the people around them and were able to freely exercise their abilities beyond their normal limits.

However, even without those advantages, they moved well.

As someone who commanded the training unit at D.D.D., the leading ultralarge guild on the Yamato server, Riezé could tell. The way they positioned themselves in the front and rear. The way they launched and fielded attacks from angles that wouldn't block the vanguard. The order and composition of the special skills they chose. The way they relied on the surrounding members and stayed conscious of overall attacks, even though they weren't taking attacks from monsters personally… And the way they conveyed messages out loud. Even at level 90—no, regardless of level: In the area of player skills, from the way these five moved, you'd never have thought they were beginners.

She'd been asked, via Akatsuki, to "look after the newbies" in advance, and as someone from a training unit, she'd accepted the request as a matter of course. However, their skills seemed to be more than she'd imagined. Actually, they were at a pretty absurd level. She would have liked to scout them for D.D.D.

"I'm *sending some* your way."

"Eat 'em up, Riezé."

The voices seemed too cheerful for the situation. They belonged to Soujirou and Nazuna of the West Wind Brigade. Those two had been members of the Debauchery Tea Party once, and in a way, they were legendary. They were acting as the sub-tank and second healer for the invasion unit's second party. If the first party's role was to hold off the brunt of the enemy forces, their team's job was to provide mobile defense, to catch and stall the monsters that slipped past that first party.

These two were intentionally letting monsters pass them.

This action wasn't a standard move. It was a message: *Run through the movements you'll need for melee fighting. Polish the third and fourth parties' teamwork.* And most of all, *Help the midlevel group grow.*

As proof, the attacks unleashed from Soujirou's Dim Crossing were pasted with the icon that signaled a move speed decrease for the Ogres.

"Four Ogres have broken through the vanguard!"

The girl Minori looked back at Riezé, giving a report. Of course, Riezé had been able to see them as well. Technically, the girl could have left the action undone. She hadn't, though. She'd done it to send a message: *Requesting orders.* Minori had an outstanding eye for tactics. Or rather, she was sensitive to the thoughts of the people around her. She was trying with all her might to sense what they wanted to do. As she did so, she looked like a small, very wary animal.

"Richou, switch to backup! Minori, lead the unit and attack with everything you have!"

The group of five sprang forward. As she watched them, Riezé's eyes narrowed in a smile. It was a good use of a unit.

On the other hand, the commander had been a disappointment.

There were many elements that determined whether a raid succeeded or failed, but Riezé thought that one of the most important was its commander. This was particularly true of this capture unit, which was full of talent.

Naotsugu, the main tank, was powerfully maintaining the front line with stable taunt work. Soujirou and Nazuna, the pillars of the mobile attacks, were magnificent as well. Akatsuki and Nyanta, the attackers, had high processing abilities. In terms of individual skill, Riezé thought they were at a level where they could conquer even a server event.

For that very reason, there seemed to be nothing particularly noteworthy about the overall tactical decisions; they were mediocre, and not very decisive. Calling them "careful" sounded good, but they lacked boldness.

"What's this, what's up? You're looking glum."

Nazuna, who'd left the front line to the first party and dropped back, spoke to Riezé amicably. Riezé hesitated just a little, then went ahead and told her what she thought.

"Timid."

"What is?"

Nazuna took a swig out of a gourd-shaped canteen before asking her question lackadaisically.

"—Milord acknowledges the Debauchery Tea Party, and Shiroe was its famed counselor. I'd hoped to see him directing combat, but he isn't as impressive as I'd imagined."

"Ah-ha-ha-ha-ha-ha. Well, maybe not. Shiroe's a wimp, after all."

"He... He is?"

Nazuna's words had been unexpected, and Riezé looked up.

Nazuna must have spent a long time fighting alongside him in the Debauchery Tea Party, but she didn't seem to have taken offense at Riezé's evaluation; she was smiling her usual, teasing smile and puffing out her chest.

"Yep, that's right. He's a wimp. He's more a wimpy counselor than a famed counselor."

Riezé felt a pain in her chest.

She wanted to argue with what Nazuna was saying, and that was when she noticed: The hopes she'd been trying to force onto Shiroe were her own affair. As if he would resolve all the things she couldn't do anything about, such as the guild's current administrative problems and her unease at Krusty's absence. Like a gust of cool wind. Riezé had been hoping for that sort of omnipotence from Shiroe. She hadn't wanted him to save her personally; she didn't think she'd had hopes that naïve. However, she realized that she wanted him to show her the sort of talent that would be capable of those things. She finally realized that she had asked to join this capture unit because of that wish.

"'If it was someone Milord acknowledged, then…' I've been acting like a spoiled child, haven't I?"

Although, reaching that conclusion didn't mean she could shake off her disappointment and self-loathing.

Riezé's own hands were small, and there wasn't much she could do.

Still, even so, she had to make sure this raid succeeded. If Shiroe's commands were lackluster, then she'd have to step out in front. Loading the attack with the pain and irritation she felt, Riezé sent a Freezing Liner at the cluster of enemies that had appeared up ahead.

▶ 5

After they'd entered Fortress of the Call, the monster attacks grew more ferocious.

"These guys are tough to fight."

"Naotsugu, a little farther forward! Miss Mari!"

"Gotcha! Reactive Heal!"

As Shiroe pushed the front line up, he desperately scanned the surrounding situation.

It wasn't that the monsters' individual combat abilities were high. Monsters that appeared in proper raid zones were Raid-rank monsters. About 70 percent of the monsters that showed up in this zone were Party rank. Even if their levels were high, if they used concentrated attacks and teamwork that made use of their class characteristics, the individual monsters were easy to destroy.

The problem lay in the structure of this zone and the continuous reinforcements.

As a player town, Shibuya had been an open field area. Spain-zaka

Slope was complicated, but the road was more than five meters wide in most places, and there had been plenty of room to form ranks or execute team plays. However, this ancient ruin, which was said to have been a broadcasting station in the old world, was an interior zone. Its corridors were complex, mazelike, and barely three meters wide, with lots of corners and bad visibility.

The high-carbon steel doors, which showed no signs of deterioration, all looked the same. If they weren't careful, there was a danger that they'd lose track of which way was forward and which way was back.

And from the depths of that labyrinth, an inexhaustible supply of monsters welled up, like some sort of waste product. There were Ogres and Minotaur Warriors, but the majority were Eternal Moths and Moon Rabbits.

Having to check every single door put stress on the speed of their progress as well.

Fortress of the Call had many large rooms. The spaces were high-ceilinged and empty, but they weren't linked to the ends of corridors or to corners. They were on the other side of identical-looking steel doors. For the most part, they didn't have monsters lurking in them, but the walls of the rooms were often densely covered with Moon Rabbits in translucent eggs and with cocoons wrapped in white thread.

When they got close to them, the eggs burst and the Moon Rabbits sprang at them, or the Eternal Moths hatched. If they left them alone, it was possible they'd close in on Shiroe's capture unit from the rear, intercept them, and launch a pincer attack. Even if that didn't happen, once the sun went down, they'd probably emerge and attack Akiba. When they thought about it that way, they had no choice but to put them down.

"Six additional bunnies manifesting," Soujirou announced.

"I'm not letting you fight all of them, Boss!" Isami called.

"Three hours and forty-five minutes remaining!"

Even as they protected their companions, a Samurai named Isami switched with Soujirou, taking over as the tank. Both belonged to the same guild, and they were used to this: She crossed with him skillfully, picking up the targets, and stepped onto the front line. It was a basic team play, meant to lighten the load. However, it shattered Shiroe.

He should have noticed that move first.

The members had used their own individual skills to cover for Shiroe's delayed commands. Inattention, hesitation, incomplete predictions: These things were making the entire raid team less efficient.

Shiroe's weakness was holding them back.

And even though he was aware of this, he was unable to take steps to fix it.

There were about three and a half hours left until moonrise. From what he could guess from the scenery outside, they should have enough time to explore this dungeon. Even so, there was a strange anxiety inside him, making him unsure of his decisions. This might be an unfamiliar area, but raids had their own standard moves. Even capture methods had them, so it was only natural that the zone design and the distribution of monsters would have them as well.

Shiroe had seen five types of monsters in this area. They'd probably seen all the patrolling and regularly stationed monsters by now. Even if there were additional ones in specific rooms or as midlevel bosses, he had a good grasp of the types of monsters that would appear in this zone. He was also gradually figuring out the dungeon's structure. It was a combination of narrow, low-ceilinged corridors and vast rooms, of generic stairwells and high-steel doors. From the corridor a short while ago, he'd seen another enormous facility outside. The enemy boss was probably either in that facility or, if not there, in Fortress of the Call's distinctive tower, where he'd initially predicted it would be.

It's all right. There's still time.

As if trying to convince himself of that, Shiroe ran over the current situation, then instructed the unit to head for the courtyard. They'd lost nearly half their MP. If it wasn't going to last all the way to the end, they'd have to recover it somewhere.

Resting in the middle was a basic tactical move during raids. It shouldn't be a bad idea. Shiroe nodded to Naotsugu, who was looking perplexed, then led the way to the courtyard, the only remaining spot of greenery.

           *   *   *

"Ooh. Oh my. Girls wiping off the sweat of battle. That sparkling scent!"

"You get along with one another well in West Wind, don't you?"

They finally managed to take a break in a courtyard about ten or so meters square, near the center of the dungeon. Although it was surrounded by several dozen meters of concrete ruin, the well-like space felt open and airy. It might have been a garden once: Ornamental plants and tall, broadleaf trees grew on the lawn.

"Well, Boss is strict, you see. No fighting allowed."

"Thanks to that, every evening is a titillating 'happening.'"

"Kurinon. Down, girl."

Although the West Wind Brigade had kicked their legs out and collapsed, exhausted, they still seemed to have enough energy for backchat.

"Bweeeh."

"You okay, Miss Mari?"

"Eh-heh-heh-heh. This full-dress stuff really is rough, isn't it?"

Meanwhile, the Crescent Moon League seemed to be very worn out. Their MP was down to 20 percent. In *Elder Tales*, there were a relatively large number of ways to recover HP, beginning with healing spells, but MP recovery methods were extremely limited.

The most effective way was to get away from the fighting and rest. If you sat quietly or lay down, you could fully recover your MP in about two hours. That was when you had no additional help; it was possible to speed it up with appropriate food items, an Enchanter's mana recovery special skills, or a Bard's songs. Now, as a raid team, they'd probably be able to recover half their maximum MP by resting for thirty minutes or so.

In the days of the game, that would have meant a break of no more than a few minutes, but things didn't work that way in this world. On top of that, it was difficult to secure a safe area in an unfamiliar raid zone. They'd been fortunate to find this open courtyard.

It was surrounded by walls on all four sides, and there were only two places that looked as if they could be used to get in or out. Apart from the Return Point near the entrance of Fortress of the Call, where Li Gan was waiting, it seemed like the safest place.

Shiroe sat down and gazed steadily at his MP display.

Like water filling a cup, the display bar lengthened. As an Enchanter, Shiroe recovered MP faster than any other class. He also had a lot of equipment with effects that emphasized recovery speed.

The other ones who recovered quickest and were surprisingly energetic were the younger group. Although they were tense, they were sitting back to back, their expressions watchful, keeping an eye on all four directions as they rested.

Soujirou, Nazuna, Naotsugu, and Captain Nyanta were speaking to tired team members and passing out drinks. They looked exactly the way they had back during the days of the Debauchery Tea Party, and it made Shiroe feel like smiling.

The Crescent Moon League group—Marielle, Henrietta, Shouryuu, and Hien—had their heads bowed, and they were breathing so roughly that their shoulders heaved. From what he heard, this was their first time on a serious raid, so that was probably only natural. Marielle in particular was a member of the first party and had been acting as Naotsugu's dedicated healer, so she'd been concentrating the whole time. Tetora's plentiful combat experience had assisted the Cleric countless times, but even so, Marielle's mental fatigue was bound to be pretty serious. *It might be better to change our formation here in this courtyard*, Shiroe thought. That said, it wasn't easy to come up with alternatives. Nazuna certainly was a skilled healer, but she was too good at working with Soujirou. It had been that way since the Debauchery Tea Party.

Shiroe's thoughts spun through a variety of expressions, toying with him. It was a little better during combat, but while he was resting, apprehension and anxiety flooded him.

He was worried about the depression in Akiba that Ains had talked about. Even though Isaac and the others had gotten them out of a tough spot, the assassins who'd attacked Maihama were harbingers of the coming deterioration of the relationship between the Holy Empire of Westlande and Eastal, the League of Free Cities. The unfathomable sense of wrongness he'd felt when he'd heard of the Spirit Theory. The post-Catastrophe world, which was cycling through endless changes. The group that called themselves Travelers, and Roe2, who should have been Shiroe's sub-character.

The Odysseia Knights and Boreas' Moving Temple.

There was a flood of countless conflicts, things that were too much for Shiroe to handle, but which, at the same time, he couldn't ignore. No, that was probably self-serving, under the surface. He wasn't that arrogant and conceited. This was a more personal problem: He didn't feel settled regarding the decisions he'd made. He wasn't satisfied. He thought that was all it was.

When he'd established the Round Table Council, when he'd backed Raynesia's speech, when he'd saved Rundelhaus, and when he'd sought the gold of the Kunie, he'd made his decisions resolutely. He'd been satisfied with them, and even if those choices had resulted in losses, he would have had no regrets.

When he looked back, he wasn't prepared now. He wasn't satisfied enough with his choices. That was why he was afraid they would fail, and why he wasn't able to believe in the future he'd chosen. That was all it was.

Abruptly, the light dimmed.

Several dozen Ogres plummeted down from directly above the open courtyard, blocking out the blue sky.

For a moment, Shiroe was very nearly disoriented, and as if to strike an additional blow, fissures ran up the east and west walls, and minotaurs leapt through them, sending rubble flying like an explosion.

"Enemy attack!"

"Wasn't this supposed to be a safe area?!"

"Where did they come from?"

"—They're working together—"

"Wait, not yet, I'm not—"

"Eeeeeeeeek, not good! This ain't good!!"

It was a bolt from the blue.

Powerful monsters had attacked their safe zone. On top of that, they hadn't done it through the doors they'd been watching, but from other angles.

"These guys are Raid rank!"

"I'll take the right! Go ahead and take the left, Mr. Naotsugu!"

The two tanks split, heading right and left. However, the healers weren't able to follow them. Marielle had been in the middle of changing equipment and was caught off guard, so she got a late start, and Nazuna and Soujirou had been a good distance apart. To fill the gaps, Minori and Serara cast spells in rapid succession with all their might, but the courtyard was instantly filled with confused fighting.

Their ranks had completely disintegrated.

And once again, it was individuals' skills that were trying desperately to keep them afloat.

"So they're not gonna let us rest, huh?"

"Raids are always like this, aren't they?"

The group from D.D.D. had the most raid experience of any of the members. They managed to regain their poise before anyone else, then sprang into action, beginning to build battle lines. The Monk Richou was in the lead, and Kushiyatama, a vanguard-type Kannagi, followed.

"Well, this warrior has been prepared since the moment he heard he'd be with you, Miz Buzzkill."

"You wouldn't be thinking of me as a plague god, would you? You'll make me cry. And I'm absolutely going to make you cry for that 'this warrior' nonsense later!"

"I'm going, too!"

"I'll cover you. Dread Weapon!"

They carved their way through the enemy forces with ferocious speed, bantering the whole time. Koen the Assassin, Yuzuko the Summoner, and Riezé the Sorcerer followed.

"Rrraaaaaaargh!"

The Ogres bore down on them, bellowing.

They were a type of giant, and they had enormous heads and thick limbs. They were only about three meters tall, but they probably weighed close to a ton. Their jaws were as sturdy and powerful as construction machinery, and although the teeth that lined them weren't sharp, they looked like something out of a nightmare.

Richou was a big guy, and his fists detonated on the arm of a giant Ogre that was easily taller than he was. It staggered, and Koen grabbed the opportunity to dash in. Yuzuko's Salamander breathed fire on it, finishing it off.

The balance of their five classes wasn't bad. They had one tank, one healer, one close-combat fighter, and two long-range magic attack types. In fact, as Shiroe watched, the five from D.D.D. put down close to ten monsters.

All in all, this was an intrinsically bad move.

A twenty-four-member raid was composed of four parties, numbered One through Four. Each of these four parties was composed of six members and had been calculated to fulfill its own function. What happened when five members abruptly dropped out of those four parties? The balance of the remaining nineteen fighters broke down.

If this had been a full group from D.D.D., that probably wouldn't have happened. Their training almost certainly covered recombining team members in unexpected situations like this. However, this was a patchwork team put together specifically to capture Fortress of the Call.

"Yeep!"

"Serara!"

Serara had turned around, eyes wide, and had instantly frozen. Nyanta shielded her.

Hien had attracted a monster's aggro with Assassinate, and he retreated. Eternal Moths flew in through that slight gap in the ranks and scattered golden scales around. They were inhibiting magic. Like a pitch-black river of terror, Minotaur Warriors poured in.

In order to rebuild the confused battle lines, Naotsugu yelled out Front Line. For the moment, he was trying to draw the frontline enemies to himself. When he'd made that decision, he'd been prepared to die. To save Naotsugu, Shiroe broke off Force Step, but he couldn't think of the next move. Tetora was comparatively calm. Raising Resonant Jewel Rod, the idol began to chant Aurora Heal. Even in the midst of this lethal melee, the powerful overall recovery spell would probably prolong all their companions' lives by ten seconds or so. They just had to use that leeway to put together a scheme that would let them turn the tables. Right now, that was the calmest, most strategic idea.

However, as Tetora looked around in order to set the center of Aurora Heal, the ground split wide open.

As if mocking Shiroe's and the others' efforts, a plant monster with enormous tentacle-shaped vines appeared, sending the soil in the courtyard flying.

"New enemy! Venom Hydrangea!!"

A level-93 Raid-rank enemy.

Its tangled shape was actually multiple individuals. A handful of vanguards wouldn't be able to provide enough support.

The ground cracked as if it were boiling, pushing out rubble that was taller than they were, opening the jaws of the abyss.

"Ah—yeeeeek?!"

"Noooooo!"

Tetora gave a cute little scream and was on the verge of being swallowed derriere-first when Marielle shoved the idol out of the way. The idol gazed at Marielle with round, wide eyes. Marielle was a beginner at raids, and she'd just tried to save Tetora, a seasoned veteran. It was pointless, of course. After shoving the other Cleric away, Marielle got caught up in the collapse, and Tetora was run through by the Venom Hydrangea's purple spear-roots. The raid team was on the brink of annihilation.

Nevertheless, in the midst of that, Marielle had shown good will.

"It's no good! My Four Quarters Prayer won't last a moment!"

Everywhere, the battle lines were tearing like paper.

The emergency recovery spell barrier that Minori had chanted couldn't hold back ferocious attacks of this rank. The sound of shattering glass signaled its destruction.

Shiroe, who was stopping several monsters with Astral Hypno, felt his back freeze immediately. This was as futile as throwing water on hot stones. Nyanta, Marielle, Touya, Olive, Koen—they all turned into rainbow-colored bubbles of light and burst.

"Three lost! Five dead!"

Beyond the dust clouds, he heard a voice scream.

Shiroe's error had caused this tragedy.

Carelessness in assuming this place was safe. Reluctance to give up, insisting they could regroup. Both had increased the damage.

The capture team was already almost beyond saving. The well-shaped courtyard that should have been a sanctuary was like the inside of a blender, filled with rampaging monsters. *Was it a trap?* The thoughts just circled around and around inside his head, and he wasn't able to respond intelligently.

"Mr. Shiro!"

"Shiroe, we can't hold out any longer!"

As if the urgent voices had kicked him in the back, Shiroe bit his lip. His body was so cold that it might already have been in the land of the dead, and his heart was as heavy as if it had been frozen.

"—Retreat! Flip Gate!!"

Enveloped in a severing light, with half its forces lost, the Fortress of the Call capture team retreated.

The ruined courtyard echoed with the victory cries of monsters from another world.

▶6

A dizzy sensation dragged on.

It was the disorientation that always accompanied teleportation. The vague sensation of movement felt during Call of Home or when being sent to the Temple.

He'd used Flip Gate several times during the capture with Silver Sword. The spell teleported everyone on the team to the emergency safe area within the active raid zone. In most cases, safe zones were either at the zone entrance or in spaces near it where monsters didn't appear. Now that Theldesia had turned real, there was no telling how safe they would actually be, but for now, there didn't seem to be any enemies in sight.

Team members had been sacrificed in the fight. "Lost" meant that resurrection spells hadn't been cast in time after they'd died, and they'd been sent to the safe area at the zone entrance; in other words, here. After some time had passed, the "dead" members were also switched to "lost;" therefore, a total of eight people had met up with them through teleportation—and not from Shiroe's spell, but from death.

When he looked around, he saw that they were in a large, box-shaped space about twenty meters square. The room held no furnishings, only rubble piled up against the walls, and it looked like a storeroom.

After a few minutes, the tense atmosphere that had hung over them immediately after teleporting snapped and vanished.

He listened carefully, but the sounds the monsters made were far away. At the very least, they'd gained a minimal sort of safety. Right after resurrection, a penalty was inflicted on their ability values. High-level resurrection spells or resurrection at the Temple reduced this penalty, but coming back from death during a capture meant that almost all values, including physical strength and agility, dropped by several dozen percentage points. If a third of their members had reduced ability values, it would be hard for them to fight right away. That meant this rest was going to be a deal breaker.

In the midst of a very slightly relieved atmosphere, people began to make small talk here and there.

Since there were dead members who hadn't woken up yet, the conversations were subdued.

Some of the D.D.D. members were joking about how they hadn't been on a raid like this one in a while. Since Shiroe had been to the Abyssal Shaft, he understood this, too: Raids weren't the sort of thing you beat on the first try. You were wiped out over and over, and in the process, you figured out how to capture them.

However, he didn't see their current battlefield as a raid in the purest sense of the word. As proof, this zone was small compared with the Shaft, the corridors were narrow, and the majority of the monsters that appeared were Party rank. The zone clearly hadn't been designed as a raid area. It was a facility that had been abruptly requisitioned by some unknown factor. Because of Roe2's letter, Shiroe knew, dimly, what that factor had been, and his companions had also probably guessed that it was the work of the Geniuses.

Shiroe had gone into the capture with a decent shot at success.

In the end, though, they'd retreated following the collapse of their battle lines.

"I'm sorry, Miss Mari. I was right there, and it broke through anyway."

"It's fine, hon. You can't predict that somethin's gonna come up through the ground and go 'Graaah!' like that. I knew what I was gettin' into when I signed up for this. I got some raid practice in with Akatsuki."

The sight of Naotsugu and Marielle exchanging whispered apologies made guilt well up inside him.

He didn't think they hadn't been capable of lasting through that surprise attack. The enemy's level and numbers hadn't been anything they couldn't have dealt with, if he'd only seen it coming. And he should have seen it coming. This had been Shiroe's mistake.

"I'm sorry, you guys..."

So this was what it felt like to be disgusted with yourself.

He'd brought a crowd of friends to this battlefield on the strength of an imperfect decision. Shiroe was the raid conductor. Being in that position meant he should take responsibility for this raid. However, he didn't know what he should be responsible for. Victory, he thought. But what would victory look like? He'd been trying to convince himself that it meant defeating the Geniuses. Doing that wouldn't solve anything, though. It wouldn't save the people who were sinking in despair in Akiba, or the young man that Nyanta had met, or the Odysseia Knights.

Even now, Shiroe wasn't able to reach a clear conclusion. He felt it was spineless of him, and he was irritated.

In the end, what Ains said is bothering me.

He'd understood a sliver of something he hadn't been able to put into words before.

This world was small.

Its narrowness was the reason Shiroe was feeling suffocated.

He understood the "people who can't move" that Ains had told them about. Shiroe didn't think the assistance Ains wanted was wrong.

However, if he accepted that request, the majority of people in Akiba would probably object. The major guilds might break up.

Wondering which choice was right was probably a trap in and of itself.

The world was small. At present, there were a little under thirty thousand Adventurers on the Yamato server. According to their estimates, there were several dozen times that many People of the Earth. Altogether, the population of Arc-Shaped Archipelago Yamato was only about a million, and it was likely that those numbers weren't much different across the whole of Theldesia.

In addition, the Adventurers were too powerful. In terms of combat abilities alone, they probably had a hundred times what the People of the Earth did. It was likely that their production abilities were even further removed.

A small population and excessive abilities were shrinking this world to the point where, if a person was unhappy, they immediately convinced themself that it was someone else's responsibility. That was why fissures opened up between the haves and the have-nots, and why enmity grew between people who thought returning home was the most important issue and people who didn't share that opinion. Each thought the other was to blame. The fact that the distance between them was so small, and that there was no one else in the world, meant they couldn't help but think it.

The world was sealed, as if trapped in the curse of a zero-sum game, and there was nowhere to run. In this world, everyone was a victim and an interested party.

Of course Shiroe didn't think that was true. However, he understood what it felt like to believe it implicitly.

He understood that that was probably the reason his heart had been choked on this raid capture.

In this small world, defeating the Geniuses and saving the People of the Earth, and abandoning the People of the Earth and defending the facility so that they could send transmissions, were both imperfect options. Both would probably put someone at a disadvantage. Actions that Shiroe and the others took, convinced that they were for the greater good, would be the acts of usurpers as far as somebody out there was concerned.

I think Captain Nyanta's suffering is probably the same, at the root...
The hunch that there was no right answer.
The pain of knowing he would fail, no matter what he chose.
These had nailed Shiroe's feet into stagnation. The path he was walking down probably didn't lead to anything.

There was a dry sound, and for a moment, Shiroe didn't understand what had happened.

His cheek felt as if it was on fire. When he raised his head, he saw his friends, looking worried. Henrietta stood at the front of the group. Apparently, she'd slapped him.

Henrietta looks like she might cry.

That was the first thing he thought. Isuzu was the same. Minori's lips were drawn and tense, and she looked determined. Touya's resolution, Serara's worry, Rundelhaus's expectations.

He saw their faces through eyes that seemed abruptly clear. He thought about those expressions very calmly, and he felt guilty and ashamed about having thought that this was someone else's problem.

Shiroe looked up at Henrietta. The lovely woman was furious.

Her soft hair fell down around her shoulders, and he thought ineffectual things like, *Truly beautiful people look gorgeous even when they're mad.* Naturally, this was escapism: He'd gotten slapped, and his mind had overloaded, that was all.

He tried to find the words to say next, failed, attempted an apology—driven by his stinging cheek and the atmosphere—then thought that that was something he mustn't do.

After all, he was the one who'd made Henrietta look like this.

"Master Shiroe."

"Yes."

"Gentlemen should live...more selfishly."

"Yes."

Shiroe nodded, reflexively.

He couldn't live that way immediately just because someone had told him to. Shiroe didn't know what was right. He couldn't just choose something, in spite of that. Yet, Henrietta was serious, and her seriousness wouldn't allow him to make excuses. In this situation, "yes" was the only possible answer. Even he knew that much.

I'm always causing Henrietta trouble, aren't I? With the Crescent Burgers, and the strategy to pull in the commercial guilds, and at the Libra Festival, and for the zone release project, and now...

Now that he thought about it, he'd probably been leaning on her too much. Feeling apologetic and spineless, Shiroe looked at his elder. Leaning on people without being aware that he was doing it could be said to be a bad habit of his.

*   *   *

"U-um… Shiroe? I… We can stay in this world."

"Minori?"

"…In Saphir, things didn't… It didn't go so well. People thanked us and told us we saved them, so we didn't completely blow it. But listen, maybe we just plain can't go home. So… I don't really get it, but…"

"Touya."

As the twins spoke to Shiroe, they sounded desperate.

"Going back to our old world would be a good thing, wouldn't it? We want to go home because we want to be happy. In that case, we've *all* got to be happy, together."

"Yes, he's right! It's wrong to abandon the People of the Earth so that we can be happy."

As they spoke to Shiroe, the meaning of what they were saying sank in, slowly. He began to understand: They were probably saying he shouldn't worry, because the Adventurers' issues could wait.

Children were shouting "You don't have to worry" at an adult. They might be putting on a bold front, but at the same time, they were demonstrating their willingness to cooperate with everything they had and that they didn't want to hold anyone back. Shouldn't he have known that better than anyone?

"Um… We don't mind waiting, either, Shiroe."

"Not that I am qualified to comment, mind you, but I'd rather not see my guild master suffer."

As proof, Isuzu and Rundelhaus spoke up after Minori and Touya. Isuzu's mouth was set in a cross line, and Rundelhaus was looking proper and stuffy. Behind them, as Nyanta watched her, Serara held her small fists in front of her chest and nodded several times.

"You heard 'em, Shiro."

"There's no need to say it, Naotsugu. My liege… Both my liege and I will be fine. Absolutely."

When he turned around, there was the pair who had stuck with Log Horizon from the very beginning. Naotsugu was wearing an encouraging, macho smile. Akatsuki's expression was a mixture of shy and morose. As the two of them sent playful kicks and shoves at each other, Shiroe finally understood the significance of what he was seeing.

While he'd lost hope in himself, these people had been putting their hopes in him.

Like a clear stream, that awareness rinsed away Shiroe's frayed thoughts. When he took another careful look, not a single one of his companions wore an expression that seemed to blame him.

Shiroe was the only one who'd been torturing himself with feelings of self-condemnation.

There was nothing the least bit good about that. In the end, he realized, he'd been full of himself, thinking he had abilities high enough to feel regret over. He was the one who hadn't been seeing himself as he was.

His friends had understood him better than he had.

"Shiroe. Woodstock is out on aerial patrol, and he's just contacted us. They've pinpointed the enemy leader's position. It's a full Raid-rank boss: Taliktan, the Genius of Summoning, level 86. They say it's at the base of the iron tower on the roof of this zone, summoning monsters with rainbow-colored light. There are thirty-four minutes remaining until moonrise. We have no time. If we are switching to a subjugation with a hundred members, this is a point at which no further changes can be made."

The D.D.D. tactical officer, with her golden curls, delivered a meticulous summary of the present circumstances. Even the antagonistic way she spoke was no more than hidden worry.

"No... Summonin'? There were a ton of enemies already, and now there's gonna be more?"

"It's probably going be a hard fight. What do you think, Chilly Specs?"

"Unless the command style changes, we won't be able to break through what's beyond this point."

"I expect that's up to Master Shiroe."

Henrietta crossed her arms and turned away sulkily. Behind her frigid glasses, her eyes were wavering. It looked like anger, but it probably wasn't. It was more likely to be expectations and trust. Even though she risked making those around them dislike her, Henrietta had tried to wake Shiroe up. He was sure it was her way of being kind, one he'd overlooked until now.

There were lots of things Shiroe couldn't see.

Even now, there were people who were trying to fulfill the selfish requests he'd been too afraid to make, and while of course the world wouldn't fulfill that request entirely, Shiroe wasn't in this alone, either. Once he understood that, it seemed only natural, but that invisible something was—in an entirely natural way—a genuine miracle as well.

"All right. Just choosing one or the other wasn't going to work, was it? The question itself was wrong. We can't aim for an answer that there's no value in aiming for. At any rate, I can't. We can capture the goal we wanted, though."

Speaking decisively, Shiroe retrieved his glasses and put them on.

Before him was the full raid that had gathered to make the groups' request come true, and there was still enough time left before moonrise to make it happen.

After all, there was always time enough to make wishes come true.

Always, just as long as they didn't give up. Hadn't Shiroe gone through that again and again with the Debauchery Tea Party?

"Thirty minutes remaining. Let's go. This is the main run of the capture operation."

If he wanted it, he always had a shot at victory. In order to clear the dungeon within the time they had left before moonrise, Shiroe began his final briefing.

CHAPTER.
5
THE PIONEERS

▶ NAME: HENRIETTA

▶ LEVEL: **90**

▶ RACE: **HUMAN**

▶ CLASS: **ACCOUNTANT**

▶ HP: **9696**

▶ MP: **9845**

▶ ITEM 1:

[CLOCKWORK ARCHERY]

A MIDSIZED COMPOUND BOW WITH BUILT-IN TRANSFORMING STRUCTURES, CREATED BY ADAPTING COMPONENTS AND TECHNOLOGY USED IN CLOCKWORK MONSTERS. IT'S HIGHLY ACCURATE, AND WHEN A SUPPORT SONG IS PLAYED, IT RESONATES WITH THE NOTES AND EXPANDS THE SUPPORT SONG'S EFFECTIVE RANGE.

▶ ITEM 2:

[THOUGHTFUL LILAC]

A PASTEL-PURPLE SKIRT INFUSED WITH A GENTLE FRAGRANCE. IT'S TOUGH AGAINST COLD AIR, AND IT GIVES OFF A SCENT THAT INHIBITS CONFUSION-RELATED BAD STATUSES IN ITS SURROUNDINGS. ALTHOUGH IT'S A PRODUCTION-CLASS ITEM, SINCE MANY GUILDS IN FRIENDLY RELATIONSHIPS WITH THE CRESCENT MOON LEAGUE PROVIDED EXPENSIVE MATERIALS, IT'S HIGH-PERFORMANCE GEAR.

▶ ITEM 3:

[SONGSTRESS'S SECRET]

AN EXTREMELY PALE PINK NAIL POLISH. IN ADDITION TO RAISING THE BASE STATUS OF THE INSTRUMENTS AND WEAPONS BARDS USE, IT PROVIDES BONUSES WHENEVER ITS WEARER SINGS OR PLAYS INSTRUMENTS. ITS MODEST, SWEET COLOR MAKES IT POPULAR EVEN WITH GIRLS WHO AREN'T BARDS.

<Account Books>
A type of notebook.
Henrietta's lethal skill.

▶1

The operation had begun, and Minori's group was right in the thick of the fighting.

The younger group was acting as attackers. This was due more to their levels not being high enough to let them act as tanks and healers than because they were particularly good at that sort of thing. Since their levels were low, no matter what they did, the damage from their attacks tended to be low as well. However, at least with that, there was a possibility that the issue could be resolved through serial attacks that made use of high-level support and MP supplementation.

Of course, they weren't able to take on monsters whose levels were in the nineties.

The midlevel group's role was to pick out the Eternal Moths and Moon Rabbits with levels from 60 to 70 and contribute through range attacks.

"We're nowhere near done yet, Rudy!"

"Understood! Orb of Lava!!

Following Isuzu's lead, Rundelhaus cast a fireball spell. Its level had gone up, and the number of small fireballs had increased. Following the blond's instructions, they punched through Eternal Moths one after another. Even if he couldn't take them down completely with one attack, if he burned their wings, he could thin out their scales and ground them.

The interior of Fortress of the Call was cramped compared with ordinary dungeons like Forest Ragranda, and it was a maze of intricate corridors—a series of intersections and straight lines in drab, inhospitable colors. This oppressive space was where Minori and the other members of the mixed unit were fighting.

"Touyacchi, let's go clean up."

"Roger that!"

Nyanta, Touya, and the wolf Serara had summoned broke into a run. They were going to finish off an enemy group that had lost its HP to a spell bombardment.

"Defense of Doctrine Barrier!!"

"Thanks!"

With Minori's ample damage interception spell protecting him, Touya swung his katana. Gazing at his back, Minori nodded once. So far, their role-sharing was going well.

There were ten or so semitransparent windows in front of her eyes. In addition to the usual status displays for all her party's members, she had displays for each leader and the main tank, for a total of about a dozen people. Even though this was only double the amount of information she normally dealt with, Minori felt as if she might drown in its constant fluctuation.

Spells to recover HP naturally consumed MP. The same was true for spells that inflicted damage and for close-combat special skills. If they went out on the front line, there was a possibility they'd get hit with a negative status effect, so they needed special skills that prevented or removed those.

As such, status figures and displays depended on each other. Should someone step out in front or fall back? As the number of people increased, the choices multiplied explosively. Simply doubling the number of display windows had increased the flexibility she had to take into account by a factor of ten. In the midst of what was practically her first raid, Minori continued to struggle desperately with that burden and kaleidoscopic motion.

She held her breath, almost as if she were diving to the bottom of the ocean, and glared at the numbers. The basic rules were the same as they were for a six-member party. HP and MP exchange. The balance between the pace of extermination and defensive abilities. The trade-off between elimination pace and replenishing abilities. However, those basic exchange rates had split into multiple tracks, tangled with each other, and turned into big waves that tossed Minori around.

In a hall that branched off the other side of the main corridor, she saw a figure with light-yellow hair streaming behind it. Focusing as if she were desperately praying, Minori checked on the situation. That hair belonged to Riezé. She was the linchpin of the current operation. Her MP was at 78 percent, and she warned Rundelhaus to be careful to match it.

"We're starting!"

A familiar voice echoed in the corridor. It was Shiroe.

Rainbow light overflowed, and she saw a fierce fluctuation in MP.

Minori had been thinking, all this time.

She'd thought for a long, long time about what the true nature of the mysterious determination inside her might be and what sort of place it meant to take her to.

Of course she loved Shiroe. He was her favorite person.

That was why, for a time, she'd mistaken the truly stubborn mass inside her for love. However, she'd realized that was a misunderstanding. After all, it showed its face even in matters that had nothing to do with Shiroe, and it gave Minori brief reviews of her own actions: That was bad, this was good, etc. Touya said it had been that way since long before they met Shiroe. He'd informed his sister that she'd been like that for ages.

According to Touya, Minori was a big sister who didn't listen and tended to run wild. She really didn't think that described her at all, so she'd been reluctant to accept the evaluation.

However, since coming to Theldesia, she did suspect that, if people said things like that about her, it might be true after all.

There was something resolute inside her that even she couldn't do anything about, and sometimes it pushed her into action. Shiroe had probably been nourished by it, and it seemed to be growing with every day she spent in Log Horizon. That made Minori happy. She was sure it wasn't a bad thing.

One night, she had been lying in bed, thoughts wandering.

It wasn't as if she was the only one with stubbornness inside of her.

Touya had the same thing, and so did Serara. Isuzu had it, and of course Rundelhaus did as well. Ordinarily, it was hidden and couldn't be seen, but when push came to shove, it emerged and began to sparkle and shine. It was unimaginable wisdom, or kindness, or startlingly intense, desperate courage. Minori had seen it many times in Ragranda and on the journey to Saphir.

It seemed to her as if people had an internal core, like hidden treasure that wasn't usually visible, and it surfaced at unexpected moments and connected with its surroundings.

Back when she'd lost hope in Hamelin, at the bottom of that constricting night to which morning never came, what she'd felt in the voice on the other end of that quiet telechat had been the treasure inside Shiroe. Even Minori and Touya hadn't dreamed that the grad student who'd played alongside them a few times would brave danger to come and rescue them when they were imprisoned.

Why had he saved them? Minori had always wondered about that. It was probably true that he'd felt kindly disposed toward them. However, the real reason had been that special quality inside of him. Shiroe didn't usually talk much, and he was so busy that he didn't have much time to spend on Minori and the others. Back then, though, his spirit had abruptly begun to shine, and it had saved them.

When Minori thought back, she realized she'd felt the same thing in her father and mother. Her parents had been her parents even when they were exhausted and irritated, but that wasn't the only side of them there was. The parents who celebrated with her and Touya on their birthday probably weren't the real ones, either. They were hidden much deeper, like the time when she and Touya had been doing their homework together in the eat-in kitchen, and their mother had bragged to them about her student days while she heated water for apple tea... Minori didn't understand it all that well, but she thought that feeling, which she'd brushed with her fingertips, had probably been an important treasure.

She'd been told that, after Touya's accident, she'd become a "good kid." However, she hadn't been acting the part of a good kid because she'd been unhappy or because she'd felt sorry for Touya or anything like that.

Minori had wanted to be on a team with her parents. She'd been on Touya's side since they were small, and she'd simply thought she'd like to have more relationships like that.

She'd wanted people to count on her.

Practically speaking, she had been just a child, and there had been far too little she could do in Japan; she'd only been able to go to school and come home again. She hadn't been able to earn money, and if she'd put herself in harm's way, she thought she probably would have worried her parents terribly. For that reason, back when she'd understood even less than she did now, she hadn't been able to persuade them, and in the end, they hadn't managed to become a team. She thought they'd been a happy family, but after all, Minori and Touya were their parents' children.

Minori could see the brightness in Touya and Serara, in Isuzu and Rundelhaus. That was proof they were partners. She was able to see it in Naotsugu, Akatsuki, Nyanta, and Shiroe, too. However, they were still of an age when others implicitly worried about them, so they weren't a true team just yet.

She might be overreaching herself, but she thought that that was what Touya had been talking about and what she herself wanted. They were still okay. As long as Shiroe and the others were nearby, her group of younger Adventurers could work a whole lot harder. For that reason, she didn't want him and the others to treat her as a burden. After all, they lived in the same house, Log Horizon. She didn't want to be left out.

"Minori, Wolfie's gone up ahead, and he's spotted a swarm of moths in the main corridor."

"We'll detour as planned. Touya, go up the next stairway on the right!"

Minori's exhale was harsh; she didn't bother suppressing her ragged breathing before turning around to check and adjust their ranks. Currently, Rundelhaus was the party member with the least health to spare. If they managed to shake him off, the party formation would collapse. That was why Isuzu, next to him, was raising his move strength with Fawn's March and encouraging him. Isuzu and Rundelhaus made a good pair, and Minori smiled a little. If this was how things were, they'd be fine for quite a while yet.

*　　*　　*

Minori had an accurate grasp of the mission she was currently carrying out, but the level wasn't as deep as those around her. Right now, on this raid capture team, the members who had a complete grasp of the operation Shiroe had proposed were Shiroe himself, Riezé, Nyanta, Nazuna, Kushiyatama, and Naotsugu, followed by Kurinon and Tetora. The tactics they were executing were so unprecedented that even the members of D.D.D., who were used to raids, didn't know what the results would be.

What was the current problem in the Fortress of the Call capture?

The unlimited reinforcements.

The cause of their defeat had lain not in the enemy's strength itself, but in the fact that their mental stamina and MP had been worn down by the frequency and sporadic timing of the enemy reinforcements.

These might be enemies they could beat, but when they ended up in combat, a certain process was necessary: The main tank accumulated aggro, the tank's defender cast recovery spells on the tank and secured their safety, and then they attacked within the range of the aggro and wiped out the monsters. If ten enemies appeared at once, they needed to go through the process only one time, but if single enemies appeared ten times, they had to run through the whole process ten times as well. If things were like that, no matter how much MP they had, they'd run out.

The maneuver Shiroe had come up with resolved this issue.

Ordinarily, whether they were being used on single targets or a range, the Warriors' aggro-increasing special skills *only worked on enemies that were within eyeshot.* That had been common knowledge in *Elder Tales.* However, just this once, there was another way to do it. Both Eternal Moths and Moon Rabbits loved MP. The monsters had actually attacked Akiba and the other towns in order to steal it. They'd left Fortress of the Call and gone to attack other areas because the MP had lured them there. "We'll use their natures and detection abilities and scatter bait," Shiroe had said.

He was using a combination of Mana Channeling and Mana Siphon to scatter high-density MP around the area. Shiroe had turned himself into live bait and was attracting monsters. The key to the first stage of the maneuver was "kiting," using Shiroe as a tank.

*   *   *

But it's a dangerous plan that makes Shiroe a target…

Minori's breathing had gone rough from the tension, and she gritted her teeth, calming it down.

"Got 'em!"

"This way, my liege!"

She heard Naotsugu's and Akatsuki's voices.

The operation was underway, and Shiroe and the other members of the first party ran, trailing rainbow light. A herd of monsters chased after them, several dozen meters behind. Ordinary aggro-increasing special skills worked only on monsters that were within eyeshot, but with this method, they'd probably affect all the monsters in the facility, or across an even wider range.

In fact, a swarm of Eternal Moths was flying right past the corridor where Minori and the others were holding their breaths, as if their group was transparent.

It was a fairly nightmarish scene: a flying swarm of giant, nearly human-sized moths. Preschool kids often drew airborne butterflies with crayons in their picture-diaries, but they only drew them there because they felt as if they should, and it was possible they'd never seen a real butterfly or moth. At the very least, it was hard to imagine they liked them enough to constantly draw them in their journals.

Seen from a distance, the patterns on their bright wings might look like fashion accessories, but up close, not to mention enlarged to an enormous size, they were spine-crawling, and they made a person feel like screaming.

"We're making for the standby point, Mademoiselle Minori."

"Right!"

"Rudy, I'm casting Nocturne of Meditation, okay?"

Weapons at the ready, Minori's group moved rapidly down the corridor. Their feelings were optimistic, but some of that was empty bravado. They were speaking loudly to raise their morale.

Using their summoned animals, the raid team had mapped this complicated floor to some extent.

They were headed for the very longest main corridor. It was Minori's group's job to set a trap in that corridor.

Having reached their position, Minori's third party joined up with the fourth, which Riezé was leading. Party Three had been rebuilt to keep Minori and the rest of the younger group together, and except for Nyanta, all its members were around level 60. Frankly speaking, it was the team's weak point. Despite that, they made it to their position.

Minori's eyes met Riezé's, and she smiled softly. As if complimenting her, she pointed into the depths of the corridor. Shiroe and the rest of the first party, who had sprinted through a complicated route, were coming their way, trailing a veritable horde of monsters.

"Are you ready?"

At Riezé's dignified question, the group nodded firmly.

The swarm of approaching monsters was frightening.

Possibly because they were on edge, they were able to see everything very clearly, even the dense fur that covered their torsos and the scales that shone faintly as they scattered. Even if that hadn't been the case, the way they jostled one another in the small space provoked a visceral disgust. A suicidal tactic, in which an Enchanter acted as the tank. The payoff was that all the dungeon's monsters had collected in this long corridor. The straight hallway was packed with hundreds of Eternal Moths, Moon Rabbits, and Ogres, all trying to steal MP.

There was an attack that was possible precisely because this was the case.

Against monsters that were concentrated this densely and couldn't run, range attacks were several times more effective.

"Concentrate your fire! Go ahead!"

She heard a shouted order. It had come from Shiroe, who had run past Minori and the others, then turned back. Akatsuki and Naotsugu leapt forward again, to shield him.

Blinding light filled the main corridor, and energy from flame, ice, and electrical spells threw steam and the smell of ions around the area.

The annihilation maneuver had begun.

Riezé's Freezing Liner, the operation's focal point, became a raging torrent that swept through the corridor. It was overlaid by Rundelhaus's Lightning Nebula, which had been expanded to its maximum range. Big spells that ordinarily couldn't be used several times in a row received chant speed acceleration support and were unleashed two or three times.

Minori fired Mystic Spell Shawl. It was an expulsion spell with a pursuit effect that acted on evil insects and spirits, and it was perfect for holding back the Eternal Moths. That attack, which seemed to be venting her disgust, went on until the dungeon grew hushed again.

▶ **2**

Meanwhile, the second party was sprinting through a completely different route, heading upstairs.

"Uh-huh, yeah... Understood. Don't you push yourself, Old Man Whiskers."

Nazuna, who was running beside Soujirou, took her hand away from her ear. Telechats were hard to manage during combat, but there was no sign of monsters near the party. All the enemies were probably stampeding into the trap, drawn by the rainbow-colored MP Shiroe was releasing.

Soujirou understood that it was a reckless strategy, although he didn't know exactly how reckless it was. A spellcaster, with his characteristically low defense and HP, was attracting enemies for an entire raid. If something went wrong, the battle lines would crumble in a heartbeat, and the maneuver would end in failure.

Soujirou wasn't all that worried, though.

"We just got a follow-up report, Souji."

"How does it look?"

"Exactly like we want it to. He's using the rooftop broadcasting tower to summon Taliktan, the Genius of Summoning. A Raid-rank level eighty-six."

"Is that right."

Soujirou laughed. It looked as if they'd be able to fulfill their role.

"Cannonball" Woodstock, the guild master of Grandale, was a skilled flying dragon rider. He was conducting aerial reconnaissance from above Fortress of the Call and had relayed the results to Nazuna. Apparently, the enemy leader's name was Taliktan. They'd confirmed its shape in a reconnaissance run at daybreak, and it had been good news.

There was a reason Soujirou and the rest of Party Two had left Shiroe and the other three groups and were acting separately.

Shiroe's tactics—to leak MP in a mock taunt and round up all the monsters in the zone—had one flaw. If the raid monster that was the enemy leader happened to be within that range, it would turn into a complete melee. The tactic of annihilating the monsters' reinforcements in a narrow corridor would fall apart the moment the boss monster got pulled in. For this tactic to work, they couldn't let the boss monster go to Shiroe. The key to the strategy was dividing and ultimately conquering them.

"You look kinda happy, Souji."

"I am!" he told Nazuna.

His body was light. It felt as if his legs had grown wings. This sharper-than-normal body was probably a reflection of his lack of hesitation. It reminded him of his Debauchery Tea Party days. Back then, Soujirou had been a newbie.

He'd played *Elder Tales* with his buddy, picked up the basics, stuck his nose into a variety of typical MMO events, gotten separated, made friends, and then found the Tea Party. The Tea Party had been the first community he'd ever encountered in online gaming, and it was a place he'd wanted to protect.

At the time, the Tea Party had been brand-new. Players who wanted to try their hand at raids had begun to gather around Kanami, but those members weren't fixed, and more than half of them were recruited on the spot whenever they executed a capture. After Soujirou had participated a few times, they sounded him out about participating in earnest, and he'd agreed readily. He'd wanted to attempt high-level high-end content more seriously, too, but what he'd really wanted was companions. There were lots of ladies who were kind to him, but he couldn't call them comrades-in-arms. Soujirou had wanted hard-hitting combat.

Back then, the senior members—Kanami, Shiroe, KR, Indicus, Naotsugu, Nyanta, Suikazura, Stallbourne, Nurukan, and Nazuna—had already joined up. Touri, Saki, ★Kurama☆, Yomi, and others joined around the same time as Soujirou, and the Tea Party continued to take shape. Soujirou's memories were nostalgic and bright.

"Because this is Mr. Shiro's maneuver."

"Ah, I see."

There was a smile somewhere in Nazuna's voice, and she sounded happy. That accelerated Soujirou forward, farther and faster.

"Gaaaah. Souji, I swear, you like Shiroe too much!! Are you gay?! You're gay, aren't you?!"

Smiling even at Kurinon's nastiness, Soujirou raced up the narrow staircase, taking the steps three at a time. As he used his high-level Adventurer physical abilities to speed up, he looked like a rocket blasting off its launch pad.

The key to this operation was dividing the enemy.

In particular, the most important task was isolating the boss.

That was the mission entrusted to Party Two, the one he led. Having finished re-forming, the party ran, kicking up a wind. They didn't have to worry about reinforcements. When Soujirou played his part, it wasn't even possible Shiroe would fail at his own post. After all, he was one of the three players Soujirou idolized.

"Now that Mr. Shiro's made up his mind, there's just one role for me."

Soujirou slashed with Sacred Blade Kogarasumaru, slicing open the high-steel door that led to the roof. Dashing out into the wash of sunset light, he immediately leapt.

"Lone Dash!"

It was a clear, open space. In the world of Theldesia, the People of the Earth didn't often make tall structures. As demonstrated by Maihama's Castle Cinderella, it wasn't that they didn't have the technology, but the costs were probably overwhelming. Fortress of the Call was a ruin from the Age of Myth, and as a result, there were no nearby buildings that compared to it in height. In Theldesia, a structure with ten aboveground floors was the equivalent of a skyscraper.

In the middle of the rooftop square, which seemed to have been flung out carelessly, an enormous iron tower jutted even higher into the air above those ten stories. This was probably the magical device that made it possible to communicate with the moon: the broadcasting tower.

At its base was a wrinkled, elderly individual with swarthy skin.

The level-86 Raid-rank monster, Taliktan, the Genius of Summoning.

"One enemy visually confirmed! Now, there's a feast. Go get 'im, Souji!"

Nazuna raised an arm over her head, and countless small footholds materialized beyond her fingertips.

Mystery: Celestial Passage. This was an ability Nazuna had acquired that surpassed the parameters of *Elder Tales*. It was based on the damage interception spell Purification Barrier, but instead of being cast on companions, it was split up and distributed across empty space to create footholds. Its ability to intercept damage nearly disappeared, but the shining, translucent platforms that appeared in space made it possible to travel through the air.

In Buddhism, "Celestial Passage" was said to be one of the six supernatural powers gained upon attaining enlightenment. It was one of the so-called divine powers. Of course, what Nazuna was using was her own unique ability, acquired by refining skills she'd had in the game, and it had nothing to do with Buddhism. However, the abilities conferred by Celestial Passage—namely, "being able to leap over castle walls and mountains" and "the ability to run freely through the air, keeping pace with the birds"—had seemed to make it the perfect name for this Mystery. The name of Souji's Mystery, Clairvoyance, had come from the same system.

Using Nazuna's Mystery as footholds, Soujirou leapt into the air.

Up on the half-eroded concrete platform, Taliktan looked like a heretical priest. Swarthy skin; white hair worn tied back; a loose white-and-purple robe; and a long, twisted staff. When Souji saw Taliktan, the name "the Genius of Summoning" made sense to him. Taliktan had been using that supernatural ability to summon limitless monsters. The rainbow-colored pillar that linked the broadcasting tower to the sky was made of bubbles of MP. The thought that this enemy had put People of the Earth and Adventurers into comas lit a fighting spirit in him, burning blue.

"Floating Boat: Helm Splitter!"

He shifted directly from a martial-arts style of movement that made use of the footholds to an attack from above. It was a head-on cleaving attack that would ordinarily have worked best with a two-handed sword. Since Soujirou was one of the few Samurai twin sword–style builds, which emphasized counterattacking, he'd equipped a katana to each hand. As a result, instead of the usual slashing attack, he had to spin to launch the technique.

The attack bit into the cap of Taliktan's shoulder.

He felt a good, solid response.

Of course, his opponent was a raid monster: a tough enemy in high-end content that had anywhere from several thousand to several tens of thousands of times the HP of solo monsters. Soujirou's single attack hadn't decreased its HP enough for the loss to show on the display. However, the attack hadn't been deflected by a barrier, and it had gone through without being blocked by armor. In any case, his opponent's level was 86. There was no way they couldn't beat that... Assuming that this world was the same as *Elder Tales*, and there were a full twenty-four members in Soujirou's group.

"Nazuna, Isami. Cover me."

"Leave it to me, Boss!"

"Yeah, yeah. On it."

When dealing with a spellcaster-type monster, using Rania's Capture was a standard move, but it failed. However, no sooner had it done so than Isami linked it directly to Whirlwind Cutter, and he didn't see any of the fear she'd felt right after the Catastrophe. Using Nazuna's cover, Secret Rite of Celestial Tread, she closed the distance between them at high speed, continuing to create vulnerabilities for Soujirou to exploit.

In response, Soujirou shifted from Helm Splitter straight into Fire-Wheel Sword. The sound of the blade splitting the atmosphere seemed to point his heart toward its destination.

Once, Soujirou had spent a long time being afraid.

...About the fact that he'd created the West Wind Brigade.

No one had ever done so, but someday, somebody might ask him, *Didn't you put that guild together as a replacement for the Tea Party?*

On the day Shiroe had turned down his invitation to join the West Wind Brigade, that fear had taken root in his heart. He'd felt a hidden uncertainty. Was he forcing crowds of people to live in ways they didn't want to live, without being aware of it?

His time with the Tea Party had been a whole lot of fun; was it possible he was just trying to reclaim those days? If someone asked him about it, what could he tell them? Soujirou wasn't good at thinking about things, so he hadn't managed to come up with anything like a conclusion. However, the questions truthfully triggered a dull pain inside him.

Both when he'd just started playing *Elder Tales* and had been all excited, and when the Tea Party had disbanded, Soujirou had humbly asked his friends to stay with him, but they'd gone their own ways. He'd thought he hadn't had any luck with friends.

And so Soujirou had been happy.

The great sword he was swinging came down, carrying delight and satisfaction with it.

Once Shiroe's command had recovered, it had been just the way it had been during their Tea Party days. Or rather, it was clearer than it had been in the past, and it permeated each member of the raid team. As he bounded through the air and twisted his body, as he ran his gaze over the icons and switched stances, he felt his companions' breathing. He couldn't actually see them, but they seemed indescribably close to him. He knew what they were thinking, what they were trying to do, and their self-restraint as if those things were his own.

People would probably say that liking combat for reasons like that meant he was a little crazy, but he could tell his lips had curved into a smile. It wasn't that he wanted to kill enemies. In the midst of the sensation that he was diffusing, then forming connections, he began to understand things he normally didn't know. It wasn't that he couldn't feel those things during ordinary battles, but with Shiroe in command, they came home to him with incomparable intensity.

In short, Soujirou had been worried for nothing.

Isami, Nazuna, Olive, and Kurinon.

They all genuinely considered Soujirou their friend. Of course, all sorts of things were probably mixed into that emotion, and they didn't all feel quite the same way, but the bonds he'd forged between himself and his companions weren't a one-way thing.

Soujirou laughed at himself, thinking that, if it took a raid to make him understand something that simple, he really was dumb.

He also felt an odd sort of destiny in the fact that Shiroe—someone he thought had left him—had helped him to see it.

"And so, Taliktan."

Sword guard clinking, Soujirou turned Sacred Blade Kogarasumaru on the raid boss in front of him. A translucent divine messenger in a fox mask stood behind him, spreading its arms like something from a Noh play. The fantasy-class blade exuded a pressure that made the air shiver, its spiritual power building.

"Dance with me for a while. I can't let you go down there."

► **3**

"Mr. Shiro, we started without you."

"We've got it all warmed up, Shiroe!"

A ruined midair garden spread out before them, jutting into space several dozen meters above the ground. The concrete was cracked, and thin, spindly weeds poked through the gaps. A single ruin seemed to float, isolated, in the darkening crimson sky.

The strong wind that buffeted his cheeks felt as if it was blowing from all four directions. In Theldesia, which had almost no tall buildings, the view from Fortress of the Call was overwhelming. They were able to see so far that, in the old world, it seemed as though the view might have encompassed all of Tokyo.

The building's square roof had no fence, raised edges, or other safety measures, so its edges were sheer. The sense of vastness was so overpowering that someone who was afraid of heights would probably have been unable to move.

By the time Shiroe and the others tumbled out onto it, Soujirou and the rest of the second party were in the middle of a protracted battle with Taliktan, as everyone had expected.

"Thank you! Reinforcements clear. Report!"

As he shouted, Shiroe signaled to the reinforcements with one hand. In response to that hand sign, the remaining eighteen members of the raid team headed for Taliktan in a long, serpentine line and started forming ranks, with Naotsugu in the lead.

The second party had been designed for mobile defense. Compared with the first—which was built to completely engage with the enemy leader, keep it locked down for long periods of time, and fight with the goal of annihilating it—the second had better all-around performance, but its defense, recovery, and long-term combat abilities were lower. Whether defending or attacking, the Samurai class had excellent instantaneous abilities. Soujirou had kept the battle going this long through his player skills. That was just like him, but even so, they should probably avoid putting any more of a strain on him.

Naotsugu, the main tank, dashed forward, and Marielle sent support at him. It was Reactive Heal. Its level was low, but in combination with Minori's Purification Barrier, it would probably last through the first attack.

"His level's not that high. His ordinary attacks are within the expected range. His attribute is physical: that staff. There are two trouble spots. He has these group attacks that make no sense."

"What's the range configuration?"

As Nazuna answered Shiroe, she cast a Purification Barrier on Soujirou. She'd practiced it so often that she could add it without paying attention. But because the wind was strong, no matter what they did, they found themselves yelling as they talked.

"We don't know. Purple electrical attacks that looked guided rampaged around. I'm the only one who didn't get hit, but I was standing in practically the same place as Souji!"

So distance isn't relevant? It's a random attack?

Using Force Step to adjust the ranks, Shiroe kept thinking.

"The damage is huge. Souji played his trump card, and even then he almost went down."

This was bad news.

The basic performance of the Samurai class was lower than the Guardian class. They weren't able to equip shields, and their attribute defense tended to be lower as well. However, in exchange, their instantaneous coping abilities were far greater. Instant Desertion was a powerful special technique that let the user completely avoid all attacks for a short period of time, and Sword of Gathering Clouds was able to cancel the attack itself and halve the damage. Shiroe knew how

Soujirou fought from their time in the Tea Party, and just hearing that he'd almost gone down while Parry was active told him how fierce the enemy's attacks were.

If they took the same attack, there was a good possibility the front line would collapse.

No wonder the rearguard fighters' HP is so far down.

Tetora, who'd opted not to compete with Marielle and was on standby in the rear instead, had begun to heal players, focusing on the ones who were the most severely injured. Reactive Heal was high performance, but as the name suggested, it was a spell system that automatically reacted to enemy attacks and recovered HP (although, naturally, not completely). The rearguard players had already taken damage and lost a lot of HP, and the only way to deal with it was to provide care using regular recovery spells. Tetora was recovering the injured members by combining spells such as Heal and Healing Light.

That was probably the correct decision.

"Sleep, all of you."

"Why are you doing this?! What is this 'sleep' anyway?!"

The voice sounded like a growl.

Even so, Shiroe answered the words that fell from the monster's lips with the response he'd planned on, loading it with his wish. This had been one of his covert goals. It was the reason he'd needed to come here.

Shiroe hadn't been able to believe everything in Roe2's letter. But even before that, it was hard to say he'd understood the content sufficiently.

Roe2 had warned them about the Geniuses, but despite that, Shiroe had been hesitant to cut them off without attempting a discussion. Now that things had come to this, it would probably be difficult to avoid fighting, but in that case, he at least wanted information.

"Sleep, all of you."

"Isn't there room to talk this out?!"

Every time Taliktan brandished his twisted staff, shock waves rampaged, and the flooring material—which should have been concrete—crumbled with absurd ease.

Shiroe looked into the eyes of the Genius of Summoning.

He had small pupils that shone like stars against a jet-black background.

Physically, he appeared to be an aged Summoner, but his expression was something entirely different. It seemed mechanical rather than alive, and the only responses Shiroe could sense were flat, inhuman ones.

"This guy's just like Camaysar. A little better, 'cos he's not a pervert."

"Mr. Shiro, you can't get through to him by talking."

Even as a storm of bullet-like shock waves cut his cheeks, Shiroe gazed straight at the Genius. There had to be some kind of clue here. As he fought, he tried desperately to uncover it.

Taliktan wanted Empathiom, too.

The result had been this sleep.

And from what Shiroe could guess, while Empathiom might be a resource, it wasn't energy in the strictest sense of the word. That they couldn't get through to the Geniuses by talking was proof of this, in a way. With that one move, he'd come a little closer to the meaning of that letter.

"Shiroe, that lightning they reported—! It's preliminary motions—"

Riezé's scream was brilliant.

She'd picked up on the preliminary motions of a monster attack she was seeing for the first time.

However, there wasn't enough time to urge the team to take evasive action. At the edge of his field of vision, he saw Naotsugu raise his large shield, but the lightning seemed to have bypassed the Guardian. Increasing all at once, it raced among the members of the vanguard, and Soujirou, Nyanta, Nazuna, and Akatsuki were run through.

"Shiroe, about a hundred and eighty seconds...!"

Even as Nazuna was thrown to the ground by the force of the electrical attack, she finished giving her report.

If an attack as powerful as this one was unleashed several times in a row, they'd never manage to fight an actual battle. With 180 seconds, they could have used a brute force approach as they recovered, but apparently, that strategy wasn't going to be possible, either.

"Mr. Shiro, don't let your guard down. He calls in reinforcements.

Eternal Moths and Moon Rabbits... He twists that rainbow-colored light—!"

Unlike the healer, Soujirou had a little leeway, and as he cautioned Shiroe, he attempted a bold charge. He'd anticipated that special ability, both when he'd seen the name "Genius of Summoning" and when swarms of Eternal Moths had appeared in Akiba. He'd predicted that the mastermind would be a being that called in reinforcements of some kind. As a matter of fact, most of the monsters that Shiroe and the others had fought their way through in this dungeon, the Party-rank monsters, had probably been summoned by Taliktan.

He'd thought up a way to deal with that.

Now that he'd come this far and had seen the battlefield, he was sure.

The problem was that he didn't really have the time to explain it.

"Third party, bring your aggro down! Naotsugu, Souji, prepare for a pincer attack. We're moving."

"Moving? What are you planning to do, Shiroe?! There's nowhere else to go!"

Shouryuu's words sounded like a scream, and they made him feel guilty.

True, this midair concrete garden wasn't the sort of place they could run from. Considered normally, that was true.

"First party, close ranks."

However, there was no time to explain the details to Shouryuu and the rest.

If the recast time for that purple lightning was 180 seconds, they should probably assume the same was true for summoning reinforcements. At the very least, he didn't have the leeway to explain slowly.

"We're moving the battlefield. We have a shot at victory. Please believe in your own strength, the strength of Adventurers!"

His eyes met Akatsuki's, and he saw her nod emphatically.

For no reason at all, he abruptly felt as if this was going to work.

This, after all that worrying I did earlier. I guess I'm pretty mercenary. Shiroe laughed at himself. Apparently, as long as he knew what he needed do, he didn't hesitate. Either way, if that tower was a magic device, *they had to tear the enemy away from it.*

"Aggro Exchange! Anchor Howl!"

A torrent of light streamed from the sword Naotsugu held high, draining something from Soujirou. Aggro Exchange was a special skill that swapped the user's aggro with the aggro of a targeted companion. Soujirou, the main force of the second party, had mounted a preemptive strike and supported the front line until just a moment ago, and now Naotsugu had taken over the vast amount of aggro he'd accumulated.

Taliktan's eyes were like red stars floating in a black, bottomless swamp. They rolled in a grotesque motion that seemed as if it should be audible, shifting to glare at Naotsugu.

"'Scuse me a sec, Miss Mari."

Naotsugu, who was now the sole target of Taliktan's aggro, turned around, winked cheerfully, then scooped Marielle up. Getting picked up sideways startled the woman, but the next second, her cheeks flushed as if they'd been boiled. Marielle attempted to protest but didn't have time.

"Let's roll, Shiro."

"Hurry, my liege."

Leaving those words behind them, the two of them leapt into the sunset sky, pursued by Taliktan.

Falling.

Shiroe and the others had jumped from a height of several dozen meters.

They plunged toward the ground like stones, falling through air that seemed to have turned solid and howled in their ears as they passed. Even though turning Fly into a range spell had weakened its braking effect, Shiroe glared up at the shape bearing down on them, silhouetted against the moon.

Come and get us.

He hit Taliktan with that thought, without speaking it aloud. This might have been a more important move than confronting the Genius. Taliktan pursued them, and the rainbow bubbles clung to him, following him. Just as Shiroe had thought, even the Genius of Summoning needed that iron tower—in other words, a channel to the moon—in order to summon Eternal Moths.

To separate Taliktan from that tower, Shiroe's group had executed a maneuver that was like diving. The Genius already begun to summon. Unless they stopped Taliktan here, the damage would be even greater. In addition, they'd probably lose their means of contacting the moon and of closing in on the heart of the mystery.

However, as Shiroe murmured to Taliktan, he wore a fearless smile.

"If this is a raid, it's my battlefield. Watch what eight years of constant fighting on countless battlefields and accumulated knowledge can do."

Before anyone heard them, the words were shredded by the wind and vanished.

▶4

"Uhhh, yes, yes. Put them all out. No, never mind that, forget about profit. Use ammunition and potions right and left, open all storehouses up to tier six, and clear out all the stock, thanks in advance, 'bye."

Right after ending his telechat with the dwarf girl who acted as his inventory manager, Calasin leaned in from the corridor and spoke to the People of the Earth maids and cooks: "I brought you some meat." Many impromptu kettles and tents had been set up in the courtyard, and the place was as noisy as a battlefield. Or rather, it actually *was* a battlefield.

Castle Cinderella, the heart of the Maihama duchy, was currently serving as a frontline base. Since the Eternal Moths attacked from the sky, castle walls and city streets meant nothing to them. In the dusk, this castle was caught up in a battle with attacking monsters.

The monsters seemed to prioritize targeting beings with high combat abilities or mana. In this world, that description was synonymous with *Adventurer*. In the urban areas of Maihama, the doors of all the houses had been shut tight, and martial law had been declared. The People of the Earth just held their breath and stared up at the sky. The city and castle were being defended by a force that had been built around the Knights of the Black Sword.

The idea of holding the Eternal Moths back in forests and highways away from the town had been suggested, but the monsters attacked Adventurers only "as a rule." They weren't intelligent enough to let People of the Earth they happened to encounter get away. In that case, Isaac, who led the Knights of the Black Sword, had decided to keep them where he could see them and guard them that way.

Calasin's motives were different, but that didn't change the conclusion.

As a result of these things, the defense operation was underway.

"Mr. Calasin."

"Oh, would you look at that! Thanks very much for the present."

Bright female voices sent up cheers.

In this castle, Calasin was even more popular than Isaac. The goods Shopping District 8 brought were useful to People of the Earth of every class, and the demand was particularly large among the kitchen personnel. Items like sauces, soy sauce, and high-purity sugar were still difficult for the People of the Earth to make on their own.

"You're real popular, GM!"

Glancing at Taro, who'd complimented him with wide, startled eyes, Calasin grumbled: "Well, sure: I'm the Young Gent." About 20 percent of those cheers had come from hungry soldiers, and 70 percent had been from the middle-aged maids and chefs who were preparing the food. Even Taro, who looked startled every time and wore expressions that said, *That's amazing. Wow, I'm jealous*, knew this and was acting that way on purpose. Calasin couldn't deal with the guy.

After he dexterously removed groceries and potions from his fantasy-class Holy Precincts of Ku Lal Bag and lined them up under the tent, his job here was done. Beside him, Taro had taken bandages out of his own shoulder bag. Having finished his work as well, he nodded firmly.

"From the southwest and the west, you think?"

As they traveled along the top of Castle Cinderella's retaining wall at a jog, Taro spoke.

Sounds that were sharp but somehow light, as if paper bags full of air were being popped, rang out one after another. It was the noise of attack spells, bursting in midair. Since they were far away, they sounded flimsy.

"That's where the Black Sword's main forces are. The People of the Earth knight brigade should be there as well."

"Is that gonna be okay?"

Calasin answered Taro's drawled question with a nod: "No worries."

It should be all right. In fact, as far as the current uproar was concerned, he predicted they'd do extremely useful work. After being trained by Isaac and company, the Glass Greaves' levels were in the high twenties. Among the People of the Earth, these abilities were considered elite, and they had combat power that civilian People of the Earth couldn't hope to match. Since their basic abilities like strength and endurance had grown as well, they'd be able to fight for a long time.

On top of that, since they were still far from the level-90 Knights of the Black Sword, the Eternal Moths wouldn't be as quick to target them. While the Knights of the Black Sword held the enemy in check from the front, they could act as guerilla fighters and attack from the flanks or direct evacuations all they wanted. In fact, Calasin had been getting reports to this effect.

"Before sunset, though, huh? I wish they'd stick to the schedule."

"There's no help for that. Trouble always crops up."

Calasin shrugged.

It wasn't clear what had happened, but the Eternal Moths had attacked without waiting for moonrise. However, Calasin was taking that as a positive sign.

"Shiroe and the others must have done something."

"'Something'?"

"Yes, something."

He had no idea what was going on, but it wasn't anything he needed to think about.

At any rate, Shiroe had taken action out on location to corner the enemy, and the schedule had shifted. Calasin had assumed that, since Shiroe had gone, he'd get it done, so there didn't seem to be any point in thinking about the details of the situation at the site. This wasn't because he trusted Shiroe or anything. It was more that he thought that, since the world was like a violent torrent loaded with unexpected happenings and hurtling downstream, there was no point in worrying about things he couldn't completely control on his own. Though, *thought* might not have been the word: Calasin had his hands full with his own territory, so he didn't have time to meddle with anything extra.

Although taking care of little Minori and other girls is another thing entirely...

Worrying about Shiroe was ridiculous. It was what was known as a wasted investment.

That said, as far as the battle in front of him was concerned, he was involved, and he'd probably have to get through it.

"Taro."

"Yessir, GM."

His contemporary straightened up and saluted, and Calasin issued several requests. Taro, who'd pulled a memo book with a paw pad mark on it out of his back pocket and was taking down notes, said "Really?" and "Really for real?" several times, making sure, then made tracks for the front line. The defensive wall around the town itself was several kilometers away, but if an Adventurer put their strong legs to work, they could get there in a bit under ten minutes.

The stock discharge wasn't a problem at all. The Adventurers of Akiba almost never used items compatible with level 30 and under anymore. You could have called the stuff backlogged inferior stock that had been sitting around since the days of the game. If they let it go here, it might not look so good on the books, but it wouldn't do them much damage. On the contrary, Calasin thought that if they had the opportunity to create some obligations, they should go ahead and do that.

Calasin entered the great hall, passed through it, then went down a colorfully carpeted corridor to the main tower. Slowly, he climbed the broad spiral staircase. There were small windows whose purpose was to let in light, and the color that filtered in through them was madder red. The tower was filled with the chilly air of an early spring evening.

He hadn't climbed up to it many times, but the top floor of this main tower probably had a view across the whole city. From what he'd just heard, Duke Sergiad was up there as well.

Partway up the spiral, Calasin and some knights on guard duty passed one another. They weren't just People of the Earth; Adventurers were in the group, too. Lezarik was in charge of security, and apparently, he was posting sufficient forces.

Although the streets he saw from a small window halfway up the tower were brimming with tension, he didn't see any fighting. It was probably just a bad angle; the fighting was over by the hills and the defensive wall.

Calasin sighed and continued on.

The situation was pretty *tiresome*. However, he thought *tiresome* might have a saturation point. Just as it wasn't possible to dissolve more than three hundred grams or so of salt in a liter of water, there was a limit to the number of exhausting things that would melt into human lives. Where did the fatigue go when it reached its limit and overflowed? It spilled over into the surrounding area. It was just like a room in chaos. There were limits to the amount that people could clean up.

Since mystery monsters had appeared with such excellent timing, further inquiries into the Iselus assassination affair had been shelved. That had been convenient for Calasin, too, so he hadn't made a fuss, but assassinations weren't the sort of thing that could be neglected, either.

Yes, there were limits to the amount that people could clean up.

Still, people were said to be creatures who could work together, and so in order to fulfill the duty in front of him and his own curiosity, Calasin climbed the tower.

"Hello."

"Oho. To think you'd come here, Sir Calasin."

Sergiad, who'd given a laid-back response to a laid-back greeting, was gazing at the battlefield from the tower balcony. His profile had been stern, but when he turned to Calasin, it was mild again. The knights who were attending him didn't look stressed, either, probably because the battle they could see from the balcony was going their way.

"How does the monster attack look?"

"Incredibly abnormal. There are no records of an attack that would require Adventurers to line the town walls in the history of Maihama."

"You look very calm, for all that."

"Well, I'm leaving everything to Sir Isaac. Panicking would be an insult to his bravery."

Duke Sergiad laughed lightly, and Calasin smiled along with him.

Inwardly, he frowned. He was like his boss in the old world. Not only that, but he wasn't a direct boss; he was something like a managing director, a member of the executive class, somebody whose station was far above the rest. He had the sort of monstrous aura that left you unable to taste what you were eating when he invited you to lunch on an apparent whim.

Come to think of it, Michitaka and Isaac seem to hit it off with him. Do sportsman types correct for things like that?

I really, really can't, Calasin thought, getting in an internal verbal jab.

With someone like this, being tactful in a halfhearted way could be nothing but a weak point. They'd predict your actions and words and end up striking them all down. He'd have to distance himself from the mind-set of competing during negotiations.

Well, it should be fine.

Calasin gave up on thinking. If there were problems left over, somebody somewhere would just have to mop them up afterward. After all, the range that one person could clean was limited.

I say "somebody somewhere," but it'll probably be Shiroe.

Internally, he clapped his hands together in apology.

"And so what will you do about diplomacy with Westlande?"

"Is the Round Table Council finally venturing into Yamato's politics?"

"Perish the thought. I'm just a petty merchant gathering information in order to protect myself."

Calasin shrugged and looked self-effacing, but he wasn't speaking in earnest. He also didn't think Duke Sergiad would accept the idea that he was only a merchant making small talk. He was speaking with the head of a political body that divided Yamato into two parts.

Calasin had thought that, if he held back, he'd only fall behind, and nothing good would come of it, so he asked question after question, wearing an intentionally audacious expression. Even if he was dripping with cold sweat internally, throwing himself on the man's mercy seemed like a patently terrible move.

"Do you think there'll be a war?"

"—I'd like to avoid that."

As he let those words fall, Duke Sergiad was gazing into the distance.

"Unfortunately, things never go as you'd like. You may ask that, Sir Calasin, but to the Holy Empire of Westlande, our Eastal is a disobedient enemy of the emperor. It isn't a question of whether to go to war or not. To them, long before that, we are rebels who must be destroyed. The only reason the Holy Empire of Westlande hasn't invaded us during the past three hundred years is that they didn't have the military force to do so."

"And when the Adventurers appeared, that broke down?"

"Westlande isn't a monolith, either. In the near future, it will probably crack."

Duke Sergiad's words were half blown away by the wind, but they reached Calasin's ears clearly.

That was a definite possibility.

Conditions in Minami were complicated. In a way, that relationship was more complex than the one between Akiba and Eastal.

Most of Akiba's Adventurers believed Plant Hwyaden was an organization of self-government that was headquartered in the Kansai area and had been created by the Adventurers: In other words, it was Western Yamato's Round Table Council. *...But this wasn't the case.*

As proof, Plant Hwyaden's Ten-Seat Council had People of the Earth members, as well as Adventurers. There weren't many people in Akiba who gave serious thought to what that signified.

"Is that, erm…? Would that be the Adventurers' fault?"

"The ambition belongs to the senate, mind you. Still, where there's oil, fire burns more fiercely."

Plant Hwyaden *was not* an Adventurer organization of self-government.

It was the new governing organization of Western Yamato. The subjects it governed were the People of the Earth, and the Adventurers who were part of Plant Hwyaden were a new ruling class, an aristocracy. The Ten-Seat Council said no such thing, of course, and it was likely that most of the Adventurers who lived in Minami weren't conscious of the fact. However, in practice, this was already the case. A system in which that was the inevitable result was already in operation.

To make matters worse, that didn't mean Plant Hwyaden was the only governing organization in West Yamato.

West Yamato already had a governing organization known as the Holy Empire of Westlande. Internally, it had a bureaucracy known as the senate and nobles in the form of the House of Saiguu. It could be said that the rivalry and cooperation between the senate and the House of Saiguu was the history of the Holy Empire of Westlande itself. The senate, which ruled the people, and the House of Saiguu, the people's hope. Plant Hwyaden had been added on top of this double-layered control.

By rights, the confusion generated by the churning inconsistencies could easily have collapsed it. However, those inconsistencies were being hidden by the safety and the new technologies—in other words, the benefits—provided by the Adventurers.

What Duke Sergiad had said seemed to support Calasin's misgivings.

"We don't know what sort of confidential talks have been carried out or who's collaborating with whom. However, someone in Westlande, probably the senate's faction, must have thought that they wouldn't mind a war. That their chances of victory were great enough."

"I wonder about that."

Calasin shrugged.

He doubted whether Zeldus had that much fighting spirit.

"The odds of victory don't really show up as numbers to that extent."

"A strange statement, coming from a merchant."

Calasin thought as he responded to Sergiad.

"No, it's because I am a merchant. Projects—new businesses—are uncertain things. Once you start them, you can't stop, and the results are mostly ambiguous. Ninety percent of the time, the outcome isn't a definite win or a loss. For example, maybe the capital you had lined up went down the drain, but you got by without losing your personnel. Or maybe your sales were bigger than you'd planned on, but it triggered a labor dispute at your new factory."

"You mean it's never a perfect win or a perfect loss, then?"

The ultimate goal of the Round Table Council, and of Shopping

District 8, was survival. In this warped world, Adventurers didn't die. However, the simple fact that they didn't die didn't necessarily mean they were living. Calasin was running a commercial guild precisely because he didn't think those things were equal.

Since there was no end, the question of how to spend that infinity became a problem.

Ultimately, they had no choice but to spend it here, quarreling and making up again. As far as Calasin was concerned, being able to talk things over was the absolute minimum. The mere thought of all-out war with an unkillable opponent made his skin crawl.

"That's right. Long story short, we're alive, so even if we're beaten hollow, there's nothing for it but to search for the next thing and look for a bright spot or two as we go. If we win big, in the future, that big win might make people arrogant and lead to another war. That's what business is: No matter how things go, it doesn't end that easily."

"You're a tough one."

"Well, in private-sector businesses, common sense is all about customers and safety management, and the budget doesn't smile on departments that don't generate profit. Unfortunately, though, we're not salaried workers. And so, Duke Sergiad: Would you sell the Round Table your inventory?"

Sergiad's eyebrows shot up, and he murmured, "What is it you need?"

Calasin responded with the straightest face he could manage. "To begin with, the slacker princess, perhaps."

With the pillar of rainbow light that climbed to the moon behind them, the two figures stood frozen like statues, and for a long time, neither of them moved.

▶ 5

Taliktan, the Genius of Summoning, had broken a huge hole in the wall and leapt through. Golden hair swinging, Riezé intercepted him: Frost Spear, a spear of ice that gushed cold air.

Of the three elements that Sorcerers controlled, cold air was less popular than the others. This was because the attack classes were meant to kill enemies, and the direct damage dealt by ice spells was relatively low. For instance, the electric spell Lightning Chamber and the fire spell Burned Stake did far more damage, but Riezé still placed her focus on ice spells. In her opinion, the balance between firepower and MP consumption was good, as were the length of the cast times and the force per strike.

In general, long cast times were considered a drawback, but if you were able to predict the enemy's movements, they turned into an advantage. That was true this time, too. A spell that used up the time the enemy spent moving on a long chant held destructive power commensurate to its cast time. When the white-haired Genius appeared in the hall, she sent it right at his nose. Another advantage was that, of the spells Sorcerers used, this one was excellent at hampering the enemy's movements.

As Taliktan tottered, Koen and Yuzuko launched full-power attacks.

"Still…," Riezé murmured.

That had been very rough.

When she'd heard about the maneuver, she'd doubted Shiroe's sanity, and even now, she thought it was preposterous. She didn't know the actual number of stories, but that broadcasting tower couldn't have been less than thirty meters off the ground. Shiroe's plan had involved not only leaping from the open rooftop, but linking that act to kiting.

The outcome had been successful, but it still struck Riezé as far too absurd. Although, truthfully, it was possible she was merely bound by fixed ideas. The maneuver actually *had* succeeded, and they'd managed to drag Taliktan into the melee in this music hall.

"This isn't like Master Shiroe…I don't think…"

"Nah, that's not true."

Nazuna leapt lightly backward in a move as if she had eyes in her back, coming to stand beside Riezé, and answered her.

"Shiro did the same thing, this counselor stuff, on the Tea Party. I dunno what the world thought about us, but we were a rough, random bunch. *Today, he's just like he was back then*, that's all. This is normal."

Nazuna, who'd leveled her katana alertly and was glaring at the enemy, smiled faintly as she boasted.

She was probably telling the truth.

Riezé had misread Shiroe. He was the driving force behind the Round Table Council. Someone who had contributed to the alliance with Eastal, the League of Free Cities. A hardworking man of the world who undertook the task of arranging things among the guilds and organizing information. An able official, a competent administrator, a worker with political abilities, a strategist—those were the concepts through which she'd seen him. Yet, they were only a part of him.

Her staff moved automatically, rapidly spinning one spell after another.

A Sorcerer's role was to concentrate firepower. Each spell had a cast time, a bind time, and a recast time. This meant it wasn't possible to use the same spell several times in a row, so they ended up using the recast time as the chant time for another spell. Sorcerers fought by combining anywhere from five to ten types of spells to create a cycle, and then repeating that cycle.

It was easy to say, but it was actually pretty difficult. Even if a spell was standardized, its performance differed slightly from Sorcerer to Sorcerer. Furthermore, the special skills, style, and equipment a player had changed recast times, so the spells that could be linked together in a play cycle changed as well.

For instance, there were some enemy monsters that had resistance to fire damage. When dealing with those monsters, the flame spells in a cycle got in the way, but naturally, when taking those spells out, the whole cycle broke down. In other words, did the Sorcerer have several types of cycles custom-made? Could they maintain the spells at the unconscious level and choose them to suit the circumstances? These were the abilities that were required from Sorcerers on raids.

As a member of D.D.D., Riezé had sufficiently mastered eight cycles. Four of those were the type that could be connected to different cycles by adding internal branch points, to cope with abrupt accidents. There weren't many Sorcerers that well trained. Among *Elder Tales* magic classes, it was one of the pinnacles of sophistication.

However, even to Riezé, Shiroe's spell cycles seemed unique.

For most spells, chant times were between two and ten seconds. That meant it took anywhere from a minute and a half to two minutes for one cycle to complete. With a simple observation, anyone could tell which spells were being used and how they were linked together. Nonetheless, she wasn't able to read the scale of Shiroe's cycles.

Even so, he wasn't simply chanting spells as he thought of them. That would have resulted in weak connections and lost time, which would have reduced the final damage output.

No such loss was visible in Shiroe's spell chants. She could see the traces of some sort of diligent study. Yet even still, she didn't understand how the cycles were structured. Had he learned such an abundance of cycles that it wasn't possible to read them entirely in a day or so of fighting together, or was this some other, different technique?

His MP isn't going down. It's falling, but the recovery is balancing it. He's maintaining the combat skills, even as he circulates the ranks and controls them. That's what the frequent instructions to break through the front line are for.

Shiroe was giving shape to an idea that would have been laughed down as a joke, even if someone had managed to come up with it. There were errors, of course. They were there, but the sort of precautionary measures that would cover for them had already been taken.

He hadn't instructed Nazuna to fall back a moment ago just to keep her MP in reserve. It had been in order to recover the recast time from the big technique Great Purification Prayer—

Actually, no, that wasn't it: It was intended to block Taliktan's gaze and line of fire, which he'd turned on Isuzu and Rundelhaus. Or rather, Shiroe had made it *look* that way, when it was really so that she could act as an observer and give Soujirou advice from the rear, as someone who was very skilled at executing team plays with him.

The true intent behind Shiroe's instructions stayed vague while only the group's effects accumulated, light racing along countless paths toward victory. Riezé was also a raid commander, and she had a Tactician subclass. It was her job to see an encounter with the enemy as a story and read it carefully. However, even for Riezé, the story Shiroe was reading now was too wild, and her comprehension couldn't keep up.

Shiroe probably hadn't chosen a protagonist for his story.

Anyone could corner Taliktan, using any method.

That was no doubt what he was thinking.

Under Shiroe's command, there was no clear casting even for the attackers and the supporters. Even Kushiyatama—the close-combat Kannagi and "rampaging *miko*"—was brandishing her blade as if it felt good.

*　　*　　*

"Count ten seconds. Requesting Barriers on Naotsugu, Nyanta, Koen, Akatsuki, and Soujirou!"

"Aye-aye, sir!"

Nazuna responded to Shiroe's directions in a teasing voice, then chanted Purification Barrier. In an instant, translucent walls that shone madder red appeared and were applied to her allies. It was a preemptive defense spell, cast when an attack was anticipated. At that command, Riezé instinctively knew that a large attack from Taliktan was on its way.

"Hurry... Four, three, two... Now!"

As Riezé glared at him, Taliktan raised his twisted staff high, unleashing purple lightning. The bolts burst at close range, and Riezé averted her face from the light, but her Mystery, Chiron Tablet, kept tracking the battle log.

The barriers had definitely obstructed the lightning attack, but even then, Naotsugu and its other targets had taken enough damage to lose more than half their HP. It had been Taliktan's most powerful attack. If the barriers hadn't made it in time, and if they hadn't defended with pinpoint accuracy, there was no question that the front line would have collapsed.

As she registered that fact, Riezé turned pale, but through her fear, she searched desperately for an answer. Taliktan's lightning had *avoided* Riezé and headed for Nyanta. Riezé had been right in its path. She hadn't had a barrier, and if it had gone straight ahead, it would have turned her to charcoal. Why had it avoided her? Why had Nyanta been targeted? More than anything, why had it been predicted so perfectly...?

"Why, huh? How did Shiro know who was gonna get hit?"

As she asked that question, Marielle was turning white. The answer was...

"An upper-rank aggro list–penetrating attack."

Shiroe and Riezé's voices overlapped.

An "aggro list" was a theoretical index of the aggro Taliktan felt. Assuming the threats the monster sensed were converted into numerical values, this attack targeted the top five names on that list.

It wasn't as if that realization had been a very big one.

In addition, except for this being very nearly the first time they'd seen it, it was a deduction that was only natural for a raid commander, nothing to be proud of. But that wasn't the problem. The issue was that Shiroe had read off the top names on that aggro list by himself, as if it were only natural.

Aggro wasn't a numerical status. Those who had inflicted great damage, those with powerful recovery spells, those who were nearby. It was something inside monsters that took all sorts of conditions into account and changed kaleidoscopically. As the main tank, Naotsugu boosted this aggro to its maximum in order to pull monsters to him, so now, when Taliktan was fighting him head-on, it was clear he was at the top of the aggro list. However, second place and below had to be deduced from the progression of the battle up to this point.

Not only that, but in the world after the Catastrophe, it wasn't possible to check the battle log in a window. She didn't think Shiroe had acquired the Chiron Tablet Mystery, so how had he known? The answer sent a strange chill through Riezé's spine, along with a sort of spooked awe.

With Chiron Tablet, it was possible to visually confirm the battle log. Everything that happened in combat—including damage inflicted, damage received, its attribute and range, frequency, recovery, and even applied effects—was converted into readable text. That was the Mystery Riezé had.

However, through observation and insight, Shiroe had simply surpassed her Mystery.

Riezé had just experienced Shiroe's Full Control Encounter.

"What's the matter?!"

At the sight of Kushiyatama, who'd rapped out the question and was racing toward the front line, her heart trembled.

Akatsuki leapt as if there was a translucent staircase in midair. Her valiant figure was splendid.

Nazuna seemed to be unleashing relentless attacks, and she was perfectly positioned to shield the rearguard from the line of fire. Riezé was able to understand her consideration.

"This is fun, isn't it, Miss Kushi?"

"Exactly!"

Riezé broke into a run as well. The gloom in her heart had cleared completely.

She'd thought that what Krusty's command had and hers lacked was charisma, but she'd been shown that that wasn't all. What Calasin had said had been true: Shiroe was the same type as Riezé. The true meaning of those words had been nothing less than that Riezé still had a long way to go. Thinking that being the same type of person meant she could do similar things was conceited and an insult to Shiroe. It was because she was similar that she understood this.

True, like Riezé, Shiroe was a rearguard-type commander. That meant he didn't have the sort of charisma Krusty did. Still, even so, he was far ahead of Riezé.

Precisely because they fought with calculations and insight and preliminary investigations, the difference in experience and the number of battles fought was brutally clear.

"U-fu-fu-fu-fu. Ha-ha-ha-ha!"

Riezé struck down rubble that had come flying toward her with Pride of Queen, then kicked the ground with her long legs.

Fun. Shiroe's command was fun.

There were still many things she couldn't see.

There was a lot of territory her hands couldn't yet reach.

Instead of humiliation and inferiority, this made Riezé feel ambitious and as if she were soaring.

"I'm afraid I was conceited. This is the legend of the Tea Party. People flattered me, as the captain of the training unit, as a member of Drei Klauen, and I grew arrogant, thinking that I had to protect things in Milord's absence, but I'm still very green. Even as a raid member— Miss Kushi, I have a request."

"Accepted!"

"No questions asked?!"

She spoke to Kushiyatama, who was paying out a storm of countless slashing attacks right next to her, and received an instant response. It was magnificent. Worries and hesitation and those gloomy days were all disappearing, like shadows dissolving in the sunlight.

"—Because you've started being open with people, Ri-Ri."

Riezé smiled at her mischievous old D.D.D. guide.

The requests she'd never been able to make properly were possible for her now.

If she couldn't do something on her own, she'd just have to ask other people. Now that Krusty was gone, D.D.D. needed all the reliable people it could get. There was no doubt that Kushiyatama had understood the request Riezé hadn't put into words. That was why she'd come along on a raid like this one with her.

"Listen to you. I'm all fired up now. I'm blazing! —Configure Lamination Syntax! Set target— Pierce it! Frost Spear!!"

The spear of ice split, warping the space in the multilayered magic circle.

Pouring all the mana she had into it, Riezé unleashed an attack spell.

▶ 6

"Defense of Doctrine Barrier!!"

Minori fired an emergency Kannagi defense spell. The barrier's level was in the fifties, and to Shiroe and the other players whose levels were over 90, it seemed fragile. However, Shiroe had been just about to order her to do that, and she'd stolen a march on him.

He smiled a little.

Minori's response had been unexpected... In a good way, naturally. As a result, the attack team had gained a very slight advantage, a few seconds' worth. The current members weren't the type to let that chance slip by them.

Their skills had already been sufficiently polished by the combat up to this point.

In the first place, all the members except for the younger group from Log Horizon already had raid experience. But even that younger group was watching how D.D.D.—who had the basics down solidly—was doing things and absorbing their methods wholesale.

Their advanced capacity for teamwork was the result of high morale and the ability to focus.

They'd meshed tightly with the personality of their enemy Taliktan as well. Taliktan, who was waving his arms around, was no more than a typical close-combat boss now. The short-range attacks he unleashed with his staff and arms were powerful; he also had that aggro list–based lightning attack that wiped out a whole range and thunder that inflicted negative statuses across a wide area— But in a manner of speaking, that was it. He was *the perfect opponent* for a raid drill.

When Taliktan turned back with a great flourish of his hand, several magic circles appeared, and goblins and giants manifested. Tension raced over the field, but Shiroe canceled it out.

"That summoning didn't use the iron tower, only his innate abilities. There aren't many of them, and there's a limit. Stay calm and deal with them."

He wasn't actually certain about that.

Still, it was important to be decisive here. As if playing off his words, Naotsugu yelled, "What, anything goes?!" in a joking voice and charged. Akatsuki followed him, hiding in his shadow; she flickered as she went, then vanished from sight.

A tremendous number of attacks were striking Taliktan. Dread Weapon clung to Hien's Assassinate. The teamwork between the Magic Attack and the Weapon Attack classes was growing more accurate as well. The powerful attack pierced a group of goblins, who sacrificed themselves to protect their master, and bore down on Taliktan.

Lightning that streaked toward Kushiyatama was repelled by Tetora's Reactive Heal.

Their opponent's defense had been pried open, and grabbing their chance, Nyanta and Koen rushed in. Soujirou's Echo Rebound kept Taliktan from striking back.

Isuzu's spell-song reinforced Rundelhaus's flame spell, and in exactly the same way, Henrietta chanted Maestro Echo, turning Riezé's ice spell into a round. The two powerful Magic Attack teams were protected by Yuzuko's golem and Isami's katana, which had Kurinon's support.

Shouryuu launched himself into a run.

He leapt across the red seats of the music hall, attacking Taliktan like a small storm of twin blades, and cut him soundly. Marielle gave a worried shriek, but he yelled, "Stay back, please," and his desperate attack dealt Taliktan significant damage. However, as a result, he was flung away and ended up getting rescued by Hien.

The battle was changing.

Naotsugu, whose back had taken many recovery spells, pressed forward in fits and starts, stirring up the Genius's aggro. The Guardians' Aggro Charge showed its true worth when it was used to protect companions.

The sound of ringing steel and the light of magic intersected in the great hall. In the midst of it, as Shiroe maintained his spell chanting cycle, he kept an eye on his surroundings. Taliktan's HP bar was down to about 30 percent. As Shiroe lasted through Taliktan's fierce attacks, issued instructions to his companions, or had them drop back to refuel, he was remembering the hesitation he'd felt up until now.

For a long time, Shiroe had searched for answers, and he'd gotten nowhere.

Even now, he wasn't sure.

However, it was likely that the time had come to make a decision. Touya's and Minori's words had urged him forward. So had Rundelhaus and Isuzu, Captain Nyanta and Serara. Actually, come to think of it, Shiroe had been surrounded by people who supported him.

What he'd hesitated over had always been the question, "Is it all right to choose that?" The world was vast and deep, and both the people around him and the people he didn't even know were living their lives with a variety of thoughts he couldn't begin to fathom. Was it okay for him to shape the world? Was it all right to touch it? That had been the worry he'd harbored. He'd been afraid of doing anything. If he acted a certain way, it might change things. Something terribly beautiful and splendid might break. That was why he'd been afraid to touch the world with his clumsy hands.

That had been cowardice.

True, if Shiroe did something, the end results might change, but that would happen even if he did nothing. For everything in the world, there was a season, a time limit, and postponing making a choice would mean he'd chosen to avoid acting at all.

When Taliktan, the Genius of Summoning, had appeared, Shiroe had been forced to understand that, whether he wanted to or not. In this world, there were things that could be broken by hesitation, and it was probable that Shiroe wouldn't be able to run from failure and regret.

Going in the direction *she*, Kanami, had indicated, had been fun, and it had made for wonderful memories, but he had to do more than that now. Shiroe had guild members who would support him and walk with him, and Marielle and William had shown him what guild masters should be.

"Rest in peace and wait."

He couldn't.

"If you go to sleep, your safety will be guaranteed."

He couldn't.

"A return home can be achieved in exchange for six hundred and forty million units. Contractors who agree, accept access, choose to sleep, and wait on standby."

He couldn't.

Accepting Taliktan's words might be the right thing to do. At this point, though, to Shiroe, that would be the same as "postponing a choice." Just gaining one option wasn't good enough.

People had an obligation to live.

They probably had an obligation to be greedy as well.

Shiroe had thought of himself as a person who could get by with being mildly satisfied, but he'd been wrong. It was easy to not get involved with other people, to avoid wanting anything. However, the more fun times you spent with your friends, the keener the prayer that began to grow inside you. You couldn't help wishing that kindness, warmth, smiles, and peace would stay just as they were for a long, long time. Because the most important things were fleeting and easily lost, Shiroe had been afraid of actively wishing for them. He'd been afraid people would think he was greedy.

However, there were things you couldn't get without wishing for them, and right now, that was Shiroe's role.

It was probably what his parents had wanted, long ago, and what the guild masters who had gathered on the Round Table Council had wished for.

None of them—not Ains or Isaac or anyone else—had wanted

things for themselves. They had all tried to be faithful to the people they wanted to protect, and as a result, they hadn't been able to reach a consensus.

Like a big sister.

Shiroe remembered a phrase from Roe2's letter.

The Travelers also prayed for light for others' futures.

When he realized that, something hot constricted his chest. His hands clenched so tightly around his staff that they ached. It wasn't unpleasant; it churned inside him.

As if severing something, Shiroe struck at the monster.

"Taliktan. I can't do that."

"*—A return from this transient world is possible.*"

Taliktan's words were the trigger.

He really couldn't accept conditions like those.

And apparently, Shiroe's companions shared his feelings.

"Forget about it."

"After all, we can't trust you."

"Mew're much too late."

Other words of refusal were spat out, along with attacks. Right now, whether or not it was true wasn't the issue.

Touya had said it: They'd go home after they'd settled everything.

In the end, we are greedy. Ordinarily, the thought would have embarrassed Shiroe, but now he was able to look at it honestly. *We want to walk this world, to travel through it on our own two feet. We don't know whether that's right or a mistake. However, because we don't know, we want to question ourselves in the midst of unexplored landscapes.*

Whether this world was transient was something for Shiroe and the others to decide. *We won't let even the gods get in our way,* William had yelled. He thought it was a blush-worthy declaration. However, Shiroe felt the same way.

The truth did exist. He'd met Naotsugu and Akatsuki, had journeyed, flown through the sky, gotten in touch with Captain Nyanta, and started his guild. He'd brought in the twins, and his number of companions had increased. He'd spoken with People of the Earth. He'd become good friends with people of very different ages. He'd stayed up late, being noisy and fooling around, and he'd tucked blankets up over sleeping faces. There was no way those things hadn't been true. Maybe they'd begun as something transient, but nothing said they had to stay that way.

That was why he couldn't respond to Taliktan's inorganic temptation.

"Sleep, all of you. Sleep, all of you."

Taliktan kept groaning in a broken-sounding way, over and over, as if he'd forgotten to keep up appearances. His body began to swell up like a misshapen water balloon. The figure, which had formerly been a brown-skinned old man, grew enormous, wrapped its white hair around Naotsugu like melted vinyl, and sent him flying.

"Fifteen percent HP remaining. It's the last phase!"

Behind him, he heard Riezé's shout. This was a characteristic called "insanity," and it was often seen in raid bosses. When their HP fell below a certain percentage, their forms and attack patterns changed. In most cases, they also grew much stronger. However, the attack team didn't shrink back. On the contrary, they launched even fiercer attacks.

A freezing wind blew from behind him. Someone had used the effect of a fantasy-class item. Nazuna and Minori were dancing Kagura Dance, and the shining madder-red effect came from the barrier spells they were casting on the frontline warriors, one after another.

Even though they hadn't discussed it beforehand, everyone understood: It wouldn't be possible to sustain a long fight with Taliktan now that his attack power had grown. They'd just have to force him down.

Shiroe shouted as if to expel the tightness in his chest, then wove together spells and released them in rapid succession. He fired Electric Fuzz as a decoy, then killed its firing range with Brain Vise. He layered Mind Bolt over Nightmare Sphere and slammed them into him.

He had become a guild master, and now he was leading this capture unit. He couldn't not choose something. Choosing was the only way he could repay them.

It was his duty to wish for a lot. For the sake of the companions who walked alongside him and for the future companions he'd meet someday.

Akatsuki had flipped high into the air, and their eyes met.

Shiroe nodded, then belatedly realized why he'd done it. The calm part of himself whispered that it had been an illusion created by the high-density combat teamwork. However, just now, he was sure he'd touched Akatsuki's soul. It had been like anger, but clearer, a fierce determination without a target, and the emotion had matched Shiroe's to a startling degree.

"I don't want that to have been temporary!" *"That shore we walked along together."*

Shiroe's Sewn-Bind Hostage struck Taliktan's white, expanding body, and purple briars manifested. Akatsuki leapt, again and again, over the howling blizzard, the lightning, and the raid team's front line as they pushed back. She flickered and blinked, and then many overlapping Akatsukis swung the short swords they held with backhanded grips.

Akatsuki's Mystery divided her shape, and her slashing attacks burst the secret-level Sewn-Bind Hostage like a rain shower. Smoothly, Shiroe released the spell he'd had ready. He slipped another Sewn-Bind Hostage in, landing it in the less than half a second that Akatsuki spent out of sight.

"We're extravagant, so…" *"This place isn't like that!"*

Akatsuki didn't stop.

She wasn't expecting to fail.

This was true for Shiroe as well, so he moved on to the next stage of the cycle without waiting to see the results.

Sewn-Bind Hostage had bound their opponent with almost no time lag. Then came Akatsuki's series of five attacks. A total of ten briars, and slashes from ten copies. The black-haired girl had pulled off that team play as if it were only natural, and she blurred, running up through empty space.

"Assassinate!!"

With the roar of an especially loud lightning strike and the sound of something scorching, Taliktan turned into dark bubbles as if he was being absorbed into himself, then immediately disappeared.

That was how the Shibuya Eternal Moth Fortress Raid that had rocked Yamato came to an end.

INTERLUDE

▶ 1

Shiroe was gazing absently into space.

Until a minute ago, he'd been sending telechats all over the place, dealing with the aftermath. This room, which was hemmed in by composite stone and magical machinery, was still Fortress of the Call. Once they'd put down Taliktan, the Genius of Summoning, the monsters he'd summoned and their eggs had turned into rainbow-colored bubbles and vanished, but they needed to make sure they were really all gone. They were currently taking in additional personnel who'd been sent from Akiba and exploring the dungeon.

Out of consideration for their fatigue, Shiroe and the rest of the raid team had been exempted from the investigation and from guarding the perimeter, but the members who had enough energy seemed to be doing things voluntarily. That said, that group consisted mainly of Tetora, who was giving a guerilla concert in the music hall, and Shouryuu and Hien, who had made preparations for a party and were cheering Tetora on. The members who were tired were resting in this studio at the base of the broadcasting tower.

Forcibly shaking his head, which felt saturated, Shiroe took a drink of water from his canteen.

He'd gotten pretty worked up during that last battle. He was a little embarrassed, but the thought that it had been the right way to go was strong as well. After all, he'd chosen to be greedy.

He wanted to save the people he could save, and he wanted to protect his companions, too.

Up until now, Shiroe had been holding back. He'd set to work quietly, covering only the range he could deal with inside himself and taking care not to get involved with anything outside that. Even when he'd gone beyond that range, he'd made sure to leave himself an escape route. However, those days were over.

Since he'd decided to want, he didn't intend to do it by halves.

He'd keep the atmosphere in Akiba from becoming any gloomier. He'd prevent violence from breaking out between eastern and western Yamato. He'd talk with the Travelers. He'd return to his old world.

Put into words, that was probably what it would be. He was overreaching himself with those goals, and Shiroe laughed a little in spite of himself. Still, it was all right—he'd decided to take action to make those things happen, and so his feelings were bright and cheerful.

For now, his first move would probably be to contact Plant Hwyaden and the Holy Empire of Westlande. It seemed likely to be troublesome, and he was aware that he'd been putting it off, but now that things had come to this, they couldn't afford not to exchange information.

Nureha had said they'd discovered a way to return home.

That in itself wasn't really worth getting startled over. He could think of several situations in which they could say something like that, and he thought there were a few methods by which they might actually have been able to. The problem wasn't whether they had technology that could get them home, or how to do it, but how to confirm that they really had returned. Even if an Adventurer volunteer disappeared from Theldesia and Minami called it "a successful return," all it would mean was that they had a missing person on their hands. It was no different from the current situation with Krusty.

The unavoidable hurdle that nearly all people who wanted to go home were ignoring was this "confirmation of return"—in other words, communication between here and Earth. Before returning, they'd have to establish a way to make contact with Earth. That was an absolute prerequisite.

If that couldn't be done, they would have to trust to luck in a big way when it came to future developments. In short, they'd have to choose their likeliest-looking "human disappearance" idea and just risk it. Even if that method worked, since there would be no way for the people who'd returned to Earth to contact them here, they wouldn't be able to confirm that it had been a success. If it had actually succeeded, fine, but not being able to confirm failure would be awful. It was conceivable they might all wind up leaping into the same trap, one after another, like a group suicide.

Exchanging information with the Travelers seemed to hold the hope of a breakthrough, but even if they did that, they'd need to discuss things with Plant Hwyaden and solidify their standing.

He did have questions about the difference between rank 2 and rank 3 that they'd mentioned, but the only thing he could say was that Minori had demonstrated it herself. Shiroe had no intention of falling to their rank 2.

On top of that, the objective he seemed most likely to find clues about was preventing conflict in Yamato before it started. The idea of getting in the middle of a military clash between political entities was so reckless he'd never even considered it, but surprisingly, of the issues on the table now, the hurdles for that foolhardy act were comparatively low. It was probably no wonder that that fact provoked a dry smile.

In short, no matter which of the objectives they prioritized, Shiroe and the others would have to discuss things with Plant Hwyaden and exchange information, at the very least.

"What's the matter, Shiroe? Are you still tired?"

Minori sat down on Shiroe's left. She'd changed out of her *miko* outfit, and was wearing a blouse and necktie that looked a bit like a school uniform.

"You're frowning again, my liege."

On his right, Akatsuki admonished him, pushing the outer corners of her eyes up with her fingertips. Shiroe smiled wryly; he didn't think he was making that sort of face.

"Technically, during battle… You know. I said some pretty overambitious stuff."

"Did you?"

Akatsuki gazed at him steadily, arms folded, head tilted to one side.

During that hectic battle, I felt as if we'd connected, but it was probably an illusion, Shiroe thought. Apparently, his worries and decisions hadn't gotten through to the petite Assassin.

When he glanced over, just to make sure, Minori was also looking perplexed. It was only to be expected, but they didn't seem to have gotten through to the group's youngest girl, either.

Maybe it was interference from the gods: *This is what humans are like. Communicate by putting your thoughts into words.* Feeling a little disappointed, and also greatly relieved, Shiroe attempted to explain:

"I think I'm going to do my best to make those wishes come true. The goals are so high and far away that I'm not sure I can even reach them. There are tons of things to do, and all of them have 'nightmare' difficulty levels. It's going to mean more work, and I don't even know where to start. That's what I was thinking about."

"Huhn. The usual, then."

"Huh?"

Akatsuki's response brusquely cut down Shiroe's confession.

What? But I learned on that harsh Susukino abyss expedition that it's important to talk things over with your friends, and that it's not good to let things build up too far...

Having what he'd said rejected in a perfunctory way with the words *the usual* was a big shock to him.

"She's right. It's the same every month, you know."

"Huh?!"

Not only that, but Minori sided with her, and he was left without anything to say.

Even so, wasn't saying it was "the same every month" a little too mean? That made it sound as if he was some miserable clerical worker who stayed shut in his office and was constantly groaning. He wasn't happy with the assessment that that was all he'd done since coming to Theldesia. He was sure he'd spent his time actively. On the Susukino expedition, for example, and in the Abyssal Shaft.

Unfortunately, he realized that Minori hadn't been there for either of those.

Looking excited, Minori got out her Magic Bag, saying, "I bought some smooth ink that's specifically for documents and some drying sand. Here, Shiroe, you look at them, too." At that point, all Shiroe could do was watch, his expression strained.

As Shiroe tried to change the subject, Li Gan ended up helping him out.

For the past little while, he'd been crouched down, fiddling with the magic circuits of the transmission device. Abruptly, it began to emit noisy static, and light returned to the room.

There was a popping noise, sparks scattered, and the loudspeaker suddenly began to vibrate.

They'd been resting in this anteroom in the first place, even though it wasn't very big, because Li Gan had said he wanted to see how damaged the transmitter was right away and to examine whether there was any residual negative influence from the Genius Taliktan.

The members who'd been napping with their eyes closed sat up, watching to see what would happen.

"What, guy, you fixed it?"

"No... It isn't fixed yet. At this point, I've only confirmed that its functions are still live."

"So can we start talkin' to the moon now?"

"Here comes my galactic debut!"

Naotsugu and the others crowded around Li Gan. He was down on all fours, doing maintenance around the back of the low device, and he answered from there. Even though it was obviously an uncomfortable position, he sounded as if he was enjoying himself. You could even have said his voice was delighted. Shiroe, who was watching the scene, murmured, "He's a hobbyist."

"—From the ancient writings of Miral Lake, I know that this is a long-distance transmitter from the age of the ancient alvs, but the facility wasn't created to communicate with the moon, you see. I've heard that your goal is to get a message to the moon, but before we attempt that, we'll need to analyze this magic device, research it, and appropriately improve and reinforce it. "

"That's some unexpectedly practical stuff."

Akatsuki looked glum as she spoke, and Shiroe soothed her: "We couldn't really expect anything else."

On hearing that explanation, Tetora said, "I'm disappointed. And here I was all ready to make my cosmic debut..." The idol clambered up Naotsugu, got pulled at by Marielle, and began screeching shrilly.

In the midst of that uproar, Shiroe finally felt himself begin to relax. The Shibuya raid was over. The series of disturbances that had begun with Roe2's letter had helped him make up his mind; in that respect, they'd been useful.

Time was moving, and they couldn't stay in the same place forever.

Starting tomorrow, they'd have to tackle a new challenge.

Riezé poked her head in from the corridor. "You're in here, Master Shiroe?" she said, stepping into the room crowded with magic devices.

"There was no hidden treasure. I'm impressed the device was safe."

"It doesn't seem to have been broken completely."

"I expect the damage was slight because we tore the enemy away from it. Excellent work, commander."

"You were a huge help, Riezé."

Shiroe smiled at her, scratching his head. He didn't really understand why Akatsuki was nodding next to him, but this girl from D.D.D. really had saved him. He felt that her organization of the rear attack ranks and constantly indicating the order in which the enemy was to be destroyed had made a big contribution to the success of the capture. She was a first-rate commander.

"I'm told the Round Table Council is receiving inquiries from all over, and they're terribly busy. Shall we go back for now? It's going to be quite some time before the transmitter is operational, isn't it?"

As she made the suggestion, Riezé put a finger to her chin, looking thoughtful.

She had a point: They couldn't stay in this ruin forever. Thinking he'd have to issue orders to move out soon, Shiroe scanned the hall.

Fortunately, more than half the members were in this room. His work as commander wouldn't be over until they made it back to headquarters.

"...lo...Hello? Can anybody hear— Hello?"

Just as he was about to address the group, however, sounds that were different from earlier, sounds that meant something, issued from the magic device. As if summoning them to a new adventure, the ancient magical equipment from the age of the alvs had brought them news from a distant land.

2

Everyone had been caught off guard, and for a moment, the room was silent.

"*...Ni hao. Bonjour, aloha. Moi! Also moikka!*"

In the midst of that hush, the magic device kept repeating oblivious greetings. The cheerful voice belonged to a young woman. No one answered. After all, they'd only been testing the device, and no one had expected to get a response from anywhere.

"*Kaliméra. Hujambo... Guten Tag... Other than that, um... 'Me eat you whole'?*"

"We can hear you. The noise is really bad, but... Who are you?"

Shiroe was the first to recover.

He'd responded mainly out of a sense of duty—as the person who was currently in charge, he couldn't just stay silent—but the reply that came back was unexpected.

"*Hmm? Your voice... That wouldn't be Shiro-boy, would it?*"

"Huh?"

At the sound of his own name, Shiroe froze up. There weren't that many people who'd know his voice. Of course lots of Akiba's Adventurers knew Shiroe, but he didn't think there were thirty people who'd be able to recognize him from his voice alone. In other words, this was a friend. "Hey, that voice... Wasn't that...?" "Meow, it couldn't be." His companions were talking behind him, but he wasn't listening to them. Lowering his own voice, Shiroe spoke to Li Gan.

"Where is this connected to? Doesn't it have some sort of detection function? Did it just connect to something nearby?"

Li Gan shook his head vigorously in response. His expression seemed to say he hadn't made a mistake, and he hadn't done anything unnecessary to the equipment. *It's not like he's a little kid who's gotten into mischief; I wouldn't get mad about something like that*, Shiroe thought. Either way, apparently Li Gan wasn't going to be any help here.

Even if this was a friend of Shiroe's, he couldn't think of anyone who'd call him Shiro-boy.

I don't like that name. It sounds sort of doglike. As far as he was concerned, "Shiro" was a name for pet dogs. He didn't hate it so much that he'd fly off the handle just because someone had called him that, but it was embarrassing, and it felt like he was being made fun of. For that reason, there was only one woman who called him Shiro-boy…and they couldn't possibly have made contact with her.

"*I knew it! Yoo-hoo! Shiro-booooy!*"

"Kanami?!"

It was impossible, but they'd reached her anyway.

"*It's been forever! How've you been?*"

"Don't give me that 'it's been forever' line!"

Shiroe responded on reflex; he felt dizzy, and his vision seemed to be dimming. It was anemia. He'd never gotten anemia before, but he was sure that was it.

Why now? He wasn't good with this person. He'd go so far as to call her a natural enemy. If someone had asked him to think of one person he'd absolutely never be able to deal with adequately, he'd have told them "Kanami."

It wasn't that he didn't like her. It wasn't that he wanted to avoid her. He just couldn't keep up with her.

He respected her, he felt obligated to her, and he thought she was a good person. Her cheerfulness and charisma were the biggest elements behind the fact that the Debauchery Tea Party had managed to spend a long time in the raid rankings, even though it wasn't a guild. Shiroe had been nothing more than a gloomy game expert, and it was thanks to her that he'd been able to experience the best part of MMOs: working together with companions to conquer content.

She'd been outrageous and impudent, but the Tea Party had been a group of people who loved partying and making noise, and he didn't think a single one of them had disliked her for it.

That boisterous personality was why Shiroe was simply not good with this woman. She was a human typhoon who treated him like her honorary little brother at every turn.

"*Oh, hey, I heard! I heard all about it. You're doing all sorts of fun stuff in Yamato, too, huh?! Like the Round Table thingummy!*"

"It's the Round Table Council. How do you know about that? And actually, Kanami, didn't you retire?! When did you come back?! Where are you?!"

And what on earth was a "thingummy"?

Shiroe, who'd knee-jerk answered, felt a little depressed again. With people who never listened to what other people said, he ended up letting his spinal nerves do the talking, too. Or rather, it was less "talking" than "retorting." Not only that, but since Shiroe's words just got ignored, it was pretty tiring.

Isn't she careless? he'd asked Naotsugu once.

Because she's a careless person, yeah. The answer he'd gotten hadn't been any kind of resolution, and it had only drained more of his energy.

"Kanami, you wouldn't be on the moon, would you?"

Through his fatigue, he did his best to ask questions in a business-like way, and her reply was, *"No, on the Chinese server.*

"We're currently on a journey, but we stumbled onto this TV station. It looked like it might work, so we messed with it. And then you picked up."

"You 'stumbled onto'…?"

Shiroe pinched the bridge of his nose.

In other words, after Kanami had moved to Europe, she must have gotten back into *Elder Tales.* The MMORPG had had players all over the world. Europe had had two servers, and it had been one of the most active regions, right up there with North America and Japan. He hadn't even considered the possibility, but if she'd changed her entire account, he could understand why there hadn't been any word from her.

Shiroe didn't know whether this was good news or bad.

There was almost nothing about Kanami that he understood clearly to begin with. He didn't want to know, he didn't think he should know, and he didn't think it would be better if he did know.

"Oh, that's right! Listen to this, Shiro-boy! My daughter turned three!"

"I know."

There were plenty of things it was better not to know.

"Huh? Did I tell you already?"

"No. I heard, though."

"I see..."

He could picture Kanami, eyes round, looking startled. She'd put her hands on her hips and puff out her chest, she'd squish up her soft-looking cheeks, and she'd nod as though she understood everything, even though she wasn't actually thinking anything at all. That was the kind of woman she was.

She had a big mouth, and she always seemed to be laughing.

Her sense of distance was busted, and she'd often tromped right into Shiroe's personal space, to the point where he and Naotsugu had formed a victims' association together.

She had outstanding energy, and she'd been that way even when they'd met offline.

Kanami's vitality had seemed inexhaustible, and she'd always done everything at full power. That had been the same both in the outside world and in the game. She was a natural leader and naturally cheerful. When you were around her, it always felt as if a summer wind were blowing.

Shiroe's parents had been very busy, and he hadn't had many friends even when he was a kid, so he'd never gone to leisure facilities to play. It was because of his friends, Naotsugu and Kanami, that Shiroe had built up experience with "going out and having fun."

To Shiroe, dealing with the impossible tasks she set up for him was what the Tea Party had been all about, which meant he'd spent the majority of his time in *Elder Tales*, since middle school, on things like that.

When he tried tallying them up again, the woman was a complete nuisance. You could even have called her destructive. It was only natural that he wasn't good with her. It was so bad that he didn't want to understand why she'd been such a hit as a charismatic leader.

Shiroe looked down for just a moment. He saw his own feet, standing firmly on the stone floor. His fists were clenched, but not hard, and they weren't trembling. He exhaled a little, steeling himself.

"I'm sorry I wasn't able to congratulate you... Congratulations," he told Kanami.

He'd thought the lines were something he'd never actually tell her, but he'd practiced them hundreds of times anyway, and he said them in a voice as close to normal as he could manage.

"I tell you what, my daughter's unbelievably cute. She zooms all over the place! She does this rocket dash and hits you—boom!—like a suicide attack, then clings to you real tight. She's a princess."

She'd left the Tea Party because she'd gone to Europe to study abroad, following the guy she'd married. Shiroe hadn't known much about him, other than he was German. He'd only found out that he was a doctor affiliated with an international NGO called Doctors of the World after the Tea Party had disbanded, and he'd learned that through KR.

That didn't mean he'd known nothing. Just before the Tea Party had broken up, Kanami had been exhilarated, so she'd told them all sorts of fragmented information, like how hairy his legs were, and that he liked sashimi, and that he'd teared up on the scream machine at the amusement park, and that he could only say *ohayou gozaimasu*—"good morning"—as "oyohan gojyamasu." Kanami had looked happy, and she'd been even more energetic than usual; it had been a serious nuisance.

Boasting about the people she was close to was part of Kanami's character. Shiroe knew she bragged about the Tea Party members all over the place, too. For that reason, when she told him about her daughter, he managed to feel warm inside.

Come to think of it, there were probably a lot of Adventurers in situations like Kanami's.

Adventurers who'd been separated from children who were still small. Getting separated from young family members wasn't the only tragedy, of course. Most Adventurers probably had people who had been hard to leave, parents and siblings, back on Earth. Shiroe thought that, for those people as well, he had to find a hint somehow.

Kanami must be traveling in search of that sort of thing, too. She was a complete terror and an awful leader, but her daughter was blameless. Feeling that it was a miracle that this sort of thing had happened on the very day he'd resolved to work toward a return home, Shiroe spoke to her.

"Is that right—? In that case, we really do have to get back. To our old world, I mean."

"...Huh? Why?"

"Huh?"

As usual, Kanami casually smashed Shiroe's idea.

"Shiro! Listen, I want to show this world to my daughter!"

"...Huh?"

Shiroe was taken aback, and the only response he could manage was a dim-sounding one.

He'd thought it many times—no, hundreds of times—before, but what on Earth was this person? He didn't understand what she meant, and his heart churned with doubts. He had no idea what she was thinking.

"Seriously. Theldesia's amazing, isn't it? I mean, it's this huge, rolling expanse of uncharted world! It's enormous and gorgeous and fantastic, and it's full of Mommy's friends, and it's a grand adventure where you meet people from all over the world. I absolutely want my daughter to do something like that!"

Kanami's voice was cheerful.

"She likes high places. I want to let her ride a griffin. I want to show her vast forests and the ocean and deserts. When she's surprised, her eyes go really round. I want to show her that the world she was born into is a beautiful place!"

But all she was talking about was her daughter.

Kanami's love was the real thing. She'd never been clever enough to lie or fake it. Her recklessness, her insolence, and everything that made bystanders think she was messing with people—all those things were just Kanami being serious.

And so Shiroe knew.

Apparently, she was actually planning to bring her daughter here.

Unexpectedly, Shiroe felt excited.

Everything he'd been worried about had started to seem ridiculous. He felt as if he'd seen Kanami talking about castles in the air, wearing an unguarded smile.

He realized that, after spending time away from her, he really had forgotten about her a little bit. Now that he was hearing her voice like this again, she was several times more absurd than he'd remembered. She really was the woman he'd been bad with.

He worried and hesitated over problems, and he suffered and drew up meticulous plans so that he wouldn't have to do those things that bothered him, but she just leapt jauntily over them. She was an exasperating hero.

"My liege."

"Shiroe?"

Akatsuki and Minori looked up at him, worried, but he was able to smile at them.

"That's fine, too... I thought it couldn't be done, and I'd given up on it, but in that case..."

After all, we're greedy. If we're trying for something, even if it's neither going home nor being buried in this world...

...that's a choice we can make.

In short, that was what Kanami had been talking about.

They wouldn't choose one or the other. They'd choose both, and they'd wish for a future beyond that. Shiroe had been desperately telling himself that that was greedy, and he felt ridiculous. Apparently, even his biggest ambition had been small as far as Kanami was concerned. Still, if that dream existed, then it would be all right for Shiroe to obtain it.

"We'll make it possible to go back and forth between Earth and Theldesia."

When he put it into words, he heard a stir run through the people around him.

He could understand that. When it came to attaining that hope, they didn't even know where to begin. People had thought, *It would be wonderful if we could do that*, but everyone had been hesitant to say it.

Even if they made it happen, Earth had a modern civilization, while Theldesia had medieval science. Earth had no magic technology, and Theldesia was a fantasy world. Contact between those two worlds was bound to have a drastic influence on both of them. It might even happen on a destructive scale.

Shiroe thought that was all right.

He didn't plan to ignore that danger or to take part in terrorism. However, if the two worlds were on a path that would put them in contact with each other, it would probably be arrogant for him to try to stop it from happening on his own. If the worlds were on a course that would prevent them from meeting, then no matter what Shiroe did personally, they'd probably never meet.

At the stage when they were deciding on a destination, both cowardice and arrogance were unnecessary emotions. There was no need to be frightened of possibilities they didn't clearly understand.

"I-is that possible?!"

"It'll work, it'll work."

His thoughts about the two worlds' influence on each other were scrambled by Kanami's incredibly bright words, until they were in danger of becoming shapeless. However, even then, Shiroe had companions.

"That's just irresponsible!!"

"Yeah, that's Kanami for ya. Real-tough-to-deal-with city."

"This person's amazing. She's startled even me, and I'm an idol."

That was why Shiroe was able to shrug his shoulders and laugh. Even firing verbal jabs at Kanami wasn't his own private penalty game anymore.

"So, Shiro-boy! Get out there and make that happen, please!"

"Are you issuing a quest?"

"Yeah, that! It's a quest."

"…I can't."

Maybe because he'd laughed for the first time in ages, his heart was bright and cheerful. Inside Shiroe, even as he teased her, the time that had passed was slowly vanishing.

"Whaaaaaat?! Did you get all mean on me, Shiro-boy?!"

Time had passed.

It was as if a scab that had been clinging to the inside of his heart, one Shiroe himself hadn't noticed, had sloughed off, leaving things clean.

Apparently, he wasn't Shiroe of the Debauchery Tea Party anymore. The realization made him feel just a little sadness and far more pride.

"Kanami. I've created a guild. It's called Log Horizon. I've made friends and companions."

"Uh-huh?"

He'd become Shiroe of Log Horizon. He was looking directly at all his companions: Minori, who was gazing at him worriedly; Akatsuki, who'd pinched up the tail of his mantle; Naotsugu, who was smirking;

Nyanta, whose eyes had narrowed in a smile; Touya, who didn't look worried at all; Isuzu and Rundelhaus; and Tetora, who was getting carried away. He had companions now.

That was why time had passed.

"As a result, I can't accept a request like that one."

"WhaaaaAAAaaat?"

"Because *we'll* complete that quest— We'll be the first ones in the world to see that view. Right; I guess we'll be competing with you, Kanami. I suppose there's no help for that..."

Packing as much retaliation as he could into his jeer, Shiroe spoke across the magic device. Like a shore washed by waves, over and over, he felt the Tea Party slowly coming to an end.

He'd probably made a mistake, somewhere along the way.

Something that should have ended hadn't done so. Those days had been magnificent. The Debauchery Tea Party had been a good place. In order to establish that as fact, they had allowed things to end. That was only natural. However, it was possible that Shiroe hadn't been able to do it very well.

Not that there's much I can do well anyway.

He had the leeway to laugh a little.

How strange: On the day he'd decided to head toward the future, the past had said its good-byes to him.

It wasn't a painful thing. At the very least, it was far more peaceful than the days when the Tea Party was disbanding, and it brimmed over with a quiet light.

The memories wouldn't disappear. On the contrary: Now the past would begin to turn into memories. This struck Shiroe as a hushed blessing, and he tucked it away in his heart, feeling something like affection.

"We're rivals now, after all."

"I see."

"Still, we do go way back. If you make it here in time, I don't mind letting you see it, too. If you're on the Chinese server, it's because you're headed this way, correct?"

If he saw her again, it felt as if he might not be as bad with her as he had been before. Shiroe almost thought that, but then he shook his head.

It wasn't as if Kanami herself had repented of anything. He considered the idea that having a child might have cured her troublemaking ways, but he decided not to get his hopes up based on wishful thinking.

"I'd expect no less from everybody's bus guide. No wonder Krus-Krus talks you up so much. I bet the girls can't leave you alone."

"Look, would you quit joking around like— What? Krusty?!"

Speak of the devil. Shiroe began to feel a dark dismay. It didn't help that, behind him, Riezé gave a wordless scream and started repeating "Milord, Milord."

Shiroe and Naotsugu were fairly used to her, but Riezé was an outsider, and the stimulation had been too much for her. As Shiroe had thought, Kanami was still Kanami. For better or for worse, she was a natural problem child who somehow managed to draw nothing but jokers. There was no other way to describe her. Why had Krusty's name come up now?

"Right, right, he's over here. Y'know, Krus-Krus almost died, but he's such a toughie you wouldn't believe it—"

"You're telling me Krusty's on the Chinese server? Kanami, what have you gotten involved in over there? Do you need help? Let me talk to Krusty—"

Even so, the questions he'd desperately asked ended up being left unfinished.

"Whoa…oh…acting up…rgh… Punch it, kick it… Argh! Tiger Echo…"

The magic device fell silent, and an indescribable atmosphere filled the room.

Shoulders slumping, Shiroe turned around.

Li Gan shook his head, pleading not guilty. Naotsugu held his head, and—unusually—Nyanta averted his eyes. Nazuna was grinning, Soujirou was smiling cheerfully, and Riezé looked unsteady, as though she'd come close to fainting.

Tetora seemed to have put some sort of idea into Minori's and Akatsuki's heads. "It's nothing. It's not like that," Shiroe told them, defending himself. Then he informed the capture unit, which was on the brink of an uproar, that they were returning to Akiba.

It was a disorganized ending, but even so, to Shiroe, it was an irreplaceable one as well. As with all endings, it held the hint of a new beginning.

Shiroe nodded and spoke to his companions. A season they couldn't escape was bearing down, not just on Log Horizon, but on the town of Akiba and on the Adventurers.

It was the eve of the season in which, through an encounter, Shiroe and the others would carve open new horizons—the beginning of the Noosphere.

<Log Horizon, Volume 10: Homesteading the Noosphere—The End>

MAP TOKYO / CHIBA

IN THE OLD WORLD, HOW LONG WOULD IT TAKE TO GET FROM AKIBA, WHERE SHIROE AND COMPANY ARE BASED, TO SHIBUYA AND MAIHAMA, THE SCENES OF THE BATTLES IN THIS BOOK?

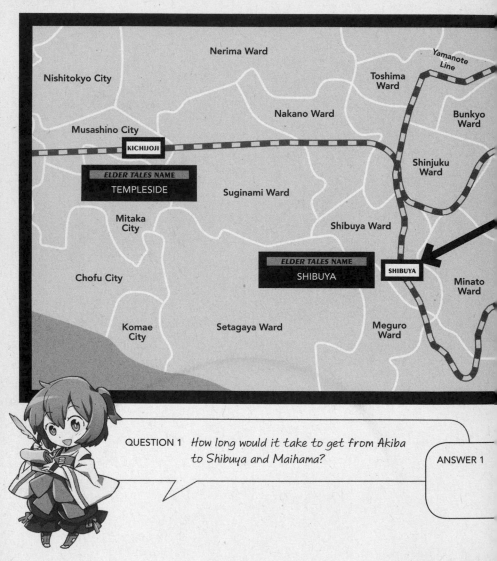

Nerima Ward

Yamanote Line

Nishitokyo City

Toshima Ward

Nakano Ward

Bunkyo Ward

Musashino City

KICHIJOJI

Shinjuku Ward

ELDER TALES NAME
TEMPLESIDE

Suginami Ward

Mitaka City

Shibuya Ward

Chofu City

ELDER TALES NAME
SHIBUYA

SHIBUYA

Minato Ward

Komae City

Setagaya Ward

Meguro Ward

QUESTION 1 *How long would it take to get from Akiba to Shibuya and Maihama?*

ANSWER 1

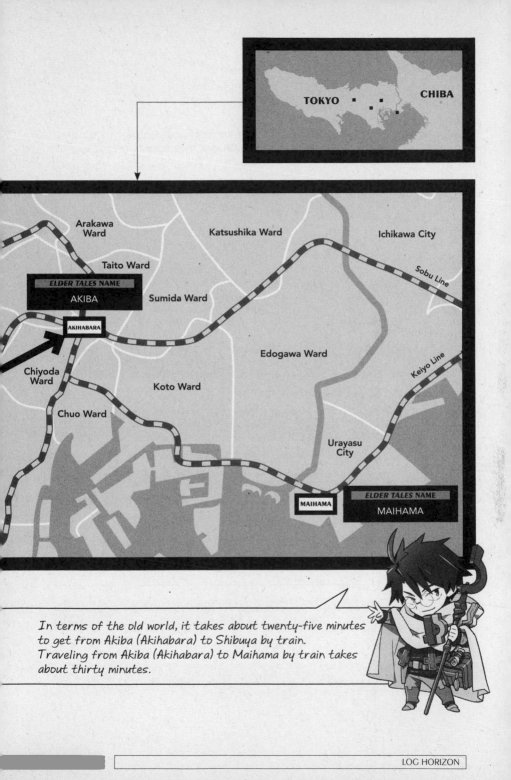

TOKYO · · · CHIBA

Arakawa Ward

Katsushika Ward

Ichikawa City

Taito Ward

Sobu Line

ELDER TALES NAME
AKIBA

Sumida Ward

AKIHABARA

Edogawa Ward

Chiyoda Ward

Koto Ward

Keiyo Line

Chuo Ward

Urayasu City

MAIHAMA

ELDER TALES NAME
MAIHAMA

In terms of the old world, it takes about twenty-five minutes to get from Akiba (Akihabara) to Shibuya by train.
Traveling from Akiba (Akihabara) to Maihama by train takes about thirty minutes.

PARTY

1

[First Party] Impenetrable Vanguard

The first party acts as the shield for the entire raid team. They are handpicked to stop attacks, not just in normal encounters, but from the powerful raid boss Taliktan as well. Due to differences in spell features, it would have been preferable to have a Druid as one of the three healers; however, out of consideration for the overall balance and because of Tetora's adaptability as a veteran healer, they used two Clerics instead. With the addition of support from Akatsuki, who acquired aggro control skills during the raid with the Water Maple Maidens, this is a lineup for long-term combat that gives total control of MP replenishment to the Enchanter Shiroe, facilitating recovery.

▸ **Naotsugu**

| **Race** Human | **Class** Guardian | **Subclass** Frontier Inspector |
| **Guild** Log Horizon | **Specialty** Anchor Howl |

"Bring it. Nobody-gets-past-me city."

▸ **Tetora**

| **Race** Human | **Class** Cleric | **Subclass** Idol |
| **Guild** Log Horizon | **Specialty** Aurora Heal |

"Yaaaaaaay! It's the first performance in galactic Idol Land!"

▸ **Marielle**

| **Race** Elf | **Class** Cleric | **Subclass** Woodworker |
| **Guild** The Crescent Moon League | **Specialty** Reactive Heal |

"I can do this! Reactive Heal!"

▸ **Kushiyatama**

| **Race** Elf | **Class** Kannagi | **Subclass** Chef |
| **Guild** Sun Path | **Specialty** Subjugating Divine Protection |

"I swear I'll make you cry! Stay right where you are!"

▸ **Akatsuki**

| **Race** Human | **Class** Assassin | **Subclass** Tracker |
| **Guild** Log Horizon | **Specialty** Assassinate, Accel Fang |

"My liege... Both my liege and I will be fine. Absolutely."

▸ **Shiroe**

| **Race** Half Alv | **Class** Enchanter | **Subclass** Scribe |
| **Guild** Log Horizon | **Specialty** (if he had to pick) Mana Channeling |

"Let's go. This is the main run of the capture operation."

▶ APPENDIX

(2) [Second Party] Mobile Unit

The role of the second party is mobile attacks. Ordinarily, this team is a bit like insurance: It's intended to deal with sudden enemy reinforcements, or to take over for the first party when it has to temporarily drop back from the front line due to any unforeseen circumstances that come up. However, during this raid, because of Soujirou's personality, it was sent on a preemptive assault. The primary axis of the second party is the teamwork between Soujirou and Nazuna. They've worked together in both the Tea Party and the West Wind Brigade, which lends a sense of history to the partnership. Many of the members of this raid were rather inexperienced, and the stability of this highly adaptable party really helped to keep the raid functioning.

▶ Soujirou
Race Human **Class** Samurai **Subclass** Master Swordsman	
Guild The West Wind Brigade **Specialty** Instant Desertion, Clairvoyance	

"Now that Mr. Shiro's made up his mind, there's just one role for me!"

▶ Nazuna
Race Foxtail **Class** Kannagi **Subclass** Gambler	
Guild The West Wind Brigade **Specialty** Purification Barrier, Celestial Passage	

"Now, there's a feast. Go get 'im, Souji!"

▶ Serara
Race Human **Class** Druid **Subclass** Housekeeper **Guild** The Crescent Moon League	
Specialty Servant Summoning: Great Wolf, Mercy Rain	

"Nyanta looks gallant when he's fighting, too. ♡ "

▶ Nyanta
Race Felinoid **Class** Swashbuckler **Subclass** Chef	
Guild Log Horizon **Specialty** Opening Gambit, Bloodletter	

"I'll tear mew to pieces!"

▶ Koen
Race Human **Class** Assassin **Subclass** Tracker	
Guild D.D.D. **Specialty** Fatal Ambush, Stealth Blade	

"Well, this warrior has been prepared since the moment I heard I'd be with you, Miz Buzzkill."

▶ Henrietta
Race Human **Class** Bard **Subclass** Accountant **Guild** The Crescent Moon League	
Specialty Mother of Mercy Anthem, Curtain Drops	

"Master Shiroe. Gentlemen should live...more selfishly."

PARTY

3

[Third Party] Magic Flank Attackers

The third party was created with a focus on attacking and annihilating the enemy. Ordinarily, with two warriors and two healers, their attack power wouldn't be that great. However, combined with the fact that the low-level members were able to charge without worrying about aggro, they produced quite good results in combat. This was probably because the Monk Richou, who would normally have been a tank, fought enthusiastically, and this meshed well with Minori and Touya's synchronized midfield support, and the magic attacks from the two members in the rear. Since it did mean their fuel consumption was bad, they took a lot of breaks during combat.

| ▶ **Richou** | **Race** Felinoid | **Class** Monk | **Subclass** Berserker |
| | **Guild** D.D.D. | **Specialty** Tiger Echo Fist, Tiger Stance | |

"You youngsters are working hard. I've got a few years on you, so let me show off out there."

| ▶ **Touya** | **Race** Human | **Class** Samurai | **Subclass** Apprentice |
| | **Guild** Log Horizon | **Specialty** Izuna Cutter, Voice-Withering Blade | |

"We'll go home after everything's settled!"

| ▶ **Minori** | **Race** Human | **Class** Kannagi | **Subclass** Accountant |
| | **Guild** Log Horizon | **Specialty** Defense of Doctrine Barrier, Protective Talisman | |

"To catch up to the one I idolize—Defense of Doctrine Barrier!"

| ▶ **Fragrant Olive** | **Race** Elf | **Class** Druid | **Subclass** Scribe |
| | **Guild** The West Wind Brigade | **Specialty** Summon Storm, Rotten Apple | |

"Oooooh, Master Sou's so manly! ...Agh. Nosebleed?!"

| ▶ **Riezé** | **Race** Half Alv | **Class** Sorcerer | **Subclass** Tactician |
| | **Guild** D.D.D. | **Specialty** Freezing Liner, Frost Spear | |

"Let's see the true skill of the famed Tea Party counselor."

| ▶ **Yuzuko** | **Race** Human | **Class** Summoner | **Subclass** Apprentice |
| | **Guild** D.D.D. | **Specialty** Servant Summoning: Salamander, Servant Forge | |

"This is for my Water Maple friends. Of course I'll do my best."

[Fourth Party] Main Physical Attackers

The fourth party was built for physical attacks. Both Shouryuu, a Swashbuckler, and Hien, an Assassin, were at the top level, and they had more than enough destructive power, but they were short on raid experience. Isuzu and Rundelhaus supported the midfield, but their levels were too low. The skills of Isami and Kurinon of the West Wind Brigade, who led those four, are worthy of respect. Rundelhaus cut down on the number of attack spells he used and applied support magic to the physical attack classes. This and other moves made them the heart and soul of damage output in this raid, in terms of the ability to keep fighting as well.

▶ **Isami**

Race Human **Class** Samurai **Subclass** Accountant
Guild The West Wind Brigade **Specialty** Izuna Cutter, Fire Wheel Sword

"If this is all they've got, I can tough it out longer!!"

▶ **Kurinon**

Race Human **Class** Cleric **Subclass** War Priest
Guild The West Wind Brigade **Specialty** Legend Cape, Pass Judgment

"Ooh. Oh my. Girls wiping off the sweat of battle. That sparkling scent!"

▶ **Rundelhaus**

Race Human **Class** Sorcerer **Subclass** Adventurer
Guild Log Horizon **Specialty** Burned Stake, Orb of Lava

"Feel the results of my training! Burned Stake!!"

▶ **Isuzu**

Race Human **Class** Bard **Subclass** Nomad **Guild** Log Horizon
Specialty Moonlit Mermaid's Lullaby, Circular Carol

"Okay, Rudy, I'll match you!!"

▶ **Shouryuu**

Race Wolf-Fang **Class** Swashbuckler **Subclass** Hero
Guild The Crescent Moon League **Specialty** Round Windmill, Discard

"At least shape up at a time like this, Madoka!!"

▶ **Hien**

Race Foxtail **Class** Assassin **Subclass** Brigand
Guild The Crescent Moon League **Specialty** Atrophy Break, Suppression Shot

"Let's get this pain-in-the-butt job done fast and go home, Shousuke."

ISUZU'S DAY

06:00 Wake up. Look out the window and decide on the morning's schedule.
06:20 Tag along on walk. Shrink back from too-energetic guild mate.
07:00 Take an early shower.
07:30 The Captain's breakfasts are the best. ♪

09:00 Go out hunting. Have finally gotten used to riding a horse. If taking a cart, may play lute.

12:30 Lunch is round bread and omelets and potatoes. Serara makes soup.
13:00 Start hunting again.
14:00 It ends fast!
14:30 Hunting is over, but if something looks noteworthy, we pick it up on the way home. Finding nuts or fruit is lucky because it makes for fancier dinners.

16:00 Arrive in Akiba. The horse went home, so carry cargo back to guild center on foot. Take souvenir to Marielle. Then there's free time. Serara comes along today.
16:30 Make rabbit stew in the Crescent Moon League kitchen. We occasionally have joint cooking days like this one. Captain Nyanta needs a break sometimes, too.
19:00 Rudy, you're cramming too much in.
19:30 Rudy, you're too discouraged.

20:00 Do stretches in living room with Minori. Shiroe and the others are chatting in the evening cool. We play card games sometimes. I play the lute.
20:30 Bath. Time to get all clean.
21:30 Mystery snack received. A present? Why? Apparently, Nyanta made it as an experiment because he didn't cook dinner. Lost to temptation and ate it.
22:30 Got sleepy, so gathering broke up. Today was a really full day, too.

RUNDELHAUS'S DAY

05:15 Wake up. Sunrise is still far off in winter, but waking early is a habit.
06:00 Finish grooming. Head out for morning training, but spend time doing warm-ups in the entry hall. One should always be thoroughly prepared.
06:30 True nobles do not neglect their training.
07:15 Return to guild and race into shower. Sometimes get very into training, so end up rushing.
07:30 Breakfast. The Captain's breakfasts are superb.

09:00 Go hunting with Touya, Minori, Isuzu, and Serara.
10:30 Arrive at hunting ground. Battle monsters while gathering items.

12:30 Lunch is round bread and omelets and potatoes. Serara makes soup.

14:00 It's a little early, but get ready to go home.

16:00 Take side trips, then arrive at Akiba. From here on out, there's free time.
16:30 Take souvenirs from the day's hunting to assembly hall. Write "Today's Expedition" in group notebook. People of the Earth friends are doing their best in Akiba, as usual
18:30 Go to Crescent Moon League to meet and act as escort.
19:00 Dinner. Isuzu helped cook tonight. It's delicious, and I eat too much... I'm a hamster? I, who have been called the snow wolf of fashionable society? That's a shock.
20:00 Informal meeting with older guild members. Time to learn all I can. Ask for stories about "Earth." Arithmetic is too hard.
21:00 Take baths by turns. Have caught Touya's love of baths.
21:30 Sneak into kitchen. Almost never do this, but heard there was hidden treasure there today. Think I've been eating more since I became an Adventurer.
22:00 Go to bed. Staying up late would drain tomorrow's energy..

6:00

12:00

18:0

24:0

3:00

A
DAY
IN
THE
MEMBERS'
LIVES
PART 2!

CALASIN'S DAY

07:00 Wake up. Make several wake-up calls with invitations to breakfast, but get turned down coldly.

07:45 Eat breakfast at guild house's café annex. Taro brings work right in the middle of the meal. Apparently, he forgot to bring it yesterday. Decide to put it in Magic Bag and "forget" it.

09:00 Field business at Shopping District 8. Tomokazu is training a newer member (cat-girl). I feel kind of depressed.

11:00 Check inventory while touring shops. Issue orders via telechat, without writing things down. Sorry, Taro, but take notes, 'kay?

12:00 Arrive in Akiba. Have lunch in dining hall. Whoo-hoo! I got a present! Even half an order of fried chicken from a girl is delicious.

13:00 Shuffle papers at Production Guild Liaison Committee. Minori helps. I feel soothed.

15:00 Write ton of letters. Can't use telechats with People of the Earth. Just can't use them. Have to get supplies from them, so although it's a pain, it can't be helped. The set of one hundred filled-in template letters Shiroe made me is incredible.

17:00 Finish work. After all, our guild is good to its workers. Mwa-ha-ha. Ride Giant Owl and head back to Maihama.

17:20 Arrive in Maihama. Land at guesthouse I'm borrowing and have staff meeting. Change clothes quickly. Hurry, hurry.

18:00 Eighth Street Dinner Show begins! Cat dancers come on from both sides. Blush.

19:00 Looks like everyone had fun, so I go around the table and give handshakes. You know, I just wanted to talk business, so what's with the handshake session? I mean, I got the contract so it's fine, but really.

19:30 Aggravating, so I make Taro the center and have a singing show.

20:00 Going to Tsukuba next week. They call it the Magic City. Bet they'll buy writing implements and books. I'll tell 'em to bulk up the purchasing.

21:30 Dinner show ends. Simple wrap party in greenroom. I pour liquor for everybody. Can't relax until the party shifts to its next destination. Okay! Where's a girl I can take home with me…?

22:15 Dinner at a tavern with Isaac. This direct-run place has great food. It's the best! Whoo-hoo, fried rockfish is the best! I'll have another beer, too. It's a reward from me to me…

23:00 Why is that gorilla drinking ten beers, even though they're not a reward for anything?

25:20 Give report to Duke of Maihama's messenger. Sleepy. Can't do any more.

25:45 Sleep in borrowed room at Maihama. This hug-pillow will make a great product…

ISSAC'S DAY

07:00 Get up, pour cold water over head, then go look in on the knights' training. Can't do boring stuff like swinging swords around first thing in the morning, so I make 'em run.

08:15 Maihama knights are so positive lately it's creepy. I send 'em all flying. They get right back up. Dammit, Lezarik, you're casting too much recovery magic on 'em. What're you guys, zombies?

10:30 Started having fun, so forgot to hold back. Just heal that with fighting spirit.

11:30 Have breakfast/lunch. Ginger-pork set meal with double the meat. Yum. Don't really get it, but the People of the Earth have been real friendly lately. Maybe because of Iselus?

12:00 Get bored. Could go to afternoon training, but it's too high-pressure. If I look in at the Round Table Council, they'll just give me more work. Decide to go to Maihama Castle. It's cool there.

12:30 Get caught by the old guy. There's no help for it; hang out with him.

14:00 Escape and borrow a guest room. Perfect for naps. Thanks for showing me in here.

17:00 When I wake up, the maid (?) who showed me the room is standing outside it with a sword. Said she ran people off so it wouldn't get noisy. Both the men and women in Maihama have a real strong sense of duty. Let's go grab something to eat sometime.

18:00 Go to training site, but the hard training is over. Should've checked by telechat.

18:30 Borrow the bath at Calasin's place, then go out drinking.

19:00 Oops. They already figured out Calasin's direct-run tavern. Leza catches me and makes me do paperwork at a corner table. All I'm doing is signing stuff Leza wrote, but still. When I yell "Beer!" they bring me barley tea. That jerk Leza.

21:00 This is endless, and the idiots around me are getting drunk and drinking toasts. Whack 'em with the Black Sword.

21:30 Finally finish. Bleh.

22:00 Calasin shows up. Says he hasn't eaten, so we eat fried rockfish. More liquor. Left the rest of the work to Leza.

23:00 Finally getting warmed up. Summer's all about beer.

23:30 Okay, bedtime!

6:00

12:00

18:00

24:00

3:00

ISELUS'S DAY

HENRIETTA'S DAY

05:00 Get up, very quietly. This is free time. Practice with dagger in room.

06:30 Dress before maids come.

07:00 Breakfast. Am eating with my aunt today.

08:30 Morning greetings over. In the afternoon, we'll ride horses into town.

09:00 Sword practice. Recently got permission to enter training facility. Can't spar with knights yet, so just do practice swings…

11:00 Practice is over. Maid said to take bath, but took cold bath with Young Isaac and had him dry my head off. For men, that's enough! It is!

11:20 Lunch with Young Isaac. Ginger-pork sandwiches are delicious.

12:00 Say good-bye to Young Isaac and get ready to go out. Have them put saddle on at stable, then go to town. This is an inspection.

12:30 It sounds like the planned inspection is over. Was there a mix-up?

13:00 Eat roasted corn I was given in Maihama with the knights who are guarding me. Watching the town children run around makes me remember the pioneer village where I went to camp.

16:00 Travel around the farmland on the city's outskirts, then return to castle. Am taken away for bath.

17:30 Dinner. Family is at dinner party with a trader, so I'm alone. I wish my sister Raynesia were here…

18:30 History and rhetoric studies. My teacher was invited from Tsukuba.

20:00 Bedtime. Good night.

06:30 Wake up. Get dressed.

07:00 Go to wake Mari. Try just speaking to her, but she won't wake up. Go to kitchen and watch the cooking while going over the guild members' schedules.

08:00 Breakfast begins. We split into several groups and go to the cafeteria by turns. What with handing out box lunches, the cafeteria is at its busiest in the morning.

09:30 Start the latest breakfast with Mari. I did not join the earlier groups, so I partake along with her.

10:00 The next two hours are vital. Give Mari papers that need her approval and ask her to check them over. There's nowhere to run.

12:00 Lunchtime. If lunch is delayed, I sometimes have no appetite.

13:00 Mari's tummy is full, and she's cheerful. See her off, then get down to some serious desk work.

14:00 Guild work is finished. Go straight to the Round Table Council office. Use the Kunie Card and move the zone release work forward. Tohoku, Hokuriku, and Kanto areas are nearly complete. It's daunting work.

16:30 Am kept on my toes by various inquiries, and time flies. It reminds me of Master Shiroe's hard work.

18:00 Look in at Water Maple Manor for a few moments. As expected, she's there: I get my daily dose of Akatsuki.

19:30 Suppertime. We're joining Log Horizon today?

21:00 Take an early bath, and talk with the younger guild members about their days.

22:00 All right: one more job. Must tell Mari about the progress of the aristocrats' council, in a casual way.

22:30 A hasty delivery to Master Shiroe. Calling late at night is impolite, but I did accept his offer of tea.

23:30 Nighttime round of the guild hall. Lights out, everyone.

24:00 Good night.

RIEZÉ'S DAY

KUSHIYATAMA'S DAY

06:30 Wake up. One advantage of this world: Setting my curls doesn't take time.

07:00 A light breakfast of toast and black tea while I deal with accumulated documents... It's sweet!! This one was Miss Takayama's!

08:30 Meeting with guild's core members. Troubles are endless. Staff members interject their ordinary, inane stories on occasion. Well, they're trying to be encouraging.

09:00 Split up and perform Round Table Council and internal guild work. Once again, I realize the weight of Milord's presence... No, I mustn't be weak! I'll give this all I've got!

13:00 Take break from work and go to Water Maple Manor. A short tea party/luncheon with Raynesia and Akatsuki. Huh? Miss Kushi was making pasta until just a moment ago? And I missed her? No...

14:00 On returning to the guild castle, the mountain of documents has grown by 20%... To be perfectly honest, this bites.

16:00 An invitation to attend raid training from Richou. Are you certain? There are still a lot of documents to... Pardon? You've brought powerful reinforcements, so leave it to you?

17:00 Leave the document processing to the veterans and head to the training raid. Miss Kushi is here to cheer us on as well, and I'm bursting with enthusiasm! All right, it's time to bust some heads!

19:30 A posttraining barbecue. Three linked hibachi grills! Enormous meat! It's wicked-hot! ... Ahem. I—I was a bit improper there, wasn't I?

21:00 Heart and body satisfied, I refresh with a bath. Ordinarily, there would be a pile of documents on my desk, but they're being considerate today. I believe I'll take them up on that.

22:00 After stretching, review the day's combat. Spell-chant-connection image training.

23:30 Thanks to all, and good night.

05:00 Hear breakfast prep noises from kitchen and fully wake up. The People of the Earth who work at the guild house won't slack off from their jobs, no matter how often I tell them to.

07:30 Breakfast with everyone in dining hall. Bacon, eggs, and honey-cheese toast today. Am mildly worried about calorie count.

08:00 Stamp documents with my personal seal at mansion. Would love to ask why I have to deal with all the cleanup work from Yae's moneymaking, but as usual, she's disappeared.

12:00 Lunch at Water Maple Manor today. Give lecture on how to make pasta carbonara, at maids' request. More calories here...

13:00 Return to Templeside and lead the low-level team's hunt. Daruta has been getting carried away again lately, so I knock him around.

16:00 Go back to Akiba. Head to D.D.D. guild castle, without letting Ri-Ri see me. Plot with Richou. No, we're not doing anything bad.

17:00 Check on Yama. Everyone's way too earnest. I think worrying about the likes of Krusty is a waste of energy.

18:00 Get pulled into the D.D.D. training raid, then plunge into a BBQ. The calories... But what's the owner of Tonsuton doing here?

21:00 My stomach is heavy. When I drag myself back to the mansion, there's a telechat from Caille of the Marine Organization. Apparently, the figures on the delivery statement don't match up. I turn the pile of documents upside down, and there's a huge scene. Yae, where did you go?!

22:00 Rice porridge. Yum.

23:00 Accidentally fall asleep on office sofa. Living like this can't be good for my looks!

6:00

12:00

18:00

24:00

3:00

▶ELDER TALES

A "SWORD AND SORCERY"—THEMED ONLINE GAME AND ONE OF THE LARGEST IN THE WORLD. AN MMORPG FAVORED BY SERIOUS GAMERS, IT BOASTS A TWENTY-YEAR HISTORY.

▶THE CATASTROPHE

A TERM FOR THE INCIDENT IN WHICH USERS WERE TRAPPED INSIDE THE *ELDER TALES* GAME WORLD. IT AFFECTED THE THIRTY THOUSAND JAPANESE USERS WHO WERE ONLINE WHEN *HOMESTEADING THE NOOSPHERE*, THE GAME'S TWELFTH EXPANSION PACK, WAS INTRODUCED.

▶ADVENTURER

THE GENERAL TERM FOR A GAMER WHO IS PLAYING *ELDER TALES*. WHEN BEGINNING THE GAME, PLAYERS SELECT HEIGHT, CLASS, AND RACE FOR THESE IN-GAME DOUBLES. THE TERM IS MAINLY USED BY NON-PLAYER CHARACTERS TO REFER TO PLAYERS.

▶PEOPLE OF THE EARTH

THE NAME NON-PLAYER CHARACTERS USE FOR THEMSELVES. THE CATASTROPHE DRASTICALLY INCREASED THEIR NUMBERS FROM WHAT THEY WERE IN THE GAME. THEY NEED TO SLEEP AND EAT LIKE REGULAR PEOPLE, SO IT'S HARD TO TELL THEM APART FROM PLAYERS WITHOUT CHECKING THE STATUS SCREEN.

▶THE HALF-GAIA PROJECT

A PROJECT TO CREATE A HALF-SIZED EARTH INSIDE *ELDER TALES*. ALTHOUGH IT'S NEARLY THE SAME SHAPE AS EARTH, THE DISTANCES ARE HALVED, AND IT HAS ONLY ONE-FOURTH THE AREA.

▶AGE OF MYTH

A GENERAL TERM FOR THE ERA SAID TO HAVE BEEN DESTROYED IN THE OFFICIAL BACKSTORY OF THE *ELDER TALES* ONLINE GAME. IT WAS BASED ON THE CULTURE AND CIVILIZATION OF THE REAL WORLD. SUBWAYS AND BUILDINGS ARE THE RUINED RELICS OF THIS ERA.

▶THE OLD WORLD

THE WORLD WHERE SHIROE AND THE OTHERS LIVED BEFORE *ELDER TALES* BECAME ANOTHER WORLD AND TRAPPED THEM. A TERM FOR EARTH, THE REAL WORLD, ETC.

▶GUILDS

TEAMS COMPOSED OF MULTIPLE PLAYERS. MANY PLAYERS BELONG TO THEM, BOTH BECAUSE IT'S EASIER TO CONTACT AFFILIATED MEMBERS AND INVITE THEM ON ADVENTURES AND ALSO BECAUSE GUILDS PROVIDE CONVENIENT SERVICES (SUCH AS MAKING IT EASIER TO RECEIVE AND SEND ITEMS).

▶THE ROUND TABLE COUNCIL

THE TOWN OF AKIBA'S SELF-GOVERNMENT ORGANIZATION, FORMED AT SHIROE'S PROPOSAL. COMPOSED OF ELEVEN GUILDS, INCLUDING MAJOR COMBAT AND PRODUCTION GUILDS AND GUILDS THAT COLLECTIVELY REPRESENT SMALL AND MIDSIZED GUILDS, IT'S IN A POSITION TO LEAD THE REFORMATION IN AKIBA.

▶LOG HORIZON

THE NAME OF THE GUILD SHIROE FORMED AFTER THE CATASTROPHE. ITS FOUNDING MEMBERS—AKATSUKI, NAOTSUGU, AND NYANTA—HAVE BEEN JOINED BY THE TWINS MINORI AND TOUYA. THEIR HEADQUARTERS IS IN A RUINED BUILDING PIERCED BY A GIANT ANCIENT TREE ON THE OUTSKIRTS OF AKIBA.

▶THE CRESCENT MOON LEAGUE

THE NAME OF THE GUILD MARI LEADS. ITS PRIMARY PURPOSE IS TO SUPPORT MIDLEVEL PLAYERS. HENRIETTA, MARI'S FRIEND SINCE THEIR DAYS AT A GIRLS' HIGH SCHOOL, ACTS AS ITS ACCOUNTANT.

▶THE DEBAUCHERY TEA PARTY

THE NAME OF A GROUP OF PLAYERS THAT SHIROE, NAOTSUGU, AND NYANTA BELONGED TO AT ONE TIME. IT WAS ACTIVE FOR ABOUT TWO YEARS, AND ALTHOUGH IT WASN'T A GUILD, IT'S STILL REMEMBERED IN *ELDER TALES* AS A LEGENDARY BAND OF PLAYERS.

▶FAIRY RINGS

TRANSPORTATION DEVICES LOCATED IN FIELDS. THE DESTINATIONS ARE TIED TO THE PHASES OF THE MOON, AND IF PLAYERS USE THEM AT THE WRONG TIME, THERE'S NO TELLING WHERE THEY'LL END UP. AFTER THE CATASTROPHE, SINCE STRATEGY WEBSITES ARE INACCESSIBLE, ALMOST NO ONE USES THEM.

▶ZONE

A UNIT THAT DESCRIBES RANGE AND AREA IN *ELDER TALES*. IN ADDITION TO FIELDS, DUNGEONS, AND TOWNS, THERE ARE ZONES AS SMALL AS SINGLE HOTEL ROOMS. DEPENDING ON THE PRICE, IT'S SOMETIMES POSSIBLE TO BUY THEM.

▶THELDESIA

THE NAME FOR THE GAME WORLD CREATED BY THE HALF-GAIA PROJECT. A WORD THAT'S EQUIVALENT TO "EARTH" IN THE REAL WORLD.

▶SPECIAL SKILL

VARIOUS SKILLS USED BY ADVENTURERS. ACQUIRED BY LEVELING UP YOUR MAIN CLASS OR SUBCLASS. EVEN WITHIN THE SAME SKILL, THERE ARE FOUR RANKS— ELEMENTARY, INTERMEDIATE, ESOTERIC, AND SECRET—AND IT'S POSSIBLE TO MAKE SKILLS GROW BY INCREASING YOUR PROFICIENCY.

▶MAIN CLASS

THESE GOVERN COMBAT ABILITIES IN *ELDER TALES*, AND PLAYERS CHOOSE ONE WHEN BEGINNING THE GAME. THERE ARE TWELVE TYPES, THREE EACH IN FOUR CATEGORIES: WARRIOR, WEAPON ATTACK, RECOVERY, AND MAGIC ATTACK. SEE THE SECTION BELOW FOR DETAILS.

▶SUBCLASS

ABILITIES THAT AREN'T DIRECTLY INVOLVED IN COMBAT BUT COME IN HANDY DURING GAME PLAY. ALTHOUGH THERE ARE ONLY TWELVE MAIN CLASSES, THERE ARE OVER FIFTY SUBCLASSES, AND THEY'RE A JUMBLED MIX OF EVERYTHING FROM CONVENIENT SKILL SETS TO JOKE ELEMENTS.

▶MYSTERY

ALSO CALLED OVERSKILL BY SOME PLAYERS. UNIQUE, POWERFUL TECHNIQUES THAT ARE UNLIKE CONVENTIONAL SPECIAL SKILLS. CREATED WHEN INDIVIDUAL PLAYERS EVOLVE AND EXPAND ABILITIES FROM THE DAYS OF THE GAME.

▶ARC-SHAPED ARCHIPELAGO YAMATO

THE WORLD OF THELDESIA IS DESIGNED BASED ON REAL-WORLD EARTH. THE ARC-SHAPED ARCHIPELAGO YAMATO IS THE REGION THAT MAPS TO JAPAN, AND IT'S DIVIDED INTO FIVE AREAS: THE EZZO EMPIRE; THE DUCHY OF FOURLAND; THE NINE-TAILS DOMINION; EASTAL, THE LEAGUE OF FREE CITIES; AND THE HOLY EMPIRE OF WESTLANDE.

▶CAST TIME

THE PREPARATION TIME NEEDED WHEN USING A SPECIAL SKILL. THESE ARE SET FOR EACH SEPARATE SKILL, AND MORE POWERFUL SKILLS TEND TO HAVE LONGER CAST TIMES. WITH COMBAT-TYPE SPECIAL SKILLS, IT'S POSSIBLE TO MOVE DURING CAST TIME, BUT WITH MAGIC-BASED SKILLS, SIMPLY MOVING INTERRUPTS CASTING.

▶ MAIN CLASSES

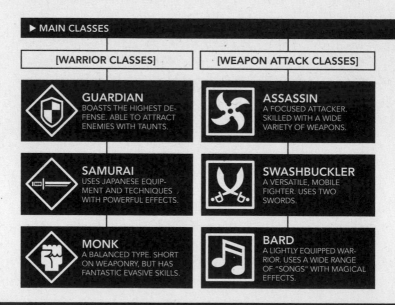

[WARRIOR CLASSES]

GUARDIAN
BOASTS THE HIGHEST DEFENSE. ABLE TO ATTRACT ENEMIES WITH TAUNTS.

SAMURAI
USES JAPANESE EQUIPMENT AND TECHNIQUES WITH POWERFUL EFFECTS.

MONK
A BALANCED TYPE. SHORT ON WEAPONRY, BUT HAS FANTASTIC EVASIVE SKILLS.

[WEAPON ATTACK CLASSES]

ASSASSIN
A FOCUSED ATTACKER. SKILLED WITH A WIDE VARIETY OF WEAPONS.

SWASHBUCKLER
A VERSATILE, MOBILE FIGHTER. USES TWO SWORDS.

BARD
A LIGHTLY EQUIPPED WARRIOR. USES A WIDE RANGE OF "SONGS" WITH MAGICAL EFFECTS.

▶MOTION BIND

REFERS TO THE WAY YOUR BODY FREEZES UP AFTER YOU'VE USED A SPECIAL SKILL.
DURING MOTION BIND, ALL ACTIONS ARE IMPOSSIBLE, INCLUDING MOVEMENT.

▶RECAST TIME

THE AMOUNT OF TIME YOU HAVE TO WAIT AFTER YOU'VE USED A SPECIAL SKILL
BEFORE YOU CAN USE IT AGAIN. THIS RESTRICTION MAKES IT VERY DIFFICULT TO
USE A SPECIFIC SPECIAL SKILL SEVERAL TIMES IN A ROW. SOME SPECIAL SKILLS
HAVE SUCH LONG RECAST TIMES THAT THEY CAN BE USED ONLY ONCE PER DAY.

▶CALL OF HOME

A BASIC TYPE OF SPECIAL SKILL THAT ALL ADVENTURERS LEARN. IT INSTANTLY
RETURNS YOU TO THE LAST SAFE AREA WITH A TEMPLE THAT YOU VISITED, BUT
ONCE YOU USE IT, YOU CAN'T USE IT AGAIN FOR TWENTY-FOUR HOURS.

▶RAID

THE TERM FOR A BATTLE FOUGHT WITH NUMBERS LARGER THAN THE NORMAL
SIX-MEMBER PARTIES THAT ADVENTURERS USUALLY FORM. IT CAN ALSO BE USED
TO REFER TO A UNIT MADE UP OF MANY PEOPLE. FAMOUS EXAMPLES INCLUDE
TWENTY-FOUR-MEMBER FULL RAIDS AND NINETY-SIX-MEMBER LEGION RAIDS.

▶RACE

THERE ARE A VARIETY OF HUMANOID RACES IN THE WORLD OF THELDESIA.
ADVENTURERS MAY CHOOSE TO PLAY AS ONE OF EIGHT RACES: HUMAN; ELF,
DWARF, HALF ALV, FELINOID, WOLF-FANG, FOXTAIL, AND RITIAN. THESE ARE
SOMETIMES CALLED BY THE GENERAL TERM "THE 'GOOD' HUMAN RACES."

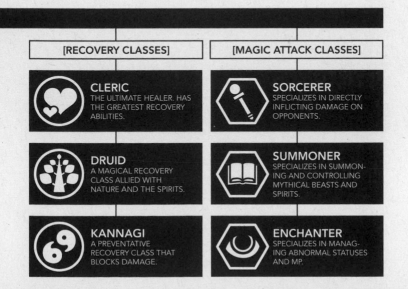

[RECOVERY CLASSES]	[MAGIC ATTACK CLASSES]
CLERIC THE ULTIMATE HEALER. HAS THE GREATEST RECOVERY ABILITIES.	**SORCERER** SPECIALIZES IN DIRECTLY INFLICTING DAMAGE ON OPPONENTS.
DRUID A MAGICAL RECOVERY CLASS ALLIED WITH NATURE AND THE SPIRITS.	**SUMMONER** SPECIALIZES IN SUMMONING AND CONTROLLING MYTHICAL BEASTS AND SPIRITS.
KANNAGI A PREVENTATIVE RECOVERY CLASS THAT BLOCKS DAMAGE.	**ENCHANTER** SPECIALIZES IN MANAGING ABNORMAL STATUSES AND MP.

AFTERWORD

This is Mamare Touno, bringing you this volume as the second season of the *Log Horizon* anime has finished airing and is starting to be rebroadcast. It's been a while... I think? It really doesn't feel that way, but I wrote this in an environment where time gets compressed and stretched out, like bread dough or something out of sci-fi. Anime really keeps you busy. If things are like this when Mr. Masuda's here, how industrious must other creators be? I think it would constantly be "Game Over" for me.

Thank you very much for picking up *Log Horizon, Vol. 10: Homesteading the Noosphere.*

In an abrupt change from the previous volume, I wrote about an uproar in Maihama and Akiba. I wanted to put in some kind of pause every five volumes, so I rushed things a little this time (although it did make the book that much thicker), but Shiroe's unexpected encounter with *her*, aka Kanami, is in this volume, too.

There are lots of things I want to say about Kanami, but she's exactly the woman anime viewers and online readers are acquainted with. She was Shiroe's guiding light when he was at a sensitive age. In the anime, her most impressive scene is her first appearance, but to Shiroe, Kanami is always "the woman who looks back at him and smiles." I'd like healthy young men to sympathize with the feeling of surrender—like an odd restlessness, a sense of defeat you can't quite reconcile yourself to—and with the feeling of wanting to defy it, even so. Ladies, please just think, *That's so dumb...* and pretend not to see it, in a tepid sort of way. If you point it out, Shiroe will probably writhe around in agony and die.

That aside, let's talk about the Season 2 heroine.

In other words, my supervising editor, Ms. F——ta.

Because Yamane Yamamoto was releasing the spin-off story *Kushi-yatama, Do Your Best!* I nonchalantly went along for the advance meeting. It wasn't my book, so it felt like a bit of a holiday to me. Yamane was pretty tense, so we were talking about all sorts of pointless stuff, when along came Ms. F——ta.

"Hisssss?"

She was waving her hand wildly. Could that be a greeting?

I quickly glanced at Yamane, and he was flabbergasted. There, see? You see? These afterwords aren't lies.

She's little, and she's bouncing around, right? "Y-yeah," he said.

Getting right down to it, we started our meeting/meal in a trendy little eatery, and both Mr. Masuda and I ate. This is off-topic, but although these hip dining areas in Shinjuku do help to raise motivation when greeting someone for the first time, I think preliminary meetings are best held in quiet family restaurants late at night. Does that mean I'm in the process of being poisoned?

Well, in any case, just when we'd finished our meal and were gearing up to really start the meeting, Ms. F——ta ordered seconds.

"Huh? You're still eating?"

"Yes."

"Seriously?"

"You can keep eating, too, right, Mr. Mamare?"

"No, I haven't been able to eat all that much lately."

"It's meat, so it'll be fine."

>choke<

Yamane, who we'd just met, was shaking next to me.

His shoulders were shaking.

They brought out a huge helping of cubed, stewed meat.

Of course, both Yamane and I partook as well. Yamane had konjac. I had a boiled egg. Ms. F——ta ate the meat, with a big smile on her face. "Hisssss!"

Still, when I listened to what was going on beside me, the preliminary book meeting had turned into a pretty heated debate. Which direction should we pare this in, should we add to it, what should we do to make it easier for readers to understand—it was useful stuff. I was pretty impressed, but then I realized feeling that way seemed like proof I don't normally do a proper job, and I regretted it.

On the way back, Yamane said, "Ms. F——ta was Ms. F——tastic!", and his smile was fantastic. Great! Now I have another ally. We'll spread the truth about Ms. F——ta far and wide, inside and out.

Hisssss.

And with that report on recent events, this has been *Log Horizon*, Vol. 10.

I think about 80 percent of writing a novel is a puzzle of sorts. You have to put preexisting pieces together in a certain way while observing the limits, and although the process is mediated by taste, it's not really all that creative. If a high-performance artificial intelligence ever shows up, it might manage it better than humans.

But is it all like that? No. The first 20 percent is the work of building the limits you'll need to observe with those puzzle pieces. That probably includes the work of creating the problem that needs to be solved.

This time, Shiroe came up against that same wall. "What should I wish for?" "What do I want to be in the future?" Those aren't questions that can be solved with puzzles. If you try to solve them with all the possibilities from the statistics and analogical reasoning based on all the conditions, you'll paralyze yourself.

That's the sort of story *Log Horizon, Vol. 10* was. Even though neither Isaac nor Iselus worries, Shiroe keeps running into this sort of wall because he's a pain—correction: because he's a clumsy young guy. There's also a theory that abuse from their creators is what makes protagonists worthwhile.

Now that he's taken aim, Shiroe is going to head straight for part three. The journey is likely to take him from Akiba to the West... Probably. Whoops, before that, I'll have to turn the camera on the middle country server for a bit. I'm getting concerned about how Log Horizon's other bespectacled fiend is doing. That means the online serial is being updated, too.

This time as well, the items listed on the character status screens at the beginning of each chapter were collected on Twitter in July 2015. I used items from @aiirorakko, @dharma0430, @falco_of_choco, @hige_mg, @highgetter, @hpsuke, @irohaniwoedo, @kazamasa504, @Landerblue_, @makiwasabi, @me_pon, @mimitabu_sub, @mine_ml, @nariril, @pons_k, @strangestar_s, @sunshine_rumi, and @tatara26. Thank you very much!! I can't list all your names here, but I'm grateful to everyone who submitted entries.

We got tons and tons of ideas this time, too! It was really hard to narrow them down to three. The presence of quite a few cuter-than-usual items might be due to His Highness Iselus's soothing powers.

For details and for the latest news, visit tounomamare.com/. You'll find information about Mamare Touno that isn't *Log Horizon*–related in the blog *Mamare Wednesday*, which is updated every Wednesday.

...Finally: Shoji Masuda, the producer, and Kazuhiro Hara, the illustrator. Tsubakiya Design, the designer, little F——ta, and Sakakibara of the editorial department! Oha, who helped me out again this time! Thank you to Tosho Printing! This time, I also got help from the anime's Studio DEEN; Director Ishihira; Nemoto, who handled the series composition; the script team; and the people of NHK and NEP. I received support for the creation of many different games, too. Thanks to the people of AZITO for creating all the mini-characters.

And. And. Yamane Yamamoto, with whom I released a book. I wrote about it in the essay, but damn. I confess I'm a bit jealous. It's exactly as I said. It would be great if lots more spin-off stories were released, though. What sort of story are you going to write next?

In any case, now all that's left is for everyone to savor this book. *Bon appétit!*

Mamare "Whoever said we'd have a cool summer this year should reflect on their error" Touno

EXCELLENT WORK.
(KAZUHIRO HARA)

▶LOG HORIZON, VOLUME 10
MAMARE TOUNO
ILLUSTRATION BY KAZUHIRO HARA

▶TRANSLATION BY TAYLOR ENGEL
COVER ART BY KAZUHIRO HARA

▶LOG HORIZON, VOLUME 10:
HOMESTEADING THE NOOSPHERE

▶FIRST PUBLISHED IN JAPAN IN 2015 BY KADOKAWA
CORPORATION ENTERBRAIN. ENGLISH TRANSLATION RIGHTS
ARRANGED WITH KADOKAWA CORPORATION ENTERBRAIN
THROUGH TUTTLE-MORI AGENCY, INC., TOKYO.

▶ENGLISH TRANSLATION © 2018 BY YEN PRESS, LLC

▶YEN ON
1290 AVENUE OF THE AMERICAS
NEW YORK, NY 10104

▶VISIT US AT YENPRESS.COM
FACEBOOK.COM/YENPRESS
TWITTER.COM/YENPRESS
YENPRESS.TUMBLR.COM
INSTAGRAM.COM/YENPRESS

▶FIRST YEN ON EDITION: FEBRUARY 2018

▶YEN ON IS AN IMPRINT OF YEN PRESS, LLC.
THE YEN ON NAME AND LOGO ARE TRADEMARKS OF
YEN PRESS, LLC.

▶LIBRARY OF CONGRESS CATALOGING-IN-PUBLICATION DATA
NAMES: TOUNO, MAMARE, AUTHOR. | HARA, KAZUHIRO,
    ILLUSTRATOR. | ENGEL, TAYLOR, TRANSLATOR.
TITLE: LOG HORIZON / MAMARE TOUNO ; ILLUSTRATION BY
    KAZUHIRO HARA ; TRANSLATION BY TAYLOR ENGEL.
DESCRIPTION: FIRST YEN ON EDITION. | NEW YORK, NY :
    YEN ON, 2017–
IDENTIFIERS: LCCN 2015038410 | ISBN 9780316383059 (V. 1 : PBK.) |
    ISBN 9780316263818 (V. 2 : PBK.) | ISBN 9780316263849 (V. 3 : PBK.) |
    ISBN 9780316263856 (V. 4 : PBK.) | ISBN 9780316263863 (V. 5 : PBK.) |
    ISBN 9780316263870 (V. 6 : PBK.) | ISBN 9780316263887 (V. 7 : PBK.) |
    ISBN 9780316470957 (V. 8 : PBK.) | ISBN 9780316470971 (V. 9 : PBK.) | .
    ISBN 9780316471053 (V. 10 : PBK.)
SUBJECTS: | CYAC: SCIENCE FICTION. | BISAC: FICTION /
    SCIENCE FICTION / ADVENTURE.
CLASSIFICATION: LCC PZ7.1.T67 LOJ 2016 | DDC [FIC]—DC23
LC RECORD AVAILABLE AT HTTPS://LCCN.LOC.GOV/2015038410

ISBN: 978-0-316-47105-3

10 9 8 7 6 5 4 3 2 1

▶LSC-C

▶PRINTED IN THE UNITED STATES OF AMERICA

▶AUTHOR: **MAMARE TOUNO**

▶SUPERVISION: **SHOJI MASUDA**

▶ILLUSTRATION: **KAZUHIRO HARA**

▶AUTHOR: MAMARE TOUNO

A STRANGE LIFE-FORM THAT INHABITS THE TOKYO BOKUTOU SHITAMACHI AREA. IT'S BEEN TOSSING HALF-BAKED TEXT INTO A CORNER OF THE INTERNET SINCE THE YEAR 2000 OR SO. IT'S A FULLY AUTOMATIC, TEXT-LOVING MACRO THAT EATS AND DISCHARGES TEXT. IT DEBUTED AT THE END OF 2010 WITH *MAOYUU: MAOU YUUSHA (MAOYUU: DEMON KING AND HERO). LOG HORIZON* IS A RESTRUCTURED VERSION OF A NOVEL THAT RAN ON THE WEBSITE *SHOUSETSUKA NI NAROU (SO YOU WANT TO BE A NOVELIST)*.

WEBSITE: HTTP://WWW.MAMARE.NET

▶SUPERVISION: SHOJI MASUDA

AS A GAME DESIGNER, HE'S WORKED ON *RINDA KYUUBU (RINDA CUBE)* AND *ORE NO SHIKABANE WO KOETE YUKE (STEP OVER MY DEAD BODY)*, AMONG OTHERS. ALSO ACTIVE AS A NOVELIST, HE'S RELEASED THE *ONIGIRI NUEKO (ONI KILLER NUEKO)* SERIES, THE *HARUKA* SERIES, *JOHN & MARY: FUTARI HA SHOUKIN KASEGI (JOHN & MARY: BOUNTY HUNTERS), KIZUDARAKE NO BIINA (BEENA, COVERED IN WOUNDS)*, AND MORE. HIS LATEST EFFORT IS HIS FIRST CHILDREN'S BOOK, *TOUMEI NO NEKO TO TOSHI UE NO IMOUTO (THE TRANSPARENT CAT AND THE OLDER LITTLE SISTER)*. HE HAS ALSO WRITTEN *GEEMU DEZAIN NOU MASUDA SHINJI NO HASSOU TO WAZA (GAME DESIGN BRAIN: SHINJI MASUDA'S IDEAS AND TECHNIQUES)*.

TWITTER ACCOUNT: SHOJIMASUDA

▶ILLUSTRATION: KAZUHIRO HARA

AN ILLUSTRATOR WHO LIVES IN ZUSHI. ORIGINALLY A HOME GAME DEVELOPER. IN ADDITION TO ILLUSTRATING BOOKS, HE'S ALSO ACTIVE IN MANGA AND DESIGN. LATELY, HE'S BEEN HAVING FUN FLYING A BIOKITE WHEN HE GOES ON WALKS. HE'S BEEN WORKING ON THE *LOG HORIZON* COMICALIZATION PROJECT WITH COMIC CLEAR SINCE 2012.

WEBSITE: HTTP://WWW.NINEFIVE95.COM/IG/

Adventurer, you whose weight is borne by your winged soul? The mystical world of Theldesia is home to dragons and giants, magical beasts, and demihumans. Fragrant green winds blow across this new yet ancient land that opens before you like a blank page. Fill it with your life

Dive into the latest light novels from *New York Times* bestselling author REKI KAWAHARA, creator of the fan favorite *SWORD ART ONLINE* and *ACCEL WORLD* series!

The Isolator, Vol. 1-2
©REKI KAWAHARA
ILLUSTRATION:Shimeji

Sword Art Online: Progressive, Vol. 1-3
©REKI KAWAHARA
ILLUSTRATION:abec

Sword Art Online, Vol. 1-7
©REKI KAWAHARA
ILLUSTRATION:abec

Accel World, Vol. 1-6
©REKI KAWAHARA
ILLUSTRATION:HIMA

And be sure your shelves are primed with Kawahara's extensive manga selection!

Sword Art Online: Aincrad
©REKI KAWAHARA/ TAMAKO NAKAMURA

Sword Art Online: Fairy Dance, Vol. 1-3
©REKI KAWAHARA/ TSUBASA HADUKI

Sword Art Online: Girl Ops, Vol. 1-2
©REKI KAWAHARA/ NEKO NEKOBYOU

Sword Art Online: Progressive, Vol. 1-4
©REKI KAWAHARA/ KISEKI HIMURA

Sword Art Online: Phantom Bullet, Vol. 1-2
©REKI KAWAHARA/ KOUTAROU YAMADA

Sword Art Online: Mother's Rosary, Vol. 1-2
©REKI KAWAHARA/ TSUBASA HADUKI

Accel World Vol. 1-6
©REKI KAWAHARA/ HIROYUKI AIGAMO

YEN ON

Yen Press

www.YenPress.com

Death doesn't stop a video game-loving shut-in
from going on adventures and fighting monsters!

KONOSUBA:
GOD'S BLESSING
ON THIS
WONDERFUL WORLD!

IN STORES
NOW

Yen Press

LIGHT
NOVEL

YEN ON

MANGA